Praise for the Jack Reacher series

"This series [is] utterly addictive."
—Janet Maslin, *The New York Times*

"Reacher [is] one of the century's most original, tantalizing pop-fiction heroes."
—*The Washington Post*

"One of the great many things about Jack Reacher is that he's larger than life while remaining relatable and believable." —James Patterson

"Jack Reacher is the thinking reader's action hero."
—*The Seattle Times*

"Jack Reacher is a wonderfully epic hero; tough, taciturn, yet vulnerable. . . . Irresistible." —*People*

"Child is a superb craftsman of suspense."
—*Entertainment Weekly*

"Tight, sinuous, and addictive." —*USA Today*

"Easily the best thriller series going." —NPR

"Shows no signs of slowing down . . . You need Jack Reacher." —*The Atlantic*

By Lee Child and Andrew Child

By Lee Child

Short Stories

By Andrew Grant

LEE CHILD AND ANDREW CHILD

Dell | New York

No Plan B

No Plan B is a work of fiction. Names, characters, places,
and incidents are the products of the authors' imagination or
are used fictitiously. Any resemblance to actual events, locales,
or persons, living or dead, is entirely coincidental.

2023 Dell Mass Market Edition

Copyright © 2022 by Lee Child and Andrew Child
Excerpt from *The Secret* by Lee Child and Andrew Child
copyright © 2023 by Lee Child and Andrew Child

Published in the United States by Dell, an imprint of Random House,
a division of Penguin Random House LLC, New York.

DELL is a registered trademark and the D colophon is a trademark of
Penguin Random House LLC.

Originally published in hardcover in the United States by
Delacorte Press, an imprint of Random House, a division of
Penguin Random House LLC, in 2022.

This book contains an excerpt from the forthcoming book
The Secret by Lee Child and Andrew Child. This excerpt has
been set for this edition only and may not reflect the final content
of the forthcoming edition.

ISBN 978-1-9848-1857-7
Ebook ISBN 978-1-9848-1855-3
International ISBN 978-0-593-72263-3

Cover design: Carlos Beltrán
Cover image: © Ktsdesign/Getty Images
Title page art adapted from an original photograph
by leon134865/stock.adobe.com

Printed in the United States of America

randomhousebooks.com

9 8 7 6 5 4 3 2 1

Dell mass market edition: June 2023

For everyone we have lost too soon

Chapter 1

The meeting was held in a room with no windows.

The room was rectangular and it had no windows because it had no external walls. It was contained within a larger, square room. And the square room was contained within an even larger octagonal room. Together this nest of rooms formed the command hub of Unit S2 at the Minerva Correctional Facility in Winson, Mississippi. Along with its sister segregation unit, S1, it was the most secure place in the complex. It was laid out with walls like the concentric rings of a medieval castle. Designed to be impregnable. From the outside, even if attacked by the most determined rescuers. And from the inside, even during the most extreme riot.

The safety aspect was welcome but the reason the hub had been chosen for this meeting was its seclusion. The opportunity it offered for complete secrecy. Because the rest of Unit S2 was vacant. There were no guards. No admin staff. And none of its 120 isolation cells were in use. They weren't needed. Not with the way the prison was run under its current management. The progressive approach was a cause of great pride. And great PR.

There were six men in the room, and this was the third covert meeting they'd held there in the last week. The men were spread out around a long, narrow table and there were two spare chairs pushed back against a blank, white wall. The furniture was made of bright blue polycarbonate. Each piece was cast in a single mold, leaving no joins or seams. The shape and material made the items hard to break. The color made it hard to conceal any parts that did somehow get smashed off. It was practical. But not very comfortable. And all left over from the previous administration.

Three of the men were wearing suits. Bruno Hix, Minerva's Chief Executive and joint founder, at the head of the table. Damon Brockman, Chief Operating Officer and the other joint founder, to Hix's right. And Curtis Riverdale, the prison's warden, next to Brockman. The man next to Riverdale, the last one on that side of the table, was wearing a uniform. He was Rod Moseley, Chief of the Winson Police Department. On the opposite side, to Hix's left, were two guys in their late twenties. Both were wearing black T-shirts and jeans. One had a broken nose and two black eyes and a forehead full of angry purple bruises.

The other had his left arm in a sling. Both were trying to avoid the other men's eyes.

"So is there a problem or not?" Brockman shrugged his shoulders. "Can anyone say for sure that there is? No. Therefore we should go ahead as planned. There's too much at stake to start running from shadows."

"No." Riverdale shook his head. "If there might be a problem that means there is a problem, the way I see things. Safety first. We should—"

"We should find out for sure," Moseley said. "Make an informed decision. The key is, did the guy look in the envelope? That's what we need to know."

No one spoke.

"Well?" Moseley stretched his leg out under the table and kicked the guy with the sling. "Wake up. Answer the question."

"Give me a break." The guy stifled a yawn. "We had to drive all night to get to Colorado. And all night again to get back here."

"Cry me a river." Moseley prodded the guy with his foot. "Just tell us. Did he look?"

The guy stared at the wall. "We don't know."

"Looking in the envelope isn't definitive," Riverdale said. "If he did look, we need to know if he understood what he saw. And what he plans to do about it."

"Whether the guy looked is irrelevant," Brockman said. "So what if he did? Nothing in there gives the slightest clue to what's going on."

Riverdale shook his head. "It mentions 10:00 A.M. on Friday. Very clearly. The time, the date, the place."

"So what?" Brockman raised his hands. "Friday's an occasion for joy and celebration. There's nothing remotely suspicious about it."

"But the photograph was in there." Riverdale jabbed the air with his finger in time with each syllable. "Eight by ten. Impossible to miss."

"And again, that means nothing." Brockman threw himself back in his chair. "Not unless the guy actually comes here. If he shows up on Friday. And even then we'd be OK. We chose very carefully."

"We didn't. How could we? We only had nine to pick from."

A smile flashed across Moseley's face. "Ironic, isn't it? That the one we picked really is innocent."

"I wouldn't call it ironic." Riverdale scowled. "And there weren't nine. There were only five. The others had family. That ruled them out."

"Nine?" Brockman said. "Five? Whatever. The number doesn't matter. Only the outcome matters. And the outcome is good enough. Even if the guy shows up, how close would he get? He'd be a hundred feet away, at least."

"He doesn't have to show up. He could see it on TV. Online. Read about it in the newspapers."

"The warden has a point," Moseley said. "Maybe it would be better not to draw so much attention this time. Maybe we should cancel the media. We could float some BS about respecting the inmate's privacy, or something."

"No need." Brockman shook his head. "You think this guy has a television? A computer? A subscription to *The New York Times*? He's destitute, for goodness' sake. Stop looking for trouble. There isn't any."

Hix tapped his fingertips on the tabletop. "Media exposure is good for the brand. We always publicize. We always have. If we change now we would only attract more attention. Make people think something is wrong. But I do think we need to know. Did he look?" Hix turned to the guys in the T-shirts. "Best guess. No wrong answer. The chips fell where they fell. We understand that. Just tell us what you believe."

The guy with the broken nose took a deep breath through his mouth. "I think he looked."

"You think?" Hix said. "But you're not sure."

"Not one hundred percent."

"OK. Where was the envelope?"

"In the bag."

"Where was the bag?"

"On the ground."

"You put it down?"

"I needed my hands free."

"Where was it when the car arrived?" Hix said.

The guy with the sling said, "On the ground."

"In the same place?"

"How could we know? I wasn't there when Robert put it down. Robert wasn't conscious when I picked it up."

Hix paused for a moment. "OK. How long was the guy alone with the bag?"

"We don't know. Can't have been long. A couple of minutes, max."

"So it's possible he looked," Hix said. "Glanced, anyway."

"Right," the guy with the broken nose said. "And the bag was ripped, remember. How did that happen? And why? We didn't do it."

Brockman leaned forward. "It was a crazy scene, from what you told us. Wreckage everywhere. Total chaos. The bag probably got ripped by accident. It doesn't sound like some major clue. And the other two haven't reported that he looked."

The guy with the sling said, "They haven't reported at all. We don't know where they are."

Brockman said, "Must still be on their way back. Phone problems, probably. But if there was anything to worry about they would have found a way to let us know."

"And the guy didn't mention anything about it to the police," Moseley said. "I've talked to the lieutenant over there a couple times. That has to mean something."

"I still think he looked," the guy with the broken nose said.

"We should pull the plug," Riverdale said.

"That's the dumbest thing I ever heard," Brockman said. "We didn't set the date. We didn't pick the time. The judge did when he signed the release order. You know that. We pull some bullshit delaying tactic, we wind up ass-deep in inspectors. You know where that would land us. We might as well shoot ourselves in the head, right here, right now."

Riverdale scowled. "I'm not saying we delay. I'm saying we go back to the original plan. The switch was always a mistake."

"That would solve Friday's problem. If there is

one. But then we'd have no way out of the bigger jam we're in. Carpenter's situation."

"I said from the start, the solution to that is simple. A bullet in the back of his head. I'll do it myself if you're too squeamish."

"You know what that would cost? How much business we would lose?"

"We'll lose a lot more than money if this guy joins the dots."

"How could he do that?"

"He could come down here. You said so yourself. He could dig around. He was a military cop. It's in his blood."

"It's years since the guy was an MP," Moseley said. "That's what the lieutenant told me."

Hix tapped the tabletop. "What else do we know?"

"Not much. He has no driver's license. No employment history, according to the IRS. Not since he left the army. No social media presence. No recent photographs exist. He's a hobo now. It's kind of sad, but that's the bottom line. Doesn't sound like much to worry about."

Brockman said, "Hobo or millionaire, what kind of crazy person would travel halfway across the country because he read a few documents and saw an innocuous picture?"

"Speculate all you want but this still worries me," Riverdale said. "Each time we met, we thought we had the problem contained. Each time we were wrong. What if we're wrong again now?"

"We weren't wrong." Brockman slammed his palm

into the table. "We handled each situation as it came up. Ninety-nine percent."

"Ninety-nine. Not one hundred."

"Life isn't perfect. Sometimes there's broken glass to sweep up. Which we've done. We found out there was a leak. We plugged it, the way we all agreed to. We found out about the missing envelope. We retrieved it, the way we all agreed to."

"And now this strange guy has looked in the envelope."

"He may have. We don't know. But you have to admit, it's unlikely. He didn't tell the cops. We know that. And he didn't tell the FBI or the Bureau of Prisons. We would know that. So say he figured everything out from a couple of seconds alone with the envelope. Why keep the knowledge to himself? What's he going to do with it? Blackmail us? And you think he's somehow going to schlep twelve hundred miles before Friday? Come on."

"Gentlemen!" Hix tapped the tabletop again. "Enough. All right. Here's my decision. We can't know if the guy looked in the envelope. It seems unlikely, so we shouldn't panic. Particularly given the consequences. But at the same time it pays to be cautious. He's easily recognizable, yes?"

The guy with the broken nose nodded. "For sure. You can't miss him. Six-five. Two hundred fifty pounds. Scruffy."

"He's banged up pretty good, remember," the guy with the sling said. "I took care of that."

"You should have killed him," Brockman said.

"I thought I had."

"You should have made sure."

"How? *Make it look like an accident.* Those were our orders for the other two. I figured they applied to this guy, as well. Hard to sell that story if I put a bullet in his brain."

"Enough!" Hix waited for silence. "Here's the plan. We'll mount surveillance. Round the clock. Starting now, through Saturday. If he sets one toe in our town, we'll be waiting. And here we don't have to worry about how anything looks."

Chapter 2

Jack Reacher arrived in Gerrardsville, Colorado, mid-morning on a Monday, two days before the Minerva guys met in secret for the third time. He had hitched a ride in a truck that was delivering alfalfa bales to a farm south of the town so he covered the final mile on foot. It was a pleasant walk. The weather was warm, but not hot. Tufts of cloud drifted across the wide blue sky. The mile-high air was thin and clear. As far as he could see, the land was flat and green and fertile. Watering gantries marked the boundaries of endless fields and between them stalks and leaves of all sizes and shades stretched up toward the sun. To the left, the horizon was dominated by a line of mountains. They jutted straight out of the ground, no gentle buildup, no smooth foothills, and their peaks, capped with snow, cut into the atmosphere like the teeth of a saw.

Reacher continued until he came to the town's main drag. It carried on for about a half mile, and there was only one block on either side before the stores and offices gave way to the residential streets. The commercial buildings were uniform in size. They were two stories high and they all had similar designs. They were all a similar age, too—late nineteenth century, based on the dates carved into some of the lintels—which gave the place a kind of time-capsule feel. A time when craftmanship was still valued. That was clear. The facades were all made from stone or marble or granite. The woodwork around the doors and windows was intricately carved and lavishly picked out with gold leaf. And every aspect was flawlessly maintained. Reacher appreciated what he saw. But he wasn't in town to admire its architecture. He was there to visit its museum.

The previous day Reacher had picked up a newspaper someone had abandoned in a diner. He found an article about a dentist and a metal detector. The gadget had been given to the guy as a retirement gift. Some kind of an in-joke based on his reputation for finding fillings done by other dentists in new patients' teeth and insisting on replacing them. Anyway, to occupy his sudden leisure time the guy reinvented himself as an amateur archeologist. He'd long been obsessed by the Civil War so he set out to visit a whole series of battle sites. Big and small. Famous and obscure. And at Pea Ridge, Arkansas, he found a bunch of artillery fragments and other artifacts. These got rolled into a traveling exhibition about the evolution of Union tactics, which caught Reacher's eye. Gerrardsville was one of the venues for the display. And as he was only a few miles away while the show was still open, Reacher figured he'd take a look.

Reacher had a cup of coffee at a café he happened to walk past and got to the museum before lunchtime. He stayed until it closed. When he had to be shooed out by one of the curators. Her name was Alexandra. Reacher struck up a conversation with her about the exhibit. The subject turned to the kind of restaurants there were in the town, and they wound up going for a burger together. Alexandra picked a scruffy kind of place. It had rough wooden tabletops. Long benches. Creaky floorboards. Old LP covers were tacked up all over the walls. But the food came fast. The plates were piled high. The prices were low. Reacher liked everything about it.

While they ate the subject changed to music and they wound up at a bar together. It was small. Intimate. Dark. A blues band was playing. Mainly Magic Slim covers with a handful of Howlin' Wolf songs sprinkled through. Reacher approved. Alexandra ordered a couple of beers and as they drank the subject changed again. It led them in a whole different direction this time. And all the way to Alexandra's apartment.

Her apartment was above a store near the main intersection in the town. It was a small place. The style was minimalist. It didn't have much in the way of furniture. Or décor. But it did have a fridge, so they had another beer. It had a CD player, so they listened to some more music. It had a bedroom. And once they reached it, there wasn't much need for more of anything else.

Chapter 3

The museum didn't open the next day until 10:00 A.M. so Reacher and Alexandra stayed in bed until the last possible minute.

They stayed in bed, but they didn't spend all their time sleeping. Alexandra knew she was cutting it fine but she took a quick shower anyway. She felt it was wise after their recent level of activity. Reacher made coffee. Then she kissed him goodbye and hurried away to her chosen slice of the past. Reacher took a more leisurely shower then made his way down the stairs and out onto the sidewalk. He was thinking about his more immediate future. He paused to gaze at the mountains for a moment. Then he saw a woman walking toward them. She was on the other side of the street, heading west, almost at the intersection. The *Don't Walk* sign was lit up. A guy was standing on the opposite corner, waiting for it to change. And a bus was heading north, about to pass between them.

The bus driver only saw movement.

Not much more than a blur. Low and to her right. A spherical object. Swinging down and around through a quarter of a perfect circle. Like a melon had somehow been attached to the end of a rope, she told the mandatory counselor the following day. Only it wasn't a melon. It was a head. A human head. It was female. Inches from the windshield. There. Bright and pale in the sunlight, like it already belonged to a ghost. Then gone. But not because the driver had imagined it. Not because it was an illusion, like she prayed for it to be. Because it continued on its arc. All the way to the ground. In front of the bus.

Then under it.

The driver veered hard to the left. She threw all her weight onto the brake. No hesitation. No panic. She was well trained. She had years of experience. But she was still too late. She heard the tires squeal. Heard her passengers scream. And felt the impact. Through the steering wheel. Just a slight, muted ripple running around the hard plastic rim. Less of a jolt than if she'd driven through a deep pothole. Or hit a log. But then, asphalt doesn't have bones that crush and shatter. Wood doesn't have organs that rupture and bleed.

The driver shut her eyes and willed herself not to vomit. She knew the kind of scene that would be waiting for her on the street. She'd been an unwilling partner in a stranger's suicide once before. It was an occupational hazard.

The guy on the opposite corner saw a lot more.

He saw the bus heading north. He saw a woman arrive at the southeast corner of the intersection. He had an unobstructed view. He was close enough to be credible. In his statement he said the woman looked nervous. Twitchy. He saw her check her watch. At first he figured she was in a hurry. He thought she was going to try to run across the street before the bus got too close. But she didn't. She stopped. She stood and squirmed and fidgeted until the bus was almost alongside her. Until there was no chance for it to slow or swerve.

Then she dived under its wheels.

The woman dived. The guy was certain about that. She didn't trip. She didn't fall. It was a deliberate act. He could tell from the timing. The way her body accelerated. The curve it moved through. The precise aim. There was no way it could have been an accident. She had done it on purpose. He could see no other explanation.

Reacher was the only one who saw the whole picture.

He was about fifty feet from the intersection. His outlook was also unobstructed but he had a wider angle of view. He saw the woman and the guy waiting to cross in opposite directions. And he saw a third person. A man. Around five foot ten. Wiry-looking. Wearing a gray hoodie and jeans. On the same side as the woman. Eight feet away from her. A foot back from the curb. Standing completely still.

The guy had picked his spot carefully. That was clear. He was in the general vicinity of the crosswalk so he didn't attract attention the way someone loitering aimlessly might. He was far enough away from the woman that he didn't appear to be connected to her in any way. But he was close enough that when the bus approached he only needed to take a couple of steps to reach her side. His movement was smooth. Fluid. He was more like a shadow than a physical presence. The woman didn't notice him appear next to her. She didn't notice his foot snake around in front of her ankles.

The guy planted his hand between the woman's shoulder blades and pushed. It was a small motion. Economical. Not dramatic. Not something most observers would notice. But sufficient for the guy's purpose. That was for sure. There was no danger of the woman stumbling forward and bouncing off the front of the bus. No danger she might get away with broken bones and a concussion. The guy's foot took care of that. It stopped the woman from moving her own feet. It made sure she pivoted, ankles stationary, arms flailing. And it guaranteed she slammed horizontally onto the ground.

The impact knocked the breath out of the woman's body. Her last breath. Because half a second later the bus's front wheel crushed her abdomen as flat as a folded newspaper.

Chapter 4

The bus came to rest at an angle from the curb like it had been stolen by a drunk and then abandoned when the prank lost its gloss. The front end was partly blocking the intersection. Reacher saw the route number on the electronic panel above its entry door switch to a written message: *CALL POLICE*. He also saw the dead woman's legs. They were jutting out from under the bus, about halfway between its front and rear wheels. One of her sneakers had fallen off. The guy who had pushed her took a black trash bag from the back pocket of his jeans. He shook it open. Crouched down next to her bare foot. Stretched an arm under the bus. Snagged something and pulled it out. Reacher realized it was the woman's purse. The guy slipped it into the trash bag. Stood up. Adjusted his hood. And strolled away, heading south, disappearing from sight.

Reacher ran across the street, diagonally, toward the bus. The sidewalk was starting to fill up. People were spilling out of the shops and cafés and offices to gawp at the body. A man in a suit had stopped his car and climbed out to get a better look. But no one was paying any attention to the guy in the hoodie. He was melting away through the fringe of the crowd. Reacher barreled through the spectators, shoving people aside, knocking one of them on his ass. The guy in the hoodie cleared the last of the onlookers. He picked up his pace. Reacher kept going, pushing harder. He barged between one final couple and broke back into a run. The guy was sixty feet ahead now. Reacher closed the gap to fifty feet. Forty-five. Then the guy heard the footsteps chasing him. He glanced over his shoulder. Saw Reacher bearing down on him. He started to run, still clutching the trash bag in one hand. He slipped his other hand up inside his hood. Jabbed at a device that was jammed into his right ear. Barked out a couple of sentences. Then veered off into an alleyway that stretched away to his left.

Reacher kept running until he was a couple of feet from the mouth of the alley. Then he stopped. He listened. He heard nothing so he knelt down, crept forward, and peered around the corner. He figured if the guy had a gun he'd be looking for a target at head height. If he had a knife he'd be winding up for a lunge to the gut. But Reacher didn't encounter any threat. There was no response at all. So he got back to his feet and took a step forward.

The alley was the cleanest he had ever been in. The walls of the adjoining buildings were pale brick. They looked neat and even. There was no graffiti. None of the second-floor windows were broken. The fire escapes looked freshly painted. There were dumpsters lined up on both sides. They were evenly spaced out. Some were green. Some were blue. All had lids. None was overflowing, and there was no trash blowing around on the ground.

The guy was thirty feet away. His back was against the left-hand wall. He was standing completely still and the trash bag was on the ground at his feet. Reacher moved toward him. He closed the gap to twenty feet. Then the guy lifted the hem of his hoodie. A black, boxy pistol was sticking out of his waistband.

The guy said, "Hold it. That's close enough."

Reacher kept moving. He closed the gap to ten feet.

The guy's hand hovered over the grip of his pistol. He said, "Stop. Keep your hands where I can see them. There's no need for anyone to get hurt. We just need to talk."

Reacher closed the gap to four feet. Then he said, "Anyone else."

"What?" the guy said.

"Someone already got hurt. The woman you pushed. Was there a need for that?"

The guy's mouth opened and closed but no words came out.

Reacher said, "Down on the ground. Fingers laced behind your head."

The guy didn't respond.

"Maybe there is no need for anyone else to get hurt," Reacher said. "And by *anyone,* I mean *you.* It all depends on what you do next."

The guy went for his gun. He was fast. But not fast enough. Reacher grabbed the guy's wrist and whipped it away to his right, spinning him around so he was facing the wall.

"Stop." The guy's voice was suddenly shrill. "Wait. What are you doing?"

"I'm going to see how you like it," Reacher said. "There's no bus. But there are bricks. They'll have to do."

Reacher let go of the guy's wrist. Moved his hand up. Planted it between the guy's shoulder blades. And pushed. It was a huge motion. Savage. Wild. Way more than sufficient. The guy tried to save himself but he had no chance. The force was overwhelming. He smashed into the wall, face-first, and flopped onto the ground like the bones in his legs had dissolved. Blood was sluicing down from the gashes in his forehead. His nose was broken. There was a serious chance he could suffocate. Or drown.

Neither of those outcomes would have worried Reacher too much.

Chapter 5

Reacher's plan had been to scoop the guy up and carry him back to the bus. That way he'd be ready for when the police arrived. But when he retrieved the trash bag, he paused. The woman's purse was inside. And something in her purse was worth killing for. Reacher had been an investigator in the army for thirteen years. Old habits die hard. And he couldn't hear any sirens yet. He knew he had a little time.

Reacher picked up the fallen gun and tucked it into his waistband. Then he wrestled the guy into the recovery position at the foot of the wall and started with his pockets. There was nothing with a name or an address, as Reacher expected, but the guy did have a bunch of keys. Reacher selected the sharpest one and used it to hack a pair of rough, broad strips from around the top of the trash bag. He wrapped the strips around his hands and took out the purse. It was eighteen inches square, made from some kind of faux leather, tan color, with a long narrow shoulder strap as well as regular handles. One side was speckled with blood. The opening was secured with a zipper. Reacher unfastened it. He rummaged inside. The first thing he pulled out was the woman's wallet. It held a Mississippi driver's license with the name Angela St. Vrain and an address in a town called Winson. There were three dollars in singles. A wad of receipts from a supermarket and a drugstore. And a photograph of Angela with a little girl. Maybe three years old. The family resemblance was clear. Mother and daughter. Reacher had no doubt.

Reacher set the wallet on the ground and delved back into the purse. He pulled out a laminated card on a pale blue lanyard. A work ID. It showed that Angela was a prison employee of some kind. At a place called the Minerva Correctional Facility, which was also in Winson, Mississippi. He found a hair-brush and a bunch of makeup and other personal items. A key ring, with three keys on it. And an enve-lope. It was regular manila style. Letter size. But it was addressed to someone else. Another resident of Winson, Mississippi, called Danny Peel. And it had been opened.

The envelope contained one black-and-white photograph—a mug shot dated sixteen years ago—and a stack of papers. The photograph was of a young adult male. His face was drawn and pinched and he had a smattering of close-cropped hair. A recent cut, Reacher thought, based on the pale skin shining through the stubble. He was also drawn to the kid's eyes. They were set close together, and they were wide open, looking half-frightened, half-confused. And the kid had another unusual feature. One of his earlobes was missing. His left. It looked like it had been sliced off. Its edge was straight and raw and a scar was visible on his neck, running around the back of his head. Done by a straight razor, Reacher thought. Someone must have slashed at the kid, going for his throat, and the kid must have twisted and hunched and pulled away. Not fast enough to avoid getting cut. But fast enough to not get killed. Which was something, Reacher thought. Maybe.

The papers broke down into two groups. The first set was marked Mississippi Department of Corrections and it began the life story of a guy named Anton Begovic. Of his adult life, anyway. They told how Begovic had gotten in trouble at eighteen. He was implicated in a burglary. A bunch of other offenses were linked to him. The weight of the charges grew until he wound up behind bars. An apparently inevitable progression. And things only got worse for him in prison. Within three years he was in solitary. He stayed there for the next seven. But with the second set of papers Begovic's life turned around.

The change coincided with the prison being taken over by Minerva Correctional. Angela's employer. Begovic was returned to the general population. His behavior improved. The prison company sponsored an appeal. A PI turned up a deathbed confession from an ex-con who admitted to the offenses that had been pinned on Begovic. The detective who put the case together was found to have killed himself a decade ago, neck-deep in gambling debt. And a judge ordered Begovic's release. It was imminent. According to the final record, he was going to be set free at 10:00 A.M. that coming Friday.

Reacher slid the photo and the documents back into the envelope. He put the envelope back into the purse and loaded up Angela's other possessions. He zipped the purse closed and dropped it into the trash bag. Then he unwound the plastic strips from his hands and jammed them into his pocket. He was thinking about the contents of the envelope. The tragic tale of a wrongly convicted man. He wondered what it had to do with Angela. Which made him think of another tragic tale. One that was just beginning. For the little girl in the wallet photo. Angela's daughter. Who would now have to grow up without a mother.

Chapter 6

A car nosed into the entrance to the alley. A black sedan. It was shiny. Sleek. A BMW. Reacher could tell from the blue and white emblem on its hood. It was supposed to represent sky and clouds. Reacher had read about it somewhere. That it harked back to the company's roots as an aero engine manufacturer. He had no idea which model it was, though. He was no kind of a car guy.

The BMW crept forward. The driver was also wearing a gray hoodie. He slowed to a stop, lowered his window, and said, "Hands where I can see them. Then step away."

Reacher didn't move.

The driver shifted into Neutral and revved the engine. He floored the gas pedal twice, three times, then waited for the angry sound to subside. "I said, step away."

Reacher stayed still.

The car was ten feet from Reacher and eight feet from the wall. The unconscious guy was on the ground, six inches from Reacher's heels. Presumably he was the driver's buddy. Which would be why the driver wanted Reacher to move. To avoid harming both of them.

Reacher stayed still.

The car crept forward. The driver pulled on the wheel. He kept going, inching across until the gap between Reacher and the front fender was down to four feet. Then he straightened up and hit the gas. The car surged ahead. The driver held the wheel with his right hand. He worked the door handle with his left. He pushed the door all the way open and kept it there like he was a knight on horseback trying to bludgeon his opponent with his shield. Trying to knock him down. Or back him away from his safe position, at least.

Reacher didn't back away. Instead he took a step forward. Toward the car. He raised his knee and drove the ball of his foot into the door. He put all his strength into the kick. All his weight. He connected with the center of the panel. The metal skin warped and shrieked and deformed. The door slammed shut. The car fizzed past Reacher then swerved away to the right. The driver fought the wheel. He braked, hard, but he was a moment too late. The front right corner of the car slammed into a dumpster on the other side of the alley. Its headlight shattered. The driver slammed into Reverse and hit the gas again. He tugged on the wheel. The car slewed around then straightened. Its back left corner was lined up with Reacher's legs. The guy on the ground would be fine. He would be safely beneath the car's rear overhang. But Reacher wouldn't escape. Not at that angle. He'd be crushed against the wall.

Reacher dived toward the mouth of the alley, rolled over once, and scrambled back to his feet. The car hit the wall. More glass broke. Shards showered down over the unconscious guy's chest and abdomen. But they weren't sharp enough to cut through his clothes. And the impact wasn't sufficient to immobilize the car.

The driver had stayed in his seat throughout. That was understandable. Avoiding a fist fight was a smart move. But he'd made no attempt to shoot. Reacher figured he must want whatever happened to look like an accident. That would be a little suspicious, given how close they were to the place where the bus had crushed Angela St. Vrain. But a lot less suspicious than leaving a body with a fatal gunshot wound.

Reacher was under no such constraint. He drew the gun he'd taken from the guy on the ground and stepped around the car. He was going for a shot through the passenger window. The driver saw what was happening and lurched forward, straight down the center of the alley. Reacher fired three shots at the rear window, instead. The first turned the glass into a dense mesh of opaque crystals. The second knocked the whole mass onto the car's backseat. The third hit something inside. Reacher was sure about that. But he couldn't tell if it was the driver. Or the head restraint. Or some other random component.

The car stopped. It paused for a moment. Then its one remaining reverse light came on. Its tires squealed. It sped backward. Reacher fired three more shots. All of them hit the driver's seat. But the car kept on coming. Straight at Reacher. No sign of slowing. No sign of swerving. The driver must have been hunkered down low. Maybe halfway into the foot well, if he was small enough. Reacher figured the guy was using the backup camera to see where to steer. He raised the gun, wondering where the lens would be. Then he pushed the thought away. There was no time. He feinted left then darted to his right. He wanted another try for the passenger window. It was close. A couple more seconds and he'd have a clear shot. Then he would finish the guy. That was for damn sure.

The driver swerved hard right. Reacher was penned in by the wall on one side. He'd be hit by the car if he moved the other way. Or if he went forward. Or if he went back.

The car was moving fast. The rear wing was inches away.

There was nowhere for Reacher to go.

Except up. If he timed it just right.

Reacher jammed the gun into his waistband. Waited another fraction of a second. Then sprang onto the car's trunk and kicked down. Hard. With both legs. He threw his arms above his head for extra lift. His fingertips brushed metal. Rough, cold iron. Part of one of the fire escapes. A rung on its lowest section. Folded into its dormant, horizontal position, like a set of monkey bars in a gym. He grabbed hold. Gripped tight. And swung his legs up to clear the roof of the car.

Reacher almost made it. The top of the empty rear window frame caught his toecaps. He felt an almighty jolt. It slammed through his ankles and his knees and up his body and along his arms and his hands and his fingers. Which loosened. A little. But Reacher didn't let go. He tightened his grip. He watched the car's hood pass beneath him. He straightened his legs, ready to drop down and spin around and take another shot. Through the windshield this time. Straight into the front section of the cabin. Where the driver would have nowhere to hide.

Reacher heard a sound. Above him. It was metal, grating and groaning and tearing. There was a *bang*. Sharp and loud like another gunshot. There was a second noise. A third. From the ironwork. Something was being pulled apart. Maybe because of Reacher's weight. Maybe because of his weight multiplied by the impact with the car. Or maybe because the equipment wasn't as well maintained as it appeared from the ground. Maybe the coats of shiny paint concealed all kinds of structural defects. But whatever the reason, the struts connecting the ladder and the gangway to the framework on the next level were failing. The whole section vibrated. It shook. It started to tilt outward, away from the building. Ten degrees. Fifteen. It stabilized for a moment. It settled. But in a new position. It was canted downward now. At an angle the anchor points had never been designed to support. They started to pull free. They screeched and juddered and pulled their sockets right out of the brittle tuck pointing.

Reacher saw what was happening. He let go of the rung. His feet hit the ground. He took half a step. And a twisted mass of iron landed right on top of him.

Chapter 7

For the first fifteen years of his life Jed Starmer didn't give much thought to the concept of the law.

He was aware that laws existed. He understood that they somehow shaped and controlled the world around him, but only in an invisible, abstract sense, like gravity or magnetism. He knew that there were consequences if you broke them. Penalties. Punishments. All kinds of unpleasant outcomes. He had seen huddles of people in orange jumpsuits at the side of the highway being forced to pick up trash. He had listened to his foster parents' warnings about juvenile hall. And jail. And ultimately Hell. But still, none of that struck much of a chord. It didn't seem relevant to his life. He wasn't about to rob a bank. Or steal a car. He didn't even cut school very often. There were other things for him to worry about. Far more urgent things, like not being kicked out of the house and forced to live on the street. And how to avoid getting stabbed or shot any time he wanted to go anywhere.

Jed's perspective changed completely on his fifteenth birthday. That was two weeks and two days ago. It was a Sunday so while his foster parents were at church Jed took the bus five miles, deep into South Central L.A., where he had been told never to go. He walked the last two hundred yards, along the cracked sidewalk, trying not to look scared, staring straight down, desperate to avoid eye contact with anyone who might be watching. He made it to the short set of worn stone steps that led to his birth mother's apartment building. Scurried to the top. Pushed the door. The lock was broken, as it had been each time he'd snuck over there in the last couple of years, so he stepped into the hallway and started straight up the stairs. Two flights. Then along to the end of the corridor. He knew there was no point trying the buzzer so he knocked. He waited. And he hoped. That his mother would be there. That she would be sober. And that even if she didn't remember what day it was, she would at least remember him.

It turned out Jed's mother did remember. The day, and the person. She was perfectly lucid. She was even dressed. She opened the door, cigarette in hand, and led the way through the blue haze to the apartment's main room. The shades were closed. There was junk everywhere. Clothes. Shoes. Purses. Books. Magazines. CDs. Letters. Bills. All heaped up in vague piles like some halfhearted attempt at organization had been made by someone completely unfamiliar with the concept. She stopped in the center of the mess for a moment, sighed, then gestured toward the couch. Jed squeezed by and took a seat in one corner. She sat at the opposite end and crushed out her cigarette in an ashtray on the side table next to her. It was already overflowing. A river of ash cascaded onto the carpet. She sighed again then turned to face Jed. She said she'd been expecting him. She hadn't gotten him a present, obviously, but she was glad he had come because there was something she needed to tell him. Two things, in fact.

The first thing was that she was sick. She had pancreatic cancer. Stage four. Jed didn't have a strong grasp of human biology. He didn't know what the pancreas did. He wasn't sure what the number signified. But he gleaned through his mother's tears that the gist was bad. It meant she didn't have long left to live. Months, possibly. Maybe weeks. Certainly not longer.

The second thing Jed's mother told him was the truth about his father. Or what she believed to be the truth, at least.

The first piece of information made Jed feel guilty. It was an unexpected response. He had observed over the years that people generally got upset when they learned close relatives were on the verge of dying. But after the news had sunk in he realized he wasn't sad. He wasn't miserable. He was relieved. Which he knew was wrong. But he couldn't help it. It was like he had been swimming against the tide his whole life with a weight tied around his waist. Caused by worry. The constant fear that the police would show up at the house. With news about his mother. That she had overdosed. Or had been murdered. Or had been found dead and festering in some filthy squat. That he would have to go and identify her body. Or even worse, that she would show up herself, on the doorstep. In who knew what kind of a state. His foster parents disapproved of his mother. Strongly. They made that clear. At every opportunity. The last thing he needed was more guilt by association. But now he could stop worrying. He knew how his mother's story was going to end. And when. The rope was about to be cut. He could swim free at last.

The second thing Jed learned had a different kind of effect. His mother's words worked like a light shining into a corner of his past that had previously been hidden. They picked out the dots that joined his life to the law. Showed him a connection he hadn't seen before. Something very personal. A link that had shaped his entire existence. It left him with a whole new respect. A determination to never break the law himself. To break the cycle, instead. To not let history repeat itself.

Jed's resolve lasted for exactly two weeks. Then it was lifted to a whole new level. Because of the time he spent online while his foster parents were out at that week's Sunday service. First, he ran a Google search based on the story his mother had told him about his father on his birthday. The results led him

to an article on a news site. A long, complex account
of events that unfolded over many years. Jed read it
carefully. He noted every detail. Every discrepancy.
And when he finished he felt like a searchlight had
been switched on in his head. A million watts of
blinding revelation. His mother's version seemed ri-
diculously pale in comparison. Like she had illuminated the important parts with a candle. Or a glow
worm. She had missed the crux entirely. Now Jed
didn't just see the power of the law. He also saw the
danger it brought.

The light from Jed's new knowledge didn't just
spill back toward his past. It also shone forward,
showing him what he needed to do. And where he
needed to go. Which was away from his foster home,
for a start. Then away from California altogether.

Jed took two days to plan. To do his research. To
build up his courage. Which explained why, at the
same time Reacher stepped into the alley in Gerrardsville, Colorado, Jed was standing in front of a dresser
in his foster parents' bedroom. The top drawer was
open. His foster mother's tired, stretched underwear
was pushed to one side. The wad of twenty-dollar
bills was exposed. And Jed was in a quandary. He
needed the money. Badly. But he didn't want to steal
it. He was desperate not to break the law. So he was
trying to convince himself that taking it wouldn't
count as stealing. Not if the money was already stolen. Which in a way, he figured it was. It had been
provided by the state to pay for his food and shelter.
His, and the other three foster kids he lived with. And
yet the cash was there, unspent, while they wore

clothes that were too small and went to bed hungry each night.

The bottom line was that Jed didn't want to commit a crime. But neither did he want to starve. Or have to hitch a ride across more than half the country. Because regardless of what he wanted, three things were certain. He had a long way to go. Not much time to get there. And he could not afford to be late.

Chapter 8

Reacher's ears were ringing when he came around. There was a sharp pain in his head. The weight of the metal on his chest made it hard to breathe. It took him a moment to figure out what was pinning him to the ground. Then another five minutes of shoving and heaving and scrabbling before he was able to wriggle free.

A small crowd had gathered at the mouth of the alley. Reacher recognized some of the people. They had been gawping at the bus after it crushed Angela St. Vrain. The excitement out there must have died down. They must have gambled that the action in the alley would be more interesting. They were certainly more interested in watching than getting involved. It was only when Reacher had almost extracted himself that a couple of the younger men stepped forward and tried to take his arms.

Reacher pushed them away.

One of them said, "You OK, buddy?"

Reacher said nothing.

"Because we thought we heard gunshots." The guy shrugged. "Guess it must have been the metal breaking."

Reacher took several deep gulps of air while he waited for the crowd to disperse then got busy checking the alley around him. There were tire marks on the pavement. Paint transfer in a couple of spots on the walls. A big dent in the nearest dumpster. A scattering of broken glass here and there. But no gun. No guys in hoodies. No car. No trash bag. No purse. And no envelope.

The emergency services were out in force by the time Reacher made his way back to the street. The traffic in all directions had been stopped by four pairs of patrol cars, formed up in Vs with their light bars popping and flashing. A tent had been set up over the area at the side of the bus where Angela St. Vrain's body had been. More to protect the scene from TV crews in helicopters and journalists with long lenses than the weather, Reacher thought. It's not like there was any great mystery about what killed the woman. The *who* was a different story, though. And so was the *why*.

Reacher saw four uniformed officers canvassing the last stragglers in the crowd. He kept on looking until he spotted a guy in a suit emerge from the far side of the bus. The guy was wearing nitrile gloves and he had a small black notebook in his left hand. Reacher thought it said something about the level of crime in the town if they sent a detective to what would seem like a routine traffic accident in many places. He wasn't complaining, though. It saved him the time it would take to find the station house.

Reacher figured the detective would be in his early thirties. He looked to be six feet even and was clearly in good shape. His hair was buzzed short. His suit pants had a razor-sharp crease down the front and back. His shirt was freshly ironed. His tie was neatly knotted. And his shoes gleamed like mirrors.

The guy felt Reacher looking at him so he walked over and held out his hand. "Detective Harewood. Can I help you?"

Reacher laid out what he had seen at the intersection and what had happened subsequently in the alley. He took it slow and broke the information into manageable chunks. Harewood wrote it all down in his book. He didn't skip anything. He didn't summarize. And he didn't waste any time with undue questions about Reacher's address or occupation.

When they were done with the formalities Reacher took Harewood's card and promised to call if he remembered any further details. Then he walked away. He was confident the case was in good hands. He considered looking for a ride out of town, but came down against it. His head hurt. His body was stiff and sore. He decided a good night's sleep was preferable. It would help him heal. And there was something else. The guys in hoodies might come back. They would have to replace their vehicle, obviously. And they'd probably want to hand off the envelope. Or secure it somewhere. But then they might be worried about the witness they left behind. They might want to do something about that.

Reacher certainly hoped they would try.

The town wasn't big. Reacher spent the afternoon staying as visible as possible. He alternated between quartering the streets, looking in store windows, jaywalking, and sitting outside cafés drinking coffee. It started out as a pleasant way to kill time. The central district was dotted with pedestrian areas and trees and places to hang out. The local population seemed to be a mix of students and new parents with babies in strollers and hipsters and young professional types in exaggeratedly casual suits. But the longer Reacher kept the search going, the more frustrated he got. He had to face facts. If he was the worm, he was attracting no fish. So he bagged the proposition and headed south, out of town, toward a pair of hotels he remembered from when he arrived the day before.

Reacher was wrong.

He realized before he had covered two blocks. He was being watched. Someone had their eyes on him. He could feel it. A chill spread up from the base of his neck. A primal response. A warning mechanism hard-wired into his lizard brain. Finely tuned. Highly reliable. Never to be ignored.

Reacher stopped outside the next store he came to. It sold fancy chocolates in brightly colored packages. He stood and looked at the window. Not at the display of old tins and giant heaps of truffles. At the reflection of the street.

A black truck with raised suspension and chrome wheels went by. There was no one in the passenger seat. Its driver paid Reacher no attention. Next to pass was a silver Jeep with a pair of kayaks on the roof and red mud sprayed up the side. Its driver was only looking at the back of the black truck. Then came a white sedan. A Toyota Corolla.

Reacher felt a flicker of recognition. He couldn't be certain he'd seen this particular car before. Corollas are popular vehicles. Then it rolled up closer to him. The chill in his neck grew more intense. He could see the guy in the passenger seat. Mid-twenties. Stocky. Cropped hair. Blue T-shirt. He could have been the clone of the guy who had pushed Angela St. Vrain under the bus, only his face was still intact. And he was looking at Reacher. That was for sure. He stared as the car drove past, glanced down at his phone, then turned to peer over his shoulder.

Reacher started walking again. The Corolla took a right at the end of the next block. Reacher pictured it taking the next right. And the next. He estimated the time that would take. Then he crossed the street. That gave him an excuse to look the opposite way without signaling his suspicion. The Corolla was waiting at the previous intersection. Reacher kept going. Not rushing. Not dawdling. Not doing anything to high-light the fact that he was aware of the car following him. Then he turned into the next alley he came to. It was similar to the one he had chased the guy into after the murder. It was clean. Tidy. There was a line of dumpsters. Fire escapes that looked to be sound. But one big difference. A scaffolding tower was set up against the left-hand building where a section of gutter was missing from the base of its roof.

The Corolla had not gone by.

Reacher pressed his back against the wall and edged toward the sidewalk. He saw the nose of a white car stopped at the side of the road, far enough from the mouth of the alley to not be conspicuous. He moved along the wall the opposite way, toward the scaffolding. The metal poles were all fixed together with brackets and bolts. They were rock solid. There was no way to remove any. Not quickly. Not without tools. So he tried the wooden planks that formed the lower platform. The central one was loose. He pried it up. Pulled it out. Carried it toward the street. The car was still almost opposite. Reacher hoped the guys who were looking for him were impatient. He hoped they would get bored waiting for him to come out. Decide to force the issue. Swoop into the alley, like the guy in the BMW had done earlier. Because then he would step forward and ram the plank through the windshield. Hit the driver in the chest. Crush his ribs. Or maybe catch him in the head. Take it clean off his shoulders. Leaving Reacher and the guy in the passenger seat with some time alone.

The Corolla didn't move.

Ten minutes passed. Twenty. Half an hour.

The Corolla didn't move.

Reacher was a patient man. He could outwait anybody. It was a skill he learned during his years in the army. A skill he had honed in the years since then. But he was also realistic. He knew some things never happen, however long you wait for them. The guy in the Corolla had looked at his phone. So he had a picture, or at least a description. That must have come from the guys Reacher had encountered earlier. They might have outlined what happened. Or the four might have gotten together for a debrief. The current pair might have seen the result with their own eyes. They could be cautious. They could be smart enough to hold out for somewhere safer to make their move.

Or somewhere they thought would be safer.

That was fine with Reacher. He was a patient man. He carried the plank back to the scaffolding and slid it into place. Then he stepped out onto the sidewalk and continued on his way.

One of the hotels on the outskirts of the town looked pretty new. It was part of a chain. And therefore anonymous, which usually appealed to Reacher. The other place was on the opposite side of the main street. It must have dated back to the 1930s. The building was long and low with a flat roof. The external walls were rendered and painted pink. It had twelve rooms, each with a number on its door in a mirrored, art deco frame. The office was at the end farther from town. A pole rose from its roof. At the top there was a cartoon figure. A pineapple in a dress, picked out in yellow and turquoise neon. It had a wild grin on its face. Reacher wasn't sure if it looked friendly or demonic.

Reacher came down in favor of The Pineapple. In his experience small independent places were better suited to his needs. They were less likely to fuss about expired IDs or to insist on credit cards for payment. He headed for the office and found himself surrounded by mirrors and neon and art deco shapes. The reception desk was covered with them, too. A guy appeared from somewhere in the back corner. He was thin. Unhealthily so, with patchy gray hair, which made it tough to guess how old he was. His shirt was covered with pictures of parrots and palm trees. His turquoise shorts were baggy on his shriveled hips and their brightness made his pasty legs look almost blue.

The skinny guy offered Reacher a room for $60. Reacher countered with $80 in cash for a room with no one on either side. The guy happily agreed. He pocketed the extra twenty and handed Reacher the key to room twelve followed by a dog-eared ledger and a pen for him to sign in with. Reacher scrawled a name and a signature then walked the length of the building and let himself into his room. There was a bed. A closet. A chair. A bathroom. Standard motel fare. The fruit theme didn't extend to the inside of the building. It was a little scruffy in places but Reacher didn't mind. He kept the light on for ten minutes then switched it off and crossed to the bed.

Chapter 9

Ticket first, Jed Starmer thought, *then something to eat.*

Not that Jed was any kind of an expert traveler. This was only going to be the second time he'd left Los Angeles County since his mother brought him there when he was a baby. Now he was leaving for good and so far he wasn't enjoying the experience. He'd had to pack, which was a problem because he didn't have a suitcase or a duffel. He didn't want to steal one from his foster parents or the other kids he lived with and there was nowhere in his neighborhood that sold them. So he did the only thing he could think of. He opened up his school backpack and dumped all the institutional crap into the trash. He replaced it with clothes. Just the basics, snatched at random from his closet, as many as would fit. He grabbed his toothbrush from the bathroom, more or less as an afterthought, and jammed it in his pocket. Then he took a final look around the house. He had hated the building the moment he first set foot through the door. He had been miserable pretty much every minute he had spent there. Now it seemed like the most welcoming place in the world.

Now that he was never going to see it again.

Next up was an issue with the bus that Jed needed to catch. It didn't show up when it was supposed to. Which wasn't a concern in terms of time. Jed had built plenty of slack into his schedule. It was a question of exposure. Jed's foster mother got off work early on Tuesdays. She drove home down the street where the bus stop was located. Jed was standing there alone. He was totally exposed. There was no way she could miss him. And if she caught him there with a pocket full of her cash, he would have hell to pay.

Ten minutes ticked by. Twenty. There was no sign of any public transport. No sign of his foster mother. Another five minutes crept past. It couldn't be long until she appeared. She had to be close. Jed couldn't keep still. He started looking around for bolt holes. Anywhere he could hide if he saw her coming. Then the bus wheezed into sight. It dawdled along the street and ground to a halt next to him. He had severe reservations about its state of maintenance but he couldn't afford to wait for the next one. Not without inviting disaster. So he climbed on board, paid his fare, then hustled to the back and tried not to draw attention to himself through the long, stop-start trek to 7th and Decatur.

Jed jumped down directly across the street from the Greyhound station. He was glad he was no farther away. He didn't like the feel of the neighborhood. Not at all. It was only a couple of blocks from the old Skid Row. He had heard stories. Seen movies. Some guys were hanging around on the sidewalk. A dozen of them. They were skinny. Half of them were smoking. All of them were watching him. Like jackals, he thought. Or hyenas. Like he was their prey. There was another bunch of guys in the parking lot out front of the station. They looked a little older. But no more welcoming. Jed lowered his gaze. He snaked his way around both groups and followed the signs to the terminal entrance.

Things got better once Jed was inside. The terminal building was spacious and bright. There were people standing in line for the ticket counter and others were sitting and sprawling on the rows of blue wire seats, but no one was paying him undue attention. He skirted around the edge of the room and made for the array of self-serve machines. The one he picked was slow. Its screen was smeared with some kind of oily residue but he still managed to navigate the menus and pick his destination and class of service. He took ten $20 bills from the wad he'd taken from his foster home and fed them, one by one, into the cash receptacle. He supplemented them with four quarters of his own. Started to panic when the machine seemed to freeze. Then relaxed when his ticket nosed its way out of its slot.

Jed ignored the vending machines and moved straight across to the food counter. He studied the menu. He was starving. He wanted everything on it. This was going to be his first meal as an independent citizen and he felt like he deserved a major splurge. The place had the same kind of choices as a McDonald's, as far as he could remember. It was a while since he'd had fast food. His foster mother didn't like him eating it. Or she didn't like paying for it. He wasn't sure which. But either way, it didn't matter. He didn't have to worry about her preferences anymore. But he did have to think about his cash reserve.

In the end Jed had taken the entire stash from his foster mother's drawer. He had come to the conclusion that it would be illogical not to. Either he was entitled to the money, so it would be stupid to leave any behind. Or he was stealing it, in which case he was dooming himself anyway. After paying for the ticket he had $300 left. Accommodation for that night wouldn't be a problem. Or for the next. He would be on the bus. He would sleep there. He had no choice. But he would need somewhere to stay on Thursday night. A hotel room, maybe, or a bed-and-breakfast. Those were probably expensive. He would need food and drink along the way. And he would need onward transportation on Friday morning. Quite a long distance. He wasn't sure what form that was going to take, yet. He hoped he could find some random driver going the same way and pay him for a ride. If not he would have to take a cab. Either way it would cost. Probably a lot. So he decided to be sensible. He ordered a burger and fries, and a bottle of water for the road. He paid with a ten-dollar bill of his own. Slipped his ticket into one back pocket. Slid the rest of his money into the other. And waited for his food to come out.

It took Jed five minutes to finish eating. Then he spent twenty minutes watching the scrolling subtitles on a pair of silent TVs on the wall. One was showing news. The other was showing sports. He wasn't much interested in either. He just wanted something to do until half an hour before his bus was due to leave. He figured thirty minutes would be about right to find its departure point and be on board early enough to get a good seat. When the time came he dumped his tray on a rack next to an overflowing trash can and then made a quick pit stop in the bathroom. When he came out again he saw a guy, standing by the wall, waving. Jed recognized him. The guy had been behind him in line at the food counter. He'd also eaten alone, a couple of tables to the side. Jed was about to walk by when he realized the guy wasn't trying to attract some other stranger's attention. He was waving specifically at him.

At first Jed thought they were about the same age but when the guy moved closer it was clear he was older. Maybe twenty or twenty-one. He was thin and tanned and he had a mess of blond hair that looked crunchy with salt, like a surfer's.

"Hey, buddy." The guy held out his hand. He was holding something. A bus ticket. "This is yours. You dropped it."

That couldn't be true. Jed had put his ticket away carefully. He was sure about that. He patted his pocket to confirm. And his heart stopped. His pocket was empty. His ticket was gone. He checked the other side. For his money. All his cash . . . which was still there. He was OK. There was no problem. But it was still a moment before he could breathe again.

The blond guy glanced at Jed's ticket. "Route 1454? Cool. Same as me."

"Thank you for finding it." Jed took the ticket. His hand was shaking. "Can't believe I dropped it."

"No problem. Weird shit happens sometimes. So, you going to Dallas, too?"

Jed shook his head. "Got a transfer there."

"Going farther?"

Jed nodded. "Jackson, Mississippi."

"That's a long way. You visiting family?"

"I don't have any family."

"Really? None?"

Jed thought about an honest answer. He didn't want to lie. But neither did he want to get into the specifics. Not with a stranger. Not then. So he said, "Nope. Just me."

"No parents?"

"Never knew my dad. My mom—cancer."

"That's harsh, man. No brothers or sisters? Uncles or aunts?"

"Nope."

"So who's meeting you when you get wherever you're going?"

"No one. Why?"

"Just seems like you got dealt a tough hand, man, if you're all alone in the world. I'm sorry about that."

Jed shrugged. "You get used to it."

"Tell you what—let's ride together. At least as far as Texas. Keep each other company."

Jed shrugged again. "OK. If you want."

"This your first time riding the 'hound?"

Jed nodded.

The blond guy put his arm around Jed's shoulder, pulled him close, and dropped his voice to a whisper. "I'm going to ask you something. It's real important, so listen up. Your bag? The little backpack thing you got going on? You got anything valuable in there? Laptop? Tablet? Nintendo?"

"No. I don't have anything like that."

"That's good. Real good. The road's not a safe place. But all the same, never let your bag out of your sight. Don't leave it anywhere. Don't let the driver put it in the hold. And keep an arm through the straps when you sleep. You got me?"

"Sure."

"Good. Now I need to siphon the python. You go ahead. Through the doors, turn left. All the way to the end. Pier sixteen. Get us a pair of seats. Midway between the wheels, if you can. That's the most comfortable. I'll catch up in a minute."

Jed found the correct bus, climbed in, showed the driver his ticket, and made his way down the aisle. More than half the seats were already taken. Everyone on board was older than Jed. Some by three or four years. Some by sixty or seventy. Some people were traveling alone. Some were in pairs. Some were in groups. Many of them had headphones on. Some had pillows. A few were wrapped in blankets. Most had things to occupy themselves with, like books or phones or computers. Jed suddenly felt horribly unprepared. He wanted to turn around. Jump off the bus. Run back to his foster home. Pretend that he had never tried to leave. Forget everything his birth mother had told him. But instead he forced himself into the first empty pair of seats he came to. He shuffled across to the window. Hauled his bag onto his lap. Hugged it to his chest. And focused on the thrum of the engine. The hiss of the ventilation. The murmur of the conversations going on all around him. The smell of disinfectant and other people's food. He told himself that everything was going to be OK. Just as long as he could pull himself together before the blond guy showed up. He didn't need to be any more embarrassed than he already was.

Two minutes before departure time the door at the front of the bus hissed shut. Jed started to rise up in his seat. He was about to call out to the driver. To tell him a passenger was missing. That they had to wait. But he didn't make a sound. He stopped moving. Slid back down. And shifted his bag to the space next to him. Dallas was more than thirty-six hours away. He didn't even know the blond guy's name. He wasn't some kind of lifelong companion. He was grateful to have gotten his ticket back. But he didn't need a day and a half of questions and opinions and dumb-ass advice being shoved down his throat before he switched to the next bus. He was happy to be on his own.

Until 10:00 A.M. on Friday, anyway.

Whether he would be alone after that was a whole other question.

Chapter 10

The lock's mechanism clicked and whirred. Reacher's door swung open. A quadrant of light unfurled across the garish carpet. Two men crept inside. Both mid-twenties. Both holding guns. One eased the door back into place in its frame. They stood still for a moment. Then they started toward the bed. It was only semi-visible. The glow filtering through the thin drapes was pale. But the shape beneath the covers was tall. It was broad. It was what they were expecting.

The men separated, one either side of the mattress. They continued to the head of the bed. It was a warm night but the comforter was pulled all the way up over the pillows. The guy nearer the window shrugged, then prodded what he estimated would be Reacher's shoulder with the muzzle of his gun.

He got no response.

He poked again. Harder. He said, "Hey. Wake up."

The ceiling light flicked on. The guys spun around. They saw Reacher at the other end of the room. He opened the door and stepped outside. Then he darted to the side and pressed his back against the external wall.

The guys ran after Reacher. The first one's leading foot touched the ground outside and Reacher smashed him in the face with his forearm. The guy's nose shattered. His neck snapped back. He collapsed through the doorway, piled into his buddy's chest, and knocked him down. Reacher scooped up the guy's gun and followed him inside.

The first guy wasn't moving. The second had rolled onto his side and was scrabbling to retrieve his gun from where he dropped it when he fell. Reacher stamped on his hand. The guy screamed and curled up into a ball. Reacher grabbed the first guy by the arm, pulled him into the room, and closed the door.

There was a bang on the wall. A man's voice yelled, "Hey. Room 12. Keep it down."

Reacher waited for the second guy to go quiet then said, "Get up. Sit in the chair if you want. We can be civilized about this."

The guy scuttled back on his heels and his butt and his good hand until his shoulders were touching the wall.

Reacher said, "I met a couple of your friends today. Here, in town. In an alley. Where are they now?"

The guy didn't respond.

Reacher said, "Why did one of them kill a woman this morning? Push her under a bus?"

The guy didn't answer.

Reacher stepped in close and stamped on the guy's other hand. He screamed again, louder, and rolled onto his other side.

There was another bang on the wall. A man's voice yelled, "Room 12. Be quiet. Last warning."

Reacher waited for the guy to uncurl himself a little then said, "Who do you work for?"

The guy shook his head.

Reacher stamped on the guy's right knee. He screamed, long and loud.

Reacher said, "I can go on all night. Can you? The other two. Where are they?"

The guy said, "They left town."

"Where are they going?"

"Home. Winson, Mississippi."

"Why did you stay?"

"We were told to find you."

"Why?"

"Find out what you know."

"About?"

The light filtering through the drapes switched from dull gray to pulsing red and blue. Reacher peered out of the window. There were two police cars in the parking lot. One outside his room. One at the far end. An officer was already on foot, heading for the office. To talk to the clerk. To check on numbers and dispositions. And to get a passkey. None of those things would take long. Reacher figured he had sixty seconds at best. He hauled the first guy up onto his feet and turned him so that his back was to the door. He punched the side of the guy's head and let him fall to the floor again. He grabbed the second guy. Pulled him away from the wall. Smashed the back of his head into the floor. Pinched one of his earlobes to make sure he was unconscious. Dragged him forward until his feet were almost touching the first guy's. They were lying like the hands of a clock at close to 3:00 P.M. He wiped his prints off the first guy's gun and tossed it onto the floor. Went into the bathroom. Opened the window. And climbed out.

The area at the back of the hotel was not promising. There was a small pool and a bunch of white plastic lounging chairs all surrounded by a rickety wooden fence. It was eight feet tall. Ancient. No way would it take his weight. The only way out was through the office, and a pair of cops would be coming the other way any second. Two at the front. Two at the back. That was the obvious way to do it. He was trapped. And there was nowhere to hide. Not at ground level, anyway.

Reacher moved back to his bathroom window and lifted one foot onto the sill. He pushed up and grabbed the edge of the roof. Pulled with his arms. Scrambled over the lip. Rolled to the center. And lay completely still. He heard footsteps on both sides of the building. They were close. The ones at the front stopped moving. Someone thumped on the door.

"Gerrardsville Police Department. Open up."

The officers at the rear were poking around the pool furniture. One of them took a chair and set it next to the fence. He climbed up and looked over and quartered the area on the far side with his flashlight. Then he jumped down and called, "Clear."

Reacher heard the whirr of the lock and then a thump as the door to his room hit one of the unconscious guy's heels. There was a pause, the door closed, then he heard the cop's voice through the bathroom window. It sounded like he was on his radio.

"We have two male suspects, nonresponsive. Two guns secured at the scene."

A second voice said, "Looks like they got into it over something. Got into it pretty good. No ID. No smell of booze. Better send a bus right away."

The first voice came back, quieter. "They can stay in the hospital overnight. The detective can question them in the morning, if he wants to. We better seal this place, just in case."

Reacher lay on the roof and watched an ambulance arrive. A pair of paramedics rolled the two guys out on gurneys, loaded them up, and drove off. The cops left a couple of minutes later. Reacher stayed where he was for another hour, until he was satisfied that there were no cops lurking and no nosey guests snooping around. Then he climbed down and walked to the office. A couple was leaving as he went in. They looked young. Flushed. Happy. And a little bit furtive.

The same guy was at the counter, wearing the same ridiculous clothes and looking just as sickly and malnourished. He saw Reacher and said, "You're OK?"

Reacher said, "I'm fine. Why?"

"The cops let you out already?"

"They never took me in. I went for a walk. Came back and found my door sealed up with crime scene tape. What's that all about?"

"It wasn't my fault. Two guys came. Made me give them a passkey."

"Then you dialed 911?"

"I guess the guy in 11 did that. He's a real asshole."

"I told you I didn't want any neighbors."

The guy pulled a twenty-dollar bill from his pocket and handed it to Reacher. "He comes here all the time. With his girlfriend. She's also an asshole. That's their favorite room. He insisted. I'm sorry."

Reacher handed the twenty back. "Give me another room. No one on either side. And this time, no excuses."

State of Illinois. It had articles of association. Share-holders. Executive officers. Employees. Accounts with all kinds of recognizable brand-name suppliers. It had plenty of customers, most of whom were satisfied. It paid taxes. It sponsored a local kids' softball team. And it provided cover for certain other materials that Emerson had to have shipped in from a handful of less-well-known sources.

The bulk of the corporation's reported income came from sprinkler installations and alarm systems. There was no shortage of co-ops and condo buildings in Chicagoland, as well as offices and industrial premises. New ones were constantly going up. Old ones were always getting refurbished. The pickings were rich for an outfit like Emerson's. And it didn't hurt that the rules and regulations changed so frequently. Something that was up to code one year could be condemned as dangerous the next. And again a couple of years after that. Hidden interests were served. The way things had always been in the Windy City. Pockets got lined. Companies got busy. Plenty of them. Including Emerson's. Corporate clients were its bread and butter. But that didn't mean it turned its back on the little guys. Emerson insisted on offering a full range of services to the safety-conscious homeowner, too. That helped to broaden the customer base, which was good from a business point of view. And the steady flow of station wagons and minivans through the parking lot added to an impression of banal normality. Which was good for another reason.

Emerson's name might have been over the door but he had nothing to do with the banal, normal side of the business. For that he hired people who knew what they were doing. Who could be trusted to keep their fingers out of the register. And he left them to get on with it. Partly because he was naturally a good delegator. Partly because he had no interest in sprinklers and alarms or anything else that helped to prevent fires. But mostly because his time was fully occupied elsewhere. He had a parallel operation to run.

The thing he loved to do.

The jobs Emerson carried out personally fell into two categories. Those that looked like accidents. And those that didn't. The job he was just finishing would not look like an accident. That was for damn sure. It would be a thing of beauty. Unmistakably deliberate. Impossible to trace back to Emerson. Or his client. Unambiguous in its meaning. And with a signature that was distinct and unique. That way, if the recipient was sufficiently stupid or obtuse, the message could be repeated and the connection would be clear.

Emerson knew it was a stretch to say he was still actively finishing the job. The work was essentially complete. There was nothing more he needed to do. Or that he could do. His continued presence would not affect the outcome in any way. He could have been hundreds of miles away and it would have made no difference. Four of his guys already were. They were heading back to base, driving a pair of anonymous white panel vans, preparing to clean their equipment and resupply for their next project. He could have gone with them. That would have been the prudent thing to do. But he stayed. He wanted to watch. He needed to watch.

Prudence be damned.

The thing he loved to do.

Emerson was on the Talmadge Memorial Bridge in Georgia, nearly six hundred feet above the Savannah River, midway between the mainland and Hutchinson Island. The strip of land that split the waterway that separated Georgia from South Carolina. He was standing, not driving. Leaning with his forearms against the lip of the concrete sidewall on the west-bound side. Graeber, his right-hand man, was next to him. He was also leaning on the wall. His pose was exactly the same but he was just a little shorter. A little younger. A little less obsessed.

Pedestrians weren't encouraged on the bridge. There was no sidewalk. No bike lane. But back during the planning stage the architects had been fearful of vehicles breaking down or crashing into one another. The city couldn't afford for a major artery to get blocked. Even for a short time. In either direction. So they provided a generous shoulder. One on each side. Deliberately adequate to keep the traffic flowing in emergencies. Unintentionally wide enough for suitably motivated individuals to walk or run or ride at other times. And coincidentally perfect for two out-of-towners to hang out and enjoy the late-evening view.

If Emerson had been a regular sightseer he would

have been looking in the other direction. Behind him. Toward the old city. To the leafy squares and cobbled streets and gingerbread houses and domed municipal halls. A rich slice of history all wrapped up in golden light and reflected back off the swirling nighttime Savannah water. But Emerson had no interest in the tourist stuff. He didn't care about its colonial roots or how closely the layout resembled the city founder's original scheme. His focus was on the industrial section. The port area, ahead of him. A sprawling mess of gas storage tanks and container facilities and warehouses that littered the west bank of the river. He was concentrating on one building in particular. A storage unit. A large one, with white metal walls and a white metal roof.

Emerson knew that aside from a crude office nibbled out from one corner, the building had no internal walls. He knew that most of its volume was filled with sealed wooden crates. He had been told they contained kids' dolls, imported from China without the correct paperwork. He believed the part about the paperwork. But he figured the last thing he would find in the crates would be kids' dolls. From China or anywhere else. But he didn't care. He'd been given a detailed chemical analysis of the alleged dolls' components and a sample crate, fully packed, identical to the ones in the unit, for him to test. Which he did. Thoroughly. Though he didn't look inside. He wasn't one for taking unnecessary risks. There are some things it's safer not to know.

Emerson's knowledge of the building and its contents wasn't all theoretical. The previous two days had been spent on close observation. First, to gauge its security measures. And second, to ensure that the place was unoccupied, as stipulated. The first was a practical thing. The second, business. If the body count went up, so did his price. It was a basic principle. He wasn't in the game for the money but he was the best, and that had to be recognized. That was only fair. Plus he had a wife at home. And a son. The kid was in his twenties now but he was still a liability. Financially speaking. Emerson had all kinds of expenses to take care of. Cars. Food. Clothes. Medical bills. More than a quarter of a million dollars in the last year alone. And one day soon there would be college to pay for. If the kid ever got his act together. Life didn't come cheap for Lev Emerson.

After forty-eight hours Emerson concluded that there was no reason to abort and no cause to demand more money so that morning, before sunrise, the implementation phase had begun. First the alarms were disabled. Intruder, smoke, and temperature. The sprinklers were deactivated. Equipment was brought in. So were the chemicals, formulated specifically for this job, safe in their special containers. Cables were laid. Control mechanisms were installed. Measurements were taken. Calculations were carried out. Predictions were made regarding airflow and heat gain. Holes were cut at strategic positions in the walls and the roof. Crates were moved to optimize circulation. The calculations were repeated. They were checked, and checked again. More adjustments were made. And finally, when Emerson was happy, the site was evacuated. His creation was set and primed and activated. The doors were closed and locked for the final time. The panel vans departed. Emerson and Graeber grabbed a bite to eat and prepared for showtime.

The thing he loved to do.

Graeber nudged Emerson's arm. The first whisper of smoke had curled into view. It was rising hesitantly through one of the new gashes in the storage unit's roof. Still delicate. Pale. Insubstantial. A hint of what was in store. A promise. Emerson felt a flutter in his chest. He was like a music lover hearing the first gentle notes of a favorite symphony. The anticipation was exquisite. Almost too much to bear. The plume thickened. Darkened. Began to twist and twirl and dance. It climbed faster and spread and . . .

Emerson's phone rang. Which shouldn't have been possible. He wrenched it from his pocket and glared at the screen. It said, *Home calling.* Which meant his wife. Who should have known better. He'd outlined the timetable to her, like he always did. He'd been clear. And she knew not to interrupt him during the finale of a job. So he jabbed the button to reject the call. Shoved the phone back into his pocket. Turned back to the storage unit, which now had smoke billowing from five vents. Tried to control his breathing. And waited for the flames.

Thirty seconds later Graeber's phone rang. He checked it, then stepped away and answered. He spoke for more than five minutes. When he returned to Emerson's side his face was pale. His hands were trembling. But Emerson didn't notice. He only had eyes for the inferno. The storage unit's roof was gone now. Its walls were buckled and warped. The flames writhed and flailed and tormented the sky. The dark void was now bursting with color, vivid and bright, fluid and alive. Fire trucks were approaching. Racing closer. There was a whole convoy. At least half a dozen. They were using their lights and sirens. Emerson smiled. They shouldn't have left their firehouse. They were pointless. Impotent. They had more chance of blowing out the sun than dousing the fruits of his labor. Any time in the next few hours, anyway.

Graeber lifted his hand. He stretched out, slowly, like he was pushing away a heavy, invisible object. He reached Emerson's arm. Took hold of his sleeve. Gave it a cautious tug.

Emerson ignored him.

Graeber tugged again, harder. "Boss. You need to call home."

Emerson didn't turn his head. "Later."

Graeber said, "No. Now. I'm sorry. But trust me. It can't wait."

"What can't?"

"It's about Kyle. Your son."

"What's he done now?"

"Boss, I'm so sorry. Kyle is dead. He died an hour ago."

Chapter 12

The Greyhound bus was alive with sound.

The fat tires thrummed on the blacktop and thumped over every crack and pothole. The ventilation system murmured and sighed. Conflicting bass rhythms escaped from several passengers' headphones. Some of the younger guys laughed out loud at shows they were watching on their tablets and phones. Some of the older ones talked. A couple argued. A few snored and grunted and groaned. Normally an unaccustomed racket like that would have kept Jed Starmer awake. He liked quiet at night, aside from the usual sirens and background traffic noise that filtered through his window and into his bedroom. But the craziness of the last few days had taken its toll. Its sudden absence merged with the darkness and the soft swaying motion. It pulled him down into the depths of sleep. Its hold was so strong that it took a couple of minutes after the driver switched on the bright interior lights for him to surface. By then the bus was stationary, lined up next to another one just like it, and the rest of the passengers were standing and stretching and fussing with their luggage or shuffling up and down in the aisle.

Jed had pulled his backpack onto his lap at some point after the bus left its previous stop in Blythe, California. He was hunched over it, resting his head on its top flap, hugging it tight like a giant teddy bear. He straightened up and pushed the bag onto the seat next to him, not wanting to look like a little kid. Then he peered out of his window. He saw a sign on the side of the depot building in the distance. It was covered with mountain silhouettes and cartoon cacti and it said *Welcome to Phoenix, Arizona* in English and Spanish. He checked the time. It was ten after two. The early hours of Wednesday morning. Which meant they were ten minutes ahead of schedule. Their stop would be stretched to an hour and a half. It would be the only significant break they got before El Paso, Texas, which they wouldn't reach until lunchtime. Jed thought about getting out of the bus for a while. Finding something to eat. Stretching his legs. But he decided against it. He only had three hundred dollars left. He had some big expenses coming up. And his whole body felt drained. He doubted he could drag himself out of his seat. So he stayed where he was. Leaned back. Closed his eyes. And made sure not to cuddle his backpack again.

He didn't want to look like a kid.

———

Back in L.A., Jed's foster mother had not slept.

She had gone to bed at her regular time but she was too angry to get any rest. Too angry, and too busy listening for Jed's furtive footsteps. She figured he was out somewhere, carousing with friends. Or worse, with a girl. He must have thought he could break his curfew and do who knew what kind of immoral things without anyone noticing. That he could sneak back home in the middle of the night and act like nothing had happened.

He was wrong.

She was going to show him exactly how wrong.

She spent hours lying still and writing sermons in her head. Rehearsing the lectures she would give him. The admonishments. The punishments. She was practically exhausted by all the thinking when her morning alarm went off. By then the time and her tiredness were turning her anger into worry. Jed still wasn't back. It wasn't like him to stay out all night. She started to think about calling the local hospitals. Maybe the police. Then her worry morphed into full-blown fear. She went to get dressed and found her emergency fund was gone. But twenty-dollar bills don't just disappear. They must have been taken. She checked Jed's closet. Some of his clothes were missing. A strange selection, not what she would have picked if she were taking a trip, but there were definitely gaps. And to seal the deal, when she looked in the bathroom, Jed's toothbrush was gone.

Jed had run away with her money. There was no other explanation. The ungrateful, thieving brat.

Jed's foster mother abandoned the process of getting ready for work. She fetched the phone. Called her boss. Said she was too sick to come in that day. Then she dialed 911 and had a different kind of conversation.

Jed had been desperate not to break the law. To avoid the police coming after him. It hadn't dawned on him there were other reasons for that to happen. He'd been too focused on chasing his new goal. On starting his new life.

Lev Emerson hadn't slept much that night, either.

He had spent fourteen hours in his car, with Graeber, blasting north from Georgia through Tennessee and Kentucky and Indiana and then across the corner of Illinois until they reached the outskirts of Chicago. They had split the driving, which was good for safety. But not good for Emerson's state of mind. He had called his wife when he was still on the bridge in Savannah, watching the fire he had set. Her voice had been distant and mechanical, the way a dead person sounds in a dream. She had told him about Kyle. Their son. His rehabilitation had been going so well. Until suddenly it wasn't. That afternoon. His body just shut down. First his liver, of course. Then one system after another. A cascade of total catastrophic failures. She had called the doctor right away but it was already too late. Nothing could be done. Kyle had shriveled and shrunk and slipped away right in front of her. She had been powerless to stop him.

Kyle was only twenty-two. It wasn't right. Not after everything they'd done to help him. Not after the amount of money they'd spent.

While Emerson was behind the wheel he had other things to focus on. Not crashing. Not getting pulled over with the needle north of 120. Straightening that kind of thing out can cause serious delays. But when Graeber was driving Emerson found it harder to control his emotions. His wife's words echoed in his head. Memories of his son crowded in after them. Along with the regrets. So many regrets. And so much reluctance to face the scene he knew must await him at home.

Graeber's car was parked in Emerson's garage. He had left it there when they set off for Georgia. Emerson had driven the last leg so he hit the remote, waited for the door to clank up and out of the way, and pulled in alongside it. Graeber reached for the door handle but before he got out he turned to his boss. "What do you want us to do?"

Emerson thought for a moment. About the things he would have to handle when he went inside the house. How long they would take. Then he said, "Call Shevchenko. He owes us, big-time. Tell him we need a plane. Today. And maybe a chopper, tomorrow or the next day. Then meet me at the warehouse. In two hours. Bring the others. And pack a bag."

"Where are we going?"

"To find the people who sold the thing that killed my son."

Chapter 13

Jack Reacher slept lightly in his replacement room. He woke himself at 9:00 A.M. He showered. He got dressed. And he had just folded his toothbrush, ready to leave, when there was a heavy knock at his door.

"Jack Reacher? This is Detective Harewood, Gerrardsville PD. Are you in there? We need to talk."

Reacher opened the door and let the detective in. Harewood glanced around the space. He waited for Reacher to sit on the bed and then took the only chair. It was a fluffy turquoise thing with a loose arm and it wasn't at all comfortable. Harewood fidgeted in vain for a moment then put a file he'd been carrying down on the floor.

He said, "You should get a cellphone."

Reacher said, "Why?"

"So that people can call you."

"Like who?"

"Like me."

"You likely to do that often?"

Harewood paused. "No. But that's not the point. You're a hard man to find. It would have been easier if I could have called you. Asked you where you were."

"But you did find me."

"Eventually. I called all the hotels in town and asked if they had a guy named Reacher registered. Of course they all said no. So I figured you were using an alias. I remembered you told me you came to town to see the exhibition about Pea Ridge. So I called all the hotels back. Asked for a guest named Samuel Curtis. The victorious general from the battle. And boom. Here you are."

"I'm impressed. You should be a detective."

Harewood smiled, but without any humor. "About that. It's why I wanted to talk to you. I wanted to let you know that the case—the woman killed by the bus—has been closed."

Reacher thought about the two men he'd seen being wheeled away on gurneys the night before. They'd been in bad shape. Maybe the beating they'd taken had made them open to a deal. He said, "You caught the guys?"

"It's been ruled a suicide."

Reacher said nothing.

Harewood closed his eyes and shook his head. "Look, I know what you told me. About the guy in the hoodie. How he pushed the woman. I believe you. But here's the problem. Another witness came forward. He swears he saw the woman dive in front of the bus. Deliberately dive."

"He's wrong."

"I believe you. But this other guy? He's . . . respectable."

"And I'm not?"

"I didn't say that. My lieutenant—"

"This *witness* is wrong. Or he's lying. Maybe he's in on it. Or maybe he was paid off."

Harewood shook his head. "He's a solid citizen. He's lived right here in town his whole life. Has a house. A wife. A job. Doesn't gamble. Doesn't drink or use drugs. Isn't in debt. Never even got a parking ticket."

"Other witnesses, then? Passengers on the bus. Someone must have seen something."

"One passenger thinks she saw the woman jump. But she wasn't wearing her glasses so she's not much use either way. And another passenger saw you. Fleeing the scene. Which is one reason why my lieutenant—"

"Is there a note?"

Harewood paused. "She left one at her home. In Mississippi. On her kitchen table. We got prints from the ME, pulled her ID, and asked the local PD to check her house. They found it right away."

"Was the note typed?"

"No. It was handwritten. And signed. No red flags there."

"What makes you think it's genuine?"

Harewood retrieved his file, took out two sheets of paper, and handed them to Reacher. "The first is her most recent job application. The company she works—worked—for makes all their candidates fill in these forms by hand. Supposedly that reveals all kinds of hidden stuff about people's personalities. Helps to weed out sociopaths and other undesirable characters. The second is her note."

Reacher started with the job form. He didn't have much experience with employment paperwork but what he read struck him as generic and banal. The first box was headed *Please state your reasons for seeking this position.* Angela's writing was large and rounded and a little childish. She had claimed she wanted to help people. To build on the skills she had developed in previous roles. To make a contribution to the community at large. There was nothing to suggest she had been a stand-out candidate. Or that she was looking to work in a prison. It could have been an application for work as a dog warden. Or at a candy store.

The second sheet had no structure. No questions to answer or information to provide. It had started life as a regular piece of blank paper. The kind that gets used in printers and copiers in homes and offices all over the country. All over the world. Pumped out of giant factories by the million. Used and filed and forgotten. Or thrown away. Or shredded. Only this one had not wound up as something ordinary. Something trivial. The words began about an eighth of the way down, close to the edge. *If you're reading this, I'm sorry, but it's because I'm dead . . .*

Reacher compared the samples. The way the letters were formed. The size and the shape and the spacing. The punctuation. The phrasing. He factored in the passage of time. The effect of stress. He was no expert but he had to admit they did look like the work of the same person. He tucked the note back under the form where he wouldn't have to look at it anymore, passed both pages to Harewood and said, "OK. Motive?"

"A love affair gone bad."

"How do you figure?"

"Angela was an admin assistant at a prison. When we notified the local PD they contacted her work. It's a private company. They have the right to monitor their employees' personal email. It's a security thing. Built into their contracts. Most people don't know it's there. Or they forget about it. So their IT guy pulled up her account. Standard procedure in the event of a sudden death. He found a message chain going back a few weeks. Evidently Angela wanted to rekindle an old flame. With an old boyfriend who lived near here. A guy named Roth. They set a rendezvous for Tuesday. Yesterday. She implied in her last email that if it didn't work out, she didn't want to live anymore. A little passive-aggressive, if you ask me."

"*Lived* near here?"

"What?"

"You said the boyfriend *lived*."

Harewood nodded. "Roth's DOA. He had a heart attack."

"When?"

"Monday night. Late. Maybe around midnight."

"So this guy Roth died less than twelve hours before Angela was killed. You buy that as a coincidence?"

Harewood shrugged.

Reacher said, "Who found the body?"

"His ex-wife."

"Where?"

"At his apartment. Yesterday morning. He was a big guy. As in ripped. Not fat. He had a home gym. He'd been working out. Which he did regularly. And then, *bang.* Game over. Just like that."

"Steroids? Or whatever the latest thing is?"

"No indication of any."

"Why was his ex-wife at his apartment?"

"For breakfast."

"Is that normal?"

"For them, yes, apparently."

"How did she get inside?"

"She has a key."

"Sounds cozy."

"I guess."

"Maybe the ex was trying to get back into the picture. Found out about this reunion. Got jealous."

Harewood shook his head. "I don't think so. They'd been divorced ten years. She moved to the apartment next door when they split. Neighbors said they got on like brother and sister. Any kind of spark fizzled out years ago. There was no bad blood."

"Had Roth had other relationships?"

Harewood shrugged.

Reacher said, "Did the ex know about his relationship with Angela?"

"We didn't ask her about it. We had no reason to.

Roth's body was found before Angela got killed. We didn't know anything about her until we pulled her out from under that bus."

"So the ex didn't confirm the rendezvous?"

"No. That's not to say she didn't know about it. But we already verified it another way."

Harewood thumbed through his file, pulled out another piece of paper, and set it on the edge of the bed. Reacher wasn't familiar with the format but he guessed it was a transcript of the emails that the Minerva IT guys had come up with. It was certainly made up of alternating messages between two people. He assumed they were Angela and Roth but the names weren't shown in a way he could decipher. There were just bunches of letters and numbers with @ signs in the middle and .coms at the end. There were vertical lines at the left of the page, starting at the top of each separate message and running all the way down to the end of the last one. Each successive line was one space to the right so that the lowest message was all squashed up into less than half the width of the page. It was the oldest, from Angela. She had been putting out feelers about getting back together. Reacher could sense her excitement. Her trepidation. The newest message, at the top, written on Sunday morning, was also from Angela. The tone was flat. She sounded depressed. The tentative hope had faded away. All that was left was an undercurrent of despair. Plus a bunch of hints that she couldn't carry on alone. Just as Harewood had reported.

Reacher put the paper down. "If Angela came here to meet Roth, where is her purse? Her car?"

Harewood took the paper and slipped it back into his file. "Her purse was in her car. Her car was in a parking lot. The first one you come to if you're coming in from the east. Like she would have done."

"I saw the guy take her purse. They must have dumped it in her car. Was there an envelope inside it?"

Harewood checked his notes. "No. There was a wallet. Keys. Some personal stuff. But no correspondence. Why?"

"Never mind. How do you account for the blood?"

"What blood?"

"On her purse. There was blood spatter all over one side of it."

"There's no record of that. What makes you think so?"

"I saw it."

"How? Blood wouldn't stand out against black leather."

"The purse was tan. And it wasn't leather."

Harewood checked his notes again. "It was leather. And it was black."

"They must have switched it. Replaced it with a sanitized one."

"Can you prove that?"

"What about her kid?"

"How do you know she had a kid?"

"Lucky guess."

Harewood shook his head. "She made arrangements with a neighbor. A woman who often watched her."

"Permanent arrangements? With money attached? Adoption papers? Favorite toys?"

Harewood shrugged. "I only have what the officers in Mississippi passed along. They seem satisfied."

"And the BMW?"

Harewood shook his head. "That's another problem. The plates you gave me are registered to a Dodge Caravan in Oklahoma City. The owner was at work yesterday. He has a receipt from a parking garage. Timestamped, with pictures of the vehicle arriving and leaving."

"OK. Where are the shell casings? I put six rounds into that car."

"CSU swept the alley. Twice. It was clean. No trace of any brass."

"So test my hands for GSR."

"Which would prove what? That you fired a gun? Not necessarily a gun that fired missing rounds at a missing car."

"What about the fire escape? There's no hiding that."

"It collapsed. Sure. But there's no proof *why*."

"What about—"

"Listen, Reacher. I've already asked all these questions. And I've been told to stop. In no uncertain terms. The file is closed. I just came to let you know the situation. As a courtesy."

"Then I guess we're done here. You know where the door is."

Harewood didn't move.

Reacher waited thirty seconds then stood up and

dropped his room key onto the bed. "Do me a favor. Leave that at reception on your way out."

Harewood said, "Wait. I came to . . . Well, I didn't just come as a courtesy."

Reacher sat back down.

"To be completely honest, my lieutenant wants you out of the jurisdiction. He thinks you're trouble."

"So you're here to drag me across the county line?"

"No. I'm not here at all. Not officially."

"I figured. Showing evidence to a potential suspect—that can't be SOP around here."

"No." Harewood looked down at the floor. "The lieutenant would have my ass for that."

"So why did you do it?"

"I ran your record. The 110th. The special investigators. Your old unit. In the army."

"What about it?"

"Look, I'm new to this gig."

"And?"

"I don't have anyone else to ask."

"Ask what?"

"If you were me, what would you do?"

"About what?"

"My lieutenant has ordered me to drop this case. I think he's wrong. I want to keep working it. Should I do that?"

"You're talking about going against your chain of command."

"Yes, sir. I'm clear about that."

Reacher paused. "Marine Corps?"

"How did you know?"

"My father was a Marine. I know the signs."

"So? What should I do?"

"Your lieutenant—is he a crook? Is he running a coverup of some kind?"

"I don't think so. I think the guy's just lazy. He's been given a result tied up in ribbons. He doesn't want to untie them and see what's really inside the box. He doesn't want to do the work."

"What's Roth's ex's name?"

"Hannah Hampton."

"His address?"

"I'll write it for you."

"Good. Then this is what you should do. Go back to work. Business as usual. Say nothing more about this."

"I'm not asking you to work the case for me."

"I know."

"You shouldn't get involved."

"I'm already involved."

"You should get uninvolved."

"A woman was murdered. Someone has to do something about that."

"We will do something. The police department."

"Will you? With your lazy lieutenant?"

Harewood looked at the ground.

"Give me that address. Then keep your head down. I'll be in touch."

Chapter 14

Factor in the fittings and fixtures, add on the value of the art that covers the walls, and the Minerva Reception Center in Winson cost more per square foot than any corporate headquarters in the State of Mississippi. That was a sound bite Bruno Hix loved to throw around. Especially to the press. It may even have been true. Hix didn't care. He wasn't a detail man. He was all about creating the right impression. Building the center was the first thing Minerva did after it bought the prison and the brief Hix gave the architects was simple: Make sure the place reeks of money.

The Reception Center was near the entrance to the site, on the opposite side from the secure units. The building was a single story high, faced in pale stone, and shaped like a V. Partly so that it would fit in the available space, which was limited. But mainly so that its windows, which were on its inner face only, did not have a view of the cell blocks and exercise yards. Its conference room took up one whole wing. Hix hustled through the maze of fenced-in walkways that crisscrossed the complex the minute the covert meeting in S2's hub wrapped up but he still failed to get to it on time. When he burst through the double doors, a little pink and out of breath, six faces were already staring back at him. Three on one side of the long alder table. Two on the other. And one all the way at the far end. They were journalists, there to be briefed about the event planned for Friday. Plus whatever else Hix chose to spoon-feed them while they were his captive audience.

Hix waited for Damon Brockman, Minerva's other co-founder, to take a seat and dismissed the guard who'd been keeping an eye on the visitors. Then he got the ball rolling the way he always did. He stood at the head of the table, stretched out his arms like a TV evangelist, and said, "Tell me the truth. Does this room feel like it's part of a prison?"

Five of the journalists obediently shook their heads. Only the guy at the far end didn't respond.

Hix smiled and moved on to some history. His own, and Brockman's. He talked about how they met three decades ago as rookie wardens at a state facility in Lubbock, Texas. How horrified they had been at the conditions. The lack of resources. The dehumanizing treatment they witnessed. He threw in a little philosophy. Some Foucault. Some Bentham. And he pulled it all together to explain the foundation of Minerva Correctional. Named for the ancient goddess of wisdom and justice, among other things. Committed to seeing inmates for what they were: people. People who had made mistakes, for sure. Who had made bad choices. But who still had potential. Who could make a positive contribution. Who could have a future, given the right kind of environment and support. He described the vocational programs the company ran. The diet and exercise initiatives they had introduced. The proactive health screening they provided at all five of their locations. He backed up his examples with statistics. Some may even have been accurate. He claimed dramatic increases in post-release employment rates. A profound drop in recidivism. And he finished by tying everything back to Friday. The jewel in Minerva's crown. The sponsored appeal scheme for well-behaved inmates who could credibly claim to be victims of miscarried justice.

Hix paused to give his concluding point some extra emphasis, then rested his palms on the table, leaned forward, and said, "Questions?"

Hix always got asked about a bunch of mundane details. The identity of his investors. Recruitment. Employment practices. Visitation rights. Violence. The presence of gangs. He figured there would be something about the environment and the impact of Minerva's operations, too. That had become a hot potato of late. And there could be some wild cards. Spicier issues, which may or may not come up, depending on the feistiness of the audience. Issues like the morality of profiting from other people's incarceration. Whether enough was being done to prevent the sexual abuse of vulnerable inmates. Evidence of racial bias among the guards. Things that required a little more thought and finesse.

Within a quarter of an hour the five journalists sitting close to Hix had ticked all the usual boxes. Hix had tried to make it sound like he had never heard their types of questions before. Like he was interested in them. He gave what he thought would be his final answer and was about to wind the session up when the sixth journalist sprang into life. The one at the far end of the table. He was the youngest of the group. He had a round, plump face, straggly blond hair, and was dressed in faded clothes from an army surplus store. Like a wannabe Che Guevara in need of a hat and a dye job, Hix thought. And some focus. Until that point the guy had shown little interest in anything going on around him. He had shown little sign of being awake.

"The death rate in Minerva's prisons is shocking," the guy said. "Why is it so high?"

Hix glanced down at Brockman and paused for a moment. Then he wet his lips and said, "The mortality rate at our centers is not high. What makes you think otherwise?"

Brockman slipped his phone out of his pocket. He held it low down, next to his leg, so no one could see him tap out a message with his thumb.

The Guevara guy said, "I have my sources."

"Which you can't reveal?" Hix said.

"Correct."

Hix smiled. "You're fishing, aren't you, my friend? Well, you're casting your hook in the wrong pond.

The health and life expectancy of our inmates is significantly better than at comparable institutions. And that's not down to chance. Or luck. It's thanks to our unique, progressive, humanitarian policies. If fate leads you down the unfortunate path to incarceration, a Minerva facility is where you want to end up. There's no question about that."

"You're saying your death rate isn't sky high?"

"That's exactly what I'm saying."

"You have the data to back it up?"

"Of course."

"Then why don't you publish it?"

"To what end? There's nothing to see."

"You should publish it anyway. For transparency."

"We publish everything we're required to by state and federal law."

"Which is a fraction of what state and federal facilities have to publish."

Hix shrugged. "We don't make the law. We just comply with it. Scrupulously."

"You're using it as a smokescreen. You have a serious drug problem in your jails and you're trying to hide it. Whenever an inmate overdoses and has to go to the hospital, you pass it off as some kind of preventative measure coming from your so-called humanitarianism. You've gotten good at hiding the truth about the ones who recover. But when they die? That's where the real story is, right?"

"Wrong. Look, can I hand on heart say there won't be a single drug taken in any of our facilities today? No. We live in the real world. I'm not naïve. But when it comes to drugs, just like everything else, Minerva is streets ahead of every other operator in helping and protecting our inmates. The idea that addicts are dying in droves in our care is ridiculous."

"Prove it. Show us the data."

"I—"

There was a hard rap on the door behind Hix and the guard who had been watching the group came back into the room. He said, "I'm sorry to interrupt, sir, but there's a phone call for you."

"Tell whoever it is I'll call them back. I'm busy here."

"It's the governor, sir."

"Oh. What does he want?"

"He didn't say. Just that it was urgent."

"OK. I guess I shouldn't keep him waiting, then. Could you help these good folks find their way to the exit?"

The guard nodded. "Happy to."

Hix turned back to the journalists. "I'm sorry, but we're going to have to draw a line at this point. Which is a shame because I was really enjoying the debate. My friend at the end of the table, I'll get you those mortality numbers. Assuming our legal guys give me the green light. We have to be careful about privileged information, SEC regulations, things like that. And I'll also have a word with one of our inmates. See if he'll talk to you. When Minerva took this place over the guy had something going on with one of his eyes. Damon and I had seen the same thing with a prisoner years ago, when we were working for a different corrections provider. That company wouldn't bring in a doctor because of the cost. They didn't provide insurance. The condition got worse and worse, and long story short the prisoner was left completely blind. The same would have happened to our guy, only we got him proactive treatment. Now he's an artist. He paints watercolors. Some of them are on display in a gallery in Jackson. He can give you the real scoop on our humanitarian policies. With no dead junkies involved. I guarantee."

Hix shook each journalist's hand and when the last one had filed out of the room he flopped down into the seat at the head of the table. "Bad moment, back there. High death rates? That was a little too close to home."

"Who is that kid?" Brockman said. "I like him. Great way to trace drug deaths. We should try it on those assholes at Curtis Correctional. Dig up some dirt. Hit them right when their contract is up in Kansas."

"We have more urgent issues. That kid needs to be watched. Twenty-four/seven, until he leaves town."

"No need. He's no danger to us. He knows nothing. Like you said, he was fishing."

"He's no danger yet. But we can't have him poking around. Asking questions. Not if he's looking for drugs."

"So what if he's looking for drugs? He won't find any. None he can connect to us, anyway."

"You're missing the point. Drugs don't appear out of thin air. They have to be smuggled. And we can't have anyone watching for packages getting taken into the prison. Or more important, out."

Brockman thought for a moment. "You're right. Leave it with me. I'll have the guy watched. And discouraged, if necessary."

"Good. But this leads us to something else. The guy from Colorado. Who may have looked in the envelope. I had thought it would be safe to wait and see if he showed up in town."

"He won't."

"He might. And if he does, I don't want there to be any chance of him crossing paths with the journalist kid. Or of us having to deal with the guy and the journalist getting wind of it."

"You're worrying over nothing."

"I'm keeping us safe. And protecting our investment. So we're going to make a change to the plan."

"We're not canceling the ceremony. Or doing it behind closed doors. Don't listen to Riverdale. That guy . . ."

"I'm not worried about the publicity. I want it. And it can't hurt us. Worst case? The guy sees a video or reads a report that has a picture with it. After the event it's too late for him to make any waves. The danger is if he shows up. Causes a scene in real time. Gets that nosey kid all fired up. So this is what we're going to do. We're going to push the cordon farther out. Figure out how the guy might try to get here. He's homeless, after all. That has to limit his options. So we'll identify any potential approach routes and post our people at strategic locations."

"Can't hurt, I suppose. But I still don't think he'll come."

"Assume he will. The question is, how? He doesn't have a car. He can't rent one because he doesn't have a license."

"He could steal one."

"That's possible. What else?"

"Someone he knows could drive him. Or he could hitch a ride with a stranger."

"Possible. What else?"

"He could go old school. Take the bus. If he could afford a ticket. There's a Greyhound station in Jackson. That must be the closest."

"He could do that, I guess. In a pinch. Time would be tight if he hasn't already set off. What else?"

Brockman was quiet for a moment. "That's all I got."

"OK. So here's what I need you to do. Put two men on the Greyhound station in Jackson. Have them check every bus that comes in from anywhere west of here. Also put two men at the truck stop on I-20. If the guy tries to hitch a ride, what are the chances of finding one driver going all the way from Colorado to Winson? Zero. He'll need to get multiple rides. The final pickup would have to be quite a distance away. Everyone knows better than to stop for hitchhikers near a prison. Put two more men at the intersection with US 61, in case he tries his luck there instead. And two more where there's construction on US 87, halfway from Jackson. In case the guy stole a car or got a ride with a friend. It's down to one lane, right there. And it's slow. Easy to see who's driving. Or being driven."

"That's a lot of manpower."

"There's a lot at stake."

"What about the prison? And Angela's house? Do we still watch them?"

"Of course. There's no guarantee the guy won't slip through."

"That's even more manpower."

"We don't have a choice. Pull a couple of guards out of each unit. Minerva people only. No legacy grunts. Cancel days off and double enough other shifts to pick up the slack. And find the biggest man we've got. Hold him in reserve. The idiots we sent to Colorado as well. If anyone calls in a sighting have them check it. If the ID is positive, dispatch them. Make sure the guy is properly neutralized this time."

"If they get there fast enough. And if our guys spot him. They're going to be stretched pretty thin."

"I have an idea about that. Some insurance, in case he does somehow get through. Something that'll throw him off the scent. I'll take care of it while you handle the other logistics."

"Understood. And I'll tell Moseley to send out extra patrols. And make sure all his units have this Reacher guy's description."

"OK. But I want the cops on a watching brief only. We need to handle this ourselves. No official record. And, Damon? Double-check everything. Triple-check it. Make sure everyone is at the top of their game. You know what will happen if anything gets screwed up on Friday."

Chapter 15

Sam Roth's apartment building looked just like all the others on its block. Two stories. Stone fronted. Solid but plain. Nice but ordinary. There was nothing to suggest a man had died there within the last thirty-six hours.

Maybe from natural causes.

Maybe not.

Detective Harewood said Roth's death was caused by a heart attack. There was nothing suspicious about that. People die from heart disease all the time. Nearly seven hundred thousand people every year in the United States. More than the population of Vermont. More than one every forty-six seconds.

If heart disease had been the only factor Reacher might not have been so skeptical. If Roth had not been fit and accustomed to exercise. If Harewood's lieutenant had not been lazy. If Roth had not died hours before he was due to meet Angela St. Vrain. If Angela had not been murdered . . .

Too many *ifs*, Reacher thought. And too few answers.

The buildings fronted onto a wide, leafy street but the entrances were around back on a strip that was too small to be called a road but too nice to be called an alley. It was neatly paved. Clean and tidy. There were trees and shrubs. Most of the homes had sun terraces or decks on that side. Roth's building had two terraces, covered for shade, with a pair of doors between them. Both were painted blue. The same shade of navy. There was a parking space on each side. Both were occupied. One by a truck, all red paint and chrome and black glass. The other by a small hatchback. It was silver and sleek and a thick cable snaked from a flap on its rear wing to a box on the wall by the left-hand door.

Roth's apartment was on the right, according to the address Harewood had provided. Reacher knocked on the door to the left. He almost hoped no one would answer. Breaking the news that somebody's loved one was dead was a miserable job. Reacher knew from experience. He also knew that suggesting somebody's loved one might have been murdered was almost as bad.

The door jerked open after two long minutes. A woman stood in the entrance. She was wearing three-quarter-length white pants and a plain blue T-shirt.

She had nothing on her feet. Her hair was blond, streaked with a little gray, maybe shoulder length. She had it pulled back and tied in a ponytail with a plain elastic band. Her face was ghostly pale except for the deep red circles under her eyes. Reacher figured she would be in her mid-forties, although the circumstances made it hard to judge.

The woman took a moment to size Reacher up then said, "Sam's not here. He's . . ."

"I know," Reacher said. "I'm not looking for Sam. I need to talk to you."

The woman looked blank. "About Sam. You see, something happened and, Sam, he's . . ."

"It's OK. I know about Sam. Are you Hannah? Hannah Hampton?"

The woman blinked, then nodded. "Who are you?"

"My name's Reacher."

"What do you want?"

"Do you know a woman called Angela St. Vrain?"

"Angela? Oh God. I should tell her about Sam."

"You do know her?"

"Know her? Knew her? Haven't seen her for years. She moved to Mississippi. Oh God, Danny. I should tell him, too."

"Danny?"

"Danny Peel. He moved out there, too. He got Angela her job."

"Did Sam know Angela?"

"Of course. They worked together. A few years ago. Sam was her boss. More of a mentor, really."

"Did Sam know Danny?"

Hannah nodded.

Reacher said, "Did they keep in touch?"

"Danny, not so much. Angela, off and on. She sometimes reaches out to Sam for advice. With work, mainly. Why all these questions?"

"Had Sam and Angela been in touch recently?"

Hannah paused. "Over the weekend. She sent him some stuff on email."

"Work stuff? Or personal?"

"Work."

"Did Sam say what it was?"

"Some dumb accounting thing. Angela didn't know what to do about it. She was in a state. She was often in a state. Sam shouldn't have gotten involved this time. I said to him, tell her to figure it out for herself. He had more than enough on his plate. But no. That was Sam. He would never turn his back on a friend."

"What kind of accounting thing?"

"I don't know. Something about a number that didn't add up. Sam didn't go into detail." Hannah was silent for a moment. "Wait. What's all this about? You're starting to freak me out. What's going on with Angela? And what's it to you? Tell me or I'm done answering questions."

Reacher paused. "Hannah, I have some news. About Angela. It's not good news. Is there somewhere we could sit?"

Hannah took a step back. "Who are you, again?"

"My name's Reacher. Do you remember Detective Harewood? You spoke with him yesterday after you found Sam. I'm sure he left you a card. Call him. He'll vouch for me."

The door closed, and two minutes later it opened again. Hannah gestured for Reacher to come inside. He followed her into the apartment's main living space. There was a lounge area, all pale wood furniture with soft-colored fabrics plus a couple of low bookcases and a small TV in the corner. Then an oval glass dining table surrounded by white leather chairs. And a kitchen at the far end, tucked away behind a breakfast bar. There were two high stools next to it. Hannah made her way across and perched on one. Reacher followed and took the other.

Hannah rested her elbow on the countertop. "You're going to tell me Angela's dead, too."

Reacher said, "How did you know?"

"Detective Harewood told me you used to be a cop. In the army. Well, a cop shows up at your door? He asks about someone, then says he has bad news? Doesn't take a genius. What happened to her?"

"She got hit by a bus."

"Seriously?"

Reacher nodded.

"I'm sorry. That's awful. Was it an accident?"

"No."

"Wait. Was it . . . She didn't . . ."

"Jump? No."

"She was murdered? That's terrible. I told her not to move to Mississippi. People are crazy there, you know."

"It happened right here. In Gerrardsville."

"No. I don't believe it. When?"

"Yesterday."

"What was Angela doing in Gerrardsville yesterday?"

"The police think she came to see Sam."

"Why? He was helping her with that accounting thing, but on the phone. And on email. There was no need for her to come all this way."

"The police think there was something between them."

"What, like romantically?"

Reacher nodded.

Hannah shook her head. "Not a chance."

"Are you sure?"

"A thousand percent. See, one, if Sam was interested in someone, he'd tell me. And two, if he was looking for romance, you'd be more his cup of tea than Angela."

"Was that common knowledge?"

"He worked in a prison. He started when he was eighteen. Thirty years ago that wasn't the kind of thing you broadcast. Not in that environment, anyway."

"Is that why you got divorced?"

"It's why we got married. Things were different back then. For both of us. We worked together. Kind of. He was a corrections officer. I worked for a charity that helps ex-cons adjust to normal life. Still do, on a casual basis. So it made sense. But gradually attitudes changed. They improved. Or so we thought."

"I hear you. But here's the strange thing. I saw a

bunch of emails between Sam and Angela. They went back weeks. And they wound up by setting a meeting for yesterday."

Angela straightened up. "You hacked into Sam's email?"

"No. I saw printouts. They came from Angela's employer."

Hannah thought for a moment. "Sam wasn't scheduled to work yesterday. He mentioned he was planning to go out. If Angela was in town it's conceivable they were going to meet. But not to hook up. Trust me."

"So what about the emails I saw?"

"Could someone have impersonated Sam, online, to lure Angela here? If they wanted to kill her? Pedophiles do that kind of thing all the time. With kids, anyway. And Angela already knew Sam. She trusted him. It would be easier to use his identity to trick her than to invent a new one."

"Good in theory, but no. Angela initiated everything. Said she wanted to rekindle an old flame."

"But there wasn't any old flame. There couldn't have been."

"Maybe the accounting thing they were dealing with was more serious than Sam let on. Maybe they set up a meeting to talk about it. Maybe Angela was going to bring some documents for him to see. Or some other kind of evidence. But someone found out. Decided to stop them. And replaced the genuine emails between them with fake ones."

"Who would do that?"

"A co-worker with light fingers. A boss paying bribes. A supplier ripping off Angela's employer. Plenty of candidates."

"OK." Hannah shrugged. "But I don't know about planting fake emails. Why would anyone go to the trouble? Why not just delete the real ones?"

"To cover their asses. The last fake email from Angela hinted that if Sam didn't take her back, she would kill herself. The guy who killed her made it look like she jumped under that bus. Add those things together and the police have no reason to dig any deeper."

"If Sam hadn't had his heart attack, he'd have gone to meet Angela. Waited around for a while. And when she didn't show, and he was told she killed herself, what would he have done? Figured the stress of the whole thing had gotten too much for her? Maybe."

"Hannah, did you notice anyone hanging around here recently? Anyone you didn't recognize? On Sunday? Maybe Monday? Maybe in a car?"

"Wait. I'm still thinking through your idea. It might have flown. Worth a shot, I guess. As long as Sam bought Angela's death as suicide. That's the key because he wouldn't have seen whatever evidence she was bringing. And he wouldn't have known about the bogus emails because they wouldn't have shown up on his computer. They couldn't have, or he'd have been, like, *What the hell?*"

"The bogus emails couldn't have shown up, but what about the real ones? What would have happened to those?"

"They'll still be on his computer, I guess."

"You have a key to his apartment?"

"Sure. Why?"

Reacher stood up. "I need to see that computer. Right now."

Chapter 16

Hannah's hand was shaking when she tried to get the key into the lock on Roth's door.

She said, "I'm sorry. This is the first time I've been here since . . ."

Reacher said, "It's OK. You don't have to come inside."

"No." Hannah closed her eyes for a moment. She took a deep breath. "I'm doing this. For Sam. If his friend was murdered, he wouldn't want people to think it was suicide. Angela has—had—a kid. And Sam was a prison guard. He wouldn't want a murderer to go free."

The main room of Roth's apartment was laid out the same as Hannah's. It had the same kind of furniture, maybe a decade older, a little more tired, with fewer colors. There was no TV and the top of one of the bookcases was filled with a line of framed photographs. Reacher could smell incense coming from somewhere, and right away the sense of trespass he always felt when he had to search a dead person's home started to creep up his spine.

Hannah started toward an archway at the side of the kitchen area but paused when she drew level with the bookcase. She looked down at the photographs. They were all of her. There was a whole series. She was wearing the same gi in each one. In the first picture she had a white belt. By the last, the belt was brown. Hannah stretched out and flipped each photo in turn facedown. She said, "I can't believe he kept those. He knew I hated them." She sniffed and wiped a tear from her cheek.

Reacher said, "Do you still train?"

Hannah shook her head. "Not much. I haven't graded since I moved next door. I only started as a way for Sam and me to go to the gym together. Working out is so boring. He was always nagging me to step it up again."

Another tear welled up in the corner of Hannah's eye. She blinked it away and began to move again. Through the archway. It led to a doglegged staircase that opened onto a corridor with three more doors. The first one was open a crack. Hannah pushed it the rest of the way and stepped into Roth's bedroom. It was a small space. Tidy. Impersonal. The bed was made. There was no clothing strewn around. No shoes on the floor. No pictures on the walls. Just a book on the nightstand and a glass of water. The blinds were drawn. There were mirrors on the closet doors, which were closed. And in the far corner there was a small desk. It was made of metal and wood, and looked like it could fold down when not in use. There was no chair.

"Not much of an office space." Hannah took a silver laptop computer from the desk and sat down on the bed. "The other room's full of his weights and workout stuff. That was more important to him."

Hannah opened the computer and started tapping away on the keyboard and dragging her finger up and down on a little shiny rectangle below it. After a couple of minutes she turned the screen so that Reacher could see.

She said, "This is weird. There are no emails from Angela. Plenty from other people. Even a bunch of spam he never got rid of. But none from her. Not even from years ago. None in his inbox. None in any of his folders. And none in the trash. Which is extra weird because Sam had his mail set to keep deleted messages in the trash for a week. I just checked."

"Are there any emails from Danny Peel?"

Hannah tapped and swiped and clicked for another minute, then nodded her head. "A few. Mostly from before Danny moved."

"So what happened to the messages from Angela?"

"Sam must have found a way to permanently delete them. Instantly. I just can't see why he'd do that."

"Could an expert recover them?"

"Maybe. I don't know."

"Can you tell if it was definitely Sam who deleted them?"

"No one else had access to his computer. He never takes it anywhere. It's a laptop, but he only bought it because it's small. Not to carry around."

"Could they be deleted remotely?"

"I don't know. I'm no expert. They could probably be wiped off the central server remotely, I guess. But after he downloaded them? Maybe some high-level hacker could do it. Probably not a regular person."

"Have you noticed anyone hanging around the building the last few days? Any cars you didn't recognize?"

"Why are you asking that again? You think someone broke in here after Sam died and wiped his computer?"

Reacher said nothing.

"Oh." Hannah slowly closed the computer. "No. You think he was murdered? Like Angela was? No way."

"Angela was murdered on her way to meet him. In secret. Probably with some critical evidence to show him. Even if Sam believed it was suicide, he had still seen Angela's emails. He knew something was going on. He knew what kind of material she was bringing. That paints a pretty big target on his back."

"No. It was totally natural causes. I saw him, remember. I found him."

"Heart attacks can be faked. There are drugs. Chemicals."

"Not in this case. Because you know the really sad thing? When I saw him, I wasn't even surprised."

"I heard he was in good health. *Ripped,* Harewood said."

"He worked out a lot, yes. Too much, actually. It's how he dealt with stress. But healthy? Not so much."

"Sam was stressed?"

"He had a stressful job."

"He had that job for thirty years."

"The stress had gotten worse."

"How?"

"I don't know."

"New boss? Staff cuts? Some kind of disciplinary situation?"

"None of those things. He was just . . . having trouble. He didn't say anything but I know him. Knew him. Knew the signs. He wasn't eating properly. He wasn't sleeping. He was working out too much. Pushing himself too hard. I should have done more to help him. He was a heart attack waiting to happen and I knew it."

"So he was stressed. More than usual. But how did that cause Angela's emails to disappear?"

"Maybe that was done remotely, like you said." Hannah was silent for a moment, then she frowned. "Wait. Sam had dinner at my place Monday night. I was trying to get him to eat more. It didn't work. He just picked at his food then rushed off home. To work out. Again. What else would he be doing these days? I wasn't happy but I gave him a good-night kiss, like I always do. At the door. And across the way I kind of think I might have seen a car. Yes. I remember thinking it must be an Uber waiting for someone, but that it was weird because its lights were off."

"What color was it?"

"Something dark. Black, I think."

"Make? Model?"

"I'm not sure. I couldn't see too well because of Sam's truck."

Reacher thought for a moment. It hadn't rained that morning. The previous day had been dry, too. But Monday night was an unknown quantity. It had been fine earlier in the day, when he walked into town. But he had spent the evening with Alexandra. At her apartment. The weather was the last thing he was paying attention to. Still, if a vehicle had been parked for any length of time it could have left a trace of some kind. It was worth a look. So Reacher said, "Come on. Show me where the car was waiting."

The sun was high when Reacher followed Hannah outside. It was warm and bright and the air was sweet from all the plants growing in pots and urns outside the buildings. There were hardly any shadows. And the ground was bone dry. It was dusty. There were no footprints. No tire tracks. There was no possibility of any.

Hannah continued toward the opposite wall. She stopped below a spot where a pipe emerged from the brickwork. It was plastic, maybe three inches in diameter, and it ran vertically down before burrowing into the dirt. A drain, Reacher guessed. From a laundry room, or a kitchen or bathroom.

Hannah said, "The car was right here. By this pipework. On this side. So it was facing away from Sam's door. If anyone was in it, they couldn't have been watching his place."

Reacher caught up with her. He was thinking, *Cars have mirrors*. And the guy who had pushed Angela was experienced. As was his buddy, the driver. As were the two guys Reacher had encountered at The Pineapple. So they would all understand the value of discretion. Reacher was about to mention that when he noticed something about the ground near Hannah's feet. There was a patch that was a little darker than the rest. Not much. Just a fraction of a shade. But discernible. It started at the base of the pipe and fanned out in a semicircle, close to three feet in diameter, fading as it went. There must have been a leak from the drain. Just a gradual one. Not enough to turn the dirt to mud. Not foul-smelling or full of chemicals. Nothing to warrant an urgent repair.

Reacher crouched down and took a closer look at the damp section of earth. It was basically flat, though not entirely smooth. The surface had been disturbed. Probably by grit and gravel blown in the wind. But along with the natural scrapes and scratches, Reacher could see a strip made up of more regular shapes. Faint, but definitely there. A tread pattern. From a tire. It was wide, like the kind a high-performance sedan would have.

"Could you get a picture of that?" Reacher pointed at the track.

Hannah pulled out her phone and fired off half a dozen photographs. "You really think someone was watching us?"

"Too early to say."

Hannah suddenly shivered, despite the sun. "God,

I saw them. Their car, anyway. And if they were . . . then they . . . poor Sam."

"You should stay somewhere else for a few nights. Have you got family nearby? Friends?"

"No. It's just me. I'll check into a hotel."

"Make it one in another town."

"This is all too much." Hannah sighed. "No. It's not. I'll be OK. I guess I better grab some things. What are you going to do?"

"Talk to Harewood. Have him send some technicians down here."

Hannah took a step toward her apartment then stopped again. "Damn it. Look at that."

"What?"

"Sam's mailbox." Hannah pointed to a mailbox on a post next to Sam's parking space. It was a simple affair, corrugated steel, pressed into shape, and painted red just like his truck.

"What about it?"

"It's not shut properly."

Hannah was right. The mailbox's flap was open a fraction.

"Sam hated that." Hannah marched across to the box. "He liked it closed all the way. He was always chewing out the mail carrier if he didn't do it right." Hannah gave the front of the mailbox a hefty slap with her palm and its lid clicked into place. Then she grabbed it and pulled it open again. "Better see what's been delivered, I guess. Could be something urgent."

Hannah reached inside and pulled out a single piece of paper. It had no envelope and it was folded into thirds. Hannah glanced at Reacher then unfolded the page. She straightened it. Read it. Then her mouth sagged open and the paper slipped from her fingers and fluttered to the ground. Reacher scooped it up. He saw that it wasn't addressed. It wasn't signed. There were just two lines of printed words:

Wiles Park. At 1:00 P.M. Wednesday. The bench under the tree. Bring the proof. Disobey and your next-door neighbor will be in the hospital by sundown.

Reacher handed the paper back to Hannah and said, "Where's Wiles Park?"

"Near the center of town." Hannah's voice was quiet and hollow. "Fifteen minutes away, maybe. If you hurry."

The note said 1:00 P.M. The clock in Reacher's head told him that only left ten minutes' leeway.

Harewood and his technicians would have to wait.

Chapter 17

The sky gradually brightened and the Greyhound bus continued to thump and rumble its way east. It crossed the rest of Arizona, cut the corner of New Mexico, and dropped diagonally down into Texas. With every mile Jed Starmer grew more accustomed to its sounds. He became less likely to be disturbed. But also less tired due to all his hours of sleep, so one effect balanced out the other, meaning that it took him around the same length of time to wake up when the bus stopped in El Paso as it had done in Phoenix.

Jed drifted to the surface, looked around and located the depot sign. He checked his watch. They were bang on schedule. So they would be in El Paso for an hour and five minutes. It was lunchtime and he wouldn't get another decent break until they got to

Dallas in the early hours of the next morning. Which meant it made sense to get out and find some food. He was starving, but he felt more energetic than the last time he woke up. He slid across onto the seat next to the aisle. Some of the other passengers were already outside, wandering about. He waited for an elderly couple to shuffle by, then stood up and started toward the door. Then he stopped again. He didn't have his backpack. It hadn't been on his lap. He hadn't been hugging it. He hadn't wanted to look like a little kid. So he'd put it on the seat next to him. Before he fell asleep. But now it wasn't on the seat. It wasn't on the floor. It wasn't in the luggage rack. It was nowhere. It was gone.

Jed remembered the guy in the bus station in L.A. The surfer-looking dude who had found his ticket when he dropped it. The guy had warned him. Told him to hang on to his bag. To keep his arm through the strap when he slept. He should have listened. He should have . . .

Jed spotted the backpack. It was outside the bus. A guy was carrying it. He was moving quickly, along the concourse between the piers. He was almost at the depot exit. Jed started to rush down the aisle but almost at once he had to slow down. Nearly to a standstill. The old couple was in the way. Dawdling. Creeping along. It was like they were experimenting to see how slowly it was possible for human beings to move without their feet fusing with the floor. Jed hovered along behind them until they reached the door. They climbed down. Jed jumped out. He ran to the exit. There was no sign of the guy with his backpack.

Then Jed caught a glimpse of him. Through a car window. A cab. The guy was reclining in the backseat. He was cradling the backpack. Its top flap was pressing against the glass.

The cab was twenty yards away. Jed ran toward it. He waved. He yelled. The cab accelerated. Jed jumped. He screamed. He kept on running. But the cab just moved faster and faster until it was gone from Jed's sight.

Jed was left on the sidewalk, doubled over, out of breath. He was alone in a strange town, hundreds of miles from the only place he had ever thought of as home. All his worldly goods were gone. His dream of a new life was shattered. Tears blurred his vision. He slid his hand into his pocket. His fingers searched for coins. If he could find a quarter he could call his foster mother. Beg her to come and get him. To take him back. To save him.

Jed could call.

Whether his foster mother would answer was a whole other question.

Graeber and the other four guys had been waiting for an hour by the time Emerson arrived at the warehouse in Chicago. The four guys were surprised. It wasn't like Emerson to be late. But these were not normal times. Graeber had laid out some of the background for them. Not everything. Emerson was a private kind of guy. He wouldn't want his family's dirty laundry washed in public. And Graeber was ambitious. He didn't want to erode his privileged position in the organization so he stuck to the basics. Just enough to keep the others from asking too many questions. Or getting nervous and walking out.

Emerson's wife had been crazier than he'd expected when he got home. She had screamed at him the moment he walked through the door. She had wailed and pounded on his chest. She had flung things. She had blamed him for what had happened to Kyle. For the fact that the treatment had failed. Which didn't seem fair to Emerson. Not fair at all. He hadn't poured the booze down Kyle's throat. He hadn't rolled his joints or filled his syringes with who knew what. All he had done was try to get the kid better. At huge expense. And not a little personal risk.

It had taken all Emerson's strength to stay patient while his wife raged. To try to understand what was going on. And to wait for her Xanax to finally kick in.

Emerson sat at the head of the battered old table and took a moment to compose himself. Then he said, "Guys, thank you for being here. First up, you should know that this is not business as usual. It's not professional. It's personal. To me. So if anyone wants to sit this one out, you can leave. No hard feelings. No repercussions. I guarantee."

No one moved.

"Excellent." Emerson nodded his head. "So here's the plan, such as it is. We have two known points of contact with these assholes. First, we know who their front man is. Graeber and I will pay him a visit. See if we can't loosen his tongue. Persuade him to share more details of their operation. Second, there's their ship, twelve miles and an inch off the Jersey coast. It's not going anywhere. It can't. Their top guys will probably stay on board. They'll think they're safe there, and it's where they keep all their equipment and supplies. Which suits us fine, for now. As long as none of them sneaks away. So the rest of you, I want you to head over there. A friend is providing a plane. Take a basic dry kit. There's no need for finesse with this job. Then start by setting up surveillance from the shore. There's only one little boat that goes back and forth. If anyone tries to leave, intercept them. If they're customers, let them go. Maybe shake them up a little first. Make sure they know to never come back. If they're anything other than customers, put them on ice. And there's no need to be gentle. Just make sure they're still alive when I get there."

Wiles Park was badly named, Reacher thought. It should have been called Wiles Square. Because that's what it was. A square. It was a nice one. An effort had been made to turn it into a place that people would want to visit. That was clear. It was surrounded by cute stores and cafés and restaurants with fancy outdoor seating. There was a fountain in the middle, probably modeled on something from a French chateau, running at a quarter capacity, probably due to a problem with the water supply. There were all kinds of brightly colored flowers planted between tiny hedges that were cut into intricate geometric shapes. And there were benches. They were made of polished concrete and set out in a wide circle, like the numbers on a clock face. There were twelve of them. But only one was near a tree, as specified by the note in Roth's mailbox.

Reacher picked up a coffee in a to-go cup from the least pretentious-looking café on the perimeter and strolled across to the bench by the tree. He got there at ten to one. He sat down, right in the middle, and waited.

At five to one a guy stepped out from behind the fountain. He was broad, about six-two, and he was wearing jeans and a white Rolling Stones T-shirt. His hair was buzzed short and he had on a pair of black, sporty sunglasses. He halved the distance to Reacher's bench, paused, scowled, then came right up close.

The guy said, "Move."

Reacher held up his left hand and wiggled his fingers. "Like this?"

The guy's frown deepened. "Get off the bench, jackass."

"Why? Is it yours?"

"I need it. Now."

"There are eleven other benches. Use one of those."

"I need this one. I won't tell you again. Move."

Reacher stayed still. He said nothing.

The guy leaned in closer. "Did you not hear me?"

"I heard you just fine. You said you weren't going to ask me to move again. I figured you changed your mind. If you have one."

"You better watch your words. You're starting to make me mad."

"And if I don't? What are you going to do about it?"

The guy turned away. His hands bunched into fists, then relaxed again. He took a deep breath. Then he turned back to face Reacher. "Look. I'm meeting someone here, at this particular bench. In about a minute's time. It's very important. So I'd appreciate it if you would just move to another one."

Reacher said, "You're meeting Sam Roth."

The guy's scowl returned. "How did you know?"

"Because you're not meeting Roth. Not anymore. You're meeting me."

"The hell? What's going on here?"

"Change of negotiating stance." Reacher patted the smooth concrete by his side. "Sit down. Let's talk. See if we can find a solution everyone can live with."

"You got the printout?"

"It's nearby. I can get it. If we can agree on terms."

The guy hesitated for a moment, then slowly turned and lowered himself down onto the bench. He perched right on the very edge of the slab, as far away from Reacher as he could get. He said, "We need to see it. Make sure Roth changed the rota the way we told him to."

Reacher caught movement over by the fountain. Another guy emerged from behind it. He was about the same height as the guy who was now sitting. He looked a little heavier. He had the same sunglasses and similar clothes, except his shirt was plain and it had sleeves. He took one step forward then stopped and mimed an exaggerated shrug of his shoulders. The first guy shrugged, too, then beckoned for him to come closer.

The new guy marched across and stopped in front of the bench. His face was red and a vein was bulging on his forehead. He glared at his buddy and said, "What are you doing with this bozo? We have business to attend to."

The first guy said, "Relax. Sit down. He's here in Roth's place."

The new guy stayed on his feet. "The hell he is. That wasn't the deal."

Reacher said, "The deal's changed. You want the rota rewritten?"

"You know we do."

"Mr. Roth is no longer convinced that altering the rota is necessary. It's up to you to change my mind."

"Are you nuts?" the new guy said.

"I wouldn't say so. Mildly eccentric, maybe. But who am I to judge?" Reacher patted the concrete on his other side. "Sit."

"If you're not nuts then Roth must be." The new guy sat. "If what we have gets out, he's finished. His career's over. He knows that."

"What you have is bogus."

"So what? It's credible. There's no way he doesn't get investigated off the back of it. And it doesn't matter what they find. Something. Nothing. Whatever. Shit sticks. His career will be down the toilet."

"Maybe he doesn't care about that. Maybe he's ready for a new challenge."

"He cares."

"Does he?"

"You're bluffing."

"Am I?"

"Anyway," the first guy joined in. "We have insurance. In case he's too stupid to cooperate."

Reacher said, "The threat you made against his ex-wife?"

The first guy nodded. "Accidents happen. Houses catch on fire. So do electric cars. With their owners inside sometimes."

Reacher said, "I'm not a fan of assholes who threaten innocent people. I should break your legs for that."

The guy puffed himself up. "Or we could break yours."

Reacher said, "Could you?"

A witness would have said the guy fell off the bench. Just flopped sideways, hit the ground, and lay there motionless, legs bent, arms by his sides. Like when he was sitting, only rotated through ninety degrees. They would have said Reacher didn't move. Or that if he did it was only due to some kind of twitch. Nothing deliberate. Just a momentary spasm in his left arm.

Reacher turned to the new guy. "The negotiating phase is over. You're not getting the rota changed. You're not going to release the dirt you made up on

Roth. And you're not going to lay a finger on Hannah Hampton. Are you clear about that?"

The vein on the guy's forehead started throbbing again. "I don't know what your plans are, buddy, but you better cancel them. You better leave town. And fast."

"I was already planning to leave town. But I know someone who lives here. Who works in the police department. We were both in the service. If any lies come out about Roth, he'll tell me. If anything happens to Ms. Hampton, he'll tell me. I'll come back. I'll find you. And you will have the worst day of your life."

A witness would have said a very strange thing happened next. The new guy fell off the bench as well. He also flopped sideways and wound up inert on the ground, like a mirror image of his buddy. And again they would have said Reacher didn't move. Not deliberately. Although he did seem to have another spasm.

In his right arm this time.

Chapter 18

Jed Starmer stood at the edge of the sidewalk and pulled a handful of change out of his pocket. He had three quarters plus a bunch of smaller coins. They added up to more than two dollars. But Jed didn't care about the total. What counted was that he could make a call. He could get himself out of the mess he had landed in. Or at least try.

Jed figured there would be some payphones at the Greyhound station so he turned and started to make his way back there. He moved quickly at first, then slowed down and started to look around. He had been so focused on chasing the cab that the guy who had stolen his backpack had taken, he hadn't paid any attention to his surroundings. The street he was on was long and flat. The Greyhound station was far ahead, on the right. Closer, opposite him on his left, there was a weird-looking building. It was pale yellow with smooth, rounded walls. It was tall. It had no windows and its top was cut off at a steep angle. The high side was nearest him and the roof fell away sharply toward the back. It made him think of a cake, or a hat a bishop might wear in a sci-fi movie.

Around the base of the building there was a ring of sculptures. They were made of steel, all curved interlocking shapes, gleaming in the sunshine like flames. Or scimitar blades. They reminded Jed of a place back in L.A. Some kind of a fancy concert hall. He'd never been inside it but the exterior fascinated him. It was made of shiny metal, too, and the whole surface was twisted and warped like it was melting. Like a localized apocalypse was taking place. Or a scene from a fever dream. Or a sign he was going crazy. He had always found it a little menacing. Like so much in his hometown.

If L.A. still was his hometown.

A set of steps ran up to a concourse that separated the round building from a similar, shorter, wider one. Jed climbed up. He paused at the top then walked around to the far side. There was a low wall, presumably to stop pedestrians from falling down onto the street below. Jed perched on the edge. He lined up his coins on the rough concrete surface. Then he took away all of them except the quarters. Three metal circles. Dull with age. Scuffed from use. Innocuous, everyday items. But with the power to shape his future.

Jed had to decide. He could put the coins back in his pocket. Or he could feed them into a phone.

He could go forward. Or back.
Grab a new life. Or settle for his old one.

At the same time Jed was wondering what to do with
the quarters a police car pulled onto the forecourt at
the side of the Greyhound station. Two officers
climbed out. They both had a copy of a photograph in
their hands. One officer made her way inside the terminal building. She covered the whole area, showing
the picture to all the passengers who were eating or
loitering around or returning from the restrooms. The
other officer stayed outside. He focused on the line of
buses. He was looking for one vehicle in particular.
The one that had recently come in from L.A.

At the same time the officers were arriving at the
Greyhound station in El Paso, Texas, a car was rolling
to a halt at the side of the street next to Wiles Park in
Gerrardsville, Colorado. A poverty-spec Dodge Charger. Detective Harewood set his dome light flashing
on the dash, slid out, and walked across to the only
bench in the square that was near a tree. He stood for
a moment and looked at Reacher. Then he shifted his
gaze to the two guys who were still on the ground.
They were still motionless.

Harewood said, "What happened?"

Reacher drained the last of his coffee and set the
cup down on the bench. "They collapsed. Spontane-
ously."

"Seriously?"

"They were up to no good. The strain must have gotten too much."

"And you just happened to be here when it did?"

Reacher took a piece of paper from his pocket and handed it to Harewood. "They left this in Sam Roth's mailbox."

"You should have called me. Let me handle it."

"I figured they could be connected to Angela St. Vrain."

"Were they?"

"No."

Harewood checked his watch. "Did you call them an ambulance at least?"

Reacher shook his head. "I tried for a garbage truck. No luck. Apparently it's not trash day."

Harewood took out his phone and speed-dialed a number. He told someone at his office to arrange for medical assistance and a uniformed escort to remain with the guys at the hospital. Then he sat down and said, "So what kind of *no good* were these guys up to?"

"Trying to blackmail Roth. His ex-wife said he'd been under extra stress at work recently. This explains why."

"What did they want?"

"To get the staff rota rewritten a particular way. Probably to help them smuggle stuff into the prison they worked at. Possibly to help break someone out."

"Damn. What did they have on Roth?"

"Nothing real. Just some trumped-up nonsense. They admitted that. But enough to cause trouble for Roth. If he'd stayed alive."

"I'll figure it out."

"I'm sure you will."

"I'll make sense of it one way or another, but level with me. Are you telling the truth?"

"About what?"

"Did you really think these guys had something to do with Angela? Or did you just find the note and come over here looking for trouble? Because I don't see the connection."

"Turned out there wasn't a connection. Their scheme was local. Completely separate. But here's what I was thinking. The fact is, Angela wasn't linked to Roth romantically. He was her former boss. She'd gone to him for help."

"With what?"

"Some accounting thing at her work. They'd been communicating via email. That's another fact. Now for the speculation. I think Angela came to Gerrardsville to show Roth something. Some evidence relating to whatever kind of wrongdoing she had uncovered. I think whoever had her killed found this out, but only after she had left Mississippi. Hence staging her accident here. Where they knew she would be. And when."

"That would account for the timing and location." Harewood pointed to the ground on either side. "But not why you thought these guys could be involved."

"Stopping Angela from showing the evidence to Roth wasn't enough. They needed to recover it. Whatever it was. Hence stealing Angela's purse."

"How could they be sure the evidence was in Angela's purse?"

Reacher didn't answer.

A frown spread across Harewood's face. "They could have thought Angela mailed it to Roth before she left home."

"That would have been the smart move. A package is safer in the US mail than in a purse. Especially when you have a couple of killers on your tail."

"And you thought that was *the proof* demanded in the note?"

"I hoped it was. Because then we could have captured a couple of foot soldiers. Worked our way up the food chain. And it would have meant that Roth's death was an accident."

Harewood was silent for a moment. "You only try to blackmail someone you think is still alive. Not someone you know you already killed. I guess even without the evidence Angela was bringing, Roth knew too much."

"That's how I see it."

"I'll get on to the ME. Ask her to run tests for everything known to man that can induce a heart attack."

"Send some computer guys to Roth's apartment as well. Someone wiped all the emails between him and Angela off his laptop. The real ones. The ones Angela's employer found were fake."

"Will do."

"And check the area behind Roth's building for tire tracks. His ex-wife thinks she saw a car waiting there on Monday night, before he died."

Harewood shook his head.

"What? You don't believe her?"

"It's not that. I'm just thinking, my lieutenant was pissed about me wanting to investigate one death as a homicide. Now I'll have to tell him we have two."

"Here's something to soften the blow. You can tell him I'm leaving town."

"You are? When?"

Reacher stood up. "Right now."

"Why? Are you done?"

Reacher smiled. "I'm just getting started."

Jed Starmer had sat on the wall long enough for the sun to move and cast the three quarters next to him into deep shadow. He checked his watch. The bus was due to leave in ten minutes. He couldn't delay any longer. It was decision time.

Forward? Or back?

Get on board? Or make a call?

Jed didn't know which he should do. Panic rose in his throat. He felt it choking him. He couldn't breathe. But only for a moment. He swallowed the fear back down. He had already come a long way. On his own. Without needing any stuff. If he kept going he would only be alone for another couple of days. Not even another forty-eight hours. He could manage that long without a change of clothes. Losing his backpack was a setback. But it wasn't a catastrophe. It was no reason to give up. He still had his toothbrush. And he still had $300.

Jed stood up. He snatched up the coins and dropped them into his pocket. The only thing he didn't have was time. He had been planning to buy some food. He was starving, but his meal was going to have to wait. Which in a way he could take as a bonus. He could conserve his cash for a little longer. Until he reached Dallas. He could last until then without eating. He was used to being hungry. That was one thing he could thank his foster mother for.

Jed hurried down the steps and ran the rest of the way back to the Greyhound station. He scurried through the terminal building, weaving his way around the knots of slow-moving passengers, but he stopped before he reached the exit to the concourse. He had spotted a vending machine. It was by the far wall. Next to the payphones. The day was hot. Hotter than he was used to. He had been rushing around in the sun. And the machine was full of all kinds of drinks.

Going without food was one thing. But water was different. He had read that not having enough could mess up your health. Damage your internal organs. Cause lasting harm. He didn't want to start his new life all weak and sickly. But neither did he want to miss the bus. The doors closed a little before departure time. He had seen that happen in L.A., a hundred years ago. Or actually yesterday. He checked his watch. Decided it was worth the risk. Pulled the handful of change out of his pocket. Jammed the coins into the slot, one after another, and watched the total on the digital display creep up to the required amount. Then he grabbed the bottle from the delivery chute and raced to the bus.

Jed dashed up the stairs and the bus's door hissed closed before he was three feet along the aisle. He took the same seat as before. Leaned against the window. And suddenly felt exposed without his backpack. Vulnerable. He craved the way it had felt on his lap. He would have given anything to hug it tight just then. Whether it made him look like a kid or not.

"Hey, buddy!"

Jed jumped. Someone had flopped into the seat next to him. A guy, a little scruffy, maybe eighteen. Jed recognized him. He had been on board all the way from L.A. Sitting near the back. Jed had thought he was part of a group. Now he wasn't sure.

The guy said, "So. What's happening?"

Jed said, "Nothing."

The guy leaned in close. "You in trouble?"

"Me? No. Why?"

"Are the police looking for you?"

Jed felt like a steel belt had closed around his chest. His heart started to race. "The police? Of course not. Why would they be?"

"It's OK. You can tell me. It's why you didn't get back on until the last moment, right? You were waiting for them to leave."

"The police were here? On the bus?"

The guy nodded.

"I didn't know that. I was just . . . slow."

"Right." The guy winked. "*Slow*. I'm with you."

"OK, maybe they were here. But they're not looking for me."

"Are you sure? Because the cop had a photo. It was old. Four or five years, at least. But it sure looked like you. I guess no one else twigged. They just switched the driver and I bet all these old biddies are half-blind, but I could see it."

Jed swallowed hard. "What did you say?"

"Don't worry." The guy slapped Jed's shoulder. "I said I hadn't seen you."

"Thank you." Jed could finally let out a breath.

"No problem." The guy paused. "Hey, I have an idea. Maybe you could buy me breakfast? When we get to Dallas?"

"Buy you breakfast?" Jed thought about his cash supply. He was in no rush to spend any more than absolutely necessary. Then he thought about how easy it would be for the guy to dial 911. He probably had a cellphone. And even if he didn't there were seven more stops before they would reach Dallas. In places where there would be payphones. He forced a smile and said, "Sure. I'd be happy to."

"Cool." The guy swung back into the aisle and headed for his own seat. "Traveling for hours makes me hungry. See you later . . ."

Chapter 19

Twelve hundred miles away, in Winson, Mississippi, it was time for Curtis Riverdale to get busy.

Riverdale was an anomaly within the Minerva corporation. An outlier. He was unusual because he was in his post when the prison got taken over. Minerva's standard procedure was to sideline the existing warden when a new site was bought. Shift him into some kind of impotent, figurehead position. Wait for the boredom and humiliation to eat away at him until he found a job somewhere else. And if he tried to stick it out, fire him, hot on the heels of a third of his staff.

The process had gotten under way as usual. A bunch of new guards had been drafted in. Proven *Minerva people* from the company's other facilities. Tailor-made to slot in place of the guys who'd just been discarded. The new warden was installed at the same time. A tall, skinny forty-year-old who dressed like a banker and spoke like a radio host. He did all the usual new-boss things to prove he could walk and talk at the same time. But he didn't settle in Winson. He kept getting sick. He spent more time in the hospital than at work. After six months he couldn't take it anymore. He quit. And during the new guy's many absences Riverdale took the opportunity to step back up. He proved himself invaluable. Adaptable. Discreet. Able to fit into Minerva's mode of operation in a way Hix had never seen in a warden his company had inherited.

Some correctional corporations treat the business of incarceration as if they were supermarkets. They take a kind of pile-them-high, sell-them-cheap approach. But Minerva wasn't like that. Right from the start Hix and Brockman had a different view of what they did. They saw themselves as being more like prospectors in the Old West. Their goal was the same. To sort the gold from the dirt. Only they didn't use shovels and buckets and sieves. They had a system. One they had devised themselves. They had refined it. Improved it. And they used it to sift through the constant stream of inmates sent by the states they had contracts with.

The process started with the freshly convicted. The *new fish*. Lawyers evaluated their cases. Accountants reviewed their finances. Genealogists traced their family trees. Then aptitude tests were administered. Inmates with certain skills and talents were identified. Psychologists were brought in to assess their personalities. The suitable ones were selected.

The rest were sent to the doctors along with the other prisoners. A whole bunch of screening procedures were carried out. Treatments were prescribed wherever necessary. And after each individual was fully scrutinized and categorized, it was decided which facility to send them to.

The first category of prisoner had the potential for their convictions to be quashed, either for PR or for profit. They were distributed evenly throughout Minerva's sites. The second had no special potential. This was the largest group by far. The corporation's bread and butter. Dull, but necessary. Most of its members went to Minerva's older prisons but some were brought to Winson for appearance's sake. The third category was smaller. More interesting. All its members came to Winson. And the fourth category was smaller still. It wasn't interesting, exactly. But it was lucrative. Often there was only one person in it on any given day. Sometimes there were two. Sometimes there were none at all.

That afternoon there was a single prisoner in the fourth category. He was housed all alone in Unit S1. The segregation unit that was still selectively operational. So that was where Riverdale started his rounds. He had arrangements to make. Personnel to organize. Processing. Packaging. Distribution. There was a whole complex operation to keep on the rails.

That was assuming everything went according to plan on Friday. If not the place would be mothballed. Indefinitely. And a lot of Minerva staff would find themselves on their way to other prisons. Where they would wind up on the other side of the bars.

———

Jack Reacher left Gerrardsville, Colorado, on foot, the same way he had arrived two days earlier.

As he walked Reacher thought about the best way to get to his destination. Winson, Mississippi. He had never heard of the place before he saw it printed on Angela St. Vrain's driver's license. He had been planning on a detour to Gerrardsville's library to learn more about it but while they were still on the bench in Wiles Park Detective Harewood had taken out his phone. Pulled up a map. Of sorts. An indistinct multicolored tangle of roads and other features on a small, scratched screen. But enough to show Reacher the general location of the town. It was on the very edge of the state, no more than a dot, nestled into a C-shaped curve on the east bank of the Mississippi River.

Finding his way to Winson would not be a problem. Reacher was more worried about how long the journey would take. He had two dead bodies on his mind. At least one killer was on the loose. With at least one accomplice. On a trail that was getting colder by the minute. He had plenty of energy. He had cash in his pocket. But not much time.

The mountains were to his right, sawing away at the clear blue sky. The sun was turning pink and starting to dip down toward their highest peaks. It was still warm but Reacher's shadow was growing longer, dancing and skipping across the rough, bleached blacktop at his side. The air was still. It was quiet. No cars had gone by since he had crossed the town boundary. No vans. No trucks. Normally Reacher would have enjoyed the solitude. But not today. It only added to his growing impatience.

Reacher picked up his pace and after thirty seconds he heard a sound behind him. A truck's motor. A large diesel, rattling and clattering like a freight train. He looked around and saw a pickup barreling toward him. It was red. It had black glass and lots of chrome. Reacher had seen it before. He stopped walking, stepped to the edge of the road, and let it catch up to him.

The truck braked abruptly to a halt, rocked on its springs for a moment, then the passenger window buzzed down. Hannah Hampton was in the driver's seat. Her right hand was on the steering wheel. She smiled and looked at Reacher and said, "Open the door."

Reacher worked the handle and swung the door as far as its hinges allowed it to go.

The smile disappeared from Hannah's face. She brought her left hand up from the gap between her thigh and the driver's door. She was holding a gun. A short, squat, black pistol. It was an inch wide with a three-inch barrel. Less than six inches, total length. A SIG P365, Reacher thought. He had never fired one. Never even handled one. The whole subcompact thing had gotten popular after his time in the army was over, fueled by the concealed-carry craze. But he had read about that particular model. He knew it was no joke.

Hannah pointed the gun at the center of Reacher's chest and said, "Stay there. Stand still."

A repeat customer. The Holy Grail of any business. Not someone to be questioned or doubted or turned away.

Lev Emerson was counting on the guys he was after to be running their organization like a business. Albeit not a regular one. He didn't know its name. It didn't advertise. It didn't have a logo, as far as he was aware. No website. No bank details for online payments. No app. No social media presence. Just a front man. And a ship. The last, floating resort of the desperate. The place people had to go when they couldn't get what they needed anywhere else.

Emerson had paid the front man in cash the last time he had gotten involved. The only time. To get his son, Kyle, onto the ship. Kyle had certainly been desperate. But he hadn't got what he needed. He got something that killed him, instead.

Emerson had paid a lot of cash, the last time. It was a mistake he wouldn't make again. Any kind of further involvement with these guys would be a mistake. But if the front man took the bait, he would be the one making the error. That was for damn sure. Him. The people he worked for. And, most important, the people who supplied them. The ultimate source of the poison that had killed Kyle. Because Emerson didn't want to just cut off a limb. He wanted to slay the whole beast. To incinerate every cell in its body.

If the front man took the bait.

Emerson took a breath and hit Send. His laptop

made a *whoosh* sound. His message disappeared from its screen. He pictured it as a stream of ones and zeros, bouncing around the internet. Pinging from one untraceable server to another, all around the world. Maybe reaching its destination. Maybe not. Maybe being read. Maybe not. Maybe convincing the front man. Appealing to his greed. Bypassing any hint of suspicion about why such a recent customer should be getting back in the market.

Or maybe not.

Jack Reacher had lost count of the number of people who had pointed guns at him over the years. Often the person with their finger on the trigger was angry. Sometimes they were scared. Or determined. Or elated. Or relieved. Occasionally they were calm and professional. But Hannah Hampton had an expression on her face that Reacher had never seen in that kind of situation before. She looked embarrassed.

She said, "I'm sorry. Ninety-nine percent of me thinks I'm wrong. That I'm crazy. But I have to know for sure."

Reacher said, "Know what?"

"Why you showed up at Sam's door."

"I told you why."

"You told me a story. How do I know it's true?"

"You talked to Detective Harewood. He confirmed it."

Hannah shook her head. "He confirmed *what* you were doing. Looking into Angela's murder. Not *why*."

"I'm helping him out."

"Why?"

"Angela was murdered. So was Sam. Someone should do something about that."

"Yes. The detective should. It's his job. And he has the whole police department to back him up. Why does he need your help?"

"He's facing some . . . institutional obstacles."

"Such as?"

"That doesn't matter. The only thing that matters is whether you want Sam's killer to go free. If you don't, you need to put the gun down."

"What if it's not that simple?"

"It is that simple."

Hannah paused, but she didn't lower the gun. "Here's my problem. There's a little voice at the back of my head and it won't shut up. It keeps saying, you were the only one who knew Angela was murdered. You were the only one who knew Sam didn't have a heart attack. You were the only one who suggested Angela sent Sam some secret evidence. You were the only one who went looking for it."

"That's why Harewood needs my help."

"Unless there's another explanation."

"There isn't."

"If you had found the evidence at Sam's apartment, or in his mailbox, what would you have done?"

"Given it to Harewood."

"But would you, though? That's the real question."

"You think I was trying to get it for myself?"

"That's a possibility. You have to admit it. You have no legal standing here. No official role."

"So you also think I killed Angela? And Sam? That's the bottom line, right?"

Reacher kept his eyes on Hannah's trigger finger. Her knuckle gleamed white. But it didn't flex. Not yet.

Hannah said, "You know an awful lot about how Angela and Sam died. And why."

"I don't know nearly enough about that. But what I have learned, I've told Harewood. Because I am helping him. Call him. Ask if that's true."

"If you're helping, why are you leaving town? Did you find the evidence?" Hannah looked at Reacher. It dawned on her that he had no bag. No case. No bulging pockets. "Did you destroy it?"

"No."

"So why are you leaving?"

"Because I *didn't* find it. I need to look somewhere else."

"Where?"

"Winson, Mississippi."

"Where Angela lived?"

"Where she worked. Where she found the problem that led to all this."

Hannah was silent for a moment. "You're going to find out who killed Sam?"

"I'm going to try."

"You promise?"

"You have my word."

"Does that mean anything?"

Reacher nodded.

Hannah said, "If you find the guy who killed Sam? What will you do?"

"Give him the chance to surrender."

"And if he doesn't take it?"

"That'll be his problem."

Hannah lowered the gun. "OK. I believe you. I think. And I do want Sam's killer caught. So, how can I help?"

"You can give me a ride to Denver. There's a Greyhound station there."

Lev Emerson's message did make its way to the front man. It reached him almost immediately. And it found him in a trusting frame of mind. Or a greedy one. Emerson wasn't sure which. And he didn't care either way. Because the guy replied. No hesitation. No delay. It was nothing fancy. Just a time. A location. And a date.

Emerson sent his confirmation. The meeting was locked in. For the following day. At 10:00 A.M.

Emerson looked across the table at Graeber. He said, "Fetch a barrel. A big one. We have some mixing to do."

Chapter 20

Curtis Riverdale spent more than an hour in Unit S1. He checked that everything would be ready for Friday afternoon. The equipment. The right people, with the right specialized skills. And he verified the arrangements for transport. That was the part that worried him the most. It made him nervous because it wasn't under his direct control. In his gut he would have liked to run the whole operation. The entire show, from soup to nuts. But in his head he understood the value of compartmentalization. It was better all-around if no one at Minerva knew where the packages they sent out were going to end up. And it was better still if the guys who dealt with the final customers had no idea where the merchandise came from. The last thing Riverdale wanted was for the mess to land on Minerva's doorstep if anyone down the line wound up with a bad outcome.

When Riverdale was finally satisfied he left S1 and started toward the first of the three general population units. The one that housed the most interesting inmates. He set out at speed but when he was halfway along the fenced-in walkway that connected the buildings he paused for a moment. He had realized something. If everything went according to plan on Friday it would be the first time a prisoner had moved from one category to another. It would be the first time. And, he hoped, the last. All it did was increase the risk they ran. For no good reason. And in Riverdale's opinion, unnecessary risks should always be avoided.

Some people within the Minerva corporation misinterpreted Riverdale's attitude. Damon Brockman was one of them. He took it as a sign that Riverdale was timid. Cautious. Even cowardly. He didn't see that Riverdale was just a survivor. He was on to a good thing at Winson. He had worked hard for the opportunities his job offered him. And he was ready and willing to defend his position. To do whatever was necessary to save his skin.

If Brockman had been quicker he could have gotten a different perspective on the whole situation. He could have talked to the warden he had brought in to replace Riverdale. If only the new guy had paid more attention to the food that was brought to him from the prison kitchen. To its subtle, extra layer of flavor.

The food that was brought to him exclusively by members of Riverdale's old guard.

———

Hannah Hampton drove fast. She was aggressive. But plenty of other drivers around her on I-25 were faster. And crazier. They were constantly zipping past her on both sides. Cutting in front. Crowding close up behind. Reacher saw trucks abandoned in the median, facing the wrong way. Cars sitting on the shoulder with their fronts and rears stove in. There were even a couple of SUVs in the fields next to the highway. One was upside down, on its roof.

Hannah saw Reacher looking at the wrecks. She said, "Must have rained recently. People down here don't know how to drive in the rain."

Reacher said, "It's not raining now."

Hannah shrugged. "I've been thinking about this place you're going. Winson. It sounds pretty small. Off the beaten track. Do you think you can get all the way there on a Greyhound?"

"Probably not. But I'll get close."

"What will you do then?"

"Don't know yet. I'll figure something out."

Hannah hit her turn signal and pulled across to the right. A sign said the route to central Denver was coming up in a mile. Hannah slowed down, ready for the exit curve. Then she switched her foot onto the gas and swerved back onto the highway.

"Screw it," she said. "Forget the bus. I'm taking you all the way to Mississippi."

Reacher looked at her. "You sure? It must be twelve hundred miles."

"So what? This is Sam's truck. The tank's full. He paid for the diesel. He wouldn't want it to be wasted."

"Burning up a dead guy's fuel doesn't seem like the best of reasons."

"It's not the only reason. I've got to leave town for a while, anyway. You told me that. Winson's as good a place to go as anywhere. Probably. When we get there I can go see Danny Peel. Tell him about Sam in person. That's got to be better than breaking the news on the phone. And I can check that Angela's kid is OK."

"Do you know the neighbor she left the kid with?"

"No. But Danny will."

Reacher thought about the envelope he had seen in Angela's purse. The one that disappeared right after she was killed. It was addressed to this Danny Peel. He would need to talk to the guy about it. Find out how Angela came to have it. And what was so important about it. Taking someone along who knew Danny might help. It might make him more open to talk. Speed up the trust-building phase of the conversation. Make the whole process more efficient. And potentially a lot less messy.

"OK, then," Reacher said. "Thank you."

"My pleasure." Hannah looked across at him for a second. "But tell me one thing. I'm curious. Your luggage. What happened to it?"

"Nothing."

"Come on. You can tell me."

"Nothing happened."

"Really? Because here's what I think. You got to town. Met a woman. Spent the night. Maybe a few nights. You pissed her off somehow. Or you over-stayed your welcome. Wouldn't leave, despite all the hints she dropped. So she lost patience and trashed your stuff. Cut it up. Or set it on fire. Yes. Tell me she burned it. Please. Let that be it."

"OK. A woman burned it."

"Really?"

"No."

"Then where's all your stuff?"

"Right here. In my pocket."

"What can you possibly fit in your pocket?"

"Everything I need."

"Everything?"

"Everything. For now."

Bruno Hix and Damon Brockman were operating on the assumption that there were four categories of prisoner at Winson. That's what they expected be-cause that's what they had mandated. What they didn't realize was that there were actually five.

The fifth category was in fact the oldest. It pre-dated Minerva's ownership of Winson by several years. It had not been defined by professionals. No doctors were involved in the process. No psycholo-gists. No accountants. Certainly no lawyers. Its mem-bers had always been identified by Curtis Riverdale, personally. He relied on his decades of experience. His natural ability to read people. To spot certain things, however well hidden. Things like extreme des-peration. Or exceptional greed. Things that would cause an inmate to arrange for his wife, or occasion-

ally his sister, to come to the prison whenever Riverdale told him to. And then to wait, penned in on the
secure side of the glass divider, while one of the old
guard escorted the woman to his office. Where he put
his own personal spin on the concept of the conjugal
visit.

Sometimes, if Riverdale felt like spicing things up
a little, he had the prisoner brought up, too. He had
him cuffed to a steel bar he'd had attached to the wall
in the corridor for that specific purpose. And he left
his door open. Just a crack. Not so wide that the prisoner could see into the room. But enough to make
sure the sounds from inside weren't muffled in any
way.

Riverdale had a visit lined up for that evening.
With the wife of a new fish. He was looking forward
to it. If she lived up to his expectations he was thinking of having her brought back on Friday afternoon.
To celebrate Winson's return to business as usual.

Assuming everything went according to plan.

The farther Hannah Hampton drove, the less she
spoke.

She had started out pretty talkative after deciding
not to drop Reacher off at the Greyhound station.
She wanted to know all about him. To understand
what kind of guy would walk away from the army and
wander around the country with no job. No home to
return to. No definite destination. No luggage. She
asked him about his childhood. His parents. His

brother. How he felt when each of them had died. How he had been affected by growing up on military bases all around the world. She was fascinated by his life as an army cop. She wanted to know about the best case he had investigated. The worst. About any that still haunted him. Why he had left the service. And how he felt about being cast adrift after putting his life on the line for other people for thirteen years.

Reacher was happy to answer. His replies were mostly factual. They were mostly positive. He had come to terms with anything negative in his life years ago. The conversation ticked along. The tires thumped and rumbled over the joints and gaps in the road. Hannah's phone directed them onto I-70. The highway stretched away in front of them. The mountains grew smaller in the rear window, then finally disappeared into the distant haze. Hannah continued due east until they were well clear of Denver, then cut across on the diagonal, almost to the edge of the state. Then they turned again. Straight to the south this time. They plunged across the narrow strip that stretched out sideways from Oklahoma. And kept going, deeper and deeper into Texas.

The conversation began to dry up after Hannah raised the subject of relationships. Reacher turned the questions back toward her and she deflected by talking about her marriage to Sam Roth. He sounded like a nice guy. Hannah had endless anecdotes about him. About their life, together but not together. Some of her memories were tender. Some were funny. Some were wild, from way back in the day. As Hannah reminisced her voice changed. It grew quieter. She spoke more slowly. Eventually a tear ran down her cheek. Just one. She wiped it away and glanced across at Reacher with a look that said, *Your turn*.

Reacher said nothing.

Chapter 21

Damon Brockman was not the kind of guy who readily changed his mind.

When he first heard that someone might have looked in the envelope Angela St. Vrain ran off to Colorado with he didn't see a problem. He still didn't. But neither was he the kind of guy who exposed himself to unnecessary criticism. In his experience there was only one thing worse than something going wrong on his watch. That was getting the blame for it going wrong. And the only thing worse than getting the blame was when someone had previously warned you of the danger. Publicly. When they could say, *I told you so*. Especially when that person was your boss. When they could punish you for it. When they could hit you for it in the pocket. So even though

Brockman still thought the chances of Reacher showing up and causing trouble in Winson were close to
zero he decided to act as if the danger was real.

First, he brought forward the time that the sentries
were due to be in position. Bruno Hix had asked for
them to be posted by 6:00 A.M., Thursday. Brockman
changed that to 3:00 A.M.

Second, he added an extra pair of sentries. Hix
had asked for two guys to cover the Greyhound station in Jackson. Brockman put a couple more at the
stop the local bus from Jackson to Winson left from.
Plenty of people who visited the prison used that service, which made it the kind of thing anyone new to
the area without their own transport might latch
onto.

Third, he went into what-if mode. Hix had already
tried to cover every possibility but Brockman wanted
to narrow the odds. To back one horse rather than
spread his bets across the whole field. He asked himself, what would he do if he had to get across the
country with very few resources? The answer was obvious. He would steal a car. That would be quick and
easy. It would be nicer and more comfortable than the
Greyhound bus. And it would be safer than hitching
a ride. There were all kinds of crazy people out there,
preying on the broke and the homeless. He knew that
for a fact. Minerva made a bunch of money out of
confining them after they got caught.

The only danger involved with stealing a car was
that unless you lucked out in some unexpected way
the owner would notice the vehicle was missing. He
would dial 911. And if the police caught you it would

be game over, right there and then. So, to mitigate the risk you would need to switch plates. You could steal some alternatives. Which came with dangers of its own. So it would be better to clone a set. Or to have some random fake ones made. Which would be difficult for a person with limited means.

Brockman started to feel better. Car theft was the best option, but it was likely to be off the table for Reacher. Then he started to feel worse. He thought of Curtis Riverdale, of all people. Of something he had said. About Reacher being a former military cop. Some kind of a crack investigator. Reacher had witnessed Angela St. Vrain's *accident*. He had spoken to the police in the town. Maybe he had caught the local news. He could have picked up on Sam Roth's death. He could have connected the dots.

There was no danger of Reacher finding any evidence that led back to Minerva. Brockman was sure about that. But there was another problem. Dead men can't report car thefts.

Brockman took out his phone and hit the speed-dial for Rod Moseley. The chief of the local police department.

Moseley answered on the first ring. "What now? Tell me you have good news for a change."

Brockman said, "It's about Sam Roth. The other guy we offed in Colorado. We need to know the make and model of his vehicle."

Hannah Hampton and Reacher had been in Sam Roth's truck for approaching seven hours.

For nearly six of those hours neither of them had spoken. Hannah was focused on driving. It was a useful distraction for her. She was struggling to keep a lid on her grief. That was clear. At the same time Reacher was focused on nothing in particular. He had tipped his seat back a little. His eyes were closed. He was playing music in his head. There was nothing he could do to make the truck go faster. He couldn't bring their destination any closer. So listening to a few of his favorite bands was the most pleasant way he could think of to pass the time.

Hannah nudged Reacher and when he opened his eyes she pointed to a sign at the side of the road. It gave the name of a town neither of them had heard of before. Behind it the land was as flat as a board for as far as they could see. It looked dull and brown in the setting sun. A few sparse bushes poked through a crust of scrubby, scorched grass. There were a couple of stunted trees. A set of powerlines was running dead straight toward the horizon. Above them the cloud was gray and it was stretched thin like there wasn't quite enough to cover the massive expanse of sky.

Hannah said, "Time to call it a day?"

They were still heading due south so Reacher figured they hadn't gotten as far as Amarillo yet. That wasn't necessarily a problem. The sign listed the nearby town's amenities. They seemed adequate. Apparently everything came in pairs. There were two gas stations. Two diners. And two hotels. Hannah took the turnoff and a quarter of a mile after the intersection she pulled onto the first gas station's forecourt. She went inside to use the restroom. Reacher pulled the truck up to the nearest pump and filled it with diesel. He went inside to pay and when he came out Hannah was back in the driver's seat. He climbed in and she steered across the street to the first hotel. She parked in a spot at the edge of the lot, midway between the hotel and the first diner. There were only two other cars in sight so they figured competition for rooms wasn't going to be an issue. Food seemed like a more urgent priority.

The diner was set up to look like an old-world cattle station. It had rustic shingles on the roof. The walls were covered with fake logs. There were branding irons hanging from rusty pegs along with all kinds of antique tools Reacher didn't know the purpose of. Inside, the floor was covered with sawdust. The tables and chairs were made of wood. The chairs had leather seat covers the same color as the saddles in the paintings of cowboys on the walls. The tabletops were crisscrossed with burn marks and pocks and dents. They looked ancient but even so, Reacher suspected the damage had been done in a factory rather than by decades of genuine use.

There were no other customers in the place so a waitress with gray hair and a pink gingham dress gestured for them to pick where they wanted to sit. They took the table in the far corner. Reacher liked it because it let him keep an eye on the entrance as well as the corridor leading to the restrooms. The waitress handed them a couple of menus and left them to make their selections. That didn't take long. There wasn't a great deal of choice. Steak lovers were well catered for. Everyone else was pretty much out of luck.

Hannah and Reacher ordered their food. They waited in silence for it to come. Hannah's appetite for conversation had well and truly dried up. Reacher didn't have anything new to say, either. Ten minutes crawled by and then the waitress dropped off their meals. Big heaps of meat and potatoes with no vegetables in sight. Reacher was happy. Hannah, less so. She nibbled halfheartedly at the edge of her steak. Managed to swallow a couple of fries. Then pushed her plate away.

"I'm sorry." Hannah stood up. "I don't mean to be a party pooper but I'm bushed. I can't keep my eyes open. I'm going to check in next door. Get some sleep. See you by the truck in the morning?"

Reacher said, "Sure. Six A.M. sound about right?"

"Works for me. Good night."

Reacher grabbed a newspaper from a holder made of horseshoes on the wall near the door and read it while he finished his dinner. He ate the untouched food on Hannah's plate. Polished off his coffee, followed by a refill. Then he left sufficient cash to cover both meals and a tip and headed outside.

Four of the stops on the Greyhound route between El Paso and Dallas were brief. Just long enough for new passengers to join the bus or existing ones to get off. Three of the stops were longer. Twenty minutes. Or twenty-five. Sufficient for anyone who was stiff or hungry to stretch their legs or go and get some food.

Jed Starmer didn't leave his seat during any of the stops, long or short. Because he had something on his mind. The police. Officers had shown up in El Paso. With a picture of him. Only one person in the world could have supplied that picture. So only one person could have called 911. His foster mother. She had reported him missing. Or she had reported him as a thief. She was worried about him. Or she was mad at him. Jed knew which option his money was on. And he also knew that the reason didn't matter. The only question that counted was what the police would do next. They could assume that if he wasn't on the bus in El Paso, then the route was a dead end. In which case he was safe. For a while, at least. Or they could keep on looking for him, all the way down the line. All the way to his final destination. In which case he was doomed.

Jed didn't know what the police would do. And the uncertainty was eating him alive. Every time the bus came to a standstill Jed panicked. Even if it was just at an intersection. Even if it was just because of other late-night traffic. Jed pictured the door swinging open. He imagined a cop bounding up the steps. Making his way down the aisle. Shining his flashlight in every passenger's face. Asleep or awake. Comparing everyone with his photograph. Which was old. His appearance had changed in the last four or five years.

He supposed. He hoped. But he wasn't even kidding himself. The guy at the back of the bus had spotted the resemblance. There was no way the police would miss it. They were trained for that kind of thing. He would be identified. Grabbed up. Dragged off the bus. And taken back to L.A. To his foster mother. Or to jail.

The bus stopped properly seven times. Seven times the door opened. Three times someone climbed on board. But every time they turned out to be passengers. Not cops. Which meant the cops were no longer looking for him.

Or that they would be there, waiting, when the bus stopped in Dallas.

Lev Emerson's alarm went off at 2:45 A.M., Thursday morning.

It played the theme from Handel's *Fireworks Music*. Loudly. Emerson shut off the sound. He lay still for a moment, in the dark, gathering his thoughts. He was on a couch in the corner of his office in his warehouse in Chicago. He felt at home with the smell of the rough, battered leather. With how the worn surface of the cushion felt against his cheek. He had slept there many, many times over the years. But not for any of the typical reasons married men spent nights away from their beds. It wasn't because of a row he'd had with his wife. He wasn't drunk. He didn't reek of another woman's perfume. He wasn't there to take drugs or watch porn. He was there because of the nature of his work.

When someone with a regular job had an appointment in a faraway town, early in the morning, they could travel the night before. Stay the night in a convenient hotel. Eat a hearty breakfast and show up at their meeting bright-eyed and raring to go. But that wasn't an option for Emerson. Not if he had to take the tools of his trade with him. They weren't things he could fly with. They had to be transported by road. In one of his special panel vans. And he didn't like the idea of leaving one of those vans in a public parking lot. Where an idiot could crash into it. Or try to steal it. Or take too close an interest in its contents. Which meant he had to carefully calculate his travel time. Set his alarm. And get up whenever it was necessary to leave, however early the hour.

As his business took off Emerson had brought people on board to handle the bulk of the early departures. People he trusted. But he wasn't above doing the heavy lifting himself. Particularly when the job was personal. And given that his guys were currently in New Jersey, watching a ship moored twelve miles out to sea, he didn't have any option. It was down to him. And Graeber, who was asleep in the next-door storeroom. Emerson rolled off the couch. He crossed to his workbench and fired up his little Nespresso machine. He figured they both could use a good hit of caffeine before they got on the road.

Jed Starmer had never been to Dallas before but when he saw the cluster of sharp, shiny buildings in the distance, plus one that looked like a golf ball on a stick, he knew he must be close.

Jed stared out of the bus window. He was on high alert, scanning the area for blue and red lights. For police cruisers. For detectives' cars. For officers patrolling on foot. For anyone who might be looking for him. He saw storefronts. Offices. Bars and restaurants. Hotels. Federal buildings. A wide pedestrian plaza. A memorial to a dead president. Some homeless guys, bedded down at the side of the street. But no one connected to law enforcement. As far as he could tell.

So either the cops weren't coming for him. Or they would be lying in wait at the Greyhound station.

Jed felt like the bus took a week to meander its way through the city. He jumped at every vehicle he saw. And at every pedestrian who was still out on the street. No one paid any attention to him. All the same Jed hunkered down in his seat when the driver made the final turn into the depot. The last thing he saw was a sign for something called the Texas Prison Shuttle. He had never heard of anything like it and the idea made him sad. He could be on his way to prison himself, soon, and if he did wind up behind bars he knew no one would be coming to visit him. There could be convenient transport available, or not. It wouldn't make any difference.

The driver pulled into his designated slot, braked gently to a stop, and switched on the interior lights. Some passengers grunted and groaned and pulled

blankets and coats over their faces. Others got to
their feet and stretched. Then they stepped into the
aisle and made for the door. Jed stayed where he was.
If he could have wished himself invisible that's what
he would have done. Instead he had to make do with
keeping his head down and peering through the gap
between the seats in front of him. He focused on the
front of the bus. At the top of the steps. To see if anyone got on. No one did. No new passengers. And no
police. Not straightaway. But there was an hour and
five minutes until his connecting bus was due to
leave. That was plenty of time for a whole squad of
them to show up.

"Hey, buddy." The guy from the back of the bus
dropped into the seat next to Jed. "Thanks for waiting. You hungry? Come on. Time for that breakfast
you promised me."

Jed paused at the entrance of the depot and peered
inside. The space was a large rectangle with gray tile
on the floor and a ceiling that was high in the center
and low around the edges. The amenities were clustered around the sides, in the lower section. One wall
was taken up by the ticket counter, which was closed
at that time of the morning. There was a line of self-
serve ticket machines. A group of vending machines
full of snacks and drinks. Rows of red plastic seats,
with people sleeping on some of them. Then there
was the section Jed's new friend was interested in.
The food concessions. There were two of them. One

only sold pizza. The other had a full range of fast-food options.

There were no cops in sight. Yet.

Jed was intending to just get a small snack. He wanted to spend as little time out in the open as possible. And to spend as little money as he could get away with. He still had some major expenses coming up. He knew that. But then he read the menu at the fast-food counter. He smelled the bacon. And the sausages. And the fries. And all his good intentions evaporated. He hadn't eaten since L.A. He was so hungry his legs were trembling. He just couldn't help himself. He ordered the Belly Buster Deluxe, which contained pretty much everything it's possible to cook in oil, plus extra onion rings and a Coke. The guy from the back of the bus asked for the same combination. The clerk grunted some instructions to a cook who was hanging around behind her then shuffled across to the register. She hit a few keys and barked out the total. Jed had already done the math in his head. He'd already worked out how much he would have left after factoring in the tax and leaving the smallest acceptable tip.

It was less than he would have liked, but he figured he could live with it.

Jed reached into his pocket. He felt for his roll of cash. But his fingers touched nothing but lint and fraying seams. His pocket was empty. He checked his other pockets. All of them. He came up with nothing but a few coins and his toothbrush. His money was gone. All of it. He stood still for a moment, trying to make sense of what was happening. Then his knees gave way. He flopped back. His head hit the ground. The lights above him turned into fiery multi-pointed stars. They spun and danced and twirled. Then everything in his world went dark.

Chapter 22

Reacher woke himself up at a quarter past five, Thursday morning. He took a shower. Got dressed. And was outside the hotel by ten to six, as agreed. Hannah Hampton was not. And neither was Sam Roth's truck.

Reacher considered going inside and asking the guy behind the reception counter what time Hannah had checked out. Then he thought better of it. There was no point. Whether she had left five minutes or five hours before him, he wouldn't be able to catch up to her without a vehicle. And even if he could, he wouldn't. This was a volunteer-only operation. If Hannah was having second thoughts, it was better she didn't come along. It would be a mistake to take her.

There were no vehicles at the gas station on the

other side of the street so Reacher started to walk. The highway was only a quarter of a mile away. He figured he could hitch a ride when he got to the intersection. There was usually plenty of truck traffic early in the morning, before the roads got too busy. He hoped there would be at least one driver who could use some company. Who was looking for a little gas money. Or a little conversation to help him stay awake after a long night at the wheel.

The sun was starting to rise but the landscape looked no more inviting than it had the evening before. It was still flat. Still parched and brown. Still featureless. Reacher figured he must have covered a couple of hundred yards but the scene was so vast and so uniform it was like he hadn't moved at all. He pressed on, a little faster. Then he stopped. He heard a sound behind him. An engine. A diesel. Rattling and clanking like a train.

Hannah Hampton pulled up at the side of the road and buzzed down the passenger window.

She said, "What's going on? Why did you leave without me?"

Reacher said, "I figured you left without me."

Hannah checked her watch. "But it's not six yet. We said we'd meet at six."

Reacher shrugged. "Old habits. On time is late where I'm from. Anyway, where did you go? This isn't much of a place for an early morning joyride."

"To get coffee." Hannah pointed at two giant to-go mugs that were jammed into holders in the center console. "I thought you liked it. The machine wasn't cleaned in the station across the street. The morning guy was late. He hadn't gotten to it, yet. So I had to drive to the other place. It's like a mile away. Was I wrong?"

"Absolutely not." Reacher opened the door and climbed in. "I do like coffee. And it makes for a much better greeting than last time you picked me up. That's for sure."

Jed Starmer woke up a couple of hours later than Reacher. He was on a Greyhound bus. But not the one that had brought him from L.A. A different one. Heading east, approaching the border between Texas and Louisiana.

If Jed had been left to himself he might not have made it onto that bus. He had no recollection of getting up off the floor at the depot in Dallas. He just remembered finding himself on a plastic chair, propped up against a table. The guy from the back of the previous bus was sitting opposite him. Between them there were two trays, loaded with food. Belly Buster Deluxes, with extra onion rings and giant cups of Coke. Exactly what they had ordered. Exactly what he was trying to pay for when he realized his money was missing. He thought he must have been mistaken. He thought he must still have it. Relief flooded through him. He slid his hand into his pocket. He needed to touch the cash. To be sure it was there. But his pocket was just as empty as before. He was so confused.

The other guy said, "If you're wondering about the food, I paid for it."

"Oh." Jed was struggling to keep his thoughts straight. "Thank you. I guess."

The guy was staring at Jed. His expression wasn't friendly. "Tell me something. And don't lie. Are you scamming me?"

"What? No. Wait. I don't understand."

"You say you'll pay. You order the food. Then you stick me with the check."

"Not deliberately."

"The whole collapsing thing? You should get an Oscar for that."

"I don't know what you mean."

"You really thought you had the money?"

"I do have the money. I did have. Now it's gone."

"How much did you have?"

"Three hundred dollars."

"In what? Tens? Twenties? Fifties?"

"Twenties."

The guy shook his head. "So quite a roll. When did you last have it?"

Jed thought for a moment. "In El Paso. I got some water. No. Wait. That was from a machine. I used coins. It must have been in L.A. On Tuesday. I bought my ticket and a burger."

"Did you pull out the whole roll? Or just what you needed?"

Jed shrugged. "The whole roll, I guess."

"You put what you didn't spend in your pocket?"

"Right."

"Did anyone see which pocket you put it in?"

"I don't know. Probably. The bus station was pretty busy."

"Did anyone come close to you? Bump into you? Come into contact in any other way?"

"No. Wait. Yes. The guy who found my ticket. I dropped it and . . . oh."

"*Oh* is right. So. This guy. Did you talk to him? Did he ask you any questions?"

"We chatted a little, I guess. He said he was getting on my bus. But then he didn't. Now I know why."

"Did you tell him where you were going?"

"Not exactly. I was pretty vague. Why?"

"Doesn't matter. Now, come on. Eat. Before this mess goes cold."

The other guy cleared his plate then waited for Jed to catch up.

He said, "Good. Now we should get you to the hospital. Get you checked out. You whacked your head pretty good when you fell."

"No." Jed checked his watch. "No time. My next bus goes in ten minutes. And anyway, I'm fine."

"You should call 911, at least. Report the guy in L.A."

Jed shook his head.

"You need to report him. To stop him from ripping anyone else off."

"There's no point. It's too late. He'll be long gone."

"You're scared to call the police, aren't you? You're trying to avoid them. How come?"

"I'm not scared. I'm just short of time."

"You're in some kind of trouble."

"I told you. I'm not."

"Then what's the problem? Are you a runaway? Is that it?"

Jed shook his head again. "No. I'm not running away from anything. I'm just . . . relocating."

"Really? Where to? How? Where's your stuff? What are you going to do when you get there?"

"I don't know." Those were good questions, Jed thought. Although only two things really mattered. Where he was going to sleep that night after he got off the bus. And how he was going to finish his journey the next morning. The same two problems he'd faced all along. They were a little more difficult now that he had no money. But he would figure something out. There were people sleeping on the seats near him. He wasn't thrilled at the idea, but he could do the same at the depot in Jackson. It wouldn't kill him for one night. Then he remembered the sign he had seen outside. For the prison shuttle. If they had those in Texas, surely there would be something similar in Mississippi. That could be his salvation. If he could somehow persuade the driver to let him get on board. He looked up and tried to smile. "Don't worry. I'll be OK."

"Well, good luck. You're a brave kid." The guy looked at Jed for a moment then pulled two ten-dollar bills out of his pocket and slid them across the table. "Here. This is all I can spare. Take it. Just don't let anyone steal it from you this time."

Hannah Hampton's phone guided them due south until they passed Amarillo, then the highway shifted a little to the east. They would head diagonally across the state until they got to Dallas, Reacher figured. Then it would be a straight shot all the way to Mississippi. A few more stops for diesel and coffee. A few more hours to play music in his head. Unless Hannah decided she wanted to talk again. Either way was fine with him. He tipped his seat back a little farther, closed his eyes, and settled in for the ride. There wasn't much he could do while they were on the road. But when they got to their destination, he was pretty sure that was going to change. And that was also fine with him.

Lev Emerson's contact had picked a coffee shop in St. Louis, Missouri, for their meeting. The same city as their first rendezvous. A different venue. But the same line of thinking. Somewhere public. Noisy. Hard for anyone to eavesdrop or to record their conversation. And hard for Emerson to do the guy any physical harm without being seen by dozens of witnesses. The guy was cautious. That was clear. But he had overlooked one detail. Last time they met, Emerson didn't know what the guy looked like. He had no option but to wait for him inside, as agreed. But recognizing him was no longer a problem. Which is why Emerson decided to ambush him outside.

When you work with the range of chemicals involved in Emerson's line of business, getting your hands on a little chloroform is child's play. Before he left Chicago Emerson soaked a rag with the stuff and stowed it in a Ziploc bag. He timed the drive so that he and Graeber arrived at the strip mall where the coffee shop was located an hour early. He parked right by the entrance to the parking lot. Watched every car that pulled in. Spotted his contact roll up in a silver Mercedes. Backed out and followed the guy to the other side of the lot. Reversed into the space next to his, passenger side facing him. Graeber jumped out. He was holding a dog-eared road atlas. He stopped the guy and asked him for directions to an industrial park on the outskirts of the city. Emerson slipped out on the other side. He was holding the rag. He looped around the back of the van. Opened one of the doors. Stepped up behind the guy. Clamped the rag over his nose and mouth. And took the guy's weight as he sagged so that he didn't hit the ground. Graeber squeezed between them. He climbed into the van's cargo space. Emerson humped the guy's unconscious body around to the doorway. Graeber grabbed it by the shoulders. Emerson took its ankles. Together they dragged the guy inside. Then Emerson slammed the door and took a quick glance around the parking lot. The whole operation had taken nine seconds. No one had seen a thing.

Damon Brockman walked into Bruno Hix's office and sat down on one of the visitors' chairs that were lined up in front of the big wooden desk.

He said, "I just took a very interesting call. Remember Lawrence Osborn?"

Hix put down his pen. "Pepper Spray Larry? Sure.

Good guy. Came with us from Kansas City, then had to retire early. Asthma, right?"

"Right. Well, guess who just knocked on Larry's door?"

"Tell me."

"That kid. The journalist who had a bee in his bonnet about drug deaths."

"Why's he bothering Larry?"

"Seems he's going after everyone we fired when we took this place over. Figures some of them might have loyalty deficits. Might be willing to spill some beans."

"None of those guys know anything."

"Right."

"And we didn't fire Larry."

"The kid doesn't know that."

Hix drummed his fingers on his desk for a moment. "I don't like this. If the kid's hunting down our ex-employees, who knows what other kinds of digging he's doing. I don't want him here tomorrow. He's too inquisitive. Too much of a pain in the ass. It's time to get rid of him."

Brockman smiled. "Agreed. And I know an easy way to do it."

"How?"

"Larry told the kid he might be able to get some dirt on us, but he needed time to think. He said he'd get in touch if he wanted to go forward. Then he called me to give us the heads-up. See how we wanted him to play it. So, here's what I'm thinking. We have Larry contact the kid. Send him on a wild-goose chase."

"Like where? And to do what?"

Brockman shrugged. "Somewhere far away. I don't know. San Francisco. Key West. The details don't matter. We can make something up. It just has to be urgent. So the kid leaves town tonight. Tomorrow morning at the latest."

Hix picked up his pen and twirled it between his fingers. "OK. I like it. Let's do it. Just make it something convincing."

Chapter 23

The only promise Lev Emerson had to make was that he wouldn't burn the building down.

That was the opposite of the kind of condition Emerson usually signed up to but in the circumstances it made sense. He needed access to some premises. Something secluded. Where no one would hear anything. Or see anything. Or smell anything. Somewhere that was robust. Industrial. He was in a strange city. And he was in a hurry. So he had called the client he had just done the job for in Savannah. The guy owned a vintage warehouse in St. Louis. It was vacant, near the river, with no active businesses close by. Emerson already knew about the place. He remembered it because the guy had once hired him to torch a neighbor's property.

When Emerson's contact came around from the

chloroform he was lying flat on his back. He was naked. And he was in the middle of a cold concrete floor. He could smell a slight hint of gasoline. He could see walls in the distance. Made of brick. They looked ancient. A pale, chalky coating was flaking off them. The ceiling was high above him. It was stained from water leaks, and it was supported by rusty metal beams.

The guy's arms and legs were stretched out to his sides. He tried to move them but he couldn't. Because his wrists and ankles were cable-tied to six-inch stubs of steel that were sprouting from the ground. There were rows and rows of them. They were all that was left of the giant sets of shelves that had been removed and melted down when the storage business which had inhabited the building had been abandoned. The guy pulled with all his might. The plastic strips dug into his skin but the metal stubs didn't even flex.

Emerson was standing on one side of the guy. Graeber was on the other. Near the guy's feet there was a large plastic barrel. And lying on the barrel there was a ladle. The kind they use in restaurants to serve out bowls of soup.

Emerson crouched down and waited for the guy to turn his head and look at him. Then he said, "Let's not beat around the bush. I know about you. I obviously know about your ship. So the purpose of today is for you to fill in the remaining blank."

The guy's throat was dry. He managed to say, "What blank?"

Emerson said, "I want to know who your supplier is."

The guy's eyes stretched wide. "I don't know. I can't tell you."

Emerson straightened up and crossed to the barrel. He took the ladle in one hand. Removed the lid with the other. Scooped out a big dollop of thick, cream-colored gel. Crossed back to the guy. And poured the gel all over the guy's genitals.

The guy screamed and bucked and thrashed around. "Stop! What are you doing? What is that stuff?"

Emerson said, "I could tell you its chemical name but it wouldn't mean anything to you. Have you seen *Apocalypse Now*?"

"What? Why?"

"Because the name you'll know it by is napalm."

"No. Seriously? What the . . ."

"It's my own version. Better than the military kind. The key is not skimping on the benzene. The original formula only burns for a few seconds. Mine stays alight for ten minutes. Think about that. Do you feel how it's sticking to your skin?"

The guy wriggled and bounced and tried to fling the gel away from his body. It was heavy, like glue. A little came off but the bulk remained stubbornly attached.

Emerson took a box of matches from his pocket. "So. Tell me. Where does your organization get its inventory from?"

The guy stopped moving. He was struggling for breath. "We have a few sources. We get different things from different places."

"Start with what you got for my son. Where did it come from?"

"I don't know. Honestly. I only have a contact. I tell him what we need. If he can get it, he does. I don't know who he works for. That's the way the system is set up. For security. Just like he doesn't know who I work for."

"His name?"

"Carpenter. That's what he told me. It might not be his real name."

"Contact information?"

"It's in my phone. I'll give it to you. But listen. This is the truth. Four weeks ago Carpenter dropped out of sight. He might have quit. The FBI might have gotten to him. I don't know. But if you can't reach him, don't think I was lying to you."

Graeber picked the guy's pants up off the floor and pulled a phone out of one of the pockets. He said, "Passcode?"

The guy reeled off a series of numbers.

Graeber hit a few keys then said, "Carpenter? You have a picture of him. Is this a joke?"

The guy said, "He didn't know. It was in case I ever needed leverage. It's redundant now, anyway."

Emerson said, "Who cares about a picture if the guy's disappeared? How do we get around him?"

The guy said, "You can't. He was my only contact."

"So how are you placing your orders?"

"We're not. We can't. Not until a replacement gets in touch. We're using alternative suppliers right now."

"How did you pay Carpenter?"

"Cash, at first. Recently, bitcoin. It's untraceable."

"Who collects the merchandise? Where from?"

The guy missed a beat. "I don't know where from."

"So you do know who."

The guy didn't answer.

Emerson took a match out of the box.

"OK! We use a transport guy. Out of Vicksburg, Mississippi. His name's Lafferty. He's a one-man band. A specialist."

"Address?"

"In my phone."

"Good. Now, is there anything else you want to tell us?"

"No. Nothing. I've told you everything. More than I should have done. So please, let me go."

"First things first. The shipment that went to my son. You arranged that? You were a link in that chain?"

The guy closed his eyes and nodded. Just a very slight motion.

Emerson said, "Let me hear it."

The guy opened his eyes again and said, "Yes. I arranged it. Can I go now? If it's a refund you want, I can make that happen. I'm the only one who can."

Emerson took a ladleful of gel and poured it on the guy's stomach. He took another and poured it on his chest. Graeber put the lid back on the barrel and rolled it to the exit. Then Emerson struck a match.

"A refund?" Emerson said. "No. But you can go. Like my son had to go when you were done with him. Only you get to go quicker. And with maybe a little more pain."

The Greyhound bus Jed Starmer was riding reached the depot in Jackson, Mississippi, at a little after 1:15 P.M., Thursday. That was more than forty hours after he left L.A. Four people watched it arrive. Two of them were waiting for that bus, specifically. The other two were keeping an eye on everything that came in from the west.

The second pair normally worked at the Minerva facility in Winson. They had been at the station since 3:00 A.M. On a special assignment. They were bored. They were tired. And they were suspicious. Of the other two guys. Their attention had been drawn to them the moment they walked onto the covered concourse. They were young. Late teens, or early twenties at the most. They were wearing bright, short-sleeved shirts, unbuttoned, over dirty white undershirts. They had shorts on. No socks. One had sandals. The other had tennis shoes, old and creased, with no laces. Both had long, messed up, crusty hair. One was blond. The other, dark. Neither had shaved recently. Neither was a picture of respectability. That was for sure. But it was their body language that was the real red flag. Their constant fidgeting. The tension in their arms and legs and necks that they couldn't quite suppress.

Corrections officers live or die by their instincts. Their ability to spot trouble before it happens. There's no alternative given that there are times when they're outnumbered two hundred to one. Things can go south fast. Once they start, there's no stopping them.

Not without blood getting spilled. So if the Minerva guys had been on duty at the prison and the scruffy kids had been inmates they would have moved on them immediately. No hesitation. They'd have tossed them back in their cells and kept them locked away until they uncovered whatever it was they were up to. However long it took. But out there, in the free world, there was nothing the Minerva guys could do.

Except watch.

Every couple of minutes the blond kid pulled out his phone and stared at its screen.

One of the Minerva guys nudged his partner. "See that?"

"He's looking at a photo," the other guy said. "I can't see who it's of. Can you?"

The first guy shook his head. "The angle's wrong. I can make out a silhouette. That's all. But you know what it means? They're not here for anyone they know. They're looking for a stranger."

The second guy was silent for a moment. "We're here. They're here. What are the odds?"

"If they're looking for the same guy we are, they're not here to stop him. Look at the size of them. You heard what he did to Robert and Dave in Colorado?"

"So they're here to help him. He'll need a ride. Assuming they're looking for the same guy."

"Which is excellent news."

"How so?"

"Brockman sends us for one guy. We give him three. There has to be a bonus for that."

"And if they're up to something else, these kids?"

The first guy shrugged. "Then it's not our problem."

Jed was the last passenger to get off the bus. He had thought the front of the station looked inviting. It was all curved canopies and neon signs like an old-time movie theater. It was a different story around back where the loading and unloading took place. The area was covered. It was dark and full of shadows. Jed had a bad feeling about the place. He didn't want to set foot in it. He stayed where he was, pressed back in his seat, pretending he wasn't there, until the driver stood up and glared at him. Then he had no choice. He accepted the inevitable. He slunk along the aisle and climbed slowly down the steps.

It was clear to the Minerva guys that Reacher wasn't on the bus. Just like he hadn't been on the previous forty-seven buses they had watched arrive. Which meant they were going to have to wait even longer. Watch at least one more. The only question was whether they would be doing that alone. Or whether the two kids they had their eyes on would hang around, too. The kids hadn't shown any interest in any of the passengers who had streamed away.

Until Jed appeared.

Jed glanced around, got his bearings, and hurried toward the pair of swinging doors that led to the inside of the station. The blond kid checked his phone again. Then he started moving. He closed in on Jed. He came up behind him and grabbed his left arm. He stuck out his right index finger and jabbed it into Jed's kidney. He leaned down and whispered something into Jed's ear. Then they both veered away to the left. Toward the exit to the street. The dark-haired kid was already there. He checked both directions. He beckoned for them to keep moving. Then all three disappeared from view.

Chapter 24

Some people pick hotels more or less at random. Other people are more careful. They take all kinds of different factors into account. The price. The location. The amenities. The ambience. The discretion of the staff, depending on what they're planning to do while they're there. And who they're planning to do it with.

Emerson and Graeber paid a great deal of attention to their choice of hotel in St. Louis that Thursday. But for them only one thing mattered. It was all about the parking lot. It had to be large. And it had to be shaped in such a way that at least some of the spaces were positioned well away from the main building. Graeber spent a good half hour with his phone after they left the warehouse. He used a few different review sites until he found a place he thought was suitable. Then he switched to his favorite mapping app and pinched and zoomed and swiped until he had double-checked it from all angles. It looked promising on the screen. But when they arrived on-site they figured that half of the lot must have been sold since the satellite pictures they had seen were taken. Now the section they had been interested in was surrounded by contractors' hoardings emblazoned with computer simulations of a new office building.

Emerson and Graeber moved on to their second choice of hotel. The parking lot was smaller but it was early enough in the day for plenty of spaces to be vacant. Graeber pulled the van into the most isolated of them and Emerson walked across to reception. He booked one room. He paid for the whole night but he knew they would be leaving at half past one in the morning. That would give them time to get to Vicksburg, Mississippi, and still have about an hour for surveillance before the delivery guy they'd learned about showed up for work. The schedule left them with twelve hours to fill. Emerson figured they should use it to get some rest. They'd had an early start. A long drive from Chicago. Followed by a busy morning. So they would split the time into four shifts. Then take turns, one of them in the room and one in the van. The room would be more comfortable. But the van was more important. Its contents were too valuable to be left unattended. And they would be too hard to explain away if anyone in authority found them.

The car was old. It was some kind of station wagon. It was long and green and there were fake wood panels attached to the sides. The kid with the dark hair opened one of the rear doors. The blond kid moved his hand to the center of Jed's back. He shoved. Hard. Jed tried to stop himself but his fingers skidded across the dusty paintwork and he wound up facedown in the foot well. The blond kid slammed the door. He turned to his buddy. His hand was raised for a high five. Which he never received. Because his buddy was lying on his back on the sidewalk. Unconscious. One of the Minerva guys was standing over him. He had a smile on his face.

The other Minerva guy said, "Want to tell me what's going on here?"

The blond kid's mouth drooped open but he didn't speak.

The Minerva guy took a pistol from the waistband of his jeans. "This is what you need to understand. I'm a law enforcement officer. I witnessed you attempting to kidnap a minor. I shoot you, I get a medal. So if you have anything close to an innocent explanation, now's the time."

The kid didn't respond.

The Minerva guy checked his watch. There were eight minutes before the next bus was due. Which was annoying. This could be the only action he would see all day. He would have preferred to draw things out a little. Have some fun. Instead he frowned and said, "Show me your phone."

The kid didn't move.

The Minerva guy pressed the muzzle of his gun against the kid's sternum. He reached into the kid's pocket and helped himself to the phone. He glanced at it and said, "Passcode?"

The kid stayed silent.

The Minerva guy said, "OK. This phone's old. A fingerprint will unlock it. Hold out your hand."

The kid didn't move.

The Minerva guy said, "Let's recap. Passcode, or fingerprint?"

The kid didn't answer.

"OK," the Minerva guy said. "I'll go with your fingerprint. You know your finger doesn't need to be attached to the rest of you for it to work, right? Or your thumb? Or whatever you used to set it up? Maybe I'll have to snap off all your fingers, one at a time."

The kid's eyes opened wide and he blurted out a string of six numbers. The Minerva guy entered them into the phone then opened its photo library. It was full of pictures of people surfing and drinking beer and hanging out on beaches, plus one shot of someone's ass. There was nothing that seemed relevant so the guy switched to the phone's messages app. Straightaway a different picture filled the screen. It was of Jed Starmer. At the Greyhound station in L.A. Taken on Tuesday afternoon. The guy clicked and swiped and saw that the picture had been sent from a California number. There was a note attached to it. A route number. And an arrival time. He handed the phone to his partner, then said to the kid, "How much?"

The kid's eyes opened even wider. "I haven't got any money. But I can get some. I'll pay you whatever you want."

The Minerva guy slapped the kid in the face. Openhanded, but still hard enough to knock him over sideways, into the gutter. Then the guy reached down, grabbed the kid by the undershirt, and hauled him back onto his feet. "How much will you get for snatching the boy?"

"Oh. Nothing. Nada. Honest."

"Bullshit."

"It's true."

"Then why did you snatch him?"

"We had to. We don't have any choice."

"Everyone has a choice."

"We don't. We're working it off. There's a debt we owe."

"Oh yeah? Who do you owe? What for?"

"A guy we met. He gave us some drugs. A lot of drugs. We were supposed to sell them. But they got stolen. And we didn't have any money to pay him back."

"Who's the guy?"

"I don't know his real name."

"Where is he?"

"New Orleans."

"So now you supply him with runaways?"

The kid looked down and nodded.

The Minerva guy said, "You have someone at the Greyhound station in, where? L.A.?"

The kid said, "He moves around. L.A. San Fran. Austin, Texas, one time."

"He buddies up to lonely looking boys? Finds out where they're going? Makes sure no one's going to miss them?"

The kid nodded.

"How many times?"

"This is the fourth."

"How many more?"

The kid shrugged. "He said he'd tell us when it was enough."

The Minerva guy checked his watch again, then pulled a plasticuff from his back pocket. "Turn around. Hands out behind you."

"What are you going to do?"

"Call 911. You're looking at a lot of jail time, pal. Hopefully in the place where I work. I'll make sure you get a real good welcome."

"No. Wait. Please. Can't we—"

The guy spun the kid around and secured his wrists. Then he pushed him toward his partner and opened the back door of the car. He said, "We better check the boy's OK. Make sure you're not in any more trouble."

Only he couldn't check on anyone. Because the back of the car was empty. The opposite door was open. And Jed was gone.

get a fix on their current position. At first their surroundings were flat and featureless with nothing to
see apart from an occasional water tower or utilitar-
ian metal shed at the edge of the arrow-straight road.
Then a few trees and bushes appeared between the
scrubby fields. The land began to gently rise in a few
places and fall away in others. After they passed Dallas the sky became a little bluer. The grass, a little
greener. The stands of roadside trees thickened up
after they crossed into Louisiana. The farmland grew
more lush and fertile. Reacher was enjoying the slow
motion, magic lantern impression of the landscape as
it steadily unspooled outside his window. He would
have been happy to file the snapshots away in his
memory and save his energy for whatever was waiting
for him in Winson. When he would no longer be a
passenger. But when Hannah handed him the keys
after they stopped at a rest area he figured it would be
rude to refuse. And unsafe. There were dark circles
under her eyes. Her shoulders were sagging. She
struggled to heave the truck's massive door open
against a sudden gust of wind, and she was fast asleep
before they made it back onto the highway.

Another bridge spanned the river a stone's throw
away to the north. An older one. It was all solid piles
and cantilevered girders with giant rivets and flags
flying from the highest points. Reacher recognized it.
He had been shown pictures of it, and the river flowing beneath it, when he was a kid in a classroom on a
military base on the other side of the world. Before
the bridge they were crossing that day was even built.
But not in a lesson about engineering, or geography.

The idea was that the children were supposed to chant *one Mississippi, two Mississippi* to help them measure out the seconds. Reacher couldn't understand why. Even at that young age he was able to keep track of time in his head. So he ignored the official topic and focused on the bridge. It looked solid. Purposeful. Dependable. The way a properly designed structure should be. It only carried trains now. And it was a little worse for wear. Its paint was peeling. Its iron skeleton was streaked with rust. But it was still standing. Still functional. It had once been revered. Now it was surplus to requirements. That was a story Reacher knew well.

A hundred yards beyond the end of the bridge Reacher saw a sign for a truck stop. It claimed to be the largest in Mississippi. Reacher hoped that was true. And he hoped it reflected the scope of the facilities, not just the size of the parking lot. It was time for him to get a change of clothes and none of the previous places they visited had any in his size.

Hannah woke up when Reacher switched off the engine. The sleep had left her feeling brighter so they walked across the parking lot together, toward the main building. It was shaped like a bow tie. The entrance led into a square, central section that contained the restrooms, and showers for the truck drivers. The triangular area on the left was set up as a food court, with chairs and tables clustered in the center and three different outlets spread out around the edges. There was a pizza restaurant on one of the angled sides. A place selling fried chicken on the other. And a burger joint that took up the whole of the base. The store filled the entire area to the right, with shelves and racks and display cases scattered about in no discernible order.

Hannah went through the doors first and started toward the bathrooms but Reacher took her elbow and steered her into the store.

Hannah said, "What, you can't pick out a pair of pants on your own?"

Reacher checked over his shoulder and said, "You have a phone?"

"Of course. You want to call someone?"

"Does it take pictures?"

"Of course. All phones do these days."

"Do you hold it up to your eye, like a camera?"

Hannah laughed. "You hold it out in front. You see the image on the whole screen. Much better than a tiny viewfinder. Why?"

"There's a guy by the counter of the chicken place. He's lurking around like he's waiting for an order to come out. But he was actually watching the entrance. And he did something with his phone. He held it out in front and moved it, like he was tracking me with it when we came in."

"Move your arm to the side, just an inch?" Hannah peered through the gap between Reacher's biceps and his torso. "White guy, buzzed hair, T-shirt, jeans?"

Reacher nodded.

"He's still there. Another guy's with him. They look like gym buddies. He still has his phone in his hand. He keeps staring at it, like he's waiting for a message. Maybe they're supposed to be meeting someone? Who's running late for some reason and hasn't gotten in touch to let them know?"

Reacher shook his head. "He didn't raise the phone until he saw me. Then he pointed it right at me."

"Are you sure? You really think he took your picture? Why would he do that?"

"I don't know." Reacher turned around. "Let's ask him."

Reacher walked up to the guy with the phone and said, "Next time, call my agent."

Wrinkles creased the guy's forehead. He said, "What the hell are you talking about?"

"You want to take my picture, you need permission."

The guy couldn't help glancing down at his phone. "I didn't take your picture."

"I think you did."

"OK, smart-ass. So what if I—" The guy's phone made a sound like someone tapping a wineglass with the blunt edge of a knife. He checked its screen. Nodded to his buddy. Then he lifted the hem of his shirt a couple of inches. A black pistol was tucked into his jeans. A Beretta. It wasn't new. The hatching on its grip was scuffed and worn. "All right, Mr. Reacher. Enough of this bullshit. Let's finish this conversation outside."

The implied threat with the gun was ridiculous. It might as well have been a piece of lettuce. There was no way the guy was about to start shooting. Not there. Not with all the security cameras that were watching

him. The dozens of witnesses. The likelihood of col-
lateral damage that would buy him a life sentence, or
worse, if anyone died. And in any case, if he was stupid enough to try to draw the pistol he would be unconscious before the barrel cleared his waistband.
His buddy would be, too. Reacher half hoped the guy
would try it. He had energy to burn after all the hours
spent cooped up in the truck. But he knew it would
be better to wait until they were somewhere more private, so he decided to play along. He stepped back
and said, "After you."

The guy with the gun shook his head and gestured
for Reacher to move first. Reacher started toward the
exit. Hannah followed. Then the guy fell in behind
them, alongside his partner, and gave directions to
the rear of the building. They passed between the
long outside wall of the store and a parking area for
buses. Eleven vehicles were lined up in their oversized bays but there were no passengers milling
around. No drivers. The building was at the edge of
the site so there was nothing behind it. No road. No
parked cars. No people. Just a strip of cracked pavement between the wall and a fence. The fence was
made out of broad wooden slats. It was solid. There
were no gaps. No knot holes. It was ten feet high. No
one could see over it. No one could see through it.
There were no windows on that side of the building.
There were no doors. So there were no security cameras. And the walls of the food court and the store
angled outward from the bathroom block. That left a
trapezoid-shaped area that was totally secluded. No
one would see what happened there. No one would

call 911. No one would give statements to the police. No one would ever testify in court.

Reacher could see what was coming next. He knew one of the guys behind him was armed. It was safe to assume the other guy would be, too. So they would try to back him and Hannah up against the bathroom wall. That was clear. Then all the guys would have to do was stay back, and stay awake. Their plan could be to shoot Hannah. Or Reacher. Or both. To kill them. Immobilize them. Or just hold them until reinforcements arrived. But whatever the intention, it would be game over, right there.

Reacher took a half step to his right then stopped dead. Hannah was alongside him before she realized he wasn't moving anymore. She stopped, too. Reacher leaned down and whispered, "Stay behind me. Don't let the guy get a clear shot at you."

Hannah whispered back, "Which guy? There are two of them."

Reacher said, "Not for long."

Reacher heard a voice from behind him. It was the guy who'd been giving the directions. The one who was definitely armed. He said, "Keep going. No one told you to stand still."

The guy was close. Closer than when they left the building. Reacher could tell from the sound of his voice. The guy must have taken a couple of extra steps after Reacher stopped, just like Hannah had done. Reacher gauged the distance between them. He pictured the guy's height. Subtracted a couple of inches. Shifted his weight onto the ball of his left foot. Then threw himself backward. He snapped into a fast, clockwise turn, twisting at the waist to add momentum and extending his right arm. He clenched his fist. It traced a wide arc like the head of a sledgehammer. One wielded by a 250-pound maniac. The guy saw the danger. He started to duck. He fumbled for his gun. But he was too slow. The side of Reacher's fist slammed into his temple and felled him like a dead tree in a hurricane.

The second guy jumped back. He lifted his shirt and scrabbled for his own gun. Another Beretta. Reacher matched his movement. He stepped in close, stretched out his left hand, and pinned the guy's wrist against his abdomen. He took the guy's weapon. Then shoved him in the chest and sent him staggering away, too far to try to snatch the gun back.

Reacher said, "Your friend took my picture. Why?"

The guy didn't answer.

Reacher said, "You wanted to finish the conversation outside. We're outside. So converse."

The guy shook his head.

Reacher raised the gun. "Try this instead. You picked this particular spot. No witnesses. No cameras. Why was that?"

The guy held out his hands, palms up. "I don't know anything. If you're going to shoot me, just get it over with."

"You're wrong," Reacher said. "You do know some things. You know my name."

"Oh. Yeah. OK."

"You know you were sent out here to look for me."

"I guess."

"So you know who sent you."

The guy shook his head.

"You know. Who was it?"

The guy didn't answer.

Reacher prodded the body on the ground with his toe.

The guy closed his eyes for a moment. "Our boss sent us."

"Name?"

"Mr. Brockman."

"Organization?"

"Minerva Correctional."

"You work at the prison in Winson?"

The guy nodded.

Reacher said, "How did Brockman know I'd be here?"

"He didn't. He sent guys to a bunch of places. Just in case."

"How many guys?"

"I don't know. Eight? Ten? It wasn't like a regular team briefing. We got given our orders in pairs. Word filtered out between us later."

"Which places?"

"I only know one place for sure. The Greyhound station in Jackson. One of the guys who got sent there is my brother-in-law. He called me. A few minutes ago. They just caught a couple of punks trying to kidnap a homeless kid who'd come in from California. Said he wanted to see if we were having any fun like that. Which was horseshit. Really he wanted to break my balls because he knew we would be totally bored."

"Guess his call was a little premature. What were you supposed to do if you saw me?"

"Verify your ID."

"And then?"

"Stop you."

"From doing what?"

"Getting to Winson."

"Why?"

"So you couldn't cause any trouble."

"Why would I cause trouble in Winson?"

The guy shrugged. "Mr. Brockman said you were crazy. Crazy people do crazy things."

"You had to verify my ID. How?"

"We sent your picture to some guys who know what you look like."

"Which guys?"

"A couple of co-workers."

"How would they recognize me?"

"Your paths crossed a couple of days ago. In some town in Colorado."

Reacher smiled. "I see. Where are these guys?"

"In Winson. I guess. They're still out sick."

"I'll make sure to drop by their houses while I'm in town. Maybe bring them some flowers. Now, Brockman. Is he a good boss?"

"I guess."

"Is he a nice guy?"

"If he likes you."

"Right. I saw what happens to people he doesn't like. In Colorado. So here's what I'm going to do. I will go to Winson. I will cause some trouble for Mr. Brockman. Maybe a little more than he's expecting. And when I'm done I'll make sure he knows how much you helped me."

"No. Please. Don't do that. He'll kill me."

"Sorry. My mind's made up. Unless . . ."

"Unless what? What do you want? Money? 'Cause that's no problem. I can get you—"

"Not money. Information. There's something weird going on with the accounting at Minerva. I want to know what."

The guy's eyes stretched wide. "Accounting? I don't know anything about that. How would I?"

Reacher looked at the guy for a long moment. Over the years he had gotten pretty good at sensing when people were telling the truth. Normally he encouraged that kind of response. But on this occasion he was disappointed to be given an honest answer. It meant the guy was no more use to him. So he punched him in the face and watched him crumple and collapse onto the ground.

"Was that necessary?" Hannah was standing with her hands on her hips. "He was no threat. You'd already taken his gun."

Reacher said, "What about the backup piece in his ankle holster? And the knife in his sock?"

"He has another gun? And a knife?"

"He might have. You wait to find out, you'll be the one who winds up on the ground. And you won't be getting up again. These guys are working with the people who killed Sam. Who killed Angela. And they didn't bring us out here for coffee and cakes."

Hannah was quiet for more than a minute then she moved closer to the first guy Reacher had knocked down. "Is this one dead?"

Reacher shrugged. "Could have broken his neck, I guess."

"Don't you care?"

"Would you care if you stepped on a cockroach?"

"He's not a cockroach."

"No. He's worse. He's human. He had a choice."

"You know something? You're right." Hannah took another step then kicked the guy in the ribs. "He did choose this. He chose to help the people who murdered Sam. Not just killed him. *Killed* could be an accident. They took Sam's life on purpose. For some sort of gain. They're assholes. I hate them. I think we should get every last one of them."

"You'll get no argument from me."

"Good. So what do we do next?"

up. He had overindulged. Like with any great feast, it felt good in the moment. But the aftermath was no fun at all. And thanks to the likes of YouTube, the aftermath would live forever online.

The solution lay in better preparation. Hix knew that. He had already memorized his words. He was going to knock the content right out of the park. He had no doubt about that. He just needed to work on the delivery. To make sure he hit both targets simultaneously. The real and the virtual. That would be no mean feat. So he had devised a new system. A combination of old technology and new. He had started by getting the prison's maintenance crew to install giant mirrors on one wall of the conference room. He had them build a mock-up of the stage at the opposite end. Then he had two small video cameras delivered. They were designed for people who did active sports. Things like skiing and mountain biking and kayaking. Hix didn't care about how shockproof they were. He wasn't interested in their underwater performance. But there was one feature he figured would be essential. They were voice activated. So he set one on a regular tripod by his side and aimed it at the mirror to capture the kind of distant view the crowd would get. He set the other on a mini tripod sitting right on his lectern. It was pointing straight at his face. Cropped in tight, the way the news guys would do it. His plan was to give the command to record, which would set both cameras going simultaneously. Run through his speech, several times, with different expressions and gestures and degrees of movement. Then he would play the footage back, both feeds side by side on his computer screen, and settle on the best combination.

Hix had blocked out two hours in his diary. He had told his assistant that unless the prison went on lockdown he was not to be disturbed. He climbed up on the practice stage. He switched on the cameras. He was about to begin the recording. Then the conference room door swung open.

Hix turned and yelled, "What?"

Damon Brockman stepped into the room. He stayed well away from the stage and said, "You were right."

Hix said, "Of course I was right." He looked back into the lens of the lectern camera, opened his mouth, then paused. "Right about what?"

"The drifter from Colorado. Reacher. He was trying to come here."

"Was?"

"The guys at the truck stop on I-20 are all over him."

"They stopped him?"

"They got a positive ID."

"So they saw him. I'm asking, did they stop him?"

"They've been on radio silence since they sent his picture. Probably busy keeping him on ice. I've sent Harold up there to help them."

"Harold?"

"Harold Keane. The guys call him 'Tiny.' You'd recognize him if you saw him. He's been with us ten years. We brought him over here from Atlanta. He's six foot six. Three hundred pounds. All muscle. He won silver in America's Strongest Man two years running when he worked for the Georgia state system."

"Only silver?"

"Bruno, do me a favor. Don't ever say that to his face."

"He has a short fuse? Good. But it'll take him a while to get up there. Send the guys from the Megamart as well. The intersection with US 61 is way closer."

"Will do."

"And you can stand the guys down from the Greyhound station in Jackson. No point leaving them there now."

"I'll text them. Let them know. What about the guys at the construction site on US 87?"

"Leave them for now. Just in case. Until we know for sure that Reacher's safely under wraps."

"Understood."

"Good. Send the messages. Then why don't you come back? Watch me rehearse for tomorrow?"

"You know, I'd love to. But I'm slammed with other stuff. There's all kinds of craziness going on right now. So sadly I'll just have to go ahead and pass on that very tempting offer."

The next thing Reacher did was check whether the first guy he had hit was still alive.

The guy was. He had a pulse. It was fast and faint, but it was there. Reacher didn't care either way on an emotional level. It was purely a practical matter. He needed to know if he had trash to dispose of, or an opponent to keep off the field.

Reacher collected the unconscious guys' Berettas. He found their phones, smashed them against the ground with his heel, and threw the remains over the fence. Then he and Hannah searched the guys' pockets. They didn't yield any surprises. They each had a wallet with a single ATM card, a driver's license, and a Minerva Correctional ID. One had $40 in twenties. The other had $60. Reacher kept the cash. He still had new clothes to pay for. He also took a car key. It had a Mercury logo on its chunky plastic body and a remote fob on its ring.

Next Reacher pulled off the guys' boots. He tossed them over the fence. He removed the guys' jeans and T-shirts. He tossed them over the fence, too. Then he peeled off the guys' socks. They were thick. Heavy duty. The kind people wore for hiking and other kinds of vigorous sport. They were slightly damp. Reacher tried to ignore that and tested one for strength. He pulled it to see if it would stretch. Or snap. It gave a little, but it didn't break. He figured they would slow the guys down if nothing else, so he used the socks to secure their ankles and tie their wrists behind their backs. Then he dragged the guys across to the base of the wall for maximum concealment. He was ready to leave them there when a different thought crossed his mind.

He said, "Hannah? Come with me for a minute?"

Reacher led the way to the parking area at the side of the building. One of the buses had departed, leaving ten others in a tidy row. There were still no passengers in sight. No drivers. No other passersby. Reacher asked Hannah to keep a lookout then he tried the handles on the nearest bus's luggage compartment hatches. There were three on each side, low down, beneath the windows. All of them were locked. He tried the next bus. All of its hatches were locked, too. It was the same thing with the third bus. But the fourth bus was older. It had come all the way from British Columbia, Canada, according to its license plates. The first of its hatches was not secured. It pivoted out and up with no effort at all. Reacher left it open. He hurried back to the space behind the building. Picked up the first unconscious guy. Swung him onto his shoulder. Carried him to the bus. Posted him through the hatch and into the cargo hold. He fetched the second guy. Dumped him in the hold next to his buddy. Then he closed the hatch. He pressed his knee against it. Pulled the handle out. And twisted it back and forth until the mechanism failed and it came off in his hand. He did the same to the other five hatch handles. Threw them over the fence. And led the way back to the entrance to the building.

Reacher went into the bathroom to wash his hands. Then he moved on to the store. There was a basic selection of work clothes in the section that catered to truck drivers so he picked out the one pair of pants that looked long enough, a T-shirt, some underwear, and because he'd been to Mississippi before, a light rain jacket. He found a road atlas of the state. Grabbed two large cups of coffee. Paid for everything with the money he'd taken from the Minerva guys. Then he went outside and caught up with Hannah at the truck.

Hannah was happy to take her drink but she was surprised when Reacher climbed into the passenger seat and set a paper map down on the center console between them.

She said, "Why did you waste your money on that? My phone will give us directions. Anywhere we want to go. Right to the front door."

"This isn't for directions." Reacher opened the atlas to the page that showed the truck stop. It was near the western border of the state—the river—and roughly halfway between the Gulf to the south and Tennessee to the north. Jackson was to the east, roughly a third of the way to Alabama. Winson was to the southwest, nestling in a deep oxbow on the edge of the riverbank. "That Minerva guy said that ten people had been sent to watch for me. He said they're deployed in pairs, so that means there are five ambush sites. We know two of them. Where we are now, and the Greyhound station in Jackson. We need to figure out where the other three could be."

"OK. Well, clearly they anticipated we'd be coming in on I-20. But they couldn't have been sure we'd hit the truck stop. Not unless they knew about your strange wardrobe arrangement. Without that we would have kept going, then turned south here. Onto US 61." Hannah pointed at a line on the map. "Somewhere farther along there would be the next logical place to try and catch us."

"No. They would try at the intersection. They can't know you're taking me the whole way to Winson. They'll assume that if I'm on the road I either stole a car or I'm hitching rides. If I stole a car, that's where I'd turn. If someone had picked me up farther west and was continuing to Jackson or Meridian, or even Tuscaloosa or Birmingham, that's where they would let me out. So it's where I'd hang around, looking for my next pickup."

"Makes sense." Hannah took a pen from her purse and circled the spot where US 61 crossed I-20. "That's potential ambush site number three. Now, if we'd taken the more central route from Colorado through Kansas and Missouri, we'd have wound up coming down I-55 into Jackson. Then we'd have come west again. And there's only one route into Winson, wherever you're coming from. They'll put their backstop somewhere on that road."

Reacher picked up the map, studied it closely for a moment, then set it back down and pointed to a spot near the town boundary. "There. Look at the contours. It only rises a hundred feet but it's the steepest hill for about a hundred miles. Enough to slow down any trucks, and the rest of the traffic along with them. Slow-moving vehicles are easier to see into. And they're easier to stop."

Hannah circled the place Reacher had indicated. "Number four, done. Where's five going to be?"

"Jackson."

"You think? Would they put another team there? They already have the Greyhound station covered."

"Right. But what if I came in by train? Or got a ride there? How would I get the rest of the way to Winson? There's bound to be a shuttle, or a local bus service. Probably owned by Minerva. Just like they probably own the hotels near the prison."

"They can do that?"

"Of course. Why only profit off the prisoners when you can make money from their visitors, too?"

"You're so cynical." Hannah stopped with the pen poised above the map. "But I guess you're right. So where in Jackson would this bus be?"

"Doesn't matter. I'm not going to Jackson. It's too far out of my way. I'll just take care of the intersection and the hilltop for now."

"*Take care of?* Don't you mean *avoid*?"

Reacher shook his head. "Basic tactics. If you have the opportunity to degrade the enemy's capability, you take it."

"Oh. We're going to *degrade* their *capability*? Awesome. I'm up for that. Just tell me what you need me to do."

"Find a hotel. For tonight."

"OK. In Winson? For when we're done with the degrading?"

Reacher shook his head. "No. There's something I want you to think about. I want you to consider going somewhere else. On your own. For a couple of days."

"The hell I will. I'm going wherever you go. You can't make me drive you all this way then dump me. Talk about a dick move."

"I didn't make you. I'm not dumping you. But we have new information now. We should be smart. Act accordingly."

"What new information?"

"We've lost the element of surprise. Minerva knows I'm coming. They know my name. They have my description. They now have a current photograph. Their people are competent. They're out in force, looking for me. Sticking with me now will expose you to a higher level of risk. Much higher."

"OK. The risk is higher now. I get that. But you know what? I can take any level of risk I damn well want. You don't get to decide that for me."

"I'm not deciding. I'm advising. Your goal is to get the people who killed—murdered—Sam. You can't do that if they murder you first. So why don't I go ahead, like an advance party. Get the lay of the land. Sweep out any low-level operatives I find skulking around. Then when the risk is lower, I'll call. You'll join me. And we'll get to the heart of the thing together."

Hannah was silent for a moment. "You say the risk is higher. But here's what I don't understand. If we're right, the Minerva guys killed Angela because she uncovered something fishy in their accounts. They killed Sam because Angela told him what she found. So why are they coming after you? What's the connection? What aren't you telling me?"

Reacher paused for a moment, then he talked Hannah through what had happened in Gerrardsville after he witnessed Angela getting pushed in front of the bus. He told her about chasing the guy in the hoodie into the alley. Taking Angela's purse from him. Looking inside. Finding the envelope. The guy's partner showing up in the stolen BMW. And how they got away when the fire escape collapsed.

Hannah punched Reacher in the shoulder. "Why keep all that a secret? I've gone way out on a limb for you. I don't deserve to be kept in the dark."

Reacher shrugged. "Suppose those guys show up in the hospital sometime soon. Or at the morgue."

Hannah was silent for a moment. "Fair, I guess. I can see why you wouldn't want to advertise a grudge against them. But that's not the key point here. You hurt a couple of Minerva's guys. Maybe saw some incriminating evidence. That's reason for them to come after you. Not the other way around. So why are they expecting you? What else are you holding back?"

"Nothing."

"You swear?"

Reacher nodded.

"OK," Hannah said. "Maybe they know you connected them to the murders?"

Reacher shook his head. "I told the Gerrardsville police that Angela didn't kill herself but I hadn't factored Minerva in, back then. And the police ignored me, anyway. Angela's file is closed. So is Sam's."

"Then it has to be about Angela's purse. The Minerva guys took it, so there had to be something important inside."

"Maybe. Maybe not. They might have thought something important was. They might have hoped. Doesn't mean it was there."

"Tell me again what was in her purse?"

Reacher listed everything he had seen.

"Could anything have been sewn into the lining?"

"I was a military cop. I know where people hide things."

"So we're back to the envelope. Tell me about that again."

"It held a file on a guy called Anton Begovic. Wrongly convicted, due for release tomorrow. Minerva sponsored his appeal."

"Those jackasses."

"There's something wrong with setting an innocent man free?"

"No. Of course not. It's just—Minerva. With them everything's about PR. Their head dude is a guy called Bruno Hix. He's notorious. He doesn't take a dump without bringing in an image consultant to exploit it. I bet they got some lawyer who owed them a favor to do the appeal work for free. Then they'll stage a huge hullabaloo and make it look like the whole corporation is run by saints and angels and it'll cost them nothing. Sam was always suspicious of them."

"Why?"

"If something sounds too good to be true, then it isn't true. That's what he always said. Like with their wages. They pay twenty-five percent above the industry average, across the board. They made sure everyone knows about it. Then they make sure no one gets any overtime."

"Where did—"

"Wait! I have an idea. What if this Begovic guy isn't really innocent? What if he paid Minerva to help fix the appeal? Or his family did? Minerva could have tried to wash the money through the books. Not very well. And Angela could have smelled the rat."

"If there is dirty money, why would they let it anywhere near the business? Why not take it in cash?"

Hannah shook her head. "See, that's the kind of question you only ask if you've never bought a house. Or a car. Or a spare pair of pants. A big heap of cash is the biggest red flag there is. You'd have the IRS so far up your ass you'd see them when you brush your teeth. No. I think I'm on to something. And you clearly shouldn't be let out on your own. So here's the deal. I'm coming with you. But while you're busy *degrading the enemy* or whatever, I'll hang back at the hotel. I'll dig into Begovic's background. Find out all about his conviction. His appeal. What it was based on. Why it took so long. I'll maybe talk to some of Sam's contacts. Tap into the industry scuttlebutt. Find the real story."

Chapter 27

Five words were ringing in Jed Starmer's ears as he crouched between a pair of dumpsters in an alley on the other side of the Greyhound station: *I'm a law enforcement officer.*

The guy's voice had been a little muffled from where he lay on the floor of the car but Jed was sure about what he heard. Although he wasn't sure what kind of officer the guy was. He hadn't been wearing a uniform. Neither had his partner. So Jed figured they must be detectives. Or FBI agents. Something high up. Important. But he wasn't too concerned about which organization they belonged to. Or what rank they held. He was just glad they had shown up when they did. He had no idea what the scruffy guys had wanted with him but it didn't take a clairvoyant to see it wasn't going to be anything good.

Jed was glad the officers had shown up, but at the same time he was horrified. Because it meant they must have been looking for him. That was certainly what it sounded like from the exchanges he overheard. The guy from his first bus must have called them. After they finished their breakfast in Dallas. He'd kept nagging Jed about going to the police. When Jed refused the guy must have taken matters into his own hands. Which meant Jed would have to change his plans. He had been intending to sleep on the seats in the Greyhound station that night and then make his way to Winson the next morning. He couldn't risk staying in town now. Not in a public place. Not somewhere out in the open. He had no option. He had to leave. Immediately.

Reacher left the atlas, one of the captured Berettas, and the last dregs of his coffee in the truck with Hannah and walked back to the main building to change his clothes. After that his plan was simple. He was going to find the next pair of Minerva guys at the nearby intersection and give them exactly what they wanted.

For a moment, at least.

He figured that the guys would be looking for him in a car, or at the side of the road as he tried to hitch a ride. If they spotted him in a car, things could get complicated. They wouldn't be able to stop him right away because of the whole identification rigmarole. They would have to take his photograph, send it off to the guys who had seen him in Colorado, and wait for their response. So they would have two choices. They could follow his car and intercept it if his ID was confirmed. Or they could stay put and send the intel to the guys who would be stationed at the outskirts of Winson. Neither of those options appealed to Reacher. Forcing a car off a highway at speed in heavy traffic is dangerous. There's plenty of scope for injuries. Maybe fatalities. Maybe involving other vehicles with innocent drivers and passengers. And if the guys passed the information along the chain, that would be no immediate help, either. Reacher would be miles away by then, out of contact, and it would only make his life more difficult when he arrived in the town. So the smart move was to stand where the guys would be hoping to see him, stick out his thumb, and hope no regular motorists were on the lookout for company.

From above, the intersection looked like a capital A, rotated by forty-five degrees, with a curved crossbar. One side was I-20, which swung a little north of east after clearing the river. The other side was US 61, which branched off and ran to the south. The crossbar was made up of the ramps joining I-20 east to US 61 south, and US 61 north to I-20 west. The other significant part of the picture was the space beneath the crossbar. It was taken up by a giant store. Reacher couldn't tell from the map which chain it belonged to or what sort of products it sold. And he didn't much care. The only thing that mattered to him was that it had a convenient parking lot.

The plan was simple. Hannah would pull over on the shoulder just before the east/south ramp. Reacher would get out of the truck. Hannah would continue on I-20 toward Jackson, in case anyone was already watching. She would leave the highway at the next intersection and loop around to the giant store. She would wait in the parking lot. The Minerva guys would spot Reacher. They would try to photograph him and detain him, either on the shoulder or in a vehicle. They would have the same kind of success as their buddies at the truck stop had. And when they were unconscious and immobilized, Reacher would climb down the side of the ramp, make his way to the store, and rendezvous with Hannah.

The plan was simple. But it went off the rails before it even got started.

Reacher dumped his old clothes in the trash and walked back to the truck. He opened the passenger door but he didn't get in. Because someone was in his seat. A guy, late twenties, wearing some kind of European soccer jersey, jeans, and motorcycle boots. His hair was buzzed at the sides and a little longer at the top. He had a goatee. And he was holding a gun. In his left hand. A desert tan–colored SIG P320. His grip was steady and he was aiming at the center of Reacher's chest.

Reacher grabbed the guy's wrist and pulled until his forearm was clear of the truck's doorframe. He forced it back against the pillar between the windows. Twisted, so the gun was pointing at the ground. Then he slammed the door. He threw all his weight behind it. The guy screamed. The gun fell. It clattered against the truck's running board and skittered away under the next parked car. Reacher felt the guy's wrist go limp. He'd heard the bones crack and splinter. Then he snatched the door open again. The guy's head was lolling back against the seat. Beads of sweat had sprung out all over his face. His skin looked almost green. Reacher pulled back his right arm. Closed his fist. The guy's throat was exposed. One punch was all it would take.

A voice said, "Stop." It was coming from the back-seat. Another guy was there. The same kind of age and build as the one with the broken arm. He had a plain black T-shirt on. His head was completely shaved. He was behind Hannah. Leaning forward. And pressing the muzzle of a revolver into the base of her skull.

Hannah was sitting up so straight it was like she was trying to levitate. Her arms were stretched out in front. She was gripping the steering wheel with both hands. Her knuckles were bone white. She was star-ing straight ahead and her face was twisted into the kind of scowl you'd expect from a parent who found her teenage kids hosting an orgy in her living room.

The gun looked tiny in the guy's hand. It was a Ruger LCR. A .22. Probably the guy's ankle piece, Reacher thought. It wouldn't be much use at distance. You wouldn't choose it as a primary weapon. But at close quarters it would be more than adequate. And in that situation it would be ideal. If the guy got his angle right, there was a good chance the round wouldn't break out through the top of Hannah's skull. It would just bounce around inside her head, pulping her brain, until its energy was dissipated and it came to rest in the resulting mush. Which meant her blood and cerebral jelly wouldn't be sprayed across the windshield for anyone to see. And if the bullet did emerge it certainly wouldn't have enough force left to pierce the truck's steel roof. It was as discreet an option as the guy could hope for. Although with his buddy's life on the line he might not care too much about attracting attention.

Reacher opened his hand and lowered his arm.

"Good decision," the guy said. "Now, we're looking for two of our friends. This young lady told me you could help us find them."

Reacher said, "You have friends?"

"This is no time for jokes."

"Who's joking?"

"Tell me where they are."

"How would I know?"

The guy pulled something out from under his left thigh. He held it up for Reacher to see. It was the Beretta he had left in the truck when he went to change.

The guy said, "Stop wasting time. Tell me where they are."

A vehicle rumbled past the rear of the truck. Reacher took a glance. It was a bus. The old one from British Columbia. There were no passengers on board. Only the driver. Reacher hoped he was taking it all the way to Canada. Or given the sudden shift in his mood, straight to a scrap yard. One that wouldn't check it too thoroughly before dumping it in the crusher.

Reacher said, "They're not far away."

"Tell me where."

"I'll show you."

"Tell me."

"You'd believe me?"

The guy took a moment to think. "OK. Are you wearing a belt?"

Reacher nodded.

"Take it off. Give it to me."

Reacher didn't move.

The guy increased the pressure on the gun. It dug deeper into Hannah's skin. She clenched her teeth but couldn't hold back a long, low whimper.

Reacher slipped his belt through the loops in his pants and held it out in the gap between the truck's front seats. The guy kept the gun pressed against Hannah's skull and stretched out with his left hand. He grabbed the belt, then bit it between his teeth, near the buckle. He fed the free end through. Took up the slack until he had a circle about twelve inches across. Then he pulled the gun away and flipped the belt over Hannah's head and yanked it tight around her neck and the metal stalks of the seat rest. She didn't make another sound but her scowl grew even more fearsome.

"Pep?" the guy said to his buddy in the passenger seat. "Can you move?"

Pep nodded. "Think so."

"Good. Come over here. To my door."

Pep slid out of the truck and crept around to its rear. He was clutching his left arm to his chest and moving like he had the mother of all hangovers. He

No Plan B | 221

made it to the far side. The guy holding the belt slid across. Pep climbed in behind Hannah and slumped back in the seat. He looked like he was about to be sick.

"Sit forward," the guy holding the belt said. "All the way. Get your ass right on the edge."

Pep shuffled to the front of the seat. The guy took Pep's right hand and tied the belt around his wrist so that his palm was flat against the back of the driver's seat, just below the nape of Hannah's neck.

The guy patted Pep between the shoulders then slid the rest of the way across to the passenger side, opened the door, and climbed down next to Reacher. He nodded toward Pep and Hannah and said, "Do I need to draw you a diagram?"

Reacher shook his head.

"Good. Now pick up the SIG Pep dropped. Finger and thumb through the trigger guard. Pass it to me."

Reacher fished the gun out from under the neighboring car and handed it to the guy.

"OK." The guy tucked the gun into the back of his pants and made sure his shirt was covering it. "Show me where my friends are. And you better make it quick, for the woman's sake."

Reacher led the way back toward the main building and as he walked he tried to picture the remote fob on the key ring he had taken after searching the first pair of Minerva guys. He remembered it had four buttons. The lower two were colored. One was red. It looked like it had something to do with the alarm. One was blue. It was for opening the trunk. The others were black. They had little white padlock symbols on them. The symbols were faint. They were worn almost all the way off but Reacher thought the lock on the top left button was shown as closed.

Reacher slid his hand into his pocket and felt for the fob. He found the top right button and pressed it with his thumb. He looked around the lot, hoping to see a parked car's turn signals flash.

Nothing happened.

The guy walking behind him said, "Hey. What are you doing?"

"Keeping my pants from falling down."

The guy grunted like he wasn't convinced.

They kept on walking. Reacher kept on pressing the unlock button. No lights flashed. They were almost at the entrance to the building. Reacher figured the car must be somewhere else in the lot, so he would have to take the guy around the back of the building. Do the job in two stages. He knew for sure the car wasn't over to the right because that was where the buses parked. So he rolled the dice one last time. Headed toward the left. Pressed the unlock button again. And saw a pair of orange lights give a long, slow blink.

The car the lights belonged to was in the final row, in front of the fence that continued along the perimeter of the site. There was an empty space on both sides. But it was a false alarm. A coincidence. It was the wrong kind of car. A Ford Crown Victoria. Reacher had seen hundreds of them during his time in the army. And hundreds more after he left. Although this one was much cleaner than most he had come across. Its paintwork was immaculate. Dark blue, almost black. Shiny, like it recently had been polished. It had strange wheels. A weird grille at the front. Dark tints on the windows. It seemed more like someone's personal vehicle than a detective's car or a cab. So Reacher looked at it more closely. He saw there was a Mercury logo where the blue oval should be. He didn't understand why, but he had never been much of a car guy. And he didn't waste time speculating. He just slid his thumb across to the lock button on the fob. He pressed it. The car's flashers blinked again. Just as lazily. Reacher figured it was unlikely to be a coincidence a second time.

Reacher said, "This way." He changed course and made for the rear of the car. It was almost against the fence. Its owner had backed in, ready for a quick exit if necessary. Reacher waited for the guy to catch up then took the keys out of his pocket. He hit the trunk button. The lid unlocked itself but only swung up a couple of inches.

The guy said, "Do you think I'm new? I'm not opening that."

Reacher said, "No problem. I'll do it. You don't need to get any closer. Just one question first. You work for Minerva?"

"Just hit my ten-year anniversary. Where are my friends? They better not be in that trunk."

"You were sent here to look for me?"

"We were sent to the intersection. Got moved here when the other guys spotted you. What's in the trunk? Where are my friends?"

"You had guys here. You had some at the Grey-hound station. Where else?"

"No idea. Wasn't told, didn't ask. Now, enough talking. Show me what's in the trunk."

"You're right. Talking's not getting us anywhere. It's time to—"

Reacher butted the guy in the face. He didn't pull his head back very far. He didn't want to telegraph what was coming. That meant sacrificing some power so Reacher had to rely on his height and his neck muscles. It wasn't the hardest blow he'd ever delivered. But it was hard enough. It sent the guy reeling back, still on his feet but already unconscious. He smashed into the fence. Teetered for a moment. Reacher stepped in close. He caught the guy before he hit the ground. Dragged him the last few feet to the car. Lifted the trunk lid the rest of the way. Bundled the guy inside. Then slammed it shut. Unlocked the doors and climbed in behind the wheel.

Chapter 28

Bruno Hix started his speech three times.

He started. But he couldn't finish. He couldn't get beyond the first couple of lines. He was too distracted. All he could think about was the truck stop. He couldn't help wondering what was happening up there. He'd sent four guys to take care of one drifter. That should have been a walk in the park. But there'd been no confirmation. No status reports. No news of any kind. And the drifter had already made fools out of the men he'd sent to Colorado.

Hix jumped down from the stage. He left the room and hurried along the corridor to the far end of the building's other wing. To Brockman's office. The door was closed. Hix didn't knock. He just opened it and walked in. For a moment he thought Brockman wasn't there. The desk chair was empty. The armchair was empty. Then he saw that Brockman was stretched out on the couch by the window. An abandoned coffee mug was on the floor by his side.

Hix folded his arms. "Busy, huh?"

Brockman opened his eyes. He sat up. "Very. I'm strategizing."

"No news?"

"Actually, yes. There is. Good news. One of my previous strategies has borne fruit, big-time. We know how Reacher got to Mississippi so fast. He took a pickup belonging to Sam Roth. The guy Angela St. Vrain was on her way to see. He's dead, obviously, so no one reported it stolen. The guys we moved over from the intersection located it in the truck stop parking lot."

"They found a truck?"

"Correct."

"Who cares about a truck? Where's Reacher?"

"He must still be there."

"Must be? You don't know?"

"The truck's still there. So Reacher must be, too. What's he going to do—walk the rest of the way? So, Bruno, chill. Our guys are there. They're staking it out. We'll hear the moment they have him."

"Call them. Right now. Put them on speaker."

"You need to take a valium." Brockman took out his phone and dialed a number. It rang. And rang. And rang. Until it tripped through to voicemail. Brockman hung up without leaving a message. He dialed another number. That call ended up with voicemail, too. Brockman forced a smile. "There's nothing to worry about. They must have their phones on silent. To avoid giving their positions away. They're being professional. That's a good thing."

"Try the other two."

Brockman dialed again. This time there was no ring tone. The call went straight to voicemail. The same thing happened with the fourth number he tried. "Their batteries are probably flat. They've been there since 3:00 A.M., remember."

"Something's wrong."

"Everything's fine. Give it time. Be patient."

"Did you order the guys back from Jackson?"

"Yes. Right after I left your office."

"Call them again. Divert them to the truck stop as well."

"Really? We need seven guys there?"

"We have four there already. Maybe five by now. Have they got the job done?"

Brockman called the guys who'd been at the Greyhound station and passed on Hix's instructions. He hung up. Put his phone away. Waited for Hix to leave. Then pulled his phone back out and dialed another number. He'd forgotten about the guys he had sent to watch the local bus stop. There was no reason to leave them in Jackson any longer. Which was a shame. Brockman could claim some kudos from connecting Reacher with Roth's truck. But he could have claimed a whole lot more if he'd caught Reacher in a trap that Hix hadn't even thought to set.

———

Reacher backed the Mercury into the space next to Sam Roth's truck. He was hoping that Pep would recognize it and think his buddy was coming to relieve him. Or that it was just some random person's car, on their way to use the facilities in the main building. Anything really, as long as he didn't take it as a threat. As long as he didn't start strangling Hannah with the belt.

As long as he hadn't already strangled her.

Reacher jumped out of the car. He pulled the handle on the truck's rear door. It was locked. He couldn't see inside because of the tint on the window. He couldn't see what state Pep was in. Or what state Hannah was in. He tried the driver's door. It was locked as well. He banged on the glass. Nothing happened. Hannah didn't release the lock.

She didn't. Or she couldn't.

Reacher took the Beretta from his waistband. He flipped it around so he was holding it by the barrel. Then he smashed the butt against the glass in the rear door like it was a hammer. He hit the window hard, low down in the corner at its weakest spot. The glass instantly formed into an opaque mesh of crystals. Reacher gave it a shove. It sagged. But it didn't give all the way. The film that caused the tint was too tough. And it extended too far. It went all the way up and sideways into the frame, and all the way down into the body of the door. Reacher slammed it with the heel of his hand. One side came free. He hit it again. The top and the other side loosened up. Then he hit it again and the whole sheet bent back. It curled and drooped like it was moving in slow motion. It bowed and crept down until it covered the inside surface of the door.

Pep glared out at Reacher through the empty window frame. His skin was even greener than before. His face was sweatier. And he was pulling on the belt with all his strength. Hannah was trying to claw it away from her throat. Her head was thrashing from side to side but she was making no noise. She was getting no air. Reacher stretched his arm into the truck and punched Pep in the side of the head. Hard. He flopped over sideways and rolled into the footwell. He didn't move. He was out cold. He could no longer deliberately pull the belt. But it was still tied to his wrist. His weight was still keeping it taut.

Hannah still couldn't breathe.

Reacher scrabbled for the handle on the inside of the door but he couldn't get to it. The sheet of glass and tinting film was in the way. It was hanging down too far, like a shield. He tried to tear it off. But he couldn't. The film was too strong. So he grabbed the edge and pulled it up. He took hold of the opposite edge with his other hand. Forced the sides together until the sheet and his hands would fit through the frame. He wrestled it down, out of the way. Stretched his arm back in. Released the lock and opened the door.

Reacher hauled Pep upright and pushed him forward. Hannah coughed and spluttered and wheezed as the tension on the belt finally eased. She wriggled her fingers between it and her skin. Loosened it a little further. She sucked in a desperate gasping breath. Reacher worked at the knot. It had been pulled tight by all the struggling. Pep's arm was still a dead weight. It took another thirty seconds to get it free then Reacher slipped the loose end through the buckle. Hannah flopped forward against the steering wheel. She groped for the door handle. Found it. Slid out. Collapsed onto the Mercury's trunk. She lay on her back. Stared at the sky. And breathed.

The atmosphere was foul. It was full of diesel and gasoline fumes from all the traffic in the parking lot and on the highway. Normally Hannah would be repulsed by it. She had grown up with the clear mountain air in Gerrardsville. But in that moment, she couldn't imagine how anything could taste sweeter.

Something told Jed Starmer to stop.

He had spent ten minutes hiding in the alley after he was done running from the scruffy guys' car. It had taken him that long to get his breath back. And to figure out what his next move should be. It was one thing to decide to leave town. But it was another to work out how. He had been hoping to get the rest of the way to Winson on a prison shuttle, but that was only because of the sign he'd seen in Texas. He didn't know for sure they had them in Mississippi. The sign had been in the Greyhound station in Dallas. He hadn't seen one in the station there, in Jackson. But he hadn't had the chance to look, because of the scruffy guys. And he couldn't go back now. The officers might have returned. They might be there, lying in wait for him. He didn't have a phone with internet access so he couldn't google the information. He couldn't risk wandering about at random. He might be spotted. But he could go old school. He remembered running past a stand of payphones, two blocks back. And he still had a few coins in his pocket.

First Jed called directory assistance. Then he called the Minerva facility in Winson. He told the receptionist he was an inmate's relative and he wanted to come visit but didn't know how to get to the prison. He asked if there was a shuttle service from Jackson. The receptionist said there wasn't. Not a dedicated one. Which was why most visitors used the local bus. She gave Jed the address of the stop. She even told him the departure times.

The bus was due to leave in four minutes. Jed had gotten close enough to hear the engine. It was rumbling steadily away, just around the corner. He'd had to run the last quarter mile to give himself a chance of catching it. The next one wasn't due for another hour. He didn't want to be exposed on the street for that long. But a sudden thought had struck him. Officers had been at the Greyhound station. On the lookout for him. Detectives, or agents, or whatever they were. Which meant there could be more of them at the bus stop. He could run right into them. There would be no way to avoid getting caught. It would be as bad as giving himself up.

Jed stopped. He was almost at the intersection. Then a guy on a bike ran straight into him. Some kind of a messenger. He had a satchel slung over his shoulder and he had been riding on the sidewalk. The impact sent Jed staggering forward. Past the end of the building. The force spun him around. The side of his foot caught in a gap between two paving slabs. He lost his balance. He fell. Rolled over. Came to a halt straddling the curb. Half on the sidewalk. Half in the gutter. And fully in view of everyone at the bus stop.

People were staring at Jed. Maybe half a dozen. He didn't get a good look at them. And he didn't lie sprawling on the ground long enough to count heads. He just scrambled to his feet and darted back into the lee of the building, out of their sight.

The messenger had propped his bike against the wall. He was standing next to it, watching and waiting. As soon as Jed was in range he shoved him in the chest. He said, "Idiot. Look where you're going. You could have got me killed." Then he shoved Jed again and disappeared through a revolving glass door and into the last building on the block.

Jed thought about the people he had seen on the next street. Maybe they were only waiting to get on the bus. Or maybe they were watching it. Or maybe just a pair of them were. A pair of detectives. Or agents. Jed turned to run. And stopped himself again. He had nowhere to go. No other means of transport. The bus was his only shot at leaving town. He'd be crazy not to take it if it was safe.

If.

Jed had to know for sure. So he crept back to the end of the building. He ducked down. Peered around the corner. And saw two guys. One was slipping a phone into his pocket. The guy gestured to his partner. To start moving. Which they did, straightaway. Straight toward Jed.

The guys were both around six feet tall. They were broad. Strong-looking. Their hair was buzzed short. They were wearing jeans and T-shirts and suit coats. Just like the officers at the Greyhound station. They were the same height. The same build. They had the same menacing aura. They were yards away. And they were closing fast.

Jed knew he was finished. He had seen what the other officers had done to the scruffy guys. One had been unconscious within a split second. The other had gotten a gun jammed in his chest. Jed didn't want either of those things to happen to him. But he also knew he could never get away. Not on foot. The officers would be faster than him. And they would be trained to catch people. Plus they could call for backup. Maybe dogs. Maybe air support. Jed sagged against the wall. He had come so far. He had gotten so close. Then his hand brushed against something. The front wheel of the messenger's bike.

The bike was right there. Next to him. It wasn't locked. That seemed like a sign he should take it. Jed wasn't a thief. He didn't want to steal it. But he also didn't want to get caught. And the messenger had behaved like a total asshole. So Jed decided it would be OK to just borrow the bike. Given the circumstances. Just for a little while. As short a time as possible. Then he could find a way to return it. Bike riding was not something Jed enjoyed. But it had to be better than anything those guys would do if they got their hands on him.

Chapter 29

Reacher was half expecting the truck to be gone when he got back from dumping the Mercury. He left it in the corner on the far side of the lot, tucked in at the side of a donation box for a clothing charity that didn't look like it saw much action. Then he strolled back. He wanted Hannah to have plenty of time to think. To weigh her options. She had been through a lot in the last couple of days. Finding Sam Roth's body. Learning that he had been murdered. Hearing that Angela St. Vrain had also been murdered. Almost getting murdered herself. Reacher wouldn't have blamed her if she'd jumped into the driver's seat the moment he was out of sight, headed for the highway, and put as many miles between them as humanly possible.

The truck was still there. Hannah was standing next to it. A small red suitcase was at her side. A stripey tote bag was attached to its handle and she had her purse slung over her shoulder.

She said, "We need to talk."

Reacher said, "No need to explain. Thanks for staying to say goodbye. And thanks for all your help."

"What are you talking about? You think those assholes scared me off? Screw them. I was already all in. That goes double now they laid hands on me. No. We need to talk about Sam's truck. We can't use it anymore."

"Is it damaged?"

"Apart from the window, no. That's not the problem. Those guys? Who jumped me? They recognized it somehow. They were walking by, in a hurry, heading for the building, and suddenly they stopped. I saw them checking the license plate. Then before I twigged what was happening the doors were open and they were inside, shoving their guns in my face. But the point is, they must have connected you to Sam. And if they knew to look out for his truck, their buddies will, too. At the next ambush. We'll never get through. We need to get a replacement vehicle."

"You have a point, but our options are limited here. The guys who jumped you must have come in a vehicle. We could find it. Take it. But there's a good chance their buddies would recognize it, too. So there would be no benefit. Or we could steal a car from the parking lot but it would be reported in minutes. Then we would be worse off. We might not make it to the next ambush at all."

"Taking people's cars? Stealing other ones?" Hannah smiled and shook her head. "I was thinking about something less extreme. More legal. We should get a rental car. There must be a bunch of depots in Jackson. Or if we don't want to schlep all that way we could get one dropped off here. That would be more expensive, but a lot more convenient."

"How long would that take?"

Hannah pulled her phone out of her purse. "I'll see who has a car available. Then we can figure out the quickest option." The screen lit up and her phone unlocked itself. "And there's something else. When I was waiting for you to change, before those guys showed up, I checked the map to see what the rest of the route to Winson was like. And look." She held out the phone so that Reacher could see the screen. "See that red line? It means stationary traffic. I googled it, and it turns out that's because of a construction zone. The road's down to a single lane. So this is where the ambush will be. Not the hill you found on the paper map. This is a much better place. We'll be stationary. So we'll be a sitting duck. There's no way they could miss us. Not in a recognizable vehicle. And there's no other route we could take."

Reacher thought for a moment. "Does Google say what kind of traffic management they have there? Lights? A guy with a stop/go board?"

"Google didn't. But I also found a couple of online message boards for inmates' families. There's a lot of talk about the problems people have when they go visit. One woman mentioned they're using a pilot vehicle. You know the kind of thing? Usually a pickup with a big illuminated sign in the load bed. It shuttles back and forth. Drivers have to wait until it comes and follow it to the other end. This woman said the driver was a jackass. She claimed he dawdled along extra slow and let the lines back up so much she missed half her visiting time."

Reacher said, "Can your phone show the view from a satellite?"

"Sure." Hannah hit a button at the corner of the screen and flipped it around for Reacher to see. "It's not a live feed, you know. You're not going to see the pilot vehicle moving around."

"Don't need to." Reacher studied the phone for a moment. "I just need to see the terrain." He nodded. "We can make this work for us. We could get a rental car but it would be better to use the truck. We can get a replacement vehicle delivered to the hotel, later, if you want."

"Sticking with the truck for now is the best way? You're sure?"

"One hundred percent."

"It's not about the cost? Because I'm happy to pay."

"It's not the cost. Trust me."

Hannah pointed to the truck's rear door. "What about the window? We can't drive with it in that state."

"Duct tape will fix it."

"Duct tape?"

"You can fix anything with duct tape."

"Are you serious?"

"Absolutely. Look—the tinting film is holding on to all the glass. All we need is something to secure it around the frame. Duct tape."

"And do you have any? In your extensive selection of luggage, maybe? Because oddly enough it's not something I carry in my purse."

"They sell it in the store here. I saw it earlier."

"Oh. Good. I guess."

"I'll go grab some. And some emergency road flares. We're going to need those, too."

"We are? Why?"

"We're going to do some traffic management of our own."

Bruno Hix was back on his practice stage. The cameras were running. And this time he made it to the end of his speech in one take. *Pretty good,* he thought. *But could be better.*

Hix had just started his second run-through when the conference room door opened. It was Brockman.

Hix said, "What now?"

Brockman was silent for a moment. Then he shook his head and said, "You were right again."

"About what this time?"

"The truck stop. Something is wrong up there."

"Explain."

"Harold just called. He arrived and there was no sign of our other guys. He looked in all the places it would be logical for them to use on a stakeout. Nada. So he cast his net wider. He checked the parking lot.

He cruised up and down every aisle. In the corner, the farthest one away from the building, by some charity donation thing, he found Nick's car. His Marauder. His pride and joy. Harold took a closer look. The doors were unlocked and the keys were on the driver's seat. He thought it looked low at the back. So he popped the trunk. And he was right."

"Nick was in there? Hell and damnation. Was he alone? Or with whoever he was partnered up with? Steve, wasn't it? Were they alive? Or dead?"

"They were alive. But it wasn't Nick and Steve. Get this. It was Pep and Tony. The guys we sent over from the intersection."

"How did they get in Nick's trunk?"

"No idea."

"Where are Nick and Steve?"

"No idea. There was no sign of them anywhere."

"What about the truck Pep found? The one Reacher was using."

"It was gone. Harold thought he saw a red truck leaving when he arrived but he couldn't be sure it was the same one."

Hix was silent for a moment. "OK. No point worrying about what's already happened. Call the guys at the construction zone. Give them the description of Reacher's truck. Make sure they know the plates."

Brockman said, "Already done."

"Call them again. Make sure they know what they're dealing with. Tell Harold to get down there. And the guys from the Greyhound station. This Reacher's a menace. I don't want him in my town. Not tomorrow."

Jed Starmer could finally see the appeal of riding a bike. He had never had the chance to do it very much in the past. He'd never owned one of his own. His foster parents would never have allowed it. So one day, a few months back, he badgered a friend into teaching him how to ride one. The experience had not been much fun. Jed found that steering in a straight line was next to impossible. He wobbled all over the place. Hit every crack in the pavement. Every pothole. Bumped into a parked car. Fell off four times. Hurt his knee. And his elbow. And his chin. The other kids on the street all laughed at him. He was relieved when it was time to return the bike and limp his way back home. But that afternoon in Jackson, on the messenger's bike, everything was different. At first he only had one thing on his mind. Getting away from the officers who were closing in on him. He didn't worry about staying on two wheels or hurting himself or whether he looked ridiculous. He just raced down the sidewalk, bounced down off the curb, and swooped and dodged between the cars and trucks that were grinding their way through the choked city streets. He kept going for ten minutes. Fifteen. Then something dawned on him. He was free and clear.

Jed pulled over to the side of the street. He needed to find somewhere to leave the bike where it would be safe. Then, if he could just recall the name of the messenger service he had seen on the guy's bag when they collided, he could find a phone number. He could call and tell someone where the owner would find the bike.

Jed had never intended to keep the bike for long. But he had not anticipated how useful it would be. Or how fun. And he did still have another problem. He had to get to Winson. He couldn't take the bus. He didn't have enough money for a cab. And he couldn't risk standing around in plain sight, trying to hitch a ride. The bike was the obvious answer.

Jed's notes were lost. They had been in his backpack. But he figured he had about fifty miles to go. Sixty at the most. The bike was fast. Easy to pedal. It would only take, what, a couple of hours? Maybe three? He could call the messenger service when he arrived in the town. The guy would have to travel a little farther to retrieve his bike, but that was too bad. He shouldn't have been such an asshole. Really, he was lucky it was Jed he had encountered. Anyone else would have kept the bike. Or sold it. Jed had no doubt about that. Not after having his backpack stolen. And all his money.

Chapter 30

Hannah pulled the truck over onto the shoulder when the GPS in her phone said they were half a mile from the start of the construction zone. Reacher opened the passenger door and climbed out. Hannah had the pack of emergency flares on her lap, ready to go. She grabbed her purse from the backseat and took out her gun. The little SIG Reacher had first seen outside Gerrardsville when they began their journey together. She tucked it into a gap at the side of the driver's seat, then felt Reacher watching her.

Hannah turned and looked at him. "Any other assholes try anything, I'll be ready. No one's going to sneak up on me. Not again."

Reacher said, "You had much practice with that?"

"Hell, yes. Been shooting my whole life. It was the one thing about me my daddy didn't hate."

Winson, spread out at random intervals. And little convoys, packed close together, heading east.

Reacher stayed behind the tree line until he was level with the spot where the road got cut down to one lane. He found a shallow depression, maybe left by a dried-up stream, maybe by an abandoned irrigation system. He lay down in it, pressed himself into the ground, and settled in to watch. Twelve cars were waiting behind a line that had been painted on the blacktop near a sign warning drivers not to proceed unless they were escorted by the pilot vehicle. A guy was making his way along the shoulder, heading toward the end of the row. He was wearing jeans, a gray T-shirt, and black boots. He was carrying a clipboard and he had a yellow safety helmet on his head. He leaned down and looked into each vehicle he passed, checking any passengers. Another guy, of similar height but with a white helmet, was keeping pace on the other side of the vehicles, checking their drivers. The props weren't fooling anyone, Reacher thought. These guys were obviously the next Minerva crew. The only question was whether they were just being thorough or if they hadn't been told about Roth's truck. Reacher smiled to himself. Maybe they did know about it. But if they didn't, they soon would.

The area between Reacher and the road had been flattened and a square section of grass had been replaced with gravel. It was covered with tire tracks. There were multiple sets. They partially overlapped and all of them entered the space at almost the same spot. The top right-hand corner, from Reacher's perspective. They followed the same loop around, near the edge, and led back out onto the pavement to Reacher's left, still all together. An SUV was parked in the center of the rough circle the tracks formed, perpendicular to the road, with its rear facing Reacher. A Ford Explorer. It was burgundy with gold pinstripes and chunky tires with white letters on the sidewalls. It looked old, but shiny and well cared for.

At the far side of the road, on the shoulder, there was a port-a-potty with faded blue and white plastic walls. Next to it there was a gray metal box the size of a shipping container. Reacher figured it would be an equipment store. Next to that there was a dump trailer. It was loaded pretty full with tree branches and a net was strung over the top to stop its contents from falling or getting blown out. The name, number, and web address of the hire company were stenciled on the side.

There was only one thing missing from the scene. Construction workers. There was no sign of any activity at all behind the long line of traffic cones.

Reacher heard the drone of engines approaching from his right and thirty seconds later the pilot vehicle appeared. A line of cars was following in its wake like ducklings trailing their mother. The pilot turned onto the gravel square. It looped around the Explorer, adding another set of tire tracks, and came to a stop at the side of the road. The cars it had been escorting swung back into their own lane and continued heading east. The pilot pulled out. It was facing west now.

It paused, then set off and the waiting cars began to follow.

The guys with the jeans and T-shirts walked back and stopped by the line on the pavement. They waited, but no more cars appeared from the east. Reacher saw them exchange glances, shrug, and cross to the Explorer. They tossed their helmets and clipboards onto the backseat and climbed in the front. They had been at the site for a long time. They felt they deserved a break.

They weren't going to get one.

Reacher heard another engine approaching. A big diesel, coming from his left. The guys in the Explorer picked it up twenty seconds later. They climbed out. Opened the back doors. Started to reach for their props. Then they saw what kind of vehicle was making the sound. A red pickup truck. It had black glass and lots of chrome. It slowed, then stopped in front of the warning sign. The guys checked its license plate. Then they started moving toward it. They fanned out, one on each side, and paused when they were ten feet away. Each of them had pulled a gun from his waistband.

Reacher got to his feet and started to creep forward.

The guy on the driver's side of the truck yelled, "All right. Good job getting this far. But your luck's run out. This is the end of the line. Get out, slowly, hands where I can see them."

There was no response from inside the truck.

Reacher moved a little farther.

The guy yelled, "Do as I tell you and no one will get hurt. We just want to talk. So come on. Get out."

The truck's doors stayed closed.

Reacher kept moving.

The guy yelled, "Last chance. Get out or get shot."

A noise came from the back of the truck. A piercing electronic shriek. It lasted two seconds. Then there was a whirring sound. Then a *clunk*. The truck's tailgate had opened. The guys raised their guns. They started moving toward it, slowly, trying to stay silent. They made it halfway along the side of the load bed. Three-quarters. Then all the way to the back. They paused. They glanced at each other. The guy on the driver's side held up three fingers. He folded one down. He folded the second. Then the third. Both guys took another step. A big one, on the diagonal. Their guns were raised. They were pointing directly into the load bed.

The truck started moving. It accelerated hard. The pedal must have been all the way to the floor. Its rear wheels spun and skittered and kicked up handfuls of grit. The sharp fragments flew through the air like shrapnel. The guys turned and bent and covered their faces. It was an instinctive reaction. But it only lasted for a second. They straightened up and raised their guns and started firing at the truck. Its tailgate was closing again. The guy on the passenger side hit it with one round. The guy on the driver's side was going for the tires. He did some damage to the blacktop, but nothing else. They each squeezed off another couple of shots, then the guy on the passenger side started running toward the Explorer.

"Come on," the guy yelled. "He can't get far."

The other guy followed him. They jumped inside. The guy behind the wheel pulled out his keys. He jammed one into the ignition. But he didn't fire up the engine.

Reacher was sitting in the center of the rear seat. Both his arms were stretched out. He had the captured SIG in his left hand. The Beretta in his right. He pressed the muzzles against the back of both guys' heads and said, "Open the windows."

The driver turned his key one notch clockwise and buzzed both front windows all the way down.

Reacher said, "Throw out your guns."

The guys did as they were told.

Reacher said, "Do you know who I am?"

Both guys nodded.

"Then you know you need to cooperate. I want some information. Give it to me, then you can go."

The driver said, "We can't. We don't know anything."

"You work for Minerva?"

The driver nodded.

"Is anyone else looking for me between here and Winson?"

Neither of the guys answered.

Reacher pulled the guns back. He slid the SIG between his knees. Then he leaned through the gap between the front seats and punched the passenger just next to his ear. The guy's head snapped sideways. It smashed into the window, bounced back a few inches, then the guy slumped face-first into the dashboard.

Reacher raised the Beretta again. "Hands on the

wheel. Move, and I'll blow your head off. Do you understand?"

The driver grabbed the wheel. His hands were in the ten and two position and his knuckles were white like a nervous teenager's before his first lesson.

Reacher said, "Do you know what I just did?"

"You knocked out Wade."

"I gave you plausible deniability."

The driver didn't react.

"Plausible deniability," Reacher said. "It means you can do something, then say you didn't and no one can prove otherwise. Like, you can answer my questions."

The guy didn't respond.

"You can tell me what I need to know. No one will ever find out. Then you can drive away. Lie low for a couple of days. Claim you escaped. Or I could break your arms and legs and throw you in the nearest dumpster. Your choice."

The guy glanced to his right but he didn't speak.

Reacher said, "The cavalry isn't coming. Think about it. How many lanes are open?"

"One."

"What just drove that way?"

"The truck you stole."

"Correct. So it's going to meet the pilot vehicle, head-on. The person driving it is stubborn like you wouldn't believe. No way is she going to back up again. It's going to take hours to sort that mess out."

The guy glanced to his left.

"No one can get through that way, either. We covered all the bases. It's just you and me. And you have a decision to make."

The guy was silent for another moment, then he said, "What do you want to know?"

"Has Brockman got anyone else looking for me between here and Winson?"

"How would I know? Brockman doesn't share his plans with me."

"Brockman's a smart man, I guess. Relatively speaking. So what did he share?"

"A picture of you. An old one. A description of the truck you stole. And its license plate."

"What were your orders?"

"To stop you from getting to Winson."

"Why doesn't Brockman want me to get to Winson?"

"He didn't say."

"What's happening there in the next couple of days?"

"Nothing special. Some con's getting released tomorrow. There'll be speeches. Some celebrating. It happens a few times every year. The shine's wearing off, to be honest. People are getting used to it now."

"What else?"

The guy shrugged. "Nothing."

"OK. You did the right thing. Start it up. You can go now."

The guy paused for a moment, frozen. Then his hand shot out. He grabbed the key. Turned it, and the heavy old motor spluttered into life.

"One other thing before you get on your way,"

Reacher said. "See that trailer, over on the far shoulder?"

The guy nodded.

Reacher said, "Pull up next to it for a moment."

The guy shifted into Drive, released the brake, looped around to the opposite shoulder, and eased to a stop.

Reacher said, "Get out for a moment. There's something I need you to do. You can leave the engine running."

The guy opened his door and climbed down. Reacher did the same and led the way around to the passenger side.

Reacher said, "See the net that's holding down all the junk? Peel back one corner."

The guy fiddled with the nearest cleat and released part of the net.

Reacher said, "Pull out some of those branches at the top. And the bushes. Clear some space."

The guy grabbed a few of the bigger pieces and dumped them on the ground.

Reacher said, "Good. Now get your buddy out of the car. Put him in the space you made."

The guy said, "Put him in the trailer?"

"Right. We have to make this look realistic. Brockman won't believe you escaped otherwise. He'll think you helped me. That's not what you want to happen. Believe me."

The guy was still for a moment. His mouth was gaping slightly. Then he shrugged and opened the passenger door. He pushed his buddy back in the seat. His head lolled to the side. The guy grabbed his wrists. Hauled him out. Swung him onto his shoulder. Maneuvered him to the end of the trailer. Set him down on the spoil from the construction work. Then he took hold of the net and started to pull it back into place.

"Wait," Reacher said. "I need to borrow your phone for a second."

The guy shrugged, then took his phone out of his pocket, entered a code to unlock its screen, and held it out. Reacher took it and set it on the ground.

He said, "One more question. The guys Brockman sent to the Greyhound station had to watch out for me on every bus that arrived. All kinds of people would have been milling around. Places like that get pretty chaotic. That's a tall order. The guys at the truck stop had to keep an eye on hundreds of people, coming and going. That's a real challenge. The guys at the intersection didn't know if I would be hitching a ride or already in a car, speeding past. That's like two tasks in one, and neither of them is easy. But you? All you had to do was look through a window. Why do you think you were chosen for that particular job?"

"No idea."

"No?"

Reacher punched the guy in the solar plexus. That doubled him over forward. Then Reacher drove his knee up into the guy's face. That stood him up again, unconscious, with his arms flailing helplessly at his sides. Reacher shoved the guy's chest and folded him back the other way. He was left with his torso lying on top of the trailer. Reacher grabbed his ankles, lifted, twisted, and dropped him next to his buddy. He threw the branches back in to cover them. Fixed the net in place. Then he picked up the guy's phone and dialed the number for the hire company.

A woman answered after three rings. "Reed Plant Partners. How can I help you?"

Reacher said, "I'm with the crew doing construction out on US 87. We have one of your trailers. Could you confirm when it's scheduled for return?"

Computer keys rattled then the woman's voice came back on the line. "You have it booked through the end of next month."

"Can we return it early?"

"It's a fixed-term contract. There are no refunds for early returns."

"We're not looking for a refund. We just need it off-site."

"Understood. You can bring it back whenever you like. You just have to pay until the date you signed up for."

"Could you send someone to collect it?"

"There'd be an extra charge."

"That's fine."

"I could get someone out on Monday."

"How about this afternoon?"

"All our guys are busy today."

"Look, I'm in a bind here. My boss really wants that trailer gone. If there's any way you could swing it, I'd be grateful."

The woman didn't respond.

Reacher said, "If there's an extra-extra charge,

that would be fine, too. As in the kind that doesn't show up on an invoice."

The woman was silent for a moment longer, then she said, "It'll cost you a hundred bucks. Cash. Have it ready."

Hannah had been stationary for two minutes when the next convoy came into view. The pilot led it closer. And closer. And he didn't slow down. Hannah panicked for a moment. She thought the guy wasn't going to stop. She had a vision of the vehicles plowing into the side of the truck. One after another. Blow after blow. The truck rolling over. Her getting crushed. Or burned alive. Or both.

The pilot must not have been concentrating. He had driven up and down that stretch of road hundreds of times since the construction project started. He had never come across any kind of obstruction. He had never expected to. So he noticed the truck late. But in time. Just. He threw all his weight on the brake. His wheels locked. His tires slid on the gravel. But he stopped with maybe a yard to spare.

The vehicles behind the pilot all braked, too. None of them collided. A couple honked their horns as if that would help. One driver pulled past the rest and tried to swing around the front of Hannah's truck. He left the shoulder and started to bump across the rough strip of scrubland at the side of the road. He thought he was home and dry. He flipped Hannah off. Then his wheel hit a rut. His truck shuddered to a stop. It listed down toward one corner. There was only one explanation. Its axle was broken. And given the age and the condition of the vehicle its next stop was most likely going to be the scrap yard.

The driver jumped out and marched up to Hannah's door. He tugged on the handle. It was locked so he started yelling at the window. Flecks of spittle sprayed all over the glass. Other drivers climbed down and joined him. Ten more of them. That was everyone except the pilot. He stayed in his cab and dialed 911. He figured that was his civic duty. And with that done he felt free to sit back and let the chips fall where they may.

By the time Reacher arrived there were four drivers behind Hannah's truck. They were trying to shove it out of their way and getting nowhere. There were three drivers on one side, baying and screaming, and four on the other.

"Enough." Reacher stopped six feet from the rear of the truck. "Be quiet. Get back in your vehicles."

The guy from the stranded truck said, "No way. This asshole's blocking the road. My rig's messed up because of him. He's got to pay."

"Really? Because this is my truck. It's here because I told the driver to block the road. If you have a problem with that, then you have a problem with me."

Reacher looked at each driver, one at a time. Calmly. Levelly. Right in the eyes. Most of them started to edge away. A couple stayed still. The guy from the stranded truck stepped forward. "You know what? I do have a problem. My vehicle is totaled. If that's on you then you better put your hand in your pocket."

The drivers who had been moving all immediately stopped.

Reacher gestured to the stricken truck. It looked like it was trying to bury itself in the ground. "That thing?"

The guy nodded.

"Sorry, pal. I used my last quarter in a payphone, last week. You're SOL."

The guy swung at Reacher's head with a wild right hook. Reacher leaned back and watched the fist sail harmlessly past. The guy's shoulders twisted around and he wound up horribly off balance. All his weight was on his left leg. Reacher swept it out from under him. The guy pitched forward. He fell almost horizontally. Hit the dirt with his face. Tried to get up. But Reacher put his foot between his shoulder blades, pushed him back down, and held him in place.

Reacher said, "Guys, use your heads. You want to get going. I want to get going. But none of us can go anywhere while you're hanging around like some lame-ass mob."

No one spoke. No one moved. For a moment. Then a driver at the back of the crowd turned and slunk away. The guy who had been next to him followed. A couple more began to move. Then another couple until all the drivers were shuffling toward their vehicles, grumbling and muttering and shaking their heads. Reacher leaned down and rolled the guy on the ground over. He grabbed his shirt and hoisted him onto his feet. The guy scowled but stayed silent. Reacher shoved him into the lee of the truck where no one could see what would happen next.

Reacher said, "Is your truck really a write-off?"

The guy scowled. "I think so. I felt the suspension go."

"How much is it worth?"

"Five grand."

"How much in US dollars, here on planet Earth?"

"A grand. Maybe."

Reacher pulled out his roll of cash, peeled off five hundred dollars, and handed it to the guy. "Here's half. The other half is on you. Consider this a learning experience. Use better judgment in the future. If you had stayed on the road and shown a little patience, your truck would still be running."

Jed Starmer finally admitted that he'd been right the first time. Riding a bike was a total pain in the ass.

It was a pain in the ass. The calves. The thighs. The back. The shoulders. The neck. In pretty much every part of his body. Jed had never been so uncomfortable in his entire life. All he could think was, *People do this for fun? What the hell is wrong with them?*

Everything had been fine while Jed was in the city of Jackson. The streets were level. There was plenty of traffic so the vehicles had to move slowly. The drivers seemed used to bikes weaving around them. And Jed had to pay attention to finding his way. He remembered that there was only one road to Winson. He didn't have a map so he had to watch out extra carefully for signs. Twice he thought he was lost. But he kept on going and pretty soon the buildings grew smaller and farther apart. The trees became taller and closer together. The fields stretched out beyond them. Jed raised his head and looked around. He thought his new surroundings were nice.

At first.

More things changed than the view as Jed rode deeper into the countryside. There were fewer vehicles, but the ones that were around drove much faster. They passed closer to him. He nearly got knocked off the bike half a dozen times. The nervousness from his first lesson came flooding back. And he kept coming to uphill stretches of road. It felt like massive weights were attached to his wheels. Every push on the pedals was a hundred times harder than on the flat. The sun was dipping low but the air was still hot. Jed was sweating. He was thirsty. He was hungry. He hadn't eaten for more than twelve hours. His head was feeling light. His legs were soft and rubbery. He was praying for a nice long downward slope. For a few minutes when gravity could do the work. When he could rest. When he could pick up a little speed and the wind would rush by and cool his body.

Jed slogged his way around another bend. Looked up. And found himself at the foot of the tallest mountain he had ever seen.

The road into Winson was long and straight and lined with trees. The soft afternoon sunshine filtered through the leaves and cast a web of dappled shadows all along the faded blacktop. It was the kind of image Reacher had seen in Sunday newspaper articles about places parents should take their kids for picnics on school vacations. It looked idyllic. There was nothing to indicate that a town lay ahead.

Or a prison.

Or the people who had murdered Angela St. Vrain and Sam Roth.

A couple of miles beyond the sign announcing the town boundary, the trees thinned and buildings began to appear. Mainly houses. Mainly single story ones, spread apart from one another but standing near to the street. Most of them had wooden sides with dirty white paint that was peeling in handfuls. Plenty had roofs that looked like they were one decent storm away from getting blown completely off.

"I read about this place last night in the hotel before I went to sleep," Hannah said. "It has a crazy history. Originally it was a Native American settlement. The French drove them out in, like, 1720. The British took the place from the French. The Spanish moved in when the British quit after the Revolutionary War. They were supposed to be on our side but they didn't want to hand the town over so we took it from them. It thrived while all the trade was centered on the river. There are rumors of a second town, like a shadow, at the bottom of the cliff. Stories of caves and liquor and whores and stolen gold and smuggled jewels. Even if any of that was true, it's all gone now. Blown up, or flooded. Then the river trade faded and the railroads and industry took over. Paper mills, mainly, because of all the trees that grow here. Now the industry's gone, too. Which is why there are so many old houses, I guess. And why so many of them are about to fall down."

Hannah drove in silence for a while and as they came closer to the town they saw the standard of maintenance improved. The size of the homes increased. They grew closer together. The balance shifted to mainly two-story properties. Most were still white, but their paint was fresh and bright. Some were blue. Some were yellow. Many had shutters. Most had porches running their full width. Some had verandas with solid columns and ornate wooden railings. The sidewalks that passed them were wide, and there were tall, mature trees forming a border with the road.

In the town itself wood construction gave way to brick. There were still plenty of balconies and verandas but with spindly supports and ornate iron railings painted gloss black. It felt like a small-scale copy of New Orleans, Reacher thought. The roofs were mainly flat. The windows were larger, some were square, some had curved tops. There were lots of alleyways. There was parking down both sides of all the streets. Half the spaces were empty. Reacher saw a couple of cafés. A few bars. A small church, built of brick with clumsy stained glass. It looked like it had recently been rebuilt, but on a budget. There was a range of businesses. A pawnshop with guns and guitars hanging two deep in the window. An insurance agent. A tire bay. A handful of small bed-and-breakfasts. A fishmonger. A cellphone store. A body shop.

Hannah and Reacher drove around for half an hour. They started at Main Street and quartered the blocks on either side until they had a good sense of the place. Finally they stopped outside a coffee shop.

Hannah went in and grabbed two large cups to go. She climbed back into the truck, handed a cup to Reacher, and said, "Hotel?"

Reacher shook his head. "Prison first. Then food. Then the hotel."

Chapter 32

Jed Starmer was sitting at the side of the road. The messenger's bike was lying on the shoulder, to his left, where it had fallen after he jumped off.

Jed stared at the bike and sighed. He hadn't really jumped off. He had intended to. He had tried to. But his legs weren't working the way they usually did. So he had pretty much fallen off, if he was honest. Staggered, maybe, or stumbled, if he wanted to put a positive spin on it.

The thing he couldn't put a positive spin on lay to his right. The mountain. Or really, the hill. Or the slope. He had used the minutes he'd been sitting there to rein in his imagination. He wasn't facing Mount Everest. Or the Eiger. Or Kilimanjaro. The rise was probably no more than a hundred feet. But whether it was a hundred or thirty thousand it made no difference. There was no way Jed could ride up it. He wouldn't even be able to push the bike to the top, the way his legs were shaking. He would just have to sit where he was. Probably for the rest of his life, since no one was going to come and help him.

Reacher figured that the prison was Winson's equivalent of a portrait in the attic. It was ugly. Unattractive. Hidden away to the west of the town. If it was any farther away it would be in the river. But it was what kept the town alive. What made it vibrant. That was clear. There was no other industry to speak of. No other sources of employment. Nothing else to keep the local bakers and launderettes and plumbers and electricians busy on any kind of substantial scale.

The prison's site was shaped like a D. The curved side was formed by the riverbank. Beyond it was a seventy-foot drop straight into deep, dirty, fast-flowing water. A fence ran ten feet back from the edge. It had two layers. They were twenty feet high with rolls of razor wire strung along the top. There were floodlights on stout metal poles. And cameras in protective cages. There was a fifteen-foot gap between layers, and another fence ran along the center line. It was ten feet high, and it had no wire.

The fences continued in the same way along the straight side of the site. The side facing the town. There were four watchtowers level with the outer layer of wire. And three entrances. One was in the center. It led into a building. It was a single story, built of brick, with double doors, which were closed,

and a video intercom on the doorframe. That would
be the visitors' entrance, Reacher thought. The staff
probably used it, too. The other entrances were at the
far ends. They had full height gates rather than doors.
And no signs. One was probably used for supplies.
The other would be for shipping in fresh inmates.

Inside the fence, on the river side of the site, there
were five buildings in a line. They were shaped like
Xs. Reacher guessed they would be the cell blocks.
The rest of the space was filled with twelve other
buildings and three exercise areas. The buildings
were all different sizes. They were plain and utilitar-
ian. They could have been factories or warehouses if
it wasn't for the razor wire and watchtowers that surrounded them. The exercise areas were all the same
size, but they were physically separate. Presumably to
keep the different categories of prisoners isolated in
their own allocated spaces.

The buildings and exercise areas were joined by
walkways. The walls and roofs were made of wire
mesh. Even from a distance Reacher could see it was
thick. Substantial. Anyone would need serious tools
to stand a chance of getting through it. Outside,
around the buildings and between the walkways,
there were some patches of grass. A surprising number, Reacher thought, for such a grim institution.
There were squares. Rectangles. Ovals. And twenty
feet from the base of each watchtower there was a
brick-lined triangle.

The grass was well cared for. It was trimmed short.
Edged neatly. And probably fed or fertilized, given
the way its deep green stood out against the pale walls

of the buildings and the gray blur of the wire mesh. The only other structure inside the fence was newer. It was V-shaped and shoehorned in behind the security building. It was styled like some kind of corporate headquarters and there was a three-dimensional Minerva logo on a plinth, rotating, out front. Reacher figured if any prisoners got loose that would be the first thing to get destroyed.

He said, "Did you read anything about riots happening here recently?"

Hannah said, "Nothing official. But on one of the message boards a woman was complaining about her husband getting hurt by a guard. It was during a brawl in the exercise yard. Thirty or forty guys were involved but her husband was the only one the guard laid into. She complained, and got told her husband had been trying to escape. They said they'd let it slide, but if she made trouble about his injuries he'd wind up getting his sentence extended."

"Have there been any successful escapes?"

"I don't think so. I didn't come across anything, anyway."

Reacher was not surprised. The place looked well put together. According to what he read in the file he found in Angela St. Vrain's purse, it had been built by the state. Those guys knew what they were doing when it came to locking people up. Reacher had some experience of prisons, himself. He had been a military cop. He had put plenty of people inside them. Visited suspects to take statements. Caught inmates who had broken out. Grilled them to find out how. He had even been locked up himself, a couple times.

The first precaution Reacher noticed was also the simplest. The perimeter was protected by a fence, not a wall. That meant the guards could see everyone who approached any part of the place. They could see if anyone was carrying equipment to break in with or items to throw over. And there were red triangles attached to the fences. They were spaced out at fifteen-foot intervals, and they ranged from two to six feet above the ground. Reacher was too far away to read the writing but the symbol of a stick figure flying backward after getting zapped carried a clear enough message. The fences were electrified. The outer ones would only be powerful enough to knock a person on their ass. That would serve as a warning. It would be the inner fence, all small and innocuous, sandwiched between the ones with the wire on top, that would carry the lethal voltage.

Reacher would bet there were vibration sensors in the ground that would trip if anyone got too close to the fence. Alarms that would trigger if the voltage in the fences dropped. Dogs that would be released if the power failed, or got sabotaged. The entrances would all be secured. The one for visitors and staff would be like an airport with X-ray machines and metal detectors. The vehicle gates would have an airlock arrangement so that the trucks and vans could be held between the layers of fence on their way in or out. Inside the buildings the service ducts would be too narrow for anyone to crawl in or climb up. They would have movement sensors and mesh screens, anyway. The doors and gates in the secure areas would all be centrally controlled, with no keypads for inmates to learn or guess the codes for, like you see in the movies. And if all else failed, there were the watchtowers. Two would be sufficient. The prison had four. A guard in each one with a rifle could cover the whole interior of the stockade plus five hundred feet beyond the perimeter, assuming an adequate level of equipment and training.

The area in front of the prison was laid out in a semicircle. There were swathes of grass and neat, colorful flower beds all following the same curve. They looked incongruous, like a bizarre attempt to copy the formal gardens of a European chateau. The only things missing were the fountains. But Reacher knew the real purpose was not aesthetic. It was to maintain a clear field of fire from the two central towers in the event of a breakout. Or an attempt to break in.

There was a broad paved strip around the outside of the semicircle. It was wide enough for vehicles to park in. The left was the staff area. It was half-full. Mainly with pickups. Older American models. Some were not in great shape. There were a few sedans sprinkled among them. Mainly domestic, from the cheaper end of the range. Then at the far side, separated by half a dozen empty spaces, there were three newer vehicles. A Dodge Ram in silver with chrome wheels and a shiny tread-plate tool chest slung across its load bed. A BMW sedan, larger than the one Reacher had encountered in Colorado, but also black. Its license plate read MC1. And a Mercedes, in white, with MC2 on its plate.

The visitors' parking was to the right. There was only one car in that whole area. A VW Bug. It was metallic green. It had two soft tires. Its running board was hanging off on one side. It wasn't clear if it had been parked or abandoned.

Hannah opened the driver's door and turned to Reacher. "You ready? We've been here too long. We should go."

Reacher nodded and climbed in alongside her. There was nothing more to see. But he was left thinking he knew how an epidemiologist must feel after staring at a sample from a patient with a baffling new disease. On the surface everything looked normal, but he knew there was something wrong. He just didn't know what. Yet.

Bruno Hix was sitting at his desk. He was staring at his computer screen. And his own face was staring back.

The image was magnified. Hix's mouth was gaping open. His eyes were half-shut. He looked drunk. Or demented. Or worse, ugly. Hix stamped his foot. Getting two video streams to play side by side was harder than he'd expected. One at a time was fine. But both together he just couldn't figure out. He had called the prison's IT expert but the guy had already quit for the day. He was at home, preparing dinner for his cats. He was supposedly coming back but he was taking his sweet time. A person could crawl faster. Hix was not happy. He needed to have a word with Riverdale. It was time for some staff changes. And soon.

Hix's office door opened. Slowly.

Hix turned and said, "Where the . . ."

He saw Brockman framed in the doorway.

"Oh," Hix said. "It's you. Is there news?"

Brockman nodded.

Hix said, "Good news?"

Brockman said, "Just news."

"Let's hear it."

"Harold called. He got to the construction site. Our guys were not there."

"They deserted their post? What happened? Were they threatened? Bribed?"

"They just disappeared. Brad's Explorer was there, parked in exactly the same place Harold saw it earlier. But there was no sign of Brad or Wade."

"So what happened?"

"No idea. Harold spoke to the driver of the pilot vehicle. He said there had been a weird incident. He said he was heading east, as usual, and he came across a truck blocking the road. He didn't see the plate but it was the same model as the one Reacher stole. The same color."

"Did he see Reacher?"

"It sounds like it. Here's what Harold said happened. The pilot stopped, assuming the truck was trying to turn around for some reason. He figured it would get out of the way, sooner or later. But the other drivers got antsy. They surrounded the truck. Tried to push it. And got nowhere, naturally. It was just some crazy mass hysteria thing. They were still trying when a huge guy showed up from the opposite side."

"Reacher?"

"Well, he chased these other drivers away. Ten of

them. And he kicked another guy's ass, apparently. Draw your own conclusion. Then he got in the truck and drove off."

"What did Harold do?"

"He figured Brad and Wade had gotten knocked out and the guy was dumping them like he'd done with Pep and Tony at the truck stop. The roadblock was for cover. So Harold searched for them. He found nothing. But he's still trying."

"So we still don't know where our guys are?"

"No."

"And Reacher?"

"We don't know where he is, either."

"Well, obviously he got past the roadblock. He could be in town anytime. He could already be here. Call Harold. Tell him to come back. Right now."

"What about Brad and Wade?"

"What about them? They had one job. They failed. We're better off without them."

Hannah had been using her phone to do some more research while Reacher was scoping out the prison. About food, this time. The next thing on their agenda.

She had found the place people said sold the best burgers in town. She suggested they head straight there, get some carryout, and take it to their hotel. That wasn't an approach Reacher favored. He preferred to show up and see how a place looked for himself. He appreciated a good diner. And he was totally opposed to anything that smacked of running and hiding. Reacher was wired to move toward danger. To confront it. To defeat it, or die trying. It was baked into his DNA. But he could tell that Hannah was approaching her limit. She knew people were looking for them. The same group of people who had tried to kill her. It was reasonable for her to want to get off the street. To be out of sight as quickly as possible. It would have been cruel to force her to do otherwise, so Reacher didn't argue.

The burger place was four blocks north of Main Street in a building that used to be a gas station. Its original pumps were still there, now repurposed as decorations with neon lights. The forecourt had been turned into a parking area. The tables were in the main building, behind large, curved windows and under an extravagant gull-wing roof.

The drive-through counter was where the old night-service window had been. Hannah pulled up next to it. She ordered, paid, and had a paper sack full of food in her hand inside three minutes. She had gotten one burger with a single patty, mushrooms, and truffle aioli for herself and two doubles with American cheese and nothing green for Reacher. She waited another minute for their two large coffees to come out then moved toward the exit. She entered the hotel's address into the map on her phone and a robot voice told her to *proceed to the route*. Reacher didn't find that advice helpful.

Once they were back on Main Street the phone directed them to the east, away from the center of town. The hotel was near the river, to the north. It wasn't far as the crow flies but a ridge of trees meant there was no direct route. The sun was low in the sky.

Dense branches overhead cut the available daylight further. The road was quiet. They didn't see another vehicle for five minutes. Then a car appeared. It came closer and the shape of a lightbar solidified on its roof. It passed them. Its roof bar lit up. The narrow corridor between the trees started to pulse with red and blue. Then the car turned and sped back toward the truck.

Hannah said, "Oh, please, no. What now? What do we do?"

Reacher said, "There's nothing to worry about. We haven't done anything wrong."

"We haven't? Those six guys you beat up might tell a different story."

"They're not here. And they're in no position to call 911. Trust me. This is just routine bullshit. It's going to be fine."

"What if it isn't?"

Reacher said nothing.

Hannah pulled the truck over to the side of the road. The police car tucked in behind with its lights still flashing. The cop stayed inside for a couple more minutes. Reacher didn't know if he was checking something, calling for reinforcements, or just trying to play mind games. He didn't care which, as long as the cop didn't keep it up for too long. He didn't want his burgers to get cold.

The cop finally climbed out and approached the driver's window. He lifted his hand. The knuckle of his middle finger was extended, ready to knock, but

Hannah buzzed the window down before he made contact with the glass.

The cop said, "Good afternoon, s . . . miss. Do you know why I pulled you over?"

Hannah shook her head. "I have no idea. I wasn't speeding." She glanced across at Reacher. "I haven't done anything wrong."

"You're driving a vehicle registered to an individual who, according to official records, is currently deceased."

"Currently? Are you expecting that to change?"

The cop took a deep breath. "I'll put this plainly. Why are you driving a dead man's truck?"

"The dead man was my ex-husband. We were close. I had permission. I'm on his insurance. And I'm due to inherit the truck as soon as his will is read."

"Your name, miss?"

"Hannah Hampton-Roth."

"ID?"

"In my purse. OK if I get it?"

"Go ahead."

Hannah took her purse from the backseat, rummaged in it for a moment, and pulled out her wallet. She opened it, then passed her driver's license to the cop.

The cop studied the license for a moment then said, "Registration? Insurance?"

Hannah leaned across to the passenger side, opened the glove box, and took out a clear plastic pocket. The documents were inside. She straightened and handed it out of the window.

The cop said, "Wait here." Then he walked back to his car.

Hannah stretched for the keys to switch the engine off but Reacher took her hand.

He said, "Leave it running. If the cop has his gun drawn when he gets back out, floor it. Same applies if another police cruiser shows up. Or anything that could be an unmarked car."

The cop stayed in his car for five long minutes then returned to Hannah's window. His gun was still in its holster. He handed the documents and the license back and said, "You're a long way from home, miss. What brings you to Winson?"

Hannah tucked the license back into her wallet and handed the plastic pocket to Reacher. "My ex-husband has—had—friends here. I need to let them know that Sam has passed. That's better done in person than on the phone or email, don't you think?"

"Who were his friends?"

"Angela St. Vrain. Danny Peel. They worked with Sam before Angela and Danny moved out here."

"Will you be staying with one of them tonight?"

"No. We'll go to a hotel."

"Which one?"

"We're—"

"Still working on that," Reacher said.

The cop said, "You didn't think to make a reservation before you left Colorado?"

Reacher said, "No."

"What if you'd come all this way and the hotels were all full?"

"Is that a common problem here?"

The cop was silent for a moment then he nodded toward the rear of the truck. "What happened to your window?"

Hannah sighed. "Some asshole kids tried to break in."

"When?"

"Earlier this afternoon. At the rest area, on I-20."

"Kids did this?"

"That's right."

"Did they steal anything?"

"They saw us walking back after we used the bathrooms and they ran."

"Did you file a police report?"

"I didn't think there was any point. We didn't get a good look at the kids. I wouldn't have been able to give much of a description."

"And your tailgate?"

"What about it?"

"It has a bullet hole. Someone take a shot at you?"

Hannah shook her head. "At us? No. Sam, my ex, he was a keen marksman. He was at a range outside of town one day last week and a newbie had an accidental discharge in the parking lot when he was getting his gun out of his vehicle safe."

"Did Sam file a report?"

"He figured there was no need. It was an accident. No one got hurt. The guy paid for the damage. If that was wrong, you can't blame Sam. It's up to the club to make sure the rules are followed."

"What's the name of the club?"

"I don't know. I never went. Sam just called it *The Gun Club*. He was a corrections officer. A lot of his co-workers are members, too. It's owned by a retired cop. I'm sure he did the right thing."

The cop thought for a moment. Then he said, "All right. You can go. But you need to turn the truck around."

"Thank you. But why?"

"You need somewhere to stay. The best hotel around here is the Winson Garden. It's easy to find. Follow signs for the prison, then take a left onto Mole Street. I'll follow. Make sure you don't get lost."

No one was going to come and help him. He had to face reality. So Jed Starmer forced himself onto his feet. He couldn't stay where he was. He was too visible. At least two officers had been searching for him in Jackson. Pretty soon they would accept he had given them the slip. They would have no choice. Then they would have only one place left to look. Jed's final destination. Winson. Which could only be reached via the road he was currently loitering right next to.

Jed still had no idea how he was going to get to the summit. He could barely stand. He felt like someone had stolen his leg bones and replaced them with modeling clay. His stomach was hurting. He couldn't look at any object without the thing's edges blurring and its colors twisting and dancing like it was on fire. He was a hot mess. He knew that. And he knew one other thing. He had come too far to be defeated by a hill.

Jed figured he had a couple of factors on his side. Time. And trees. There were more than twelve hours before he had to be in Winson. All he needed was rest. And someplace where he couldn't be seen from the road. He hobbled across to the bike, which was still lying on its side. Heaved it up onto its wheels. Pushed it over to the long grass at the edge of the shoulder. Set it down. Took another couple of steps. And stopped.

Jed needed rest. But he also needed to be safe. He was heading into a forest. There could be wolves lurking around. Maybe alligators. Maybe coyotes. Maybe in giant bloodthirsty packs. Jed didn't know what kinds of predators they had in Mississippi. And he didn't want to find out the hard way. So he was going to have to pick his refuge with extra care.

Chapter 33

Hannah was the one with a credit card so she took care of the check-in process at the Winson Garden. Reacher was the one with the suspicious nature so he kept watch over the parking lot. The cop was the one with the orders to observe the stranger so he parked where he had a good view of the hotel's entrance. Where he could make sure the stranger and his unexpected companion did go in. And didn't come back out.

When she was done with the form filling and the bill paying, Hannah wheeled her suitcase across the reception area and handed a card key in a little cardboard wallet to Reacher. He took it and slipped it into his back pocket. Almost immediately a phone rang on the counter behind them.

The desk clerk answered it after one ring. "Winson

Garden, Winson's premier guest accommodations. How may I be of assistance today?" He listened for a moment then said in a much quieter voice, almost a whisper, "Yes, Officer. The woman did. The name on her card is Hannah Hampton. Her home address is in Gerrardsville, Colorado. She paid for two people. Two rooms. One night." Then he nodded to no one in particular and dropped the receiver back into its cradle.

Reacher could feel the desk clerk staring at him. He could practically hear what the guy was thinking. He was wondering why the police were interested in these particular guests. Whether he would have a story to tell in the morning. And whether there would be any kind of a mess to clear up.

It took the Minerva IT guy ten seconds to get Bruno Hix's computer display set up the way he wanted it.

The guy had been forced to leave his cats to eat their dinner alone. He had been made to come back to the prison on his own time. And he had still brought his A game. No one could have solved the problem more quickly or efficiently. That was for sure. So he couldn't understand why the big boss seemed even more annoyed when the job was finished than he had been at the start.

The guy was part offended, part confused. He had done a great job, which wasn't appreciated, but he must also have committed some kind of appalling faux pas. Hix's attitude made that obvious. The problem was, he had no idea what he'd done that was so bad. He started to summon the courage to ask Hix what the problem was, but before he could speak one of his mother's favorite expressions started to echo in his head: *When you're in a hole, stop digging.* He figured that meant the smart move would be to get out of the office before he made things any worse, so he muttered a vague apology and hurried to the door. He pulled it open, glanced back at Hix, and almost blundered straight into Damon Brockman, who was heading the opposite way.

Brockman waited for the IT guy to scurry off down the corridor then said, "Good news. We just dodged a bullet."

Hix switched off his computer monitor and said, "We did? How?"

"Our guys not intercepting Reacher at the truck stop? Or at the construction zone? That was a blessing in disguise. Turns out Reacher's not working alone. He has a partner. A woman. If our guys had put Reacher on ice the way we told them to, we wouldn't know anything about her. She'd still be out there, invisible, free to do who knows what tomorrow."

"How did you find out?"

"One of Moseley's guys spotted the truck Reacher was using. Just outside of town. He pulled it over, expecting to find Reacher on his own, but a woman was driving. Reacher was in the passenger seat."

"The cop found Reacher? Where is he now?"

"At the Winson Garden. With the woman."

"You sure?"

Brockman nodded. "The cop directed them there. Followed them. Confirmed they checked in."

Hix drummed his fingers on the desktop, then said, "What about this woman? Who is she? What do we know about her?"

"The cop got her ID. Her name's Hannah Hampton. She's Sam Roth's ex-wife. She told the cop they were still close. Before he died. That she had permission to use his truck."

Hix got up, crossed to the window, and looked out through the fence toward the curved parking lot. "I don't get it. We thought Reacher was only involved because of some fluky chance encounter."

"Right."

"We bought into the idea he just happened to be in Gerrardsville. Saw what happened to Angela St. Vrain. Stuck his nose in where it wasn't wanted."

"That is what happened."

"Then how come he's hooked up with Sam Roth's widow? That can't be a coincidence."

Brockman shrugged. "Reacher stuck his nose in a bit deeper. That's all. He heard about Roth's death. He decided it didn't pass the smell test. So he started to dig. It's natural he would talk to Roth's widow. Especially given that she found the body."

"What if there's another explanation? We didn't know Roth was close to his ex. It didn't cross my mind. All the divorced people I know hate their exes. I certainly do. I'd happily grind both of mine into hamburger meat and feed them to the dogs if I could get away with it."

"I know you would. But what does it matter who Roth was close to?"

"People confide in the people they're close to. What if Roth told his ex what Angela had told him? What if the three of them figured out what's going to happen tomorrow? They would know they couldn't go to the police. So maybe they hired Reacher. He could have been in Gerrardsville specifically to meet them. Not because of some random chance. Our whole theory could be way off the mark."

"I don't see it. Why would they hire Reacher? How would they know about him? And how would they get hold of him? The guy's a drifter."

"Is he? Maybe he just wants people to think that. As cover. He's a retired cop. Lots of those guys set up as private detectives when they turn in their badges."

"He was an MP. Not a regular cop."

"So what? Same skill set. And he's capable. That's clear. Ask the guys we sent after him."

Brockman shrugged. "OK. Say you're right. He came here because the woman hired him. What difference does it make?"

"The difference is that we now have two people to take care of."

"Which is no biggie. We know exactly where they both are. The only question is whether to stick Harold and the boys on them in their rooms while they sleep, or wait till the morning and jump them when they come outside."

"Do it in their rooms. As soon as possible. Have the bodies brought out on gurneys, in case there are any other guests snooping around."

"I'll set it up with Harold."

"Good. And in the meantime, who's watching the hotel?"

"The cop."

"Too obvious. Send one of our guys."

"We haven't got anyone. Only the guys we sent to Jackson and they've been working since 3:00 A.M. We need them to back Harold up, tonight. Better for them to grab some rest. Come back fresh."

"If Reacher sees a patrol car out front, he'll know something's up. He'll—"

"If Reacher was watching he'd have seen the patrol car leave. I had Moseley send his guy back, and tell him to stay out of sight. On the street."

"Send him back? He left?"

"Only for a minute. He's supposed to be on patrol. He started to go back out. Reported to Moseley. Moseley called me. I took care of it."

"You sure?"

Brockman nodded. "Moseley had his guy check with the hotel when he got back on station. The clerk confirmed he saw Reacher and the woman heading to the elevators. He was certain they hadn't come down. He swore he would have noticed if they'd come back through reception. He knew the police were interested in them after the first phone call so he was extra vigilant."

"OK. Just make sure Harold knows he has two targets now. And tell him to take the insurance with him. The envelope. He needs to make sure it's somewhere Reacher will find it if he comes out on top."

"Harold won't like that. He'll think it shows you don't have faith in him."

"Why would I give a rat's ass what Harold thinks? Tell him anyway."

"You'd give more than a rat's ass if you'd seen the size of him. He's not the kind of guy you want mad at you. Whether you're the CEO or not."

Reacher had waited for the police car to pull a wide, lazy turn and disappear toward the center of town. Then he started along the corridor that led to the elevators and the guest rooms. Hannah followed, still towing her suitcase. They passed the elevators and continued to the end of the corridor. To the emergency exit. A sign said the door was alarmed. Reacher was annoyed by that. An inanimate object couldn't experience trepidation. It was a ridiculous proposition. And if the claim was meant as a warning, that didn't work, either. The hotel's owners wanted to keep costs to a minimum. The desk clerk's ill-fitting uniform made that clear. So did the generic prints on the walls. The coarse carpet on the floor. The flimsy handles on the bedroom doors. The kind of people who were satisfied with such low-level junk wouldn't want to get fined for false alarms. There was too much risk that a drunken guest would take a wrong turn and blunder into the latch. Or a smoker would sneak out for a crafty cigarette. Or someone would want to get outside without being seen. Someone like Reacher or Hannah.

Reacher pushed the release bar. The door swung open. No lights flashed. No klaxons sounded.

If you don't want a thing to come back and bite you in the ass, do it yourself.

That was a principle Curtis Riverdale had lived by his whole career. It meant more hours with his sleeves rolled up, for sure, but it had been worthwhile. It had always served him well. In the past. But that afternoon, for the first time in his life, he wasn't sure if it would be enough.

Riverdale had made the arrangements for the next day's ceremony himself, as usual. He had lined up the outdoor seating. The temporary fences. The podium for the TV cameras. Refreshments for the journalists. The stage, for Bruno Hix to strut and preen. A tent to shroud the prison's entrance, for security. Fierce-looking guards to be seen in the watchtowers. And the protestors. He was sure not to forget about them.

Riverdale had covered all the bases. He had double-checked everything, personally. But something else was worrying him. He'd just gotten word from his old buddy Rod Moseley, the chief of police. Reacher had made it all the way to the town. Reacher was a wild card. A factor Riverdale could not control. And a lack of control was kryptonite to a guy whose whole world was shaped by rules and procedures and timetables. Plus fences and cell blocks and steel bars.

Riverdale's fingers moved subconsciously to his chest. They traced the outline of an object beneath his undershirt. A key. It hung from a chain he wore around his neck. The chain was fine enough to be discreet but it was made from high tensile steel. It wasn't ornate. It wasn't a piece of jewelry. Nor was the key. Which was for a padlock. The strongest, most secure, most weatherproof kind available anywhere in the world.

Riverdale still hoped that the ceremony would be a success. That it would garner more kudos for the company. More business, down the line. And another special visit from the new inmate's pretty wife, the same afternoon. But if it wasn't, if the whole thing went sideways, he was ready. He would disappear. No one would ever find him. And Hix and Brockman and everyone who sneered at his sense of caution? They could burn for all he cared.

Chapter 34

Jed Starmer didn't know what he was looking for. Not exactly. He figured he was in the countryside so there might be a farm nearby. With a barn. Or a stable. Or a shed. He didn't care if there were horses in it. Or cows. Or sacks of gross animal food. Or strange spiky machines. Just as long as it had walls. And a roof. And a door, which he could close. Where he would be safe. Just until he got his strength back.

Each step he took was harder than the one before. The trees were scattered around at random. They were close together so he had to weave his way between them. The undergrowth was thick and tangled. It constantly snagged his feet and ankles and made him stumble and almost fall. The earth was damp. It had a heavy, musty smell. Jed didn't like it. It seemed dirty to him. Rotten. He imagined himself collapsing and the soil closing around him, engulfing his body, holding him forever as he slowly decomposed. He tried to go faster and some kind of insect scuttled away from under a decaying leaf. It was all legs and pincers and creepy antennae. He began to think he was worrying about the wrong size of animal. Then he heard a noise behind him. It sounded like a growl. He forced himself to keep moving. He had come too far to get eaten by some weird creature in a miserable stinking wood.

Jed squeezed between two more trees and emerged onto a track. It was wide enough for a vehicle to drive on and there were tire marks on the ground. They were broad and deep. The kind that are made by something heavy. Jed paused to get his bearings. He figured he'd been heading on a diagonal since he dumped the bike, and the track ran at a right angle from the road. So he could go left and wind up more or less where he started, which was familiar but exposed. Or he could go right. Deeper into the forest. Where he'd be hidden. But where he might be in other kinds of danger.

It occurred to Jed that the track must go somewhere specific. That was the whole point of tracks. People don't cut them through the woods with no purpose in mind. Vehicles don't drive around on them aimlessly. And the place the track led to might have some buildings. Some shelter. Which had to be better than where he was. Or the side of the road.

Jed went right.

He walked for what felt like ten miles, but he knew must only be a couple of hundred yards. There was no sign of any buildings. Nothing man-made. Not even a tree house. At least the track was easy to walk along. Jed stayed to the left and counted his steps. He tried to build up a rhythm. Then he picked up a sound. Something different from earlier. Not an animal. Jed was relieved. He thought it might be wind in the leaves, but discarded that theory. The air was too still. He realized it was water. He looked farther ahead and saw that the track came to an end at the side of a pond. A large one. Almost a small lake. Some unseen stream must feed it in a last act of independence before falling away and getting consumed by the raging Mississippi.

It was all Jed could do to not fling himself to the ground. The track must just be to support a bunch of recreational bullshit. People wanting to swim or kayak. Or fish. That thought gave rise to another. It made Jed wonder if he could catch something to eat. His stomach was a constant knot of pain. Even a tiny minnow would be welcome. Then he pushed the idea away. He had no rods or lines or hooks or whatever it was people use to snag fish. But maybe he could take a drink. If the water was fresh. If there was nothing rotting in it. Nothing that would poison him. He had seen TV shows where survivalists got all kinds of gross diseases from sipping bad water. He was scared to try. But he was also thirsty. Desperate for fluids in a way he hadn't known was possible. He took a step toward the bank. He figured it couldn't hurt to investigate a little. He took another step and through a gap in the leaves he caught sight of something unnatural. Artificial. Something with a right angle.

The right angle was the corner of a metal box, three feet by three feet by six feet. It was painted dull olive green. A color Jed associated with the army. There were military-style letters stenciled on the side, as well, in white. They read WINSON COUNTY VOLUNTEER FIRE DEPARTMENT. And below, in a smaller size: AUTHORIZED USERS ONLY. The lid was held in place by a hasp and eye. There was no padlock. Jed unhooked it and lifted the lid. It folded all the way back, so he didn't have to hold it up. Inside, to the left, there was some kind of machine mounted inside a scuffed red tubular frame. It had a handle like Jed had seen on lawn mowers, presumably to make it start. Coiled up in the space next to it there was a long flexible hose, three inches in diameter, with a mesh cage and a Styrofoam float at one end. There were two cans of gas. Two plastic containers full of pink liquid with labels attached with tables specifying how much to add to tanks of water to create fire-inhibiting foam. There was a box of flashlight batteries, but no flashlights. And two shrink packs of bottled water. Thirty-six bottles per pack.

Jed was not an authorized user. And he wasn't a thief. But he was thirsty. He was close to full-on dehydration. Which was dangerous. And the point of fire departments is to save people. To help people in distress. So Jed grabbed the bottle at the nearest corner of the top pack. He pulled and twisted until it came free. Poured the water down his throat in one unbroken stream. Then he took another bottle. He drank that one more slowly, but finished it, too. He dropped the empties in the corner of the box. Removed the pack of batteries. The containers of foam mixture. The gas cans. And the hose. He tried to move the machine but it was too heavy so he left it where it was. Then he climbed inside. Pulled the lid down, with the empty bottles sandwiched against the lip of the box's long side. That way he had some fresh air, but could quickly pull them out if any animals came by.

If any firefighters came and saw their supplies scattered around, that would take more explaining. Jed figured he'd find a way to deal with that, somehow. He'd come too far to worry about what-ifs.

Up in St. Louis, at their second-choice hotel, it was almost time for Lev Emerson and Graeber to swap places again.

It was close to six hours since Emerson had checked in. Half their rest time was gone. Emerson had spent the first shift in the room, lying on the bed, fully dressed, with the drapes closed. Then he had switched to the back of the van. It was still parked at the far side of the parking lot.

Emerson preferred the van. But not for comfort or facilities. That was for sure. It had no bathroom. No TV. No coffee machine. No air-conditioning, back in the load space. Just three cushions lined up on the floor. They were from the first couch that Emerson and his wife had bought together. It was delivered the month after they got married. He had salvaged them when his house got redecorated more than two decades ago. They fitted the space like they were designed for it but their battered leather covers were worn almost all the way through. Their stuffing was wearing thin. Emerson could feel the van's metal floor if he shifted position too quickly. But the van was familiar. He liked the smell of the chemicals. The outline of the tools that were silhouetted in the light from the one-way glass in the rear doors. The way that the space calmed him. Allowed him to control his thoughts.

In the hotel room, Emerson was besieged by memories of Kyle. He could hear his son's voice. See his face. How he'd been as an adult. As a kid. He relived snippets of birthday parties. Trips they'd taken. Random moments of everyday life that hadn't seemed significant at the time but now were more valuable than anything in the universe. In the van Emerson could focus on his work. His art. He could remember everything from his first job, burning down a hot tub factory in Gary, Indiana, to the scene in the warehouse that morning.

Emerson mopped his forehead then sent a text to Graeber. He told him he could keep the room. He preferred to stay in the van. Where he could picture the fate of the distributor they were going to meet in Birmingham. The next link in the chain that would lead to the people ultimately responsible for Kyle's death. He didn't know how many links there would be. How hard it would be to loosen each tongue in turn. But he did know one thing. However long it took he would never stop. Not until he got justice for his son.

———

The problem wasn't so much that the original owners of the Riverside Lodge had built their hotel in the wrong place. It was that they had built it at the wrong time. They had broken ground when Winson's economy was fueled by more than just the prison. When people still came to the area to explore its natural beauty, not just spend a few minutes talking to a family member or a friend through a sheet of perforated Perspex. Hence its position high on the bank of the Mississippi. It had uninterrupted views to the north and the south. And to Louisiana away to the west, so far across the water that it looked like another country. Those first investors thought their clientele would never dry up as they got funneled past within touching distance by the local roads. Then the interstate came along and siphoned the passing traffic far away to the east.

The Lodge was made up of three distinct sections. A central core, two stories high, housing the reception area, the bar, restaurant, function rooms, and admin facilities. Plus a wing on either side containing the guest rooms. The roofs were flat and the structure was built of brick. There were three colors. A dark band around the base of the building. Pale yellow for the bulk of the walls. And regular vertical strips of white. The architects had insisted on those. They were a nod to the columns that stood out front of all the finest buildings in the region. The other main feature was a porte cochere which jutted out from above the main entrance. It had been designed to protect guests from the sun or the rain when they climbed out of their cars but it no longer looked very welcoming. Or very safe. In its current state it looked more likely to injure anyone who ventured beneath it. Maybe from falling masonry. Maybe from total collapse.

Hannah stopped the truck in the center of the Lodge's parking lot and wiped her chin with a paper napkin. She had eaten her burger as she drove from the Winson Garden. She had been hoping to get to it before it went completely cold, but that ship had long sailed. It had been nasty and rubbery and congealed. That didn't stop her from finishing it, though. Or Reacher from plowing through both of his.

Hannah said, "This is not how the place looked on the website when I booked. They're taking some major liberties with their advertising. Want me to find us somewhere else to stay?"

Reacher said, "No. It'll do just fine."

Hannah looked around the lot. There were three cars close together near the hotel entrance. Generic domestic sedans. Neutral colors. Probably rentals. And an ancient VW microbus away to the right near a blue metal storage container like the one they'd seen at the construction zone. It wasn't clear if the bus was still capable of moving. Hannah said, "There can't be many guests."

"That's a good thing."

"You sure? It isn't usually a good sign."

"Today's not a usual day."

"I guess." Hannah took her foot off the brake, looped around, and slotted the truck into the gap on the far side of the container. "This won't fool anyone who's searching for us but there's no point advertising where we are, right?" She took off her seatbelt, reached for the door handle, then paused. "But here's what I don't get. The cop who stopped us wasn't on the level, was he? He was expecting you to be driving. On your own. That was obvious. He was surprised when he saw me. He stammered, then he was all over my ID, and he didn't even ask your name. And the idea that the DMV has updated Sam's records already? Give me a break. So given that the cop was bent, why didn't he shoot us? Or at least arrest us?"

"Ever heard the expression *a fish rots from the head*?"

"No. I hate fish. What have they got to do with the cop?"

"The way I see it, there's bound to be plenty of contact between the police and the prison. Escape drills. Visitors getting caught smuggling. Relatives causing a nuisance in the town. So there'll be plenty of opportunity for Minerva to get its hooks into someone. Makes sense to go for someone high up. With authority. Influence. The beat cops will just have orders to be on the lookout. For me. For the truck. To report anything they see."

"You think our guy will report that he saw us go to the Winson Garden?"

"I'm counting on it."

Chapter 35

The reception area at the Riverside Lodge had a double height domed ceiling painted to look like a blue sky with a few fleeting clouds. A chandelier hung down from its highest point. It was suspended directly over the center of a compass motif that was laid into the floor with black and white tile and gold dividers. The counter was made of mahogany. It was so shiny it almost glowed after decades of being polished by maids and getting rubbed by guests checking in and out. Reacher knew the hotel must be involved with computers since Hannah had made their reservation online, but none were visible. There was just a thick ledger, bound in green leather. An old school telephone, made of Bakelite with a brown braided cable. And a brass bell to summon attention when no one was waiting to help.

Reacher tapped the plunger on top of the bell and a moment later a guy scurried out from a back room. He looked like he was maybe twenty-five. He had blond hair, a little long but swept back in a neat, tidy style. He was wearing a gray suit. The creases in the pants were razor sharp. His shirt was pressed and his tie was properly knotted.

The guy said, "How can I assist you this evening?"

Reacher said, "I need two rooms."

"Do you have a reservation?"

"No. This is a spur-of-the-moment thing."

"Let me see what I can do." The guy opened the ledger and took a fountain pen from his jacket pocket. "How many nights?"

"Let's start with one. We'll add more if we need them."

"No problem. Our standard rate is $85 per night, per room."

"Let's say $100, cash, for rooms well away from your other guests."

The guy glanced left, then right. "We only have three other guests presently. They're all at the near end of the south wing. How about the two rooms at the far end? You won't even know the others are there."

"How about the north wing? Is it empty?"

"It is, but I wouldn't recommend it. The refurbishment program hasn't been completed yet."

"Doesn't matter to me."

"To be honest, the refurb hasn't actually started. The rooms are a bit of a mess."

"Are they infested? Is there a health hazard of any kind?"

"No. They're functional. Just a little on the scruffy side."

"You could say the same about me." Reacher glanced at the sign on the wall, which directed guests to the two wings. It showed that rooms 101 through 124 were to the north. "Give me 112. My friend will take 114. Assuming they're adjacent?"

The guy nodded. "They are. Can I have your names?"

"Ambrose Burnside. Nat Kimball."

The guy took the cap off his pen but Reacher leaned across and closed the ledger.

Reacher said, "$110 per night. You pocket the extra and save yourself the trouble of writing anything down."

The guy said, "Sorry. Can't do that."

"There's no such word as *can't*. You have a simple choice. Pocket fifty dollars for doing absolutely nothing. Or—you don't want to know about the alternative. Trust me. Be sensible. Take the money."

The guy was still for a moment. Then he put the cap back on his pen. "It's $110 every night, if you stay longer. Per room. In cash. To me only. None of my co-workers get to hear about this."

Reacher counted out $220 and placed the cash on the counter. The guy scooped it up and slipped it into his back pocket. Then he took two white plastic rectangles out of a drawer. "One key each?"

Reacher shook his head. "Two."

The guy shrugged and pulled out another pair. He

poked some buttons on a little machine that was tucked almost out of sight on a low shelf and fed each card in turn into a slot. Then he slid the cards into a pair of cardboard wallets and handed them to Reacher. "Breakfast's from six till eight. Enjoy your stay."

Reacher led the way down the north corridor. Hannah followed, towing her suitcase. The even numbers were on the left. The odd numbers were on the right. Halfway along they passed room 112, then stopped outside 114. Reacher handed one cardboard wallet to Hannah. He opened the other and took out both keys. He put them in one back pocket, and slid the wallet into the other, where the keys to the room at the Winson Garden still were.

Hannah worked the lock on her door and said, "I'm going to call Danny Peel. See if he can meet us in the morning before he goes to work."

Reacher said, "Good idea. And, Hannah—do me one favor. Don't unpack just yet."

"Why not? You getting fussy about the state of the décor after all?"

"I'll be back in a minute. I'll explain then."

Reacher walked back to reception, tapped the bell, and waited for the smart-looking guy to reappear. Then he laid one of the key cards down on the counter.

He said, "This one doesn't work. Can you reprogram it?"

The guy said, "Did you put it next to your cellphone? Or your credit cards?"

"No."

"Oh. Well, what about the other one?"

"It worked fine. I went into my room. Then I put it down and came out to speak to my friend. I figured I could get back in with this one, but no luck."

"Weird." The guy picked up the card. "No problem, though. I can fix it right away."

Reacher said, "Room 121."

The guy worked the buttons on the little machine, dipped the key into the slot, and handed it back. Reacher slipped it into his pocket. Then the guy said, "Wait a minute. You're in 112. I remember because your friend is next door. Room 114."

Reacher nodded. "Correct. Room 112."

"You said 121."

"I'm good with numbers. I know exactly what I said."

"Well, whatever you said, I programmed it for 121. My mistake, I guess. You better let me have it back. Do it over."

Reacher shrugged, pulled out the other card, and gave it to the guy. The guy worked the machine again and handed the card back.

The guy said, "I'm really sorry about that. Stupid of me."

Reacher said, "No problem. Same digits. Easy to mix them up. Forget it even happened."

———

The hands on the alarm clock crept around to 1:30 A.M. Friday morning. Bruno Hix was in bed. He had been there for hours. But he hadn't gotten a moment of sleep. He had just lain there, staring at the ceiling, thinking about the stranger who had invaded his town. First, he had thought about the operation to take care of the guy. And his female companion. Harold and the others were going to hit them in their rooms at the hotel. But that had been due to happen at 1:00 A.M. Another half hour had passed. It should have been a simple procedure. He should have heard something. Confirmation that the problem had been eliminated. Unless—

Hix's phone rang. He snatched it up from the nightstand. The display showed Brockman's number. Hix hit the answer key. "Tell me we got them."

Brockman said, "It's better than that. Getting stopped by that cop must have spooked them. They've gone."

"What do you mean, *gone*?"

"They're not in their rooms at the Winson Garden. The beds haven't been touched. And their truck's not in the lot. They must have sneaked away, somehow."

"They must be staying somewhere else."

"Not in Winson. They did have a reservation at the Riverside Lodge, prepaid, in Hannah Hampton's name, but they didn't show up. We called all the B&Bs in town and they're not at any of them. We checked their names and descriptions. They're nowhere. They're history. They're no longer a problem."

Hix dropped the phone on the pillow and closed his eyes. He breathed freely for the first time that night. He felt his heart rate slow down. He began to drift toward sleep. Then he sat up. He was wide awake again. He grabbed his phone and hit the key to call Brockman back.

Hix said, "The Riverside Lodge. Where Reacher and the woman made a reservation but didn't show. Did you ask about walk-ins? Anyone paying cash?"

Brockman said, "No. Why would I? We know they didn't—damn."

"The penny drops. It's the perfect misdirect. Or almost perfect, given they're dealing with me, not you. Find the clerk who was working yesterday evening. They were probably bribed. Or threatened. Or both. Go to their house. Loosen their tongue. And if Reacher is at the Lodge, send Harold and the guys. Immediately. I don't want this dragging on any longer."

"I'm on it. And if you think about it, this is good news. If Reacher is at the Riverside Lodge after pulling that kind of shenanigans, the asshole will think he's safe. Harold's job will be a lot easier."

By the time the LED display on the van's dashboard blinked around to 1:30 A.M. Lev Emerson was sitting in the driver's seat, in the hotel parking lot up in St. Louis, waiting. Behind him, in the load space, the three old cushions were strapped away in their dedicated space. There was no danger of them getting thrown around in traffic, knocking over chemicals or damaging equipment. Two minutes later Graeber hauled open the passenger door. He had known his boss would want to drive, despite the lack of sleep, so he had taken the time to scare up a large mug of extra-strong coffee. Caffeine and conversation. Enough to keep them on the road all the way to Vicksburg, Mississippi. He hoped.

An hour later, at 2:30 A.M., six men walked through the main entrance of the Riverside Lodge, just outside Winson. First was the clerk who had helped Reacher the previous evening. His feet were bare. He was wearing blue-and-white-striped pajamas and his blond hair was sticking out in all kinds of crazy directions. He was followed by the two Minerva guys who had been sent to Colorado. Next came the two guys who had been keeping watch at the Greyhound station in Jackson. The guy who brought up the rear looked like he was as broad as any two of the others. He was six foot six tall. A good three hundred pounds. His chest and biceps were so big that his arms couldn't hang straight down at his sides. He had no neck. His head was shaved. His eyes were small mean dots that sank beneath the sharp cliff of his forehead. He had a tattoo on his right forearm that once said *Harold & Molly 4ever* in a heart, pierced by an arrow. A cut-price attempt at laser removal had left it reading something more like *larol oily leve,* in an apple.

Harold barged to the front of the group and shoved

the kid in the pajamas toward the mahogany counter. The kid scuttled around behind it and took a card key from its drawer. He prodded some buttons on the programming machine, dipped the card in the slot, and held it out. His hand was shaking. He said, "112." Harold snatched the card and the kid programmed another. He said, "114." Harold took it, too, and stared at the cards for a moment. Then he punched the kid in the face.

The kid's body hit the floor and slid until his head was pressed against the side wall. Harold and the other four guys didn't give him a second glance. They started moving immediately, crossed the deserted reception area, and made their way down the north corridor. One of them continued to room 114. Hannah's room. The others lined up behind Harold outside 112. Reacher's room.

Harold held up three fingers.

Then two.

Then one.

At 2:30 A.M. Jed Starmer was fast asleep. He was curled up in the Winson Volunteer Fire Department's equipment locker at the side of the pond in the woods. The fresh air had taken its toll. So had the physical exertion. And the stress. He was absolutely out for the count.

Jed had no idea that a bobcat had wandered past half an hour earlier. And before that a black bear had been sniffing around. It had been interested in the coil of hose. The gas cans. The containers of foam.

But most of all it had been intrigued by the scent escaping from the gap between the sides and the lid. The bear was easily capable of lifting the lid. It could have opened the box even if the latch had been fastened. It was inches away. It was hungry. It was curious. Then the wind changed. The bear turned around. It headed back down the track toward a spot where some teenagers had parked the evening before. They had drunk beer. Eaten burgers. Tossed the wrappers into the undergrowth. And without realizing it, they had saved Jed from the fright of his life.

Chapter 36

Harold touched the key card against the pad on the door to room 112. The mechanism gave a soft click and a small light changed from red to green. Harold slammed down on the handle, shoved the door, and charged into the room like the corridor was on fire. Three guys followed him. The other opened the door to room 114. He was slower with the key. Less violent. More cautious as he stepped inside.

Room 112 followed a standard hotel layout. There was a simple closet to the left, open, with a rail and a shelf above. There was a bathroom opposite it. The room opened up beyond that with a bed and an armchair to the right. Both were loaded with too many pillows. There was a painting of a riverboat on the wall above the headboard. A window straight ahead covered with garish curtains. A desk to the left that did double duty as a dressing table. A mirror on the wall above it. And a carpet, which was threadbare in the places that saw the heaviest traffic.

Harold lumbered around to the bed and stopped. It was empty. He tapped the guy who was following him on the shoulder and pointed to the floor. The guy ducked down and lifted the bed skirt. He peered underneath, then stood back up and shook his head. Harold pointed to the bathroom. The guy nearest to it pulled back his right fist and pushed the door with his left hand. He reached inside. Flicked on the light. Took a half step. Another. Then went all the way in and checked behind the shower curtain that hung in front of the tub.

The guy came out of the bathroom and said, "It's empty. Reacher's gone. Maybe he was never here."

Room 114 was a mirror image of 112. Its furnishings were equally gaudy. Its fabric was equally worn. One difference was the quality of its air. Instead of smelling moldy and stale it felt fresh but a little damp. The drapes were pulled aside and the window was open. The Minerva guy—one of the pair from the Greyhound station—picked up on that. He paused just inside the doorway. He was thinking about cockroaches getting in. And wondering if it was a sign that the woman had fled. Or if it was part of a trap. Or if the woman was just a fresh air fiend. He'd had a girlfriend once who swore she couldn't sleep with the bedroom windows closed.

The guy started to move again. He crept forward.

He drew level with the bathroom door. Reacher was waiting inside. He stepped into the doorway and punched the guy in the side of the head. The blow sent him staggering sideways across the entryway. He hit the wall on the far side and his skull left a new dent in the plaster. His arms windmilled around and knocked the hangers off the rail, sending them rattling across the floor.

The guys in room 112 heard the noises. They turned in unison and stared at the connecting wall.

Harold said, "It's Reacher. He's next door. With the widow. Get him."

The guys rushed into the corridor. They ran to the door to 114. And stopped. The door was closed and they didn't have a key.

Reacher climbed out of the window. He jumped down and landed on a strip of grass at the edge of the parking lot.

The other Minerva guy from the Greyhound station hammered on the door. He got no response.

Reacher hurried across to the window to room 112. It was unlatched. He had seen to that, earlier.

Harold pushed the three guys aside and slammed the door with his palm. The half above the handle flexed an inch but the lock didn't give way.

Reacher opened the window, hauled himself up, and climbed inside.

Harold stepped back. He lifted his right leg and drove the sole of his foot into the door at the side of the handle. The architrave shattered. The door whipped open. It slammed into the unconscious guy's feet and bounced back into its place in the ragged frame.

Reacher crossed the room. He opened his door a crack and peered out into the corridor.

Harold barged into his door with his shoulder and shoved the unconscious guy's legs far enough aside to make a gap he could squeeze through.

Reacher stepped out into the corridor. He said, "Looking for me?"

The nearest guy turned around. The one who'd been driving the BMW in Colorado. Reacher was already moving toward him. He drove the heel of his right hand into the guy's chin. The guy's head snapped back. His feet left the ground and he slammed down on his back like a roll of carpet. The next guy in line had to jump to the side and press himself against the wall to avoid getting flattened. It was the guy who had killed Angela St. Vrain. Reacher swiveled at the waist and buried his left fist in his solar plexus. The guy doubled over. He bent at the waist. His body was momentarily horizontal. Reacher brought the side of his right fist down onto the back of his head like a club. The guy's knees buckled and he collapsed across his buddy's back in an X shape with his forehead pressed against the wall. The third guy took a glance at what was happening and began to run. Away from Reacher, along the corridor, toward an emergency exit at the far end. Reacher hurdled the tangled bodies and chased after him. But the Minerva guy was lighter. He was faster. And he was desperate. There was nothing Reacher could do. It was a race he had no chance of winning.

A door on the right-hand side of the corridor swung open. The last but one. Room 121. Hannah stepped out. She turned to face the running guy. Her feet were apart, planted securely on the ground. She was holding her SIG out in front, steadily, in a two-handed grip.

She said, "Stop." The tone of her voice made it clear she was serious.

The guy slowed, raised his hands, and stopped. Then he lunged for the gun. Hannah pulled it aside, out of his reach. She kicked him in the crotch. Hard. He doubled over. He was gagging. A scream was cut off in his throat. Hannah kneed him in the face. He fell back. He was sprawling and struggling, but still moving. For another split second. Then Reacher caught up and kicked him in the head.

Hannah switched the gun to her right hand, crouched down, and checked the guy's neck for a pulse. There was a sound from down the corridor. It was Harold. He had wrestled the door to room 114 open again. He stepped out. He was so broad he seemed to fill the entire space between the walls. Hannah straightened up and stood next to Reacher. For a moment no one spoke.

Harold broke the silence. He said, "Drop the gun, little girl. Let's talk."

Hannah raised the gun and switched back to a two-handed grip. She said, "No. And let's not."

Harold took a long step forward.

Hannah said, "Stop."

Harold's face twisted into a mean, cruel grin. He took another step.

Hannah said, "I'm not kidding. Stop."

Harold took another step.

Hannah took a breath, held it, aimed at Harold's center mass, and pulled her trigger. The noise was devastating. The spent cartridge hit the wall and fizzed down onto the carpet by Reacher's foot. Harold staggered back. He fell. And lay still.

Hannah stepped forward, already leaning down to check Harold for signs of life. Reacher grabbed her arm and pulled her back.

"Let go." Hannah tried to wriggle free. "I need to know if—"

Harold sat up. His face was twisted with fury. His shirt was ripped. Metal glinted through the hole in the fabric. He was wearing a ballistic vest. The fibers had flexed like a soccer net stopping a well struck ball. The surface had distorted. The bullet had pancaked. But the structure had done its job. The bullet had not gotten through.

Reacher had a rule for that kind of situation. Your enemy gets knocked down, they do not get back up. You finish them, there and then. No mercy. No hesitation. But Hannah's intervention had slowed him down. Cost him a second. And that was enough for Harold to haul himself the rest of the way up.

Harold's feet were spread wide. His knuckles were practically brushing the sides of the corridor. His arms and legs were as long as Reacher's. Maybe longer.

Which was a problem. It took away one of Reacher's regular advantages. In a fight he could normally stay out of harm's way and still be able to inflict massive damage. But there was no way to hit Harold without the risk of getting hit in return. Of taking some serious punishment. That wasn't a prospect Reacher was keen on. It would reduce his efficiency. Lower his odds of success.

Harold shifted his stance and squared up like some old-school bruiser. It was like he had read Reacher's mind. A mean smile spread across his face. His fists were like sledgehammers. Weight was on his side. If he could land one blow it would be game over, and he knew it.

Reacher knew it, too. But he also knew there are times when a needle is more effective than a hammer.

"Careful," Reacher said. "Don't let your knuckles drag on the ground."

Harold's eyes narrowed.

"They won't let you in the hospital if you hurt yourself. They'll send you to a vet. Lock you in a zoo afterward. Or a circus."

Harold charged forward. He launched an immense right hook. The motion was smooth. Practiced. Reacher had no doubt that if Harold's fist made contact with his skull the result would be devastating. But he was expecting it. He snapped his body back from the waist. Just far enough. Harold's fist zipped past his nose. It kept moving. And made contact with the wall. It shattered the surface and smashed through the lattice of wooden slats that supported the plaster. Harold yelled and wrenched back his arm but his hand would not come free. It was stuck like a fish on a barbed hook.

Reacher danced in close and threw a punch of his own. It was vicious. Brutal. It caught Harold right by his ear. It rocked his head to the side. It would have knocked anyone else down. They'd have been unconscious. For a long time. Maybe forever. But Harold shook his head. Spat out some blood. And grinned.

Reacher switched targets. He stamped down on the side of Harold's knee. Then he drove the heel of his hand into Harold's captive arm, just above the elbow. The joint bent the wrong way. Bone dislocated. Tendons stretched. Ligaments tore. Harold roared with pain. And anger. He grabbed his trapped forearm with his free hand and twisted and heaved with all his might. The wooden strips gave way. Their jagged ends tore his wrist and palm and the back of his hand. His arm flailed around. It was floppy and out of control. And it was spraying rivers of blood. His nails brushed Reacher's cheek. One broke his skin.

Harold took a step forward then stopped and howled with pain. His knee was too damaged. It couldn't take his weight. His right arm was hanging, useless. So he reached around with his left hand and pulled a gun from his waistband.

He started to raise it.

Reacher was already moving. He was running at Harold. Accelerating as fast as he could. But space was restricted. There was little room for maneuver. Reacher figured he had one chance. He needed momentum. He needed focus. So he charged in, leaned forward, and plowed into Harold. His right shoulder

drilled into the exact spot Hannah's bullet had hit.
Where he knew Harold's ribs would be bruised.
Where he hoped they would be broken.

Harold crashed down, flat on his back. He dropped
the gun. He howled. He thrashed his legs. Flailed his
arms. Reacher moved in, looking for a part of Harold
to punch. Or kick. Or stomp. Harold kept on squirm-
ing and wriggling. He denied Reacher a target. Then
he sat up, fast, like he was exercising at the gym. He
lunged and wrapped his good arm around Reacher's
thighs. Slid his hand lower and clamped his forearm
across the back of Reacher's knees. He flung himself
back down, straining and tugging with all his might.

Reacher's knees jackknifed. There was nothing he
could do to avoid getting pulled down. He knew that.
So he didn't fight gravity. He didn't resist. Instead he
aimed, and planted both knees square in the center of
Harold's chest.

Maybe Harold's rib cage had been damaged by the
gunshot. Maybe it had been weakened by Reacher's
shoulder charge. Maybe he just had porous bones.
But whatever the reason, Harold's sternum collapsed.
His lungs were crushed flat. So was his heart. His
liver. And a bunch of other organs. His body gave one
last spasmodic twitch. His head lolled to the side.
And then he was still.

Bruno Hix was still awake. He had done everything
he could think of to get to sleep. Herbal tea. Whiskey.
Meditation. Nothing had worked. He felt the anger
building inside himself. His big speech was hours

away. He didn't want black circles under his eyes because he was short of rest. He didn't want to fluff his lines because he was too tired to concentrate.

Hix stared at the ceiling and pictured himself at the beach on a tropical island. He'd read somewhere about relaxation techniques and this one was supposed to help. He took it a step further. Imagined what kind of drink he would have in his hand. Maybe a piña colada. Maybe a daiquiri. He was still trying to decide when his peace was shattered by his phone. It was a text. From Brockman.

"Friends" located. H & co on scene. Only a matter of time . . .

That was it. Everything was going to be OK after all. Harold would take care of Reacher. The guy's luck had to run out sometime. And if this wasn't the time, if Harold failed, it wouldn't matter. Not now that contact had been made. They could fall back on the insurance. Hix had arranged it himself, therefore he didn't have to worry. He was confident it would work if it was needed.

Hix was confident. In the insurance itself. The note was completely credible. He had put a lot of thought into it. He wasn't worried about whether Reacher would believe it. But for Reacher to believe it he would have to read it. And for him to read it he would have to find it. If he defeated Harold. And Brockman had hinted that Harold might refuse to take it due to some ridiculous sense of pride. Hix pictured the envelope abandoned at Harold's house. Left in the vehicle.

Tossed in the trash. Then he got hold of himself. Forced nice images of the beach back into his head. There was no need to borrow trouble. His plan was elegant. Sophisticated. There was no way the universe would let it get torpedoed by some petulant meathead.

Chapter 37

Reacher was worried about the gunshot. The noise it had made. Someone was certain to have heard. The night clerk. Or the other guests, in the south wing. One of them was bound to call 911. Maybe they all would. Maybe they already had. One way or another the police would soon be showing up. And Reacher did not want to be around when they got there. The stealthy approach hadn't worked. Now whoever was pulling the strings would have an emergency call and a dead body to work with. A perfect excuse to send in a couple more goons, guns blazing, no questions asked.

Winson was not a New York or a Chicago. It wasn't even a Jackson. Reacher doubted the cops would be on patrol twenty-four/seven. Any presence was likely to be confined to the station house at that time of night. The best case would be one guy. Low down the pecking order. Alone with a pot of stewed coffee and a box of stale donuts. Someone who would have to call for assistance and wait for another officer to arrive before responding. The worst case would be that a pair of old hands were on duty. Trusted guys. Ready to roll at a moment's notice. Ready to do whatever their boss told them to.

Reacher always planned for the worst. The town wasn't far away. There would be no traffic. The cops would be local. They would know the road, and they would drive fast. He figured he and Hannah had nine minutes to get clear of the hotel.

Hannah was kneeling down near Harold's head. She had checked his neck for a pulse after Reacher climbed off him. She hadn't found one. But she had discovered her legs would no longer work. She was unable to stand up. When the week began she had never seen a dead body. Now she had been up close and personal with two. And this one she felt partially responsible for. Blood was leaking from its crushed chest and oozing toward her knees. She was starting to get mesmerized by it.

Reacher helped Hannah to her feet and guided her back to room 121. He asked her to get her things together. Quickly. And while she packed he went out to the corridor. He took a pillowcase from the bed and filled it with the contents of the Minerva guys' pockets. Their guns. Phones. Wallets. Keys.

Reacher and Hannah made it down the corridor

and into reception. They had six minutes left to get clear. Plenty of time. Then Reacher noticed a pair of bare feet. Someone was on the floor, behind the counter. He detoured to investigate. It was the kid who had checked them in. He was in his pajamas. Alive, but unconscious.

Reacher crossed back to Hannah and they continued to the parking lot. The three rental cars were still lined up on the south side of the porte cochere. The VW bus had moved closer on the north side. Two other vehicles had arrived and were parked next to it. A Dodge Neon and a Ram panel van. The Dodge had lived a hard life. That was clear. It had dents in its front wings, mud sprayed around its wheel arches, a crack running the whole width of its windshield, and a couple of deep gouges in its front fender. The van was dark blue. It was spotless. It had no livery or logo, but it looked like the kind of thing a company would use to ferry stock and supplies between different sites.

They had five minutes left to get clear.

Reacher pointed at the vehicles and said, "See how they're lined up? One guy came here directly in the van. The others went to the clerk's house. Roused him. And made him drive back in his VW because there would be no room in the car. Which could help us. Wait here a minute."

Reacher went back inside and crossed to the counter. He checked the kid's pajamas. Found a key on a rabbit's foot fob. He fished a wallet out of the pillowcase. Took out all the cash and slipped it into the kid's pocket. Then he tore a page out of the ledger, grabbed a pen off the shelf, and wrote: *Will return the bus. Don't report it stolen. More $ to come. Ambrose Burnside.*

They had three minutes left.

Reacher hurried outside and tossed the key to Hannah. He said, "The cops will be looking for Sam's truck. See if you can get the VW to start. Better to use it instead." Then he looped around to the rear of the van. Its door was unlocked. The walls and floor of the cargo area had been boarded up with plywood to protect the paint. Two gurneys were stacked on each other at the right-hand side. They were folded down and secured with elastic straps. Next to them was a black plastic trash bag. Reacher looked inside. It was full of medics' uniforms. There was nothing he could use, so Reacher moved on to the front of the vehicle. He went to the passenger side and opened the glove box. There were two pieces of paper inside. The insurance and registration documents. Reacher checked the details. He was hoping for a corporate name he hadn't seen before. A new thread to pull in whatever illegitimate financial tapestry Angela St. Vrain had been talking to Sam Roth about. But Reacher was out of luck. The papers listed the vehicle's owner as the Minerva Correctional Corporation, with an address in Delaware. Reacher immediately thought, *Tax avoidance,* but he couldn't see a connection to murder.

Two minutes left.

Reacher heard the VW rattle into life. He scanned the rest of the van's cab. It was clean and empty. Then he stepped back to slam the door and spotted something white peeking out from under the passenger seat. It was the corner of an envelope. It must have slipped off the dashboard while the van was moving and slid back there. Reacher fished it out. It was standard letter size. Thin, like it only had a single piece of paper inside. And it was addressed to Danny Peel. The same name that had been on the envelope in Angela St. Vrain's purse. The same address. But different handwriting. Reacher was confident about that.

Bruno Hix was already the world's greatest living chat-show host, but the extravaganza that was about to go live was destined to cement his status as an all-time legend of broadcasting. It was going to feature the most stars ever interviewed in a single event. It would be the most expensive eight hours of television ever made. It was being filmed in the middle of the Mediterranean, on the deck of his yacht. The audience was already in place. A thousand people divided between less luxurious ships, moored on all four sides. He had a drink in his hand. The cameras were rolling. But his guests hadn't showed up. And somehow he was naked. His hair was falling out. His skin—

Hix's phone rang. His eyes snapped open. He was sweating. He threw back the comforter and lay for a moment, trying to control his breathing. Then he answered the call. It was Brockman again.

Hix said, "Talk to me."

The line was silent for a moment. Then Brockman said, "He's on the loose again."

"Who? Reacher?"

"Yes."

"And the woman?"

"Her too."

"Harold screwed up?"

"Harold's dead. Reacher literally crushed him."

"Harold. Second best again. Maybe we should put that on his gravestone. What about our other guys?"

"They're hurt. But alive."

"Where did Reacher go?"

"They don't know. Moseley's guys are searching for him."

"OK. Keep me posted."

"Bruno? I've been thinking. About tomorrow. I hate to say this. You know I've been against making any changes, right from the start. But maybe the others were right. With Reacher running around out there, maybe the full ceremony isn't the smart way to go. Maybe it's time we switched to Plan B."

"We don't have a Plan B. We've never needed one."

"Maybe it's time to think of one. We can't postpone because of the court order but the ceremony isn't important. Getting our guy released on time is all that matters. We could put out a statement. Say he was too traumatized to go through with the publicity."

"The release is the top priority, for sure. But we don't want to throw the baby out with the bathwater. The ceremony is very important. You can't buy that kind of good press. And you're forgetting the insurance. That will take care of Reacher. He'll be miles away at 10:00 A.M. And if he comes back, it'll be too late for him to do anything."

"Will it work?"

Hix reached out and took a second cellphone from his nightstand. A cheap, simple one. He checked its battery. He checked it had signal. "Of course it will. We'll have confirmation soon. Nine o'clock. Nine-fifteen at the latest."

The VW was less conspicuous than Roth's truck but it would still stand out in such a small town. People might know it belonged to the kid from the hotel. The police probably would. Reacher bet they'd pulled him over plenty of times. The way the bus stank of weed it was pretty much probable cause on wheels. Plus its reliability was unknown. Reacher didn't want faulty components or a lack of maintenance to do the cops' work for them and leave him and Hannah stranded at the side of the road. So they decided to lie low for the remainder of the night. They headed to a place near the foot of the hill outside the town. Reacher remembered seeing a track leading into a thick grove of trees. At the time he'd figured it could be a firebreak, or was created to provide access for forestry equipment. Either way, it would give them good cover until the morning.

Hannah took her hand off the wheel and picked the envelope up from the dashboard for the third time since they left the hotel. "How do you think they got a letter addressed to Danny? Maybe he took it to work, meaning to deal with it, and dropped it? Someone found it and was planning to deliver it to his house?"

Reacher said, "Let's ask him about it in the morning. What time are we seeing him?"

"Nothing's set. I couldn't get hold of him. He's an early riser so I'll try again first thing. And if he doesn't answer we can always just show up and surprise him."

The VW was fitted out with a bed and a kitchen and a table and a couch. Reacher appreciated the ingenuity that had gone into the design. And the thoroughness. Every tiny space had been used. But there was no getting away from the fact that the space was tiny. Reacher decided it would be better to let Hannah have it to herself so he dug through the cupboards until he found a bunch of old blankets. He took one. Spread it on the ground. And lay down under the stars.

There were two words on Reacher's mind as he got ready to sleep. *Brockman.* And *lockdown.* Brockman was a name he'd heard more than once. The guy from Minerva who had sent out all the thugs. Reacher wanted to find him. Kick down his door in the middle of the night. See how he liked it. And see what he knew about whatever it was that Angela St. Vrain had stumbled across.

The problem was that Brockman might not know anything. If Minerva people started getting attacked in their homes it could trigger panic. And lockdown is the default panic response of people who run prisons. It's in their DNA. So he would have to be patient. They had two leads to follow. Danny Peel, and the release ceremony. He would see what came of those. If nothing productive was uncovered, then he would go after Brockman. And whoever else was involved, until he got some satisfactory answers.

Chapter 38

Hannah woke Reacher at a minute after 7:30 A.M. She shook his shoulder and said, "Danny's still not answering his phone. I'm getting worried. I think we should go to his place. Right now."

The directions to Danny's house were already teed up on Hannah's phone. Its electronic voice ordered them back to the road, then right, which was the way to Winson. It took Hannah a couple of minutes to get the VW facing the right way. The track was narrow. The steering was heavy. The clutch was stiff. She sawed back and forward, bumping and lurching across the rough surface, until she got a straight shot forward. She picked up a little speed. Reached the mouth of the track. And almost hit a pedestrian. A kid. He looked like he was in his mid-teens. He was pushing some kind of fancy bike up the hill. Very slowly. It was like a contest. Like the bike was trying to pull him back down.

The smart money would be on the bike, Reacher thought.

The kid stopped. He was startled by the ancient bus suddenly appearing out of the trees. He stared through the windshield for a moment. Then he toppled backward and the bike landed on top of him.

Hannah jumped out and rushed up to the kid. "Oh my goodness. I'm so sorry. Are you OK?"

The kid didn't answer.

Hannah pulled the bike off him. "Are you hurt? Did you hit your head?"

"I'm fine." The kid rolled onto all fours, struggled to his feet, and took hold of the handlebars. "Give me that. I need to get going."

"Where to? What's the hurry? Do you have any water? Do your parents know you're here?"

"I've got to get to Winson. I can't be late."

"Just sit for a moment. Rest. Get your breath back, at least."

"There's no time."

"You're in no state to walk, let alone ride." Hannah snatched the handlebars. "We're going part of your way. Come on. There's a rack at the back. Put the bike on there. We'll give you a ride."

———

The bus purred up the hill. The bike rattled and bounced on the rack. The kid sat on the couch at the back of the cabin, stiff and anxious.

Hannah adjusted her mirror so that she could see him without turning around. She said, "What's your name?"

The kid said, "Jed. Jed Starmer."

"Well, Jed, why's it so important you get to Winson this morning?"

"Something's happening. I can't be late. I've come too far to miss it."

"What's happening? Where?"

"Someone's getting released from the prison." Jed took a breath. "My dad."

Reacher said, "I read about that. Anton Begovic?"

Jed nodded. "He was never married to my mom. That's why we have different last names."

"Does he know you're coming?"

"He doesn't know I exist."

The bus crested the hill and Hannah's phone announced they had a left turn coming up in a half mile.

Reacher said, "Where did you travel from?"

Jed said, "L.A."

"On the bike the whole way?"

"On the bus. The Greyhound. I just rode the bike from Jackson."

"You brought the bike with you?"

"I kind of borrowed it."

Hannah sighed. Reacher said nothing.

Jed said, "I didn't steal it. You don't understand. I

had everything planned. I was supposed to stay in a hotel, then get a taxi, but all my stuff got stolen, and my money got stolen, and two creepy guys tried to kidnap me, and some cops came, and—"

Reacher said, "It's OK. No one's accusing you of anything."

"This is important. I'm not a thief, OK? The guy riding the bike was an asshole. He rode into me, and he pushed me, and he yelled at me. Then he left it right there. On the sidewalk. Unlocked. I had no choice. I'll give it back when I'm done. I swear."

Hannah said, "Sounds like you've had an awful time. You lost everything?"

"Pretty much. All I've got left is my toothbrush. I had it in my pocket."

"What about your mom? Could she not help? Would you like me to call her?"

"You can't. She died—pancreatic cancer. It came on quick."

"I'm sorry."

Reacher said, "What's your plan when you get to the prison?"

Jed shrugged. "Meet my dad, I guess."

"How? They have some kind of big shindig planned. Press. TV. The whole nine yards. You won't be able to just stroll up and say, *Hi, I'm your kid.*"

Jed shrugged again. "I've come this far. I'll figure something out."

They came to the intersection and the phone insisted they should turn. Winson was straight on, so Hannah pulled over to the side of the road. She said, "It's flat from here. You should be OK on the bike. I'll help you get it off the rack."

Jed opened the door. "I can get it. Thanks for the ride."

Hannah said, "Hold on a sec. We need to talk real quick."

"What about?"

"If I'm understanding this right you're about to meet your dad for the first time. That's a huge thing. For both of you. It needs to be handled just right because it's going to have an impact on the whole of the rest of your lives."

Jed didn't respond.

Hannah said, "Have you ever met anyone who's been in prison?"

Jed said, "No."

"I have. A lot of times. I work with a charity that helps people when they get out. The next few months are going to be very hard on your dad. Even if he hated it, even if he didn't deserve to be there, he'll be totally used to life in an institution. The outside world is completely different. It's like he's going to be dumped in a strange country where he doesn't speak the language or understand the customs. It'll be daunting for him. It'll be frightening. He'll be overwhelmed with all the changes, and one thing he's really going to struggle with is surprises. He could react . . . in a way he wouldn't be happy about, looking back."

"What are you saying? That I shouldn't meet my own dad? Because—"

"Not at all. Meeting you, getting to know you, that'll be the best thing that ever happens to him. But finding out he has a kid, on top of all the other changes he's going to be facing, that's a huge deal. It's a transition that has to be handled carefully. Slowly. And today—release day—might not be the best time."

"But he doesn't know I was even born. He doesn't know to look for me. If we don't connect today, he'll disappear again. I'll never find him."

"That's not how it works." Hannah rummaged in her purse, pulled out a card, and handed it to Jed. "Here's what I suggest you do. Go to the ceremony outside the prison. See your dad get his freedom back. That's a big deal. It's obviously important to you, since you came all this way. And it'll mean the world to him that you did. But give him a day or two. Then get in touch. Call me when you're ready. I know how the system works. I can help you find where he's staying."

"What am I going to do for a day or two? In Winson? I have no money. Nothing to eat. Nowhere to sleep."

Reacher fished another wallet out of the pillowcase and took the cash from it. There was $240. He passed it to Jed. "Hannah's right. You should listen to her. You're at a crossroads in your life. It's important you choose the right way to go."

Jed wrestled the bike down from the rack at the rear of the bus, climbed on, and pedaled straight ahead toward Winson. Hannah pressed the clutch down, then let it back up again without touching the gear stick.

She said, "This is a bad situation. I'm worried about that kid."

Reacher said, "You're right. He's terrible on that bike. We should have made him walk."

"I'm not talking about road safety. It's the whole deal with Begovic getting released. Minerva will arrange support for him. It's all a big PR stunt so Hix will make sure it's done right. He won't want stories in the press about Begovic killing himself or committing some crime just to get locked up again. But Jed? Who's going to look out for him? If it's true that his mom is dead, he's got no one. I've seen this before. I know how it will play out. The poor kid's setting himself up to fail."

The phone prompted them to *proceed to the route* so Hannah took the left turn. Then the phone had them swing away to the south and skirt around the center of the town. The road was surrounded by trees. They were tall and mature, but there were no buildings for more than half a mile. Then they came to a house. It was huge. It was gleaming white. Four columns supported a porch and a balcony, which jutted out at the center. Further balconies ran the whole width on two levels on either side. The place was the size of a hotel and it was surrounded by a wall with a fancy iron gate. A driveway wrapped around an oval patch of grass with flowers and shrubs and a raised fountain. A car was parked between the fountain and the steps leading up to the front door. A BMW sedan. It was large and black. Reacher recognized it. The day before it had been in the curved lot outside the prison.

They continued for another three-quarters of a mile then turned to the west. The trees thinned out and houses began to appear on both sides of the street. The homes grew closer and larger and more uniform until the phone said their destination was a hundred feet ahead, on the left. That would place Danny's house on the final lot before a smaller road peeled away to the south. But there was a problem. That lot was empty.

Hannah pulled over at the side of the street and they saw that the lot wasn't completely empty. There was a stand-alone garage in the far corner, with a short drive leading to the side road. There was a mailbox mounted on a skinny metal pole. It had originally been red but the paint had faded over the years, leaving it pink, like a flamingo. And the main portion of the lot hadn't been empty long. It was full of ash. Black and gray and uneven, heaped up in some places, sagging down in others, with the scorched remnants of a brick fireplace in the approximate center.

Reacher climbed out of the VW. He could smell smoke. Hannah joined him on the sidewalk. She was blinking rapidly and her mouth was open but she didn't speak. Reacher figured there wasn't much to say. A minute later a man approached them from the next-door house. He looked to be in his sixties, tall, thin, with silver hair, a plaid shirt, and jeans that looked like they were in danger of falling down.

"Morning," the guy said. "You folks new to the neighborhood?"

Reacher said, "What happened here?"

"There was a fire."

Reacher caught an echo of his mother's voice. *Ask a stupid question, get a stupid answer.* He said, "Really? When?"

"Last Saturday. Early in the morning."

"How did it start?"

"The guy who owned the place was smoking a cigarette. That's what I heard. He woke up, lit his first of the day, then fell back to sleep."

"Was his name Danny Peel, the owner?"

The guy nodded.

Reacher said, "Where is he now?"

"We cremated him, Wednesday. Kind of ironic, given the way he went, but those were his wishes. There wasn't much of a crowd. Just me and a couple of people from his work."

"From the prison?"

The guy nodded again.

"Did people he worked with come by his house often?"

"There was one woman. Don't know her name."

"Anyone else?"

"He was a quiet kind of a guy. Didn't seem to socialize much. Not at home, anyway."

"Was anyone at his house on Saturday? Before the fire?"

"I doubt it. Like I said, it was early. And if anyone had been staying overnight, wouldn't they have found more bodies?"

"Did you see anyone in the neighborhood? Anyone who isn't normally here. Or any unusual vehicles?"

"No."

"Did you notice if any of his windows were open that morning?"

"No. I went out to get the mail. Then I heard the sirens. I didn't see anything. Why all the questions? You're not a cop. Are you from the insurance company?"

"Me? No. I'm just naturally curious."

Chapter 39

Hannah crossed the street without saying a word. She climbed back into the VW, rested her elbows on the steering wheel, and held her head in her hands. Reacher decided to take a look around. He didn't expect to find much. The fire hadn't left much trace of anything, but old habits die hard. He was curious. And he wanted to give Hannah some time to herself.

There had been a lawn between the house and the street but the grass had been torn up by the firefighters' boots and jagged channels had been cut through the dirt by runoff from the water they'd used to extinguish the flames. They couldn't have gotten there very quickly, Reacher thought. There was so little of the structure left. It was like someone had judged things very carefully. Too late to save any of Danny Peel's house. But in time to stop the flames from spreading to anyone else's. He picked his way across the rough ground until he was close to what would have been the outer wall. He wondered where the door had been. The kitchen. The bedroom. He could believe the fire had started there. And maybe that a cigarette had been involved. But not that it was an accident. He'd been around the block too many times to swallow that kind of a story.

Reacher looked inside the mailbox. There were four envelopes. All junk. Presumably delivered before the fire. Then he moved on to the garage. It had two roll-up vehicle doors leading to the side street and a personnel door that would have faced the house. He tried the handle. It was locked. The door didn't seem too stout so he leaned his shoulder against it and shoved. The tongue of the lock gouged a little strip out of the frame and it opened easily. Reacher stepped inside. There was a car in each bay. Both were Chevrolets. The closer one was a sedan, probably less than five years old. It was small and white and practical. The other was a Corvette, maybe from the 1960s. It was long and green and—presumably, if you were a car guy—fun. A wooden workbench stretched the whole width of the garage, against the far wall. Above it there were Peg-Boards that were covered with tools. Domestic ones to the left, like chisels and mallets and saws. Things for working on cars to the right, like spanners and wrenches and hammers. There was also a journal hanging from a hook, and a pen on a chain like they used to have in banks. Reacher looked in the journal. It was full of entries going back five years, neatly written in blue ink, giving details of all the jobs Danny had completed on the Stingray. He had done work on the brakes. Rust in the subframe. Water leaks. Electrical problems. A whole bunch of things, some large, some small, all faithfully recorded. He had been a meticulous guy. That was clear.

Reacher got back into the VW's passenger seat. Hannah lifted her head and looked at him. Her eyes were red.

She said, "So, what now?"

Reacher picked up the envelope he'd found in the van at the Riverside Lodge and held it out to her. "We open this. It might throw some light on what happened to Danny. And Sam. And Angela. I doubt the Minerva guys had it by chance."

Hannah was silent for a moment. "OK. I guess. But I can't. You do it."

Reacher tore open the envelope. There was a note inside, handwritten in neat tidy script, on a piece of paper with a company letterhead. The company was a firm of accountants called Moon, Douglas, and Flynn in Hattiesburg, Mississippi. The note was short. It read:

> Danny,
> I have what you asked for. What you have seen so far is just the tip of the iceberg. I can give you enough to sink the whole ship. Meet

me at 11:30 A.M., this Friday, Coal Creek
Coffee, corner table, downtown Hattiesburg.

Alan

PS—pls call to confirm you're coming. I have
arrangements to make. Use my cell, not the
office number. 399-307-1968.

Reacher handed the page to Hannah. She read it then dropped the paper onto the dashboard in front of her.

She said, "I don't get it. Is this the same thing Angela went to Sam about? The accounting thing? I can't see the connection. But it would be weird if there were two separate things going on at the same time."

Reacher said, "It's the same thing. Remember the information I told you about from Angela's purse? About Begovic's release? It was in an envelope addressed to Danny."

"How did she come to have it?"

"I was planning on asking Danny that."

"So Danny was corresponding with some Deep Throat–type person. He must have gotten Angela involved. Which got her killed. And indirectly got Sam killed. Oh, boy. Poor Danny. He would have been devastated."

"It wasn't Danny's fault. He uncovered a crime, apparently. He didn't commit one."

"Someone did. Someone at Minerva. The same people who set all those goons on us. We need to sink their ship. We need this blockbuster evidence. Whatever it is. Assuming this Alan guy checks out."

Hannah pulled out her phone and started tapping and swiping. A couple of minutes later she held it up so that Reacher could see the screen.

She said, "OK. Well, the company's real. It exists. The address, website, social media, logo, everything matches. There's a list of partners. There's one called Alan. Alan McInnes. And get this. They mention Minerva as one of their top clients. What do you think?"

Reacher said, "Dial the number."

Hannah entered the digits and hit Call plus the button for the speaker. A man answered after three rings.

He said, "McInnes. Who's this?"

Reacher said, "Danny Peel. I got your note. I'll see you at Coal Creek, 11:30."

"Wait. I'm not sure it's safe."

"Want to pick another venue? Name it."

"Not the venue. You. How do I know you're Danny?"

"How else would I know your number?"

"I don't know. OK. What's your middle name?"

Reacher looked at Hannah. She shook her head. He said, "I don't have one."

"Where did you live before you moved to Winson?"

"Gerrardsville, Colorado."

"Name of your last boss before you went to work at Minerva?"

"Sam Roth."

"OK." There was a moment's silence. "I'll meet you. But come alone. And don't be late."

Bruno Hix ended the call. He was sitting in his kitchen, in his pajamas. He didn't like to be at the prison too early on release days. There was always some kind of last minute logistical snafu and he couldn't risk encountering anything that would put him in a bad mood before his speech. He took a sip of coffee, switched to his regular phone, and called Brockman.

"No Plan B," he said. "It's confirmed. Reacher will be nowhere near the ceremony."

Brockman said, "Fantastic news. But, Bruno—you're sure?"

"Positive. I got it straight from the horse's mouth."

Hannah tried to pull a U-turn in the street but the old VW's steering was so heavy and slow to respond she bumped up onto the opposite sidewalk and almost clipped Danny Peel's mailbox. She backed up a couple of yards, hauled on the wheel with all her strength, dropped down onto the street, and started to build a little speed. The bus mustered all the acceleration of a slug.

Reacher looked back at the mailbox. He said, "Stop."

Hannah coasted to the side of the road. Reacher climbed out, walked back, and opened the mailbox lid. The junk was still there. Four envelopes, all loose.

Also in the box was an elastic band. The kind mail carriers use to hold all the correspondence for the same address together. Someone had removed it and set the separate letters free.

Reacher cut across the muddy lot toward the garage. He let himself in and picked up the maintenance log Danny had kept for the Stingray. He flicked through until he found a number of specific characters. Two capitals. The rest lower case. Then he walked back to the VW, climbed in, and said, "We're not going to Hattiesburg."

Chapter 40

The coffee was strong, but it still couldn't keep Lev Emerson awake long enough to reach the state line. He had no choice but to let Graeber drive for a while. He was counting on only napping for a couple of hours, just until he got his second wind, but when he woke up five hours had passed. The van was parked outside a square brick building, four miles north of Vicksburg, Mississippi. The building was the last in a line of three in a paved compound a stone's throw from the river. It was surrounded by trees and a rusty chain-link fence. There was a single-width gate, which hadn't been locked. Each building had two entrances. A vehicle door to the left, tall and wide enough for a van or small truck. And a personnel door to the right. Each had four windows in its second floor, square and dark beneath their crumbling concrete lintels.

Graeber waited for Emerson to get his bearings, then said, "Morning, boss."

Emerson grunted and checked his mug for any last dregs of coffee.

Graeber said, "The other two buildings are deserted. This one doesn't look much better but the locks are new. They're solid. It's in use."

"Any sign of the guy?"

"Not yet."

Emerson checked his watch. It was 8:30. He grunted again, a little louder this time.

Twenty minutes later a car appeared at the gate. A huge wallowing Cadillac coupe from the 1970s. It was burgundy. Its paint was shiny. It was well cared for. A guy climbed out. He could have been the same age as the car. He was a little under six feet tall, stocky, with a round face and brown curly hair. He was wearing a brown leather jacket and jeans. He shoved the gate open. Drove through. Closed the gate. Continued to the last building in line, and swung in next to Emerson's van.

Emerson worked on the principle that if something wasn't broken there was no need to fix it. He waited for Graeber to jump out with a clipboard in his hand, approach the guy from the Cadillac, and say he needed a quote to get a special consignment delivered. Then Emerson slipped out through the passenger door, looped around the back of the van, and clamped a rag soaked in chloroform over the guy's mouth and nose. He didn't hold it in place as long as he had done in St. Louis, the day before. They didn't have to move the guy very far. They just wanted to keep him compliant while they got set up. And because no one could notice what they were doing, there was no need for subtlety. So they let him fall to the ground when the chemical had done its job and dragged him toward the building.

Graeber took the keys from the guy's pocket and found the one he needed to open the vehicle door. There were two vans inside. Both were black. One was a few years old and displayed the kind of dents and scuffs that accrue during a life spent earning a living. The other looked almost unused. The first was empty. The second had an air-conditioning unit on its roof and its cargo area was fitted out with full length roll-out racks on both sides.

The far end of the space was set up as a mechanical bay. There were three giant toolboxes on wheels along the wall. Oil stains on the floor. And a hoist attached to a girder on the ceiling with chains hanging down for removing engines. The cogs looked seized and rusty like they hadn't seen much action for many years.

Graeber reversed both vans out into the courtyard and then watched the guy from the Cadillac while they waited for him to regain consciousness. Emerson searched the office, which was walled off in the remaining quarter of the building's first floor. He found all the usual administrative stuff. A calendar on the wall. A computer on the desk. Paperwork and stationery items in the drawers. But nothing that gave any insights into the confidential side of the guy's business. The only thing of interest was a pod-style coffee machine on a low file cabinet. Emerson used it to make a mug for himself and another for Graeber.

When the Cadillac guy woke up he was naked. He was on tiptoes in a pool of congealed oil. His arms were above his head, cable tied to the chains from the engine hoist. A barrel he had never seen before was standing in front of him, just too far away to kick. There was a ladle on top of it. The kind they use in restaurants. The guy was silent for a moment. He stayed still. Confusion creased his face. Then anger took over. He yelled. He yanked on the chains. He tugged them from side to side. He kicked out in all directions. But all he did was hurt his wrists and skin the balls of his feet.

Emerson heard the racket and came through from the office. He waited for the guy to settle down, then said, "You've probably figured this out for yourself by now, but we're not interested in you delivering anything for us."

The guy's eyes opened wide. "What are you interested in?"

"Deliveries you made in the past." Emerson opened the phone he had taken from the guy in St. Louis and called up the photograph of Carpenter. He held it out for the guy to see. "Specifically, deliveries you made for this man."

"What about them? I picked up a container. Usually just one. Took it to a place in New Jersey."

"Where did you pick up these containers?"

"It varied. One of five locations. I got told which one the day before. They're all within an hour of here."

"You knew what was in the containers?"

"No."

"Don't lie to me."

"I didn't know. I didn't ask. They didn't tell. But I'm not stupid. I guess I had a good idea."

"Good. Now, Carpenter. How do I find him?"

"I don't know."

Emerson opened the barrel, took a ladleful of its contents, and poured it on the floor about eighteen inches from the guy's feet.

The guy wriggled his toes farther away. "What's that?"

"Something to focus your mind." Emerson took out a box of matches, struck one, and lit the little creamy puddle on fire. "Another name for it is napalm."

Emerson took another ladleful from the barrel and stepped toward the guy. Who started to hop on the toes of one foot. His other leg was raised, ready to kick if he got the chance. Emerson flung the gel. It landed and spread out across the guy's crotch and thighs.

The guy screamed.

"What?" Emerson said. "I haven't lit it, yet. Tell me how to find Carpenter."

"You can't find him. No one can. He disappeared, like a month ago. I tried to reach him myself but I couldn't. He's gone. History. No more."

"Other contacts in his organization?"

"He was the only one. It was a security thing."

"That's a shame. It means you're no use to me. You're just a piece of annoying trash. And we all know the most environmentally friendly way to dispose of trash." Emerson took out another match.

"Wait! Listen. Three weeks ago, maybe four, a new guy came on the scene. He only interacted remotely, and he said he represented a different supplier, but I think it was the same one."

"Why?"

"The guy already knew the kind of bona fides I would want. They came through real quick. It was the same product. The same containers. The same destination. There've been two pickups so far. Both places the old organization used. A third pickup is scheduled, and that's at another place they used. You tell me—coincidence?"

"This is just dawning on you now? You weren't suspicious before?"

"Why would I care? I figured they must have a reason for this new name. New identity. Maybe someone was muscling in. Maybe they'd had quality issues in the past. Needed a fresh start. As long as there was regular work, good money, and no feds, I was happy."

"The third pickup that's scheduled. When is it?"

"Today."

"Time? Place?"

"At 1:00 P.M. Abandoned paper mill ten miles southeast of a no-bit little town called Winson."

"Any specific procedures or protocols when you show up?"

"I just drive in and wait. Another van comes in.

Their guys open my doors, slide in the container, and off we all go. Two minutes, and I don't even have to get out of the van."

"You use the new-looking one?"

The guy nodded.

Emerson said, "The plans for the day have changed. We're going in your place."

"OK. That's cool. What do you want me to do? Lie low for a while? Leave town for a couple of months? I can do that. And I can forget your faces. Anyone asks, you were never here. We never met. OK?"

Emerson crossed to the tool chests and rummaged through their drawers until he found a tray with three-inch sides. The kind of thing mechanics use to catch oil when they drain an engine. He said, "There's something else you need to know. One of the consignments you transported for Carpenter was destined for my son."

"So your kid got what he needed? That's a good thing, right? Demand has to be met somehow. But if this is about the price you paid that's not down to me. So how about this? I donate my fee. To him. To you. To whoever you want."

Emerson plunged the tray into the barrel and pulled it out, full. "You think the price was high?"

"I don't know the price. I was just thinking aloud."

"I'll tell you the price my son paid." Emerson darted forward and dumped the gel from the tray on the floor around the guy's feet. "He paid with his life."

"No. Please. Stop. Your son died? That's horrible. I'm sorry. But it's not my fault."

"I think it is." Emerson struck another match. "And I think it's fair you pay the same."

Hannah kept her foot on the brake and the gear stick in neutral. "How can it be a trick? The company checked out. The letter's genuine. If you don't show up the guy who sent it could get spooked. He seemed twitchy enough already. We may never get another chance to meet him. To find out what Danny discovered. Which could be our only link to whoever killed Sam."

Reacher said, "Have you still got the company information on your phone?"

Hannah nodded.

Reacher said, "Call the switchboard. Ask for Alan McInnes."

Hannah shrugged, but she did as Reacher asked.

The switchboard operator said, "I'm sorry. Mr. McInnes isn't in the office at present. Would you like his voicemail? But I should just let you know, Mr. McInnes is in Australia this week at a conference so it could be a while before he can respond."

Hannah hung up the call. She said, "How did you know?"

Jed Starmer wanted the bike to be safe until it was time to return it to the messenger so he lifted it over a little stone wall at the side of the road, a hundred yards short of the prison, and covered the rest of the ground on foot.

Jed had never seen a place like the prison before. He didn't like it. Not one bit. The metal fence with its rolls of razor wire scared him. He imagined being trapped behind it. He imagined the guards in the watchtowers shooting at him. The cameras panning from side to side on their poles, tracking him if he tried to run. The floodlights shining on him if he tried to hide. He shivered, despite the warmth of the morning sun.

Jed threaded his way through a bunch of folding chairs and wandered across to a temporary fence. It had been set up with a semicircle of sawhorses around the edge of the curved road that bulged out from the front of the prison. He picked a spot in line with a little outdoor stage. He guessed that was where the action would be. It was to the side of a building he thought might be the prison's main entrance. It was hard to be sure because a kind of tent had been set up around it. On the other side of the stage there was a car. A BMW. Black, and very shiny. It was the only vehicle he could see. It was facing a platform with two TV cameras on it. A large one on a tripod, and a small one that someone had set on the floor. The only other people who were around were wearing uniforms. They were gray with yellow trim and peaked caps, like the private cops Jed had once seen at a mall.

Jed was tired and his mind started to drift. He thought about his dad. Inside the prison. Stuck there for years even though he had done nothing wrong. Desperate to get out. Jed couldn't imagine how awful that would feel. How badly it could mess a person up.

He began to wonder if the woman in the old VW had been right. Maybe it was a mistake to just show up.

Reacher said, "I found a book in the garage where Danny kept records of car things. The handwriting was the same as the address on the envelope I saw in Angela's purse."

Hannah said, "So Danny sent that letter to himself?"

Reacher nodded.

"Why?"

"To keep it safe. He found something out that he shouldn't have. He realized he was in danger. Maybe he went to the police and picked up the same vibe you did, yesterday. Anyway, he figured if the proof was in the mail no one could find it. And take it. I bet it was a constant recurring thing. Every time it was delivered, I bet he mailed it straight back out."

"Then one day he gave it to Angela? Why change his routine?"

"He didn't give it to her. She found it."

"Where?"

"In Danny's mailbox. On Saturday morning. She heard about the fire and came by when he didn't answer his phone. I looked, myself, just now. There's some junk mail, loose, and an elastic band. The whole bunch came bundled together. Someone separated it. Took something. I thought it was Minerva, taking the letter we just opened. I was wrong. It was Angela."

"Why would Angela look in Danny's mailbox?"

"The same reason you looked in Sam's. A friend

was gone. She was checking to see if there was anything important that needed to be handled. She recognized his handwriting. Figured there was something
fishy. Maybe he'd mentioned finding something out to
her, before. Maybe she made the connection herself.
We'll never know."

Hannah was quiet for a moment. Then she said,
"The timing fits, I guess. She got the envelope Saturday morning. Emailed Sam Saturday afternoon. Left
Winson Sunday, because she needed to find someone
to watch her kid. It was maybe late-ish in the day
when she got on the road. And because she was one
person, traveling on her own with no one to share the
driving, she needed an extra overnight stop. Which
got her to Gerrardsville Tuesday morning."

Reacher nodded. "It fits."

"And someone from Minerva knew you looked in
the envelope Angela had before they got it back. They
tried to stop you getting here. They failed. So they
used another envelope addressed to Danny to trick
you into leaving again. They probably figured if you
looked in one, you'd look in another."

"It almost worked."

"That part's fine. But here's what I don't get. The
first envelope was full of stuff about this Begovic
guy's successful appeal. Which appears to be legit.
Now, Angela told Sam the thing she was into had to
do with accounting. What's the connection between
accounting and Begovic?"

"I don't know. Yet."

"Maybe we should try and figure that out instead
of going to the ceremony."

"I'm going to the ceremony. You don't have to."

"What could we possibly learn there? And it could be dangerous. Minerva people are bound to recognize us."

"That would be dangerous. For them."

"How about this? We could watch it online. Minerva has its own YouTube channel. There's no need to go in person."

"There is."

"What?"

"Someone tried very hard to stop me."

Chapter 41

Reacher counted thirty-nine people outside the prison, aside from Hannah and himself.

He knew why eleven of them were there. Jed Starmer had come to see his dad get released. The two camera operators and six security guards were getting paid. Bruno Hix, who had introduced himself as Minerva's founder and CEO, was enjoying the sound of his own voice. And Damon Brockman, who also claimed to be a founder, was standing on the stage, looking smug. Reacher was less sure about the other twenty-eight. He couldn't understand what kind of carrot or stick would make it worth the waste of their time.

Things livened up a little with just over ten minutes on the clock. Hix had been waffling about percentages and quoting philosophers, one minute waving his arms like he worked in an auction house, the next standing stiff and still like someone was shoving a stick up his ass. Then he stopped talking mid-statistic. An old pickup truck trundled into sight behind the crowd. Six people were perched in its load bed. The driver honked his horn and the nearest spectators moved out of the way. For a moment it looked set to make a run at the barrier. Reacher moved alongside Jed Starmer in case there was trouble. Then the truck stopped. The six guys jumped down. They produced placards that were covered with slogans about justice and profit. One showed a cartoon with Lady Justice's scales weighed down with dollar bills. A guy raised a bullhorn. He started yelling demands that the prison close. The crowd didn't like that. The mood turned ugly. Jeering broke out. The protestors were getting shoved and jostled. The security guards ran over to the fence, nightsticks drawn.

Hix jumped down from the stage, microphone in hand, and strode across to the fence. He said, "Stop. Let the people speak."

The guy with the bullhorn took the microphone. He was silent for a moment, then mumbled his way through a litany of complaints and accusations.

Hix nodded and pulled a series of concerned expressions, then he took the microphone back and the sound immediately became clear and louder. He said, "My young friends, I'm glad you came here today. I'm glad—" Hix locked eyes with Reacher and suddenly he couldn't find his voice. He stuttered and spluttered for a moment, then tore his gaze away. "I'm glad you care about fairness and humanity. If you were outside another correctional corporation's facility, there's a very good chance you'd be right. But here, I'm glad to say, you're wrong. Minerva cares for the health of those who reside within our walls. Minerva cares for safety. For education. For unlocking potential. And"— Hix turned and dashed back to the stage—"we care about righting wrongs wherever we find them. But don't just take my word for it. Ladies and gentlemen, I give you Anton Begovic."

A flap in the tent that was covering the prison entrance opened and a man stepped out. He was wearing a dark suit and a tie and his hair looked freshly cut. He stood for a moment, blinking in the sunlight. Then Brockman, who had done nothing up to that point, jumped down, took the guy's arm, and helped him onto the stage.

The guy took the microphone and stepped forward. "Thank you all for being here. Thank you, Mr. Hix. Thank you, Mr. Brockman. And most of all, thank you to the Minerva corporation and everyone who is associated with it. When others wanted to lock me up, they fought to set me free. I am truly grateful, and I swear with you all as my witnesses that I will make the most of every second that has been given back to me."

The guy waved, then Hix and Brockman shepherded him off the other side of the stage and into the BMW.

Jed ducked and tried to scramble under the barrier.

Reacher grabbed him, pulled him back, and wrapped an arm around his chest.

Jed wriggled and squirmed. "Let me go. I need to get to my dad. He's not messed up. You guys are wrong."

"I can't let you go, Jed," Reacher said. "Because that man is not your dad."

Lev Emerson had stood at the entrance to the workshop just north of Vicksburg and watched the flames curl and flutter. He had watched the body twitch and twist. Brighter and faster then softer and gentler until the corner with the chains hanging from the ceiling was dull and limp and ordinary once more. He crossed the courtyard to where Graeber was waiting after stowing the barrel and checking his mapping apps for an abandoned paper mill near the town of Winson.

They drove in convoy, Graeber in front in the shiny black van that was expected at the paper mill, Emerson behind in his shabby white workhorse. They took a short jog east then settled in on a steady southbound heading until they hit the outskirts of Jackson. Then Graeber pulled into a gas station. When they were both done topping off their tanks Graeber pointed to a diner at the side of the site. It was nothing fancy. Just a long, low brick building with a flat roof and a neon sign promising good food.

"What do you think?" Graeber said. "Want to grab a bite? Some coffee? We have plenty of time."

Emerson looked the place over. There were a dozen open parking spots outside its windows. It would be no problem to keep an eye on the white van. He said, "Sure. Why not?"

———

The inside of the diner was as simple and functional as the outside. There were ten four-tops, split into two lines of five. Plain furniture. A gray linoleum floor, scratched in places. A serving counter with two coffee machines. A clock on the wall. A framed map of the state. And a TV. A large one. It was the only newish thing in the place. It was tuned to a local news channel. The sound was off, but words summarizing the action were scrolling across a plain band at the bottom of the screen.

Emerson was facing the windows. He was glancing at a menu, wondering what to eat, then Graeber grabbed his forearm.

Graeber said, "The TV. Look."

The screen was filled with the scene from outside the prison in Winson. A guy in a suit with a brand-new haircut was standing on a stage, speaking into a microphone. The text said, *Exoneree Anton Begovic released from custody following successful appeal, thanks to Minerva Corporation. Minerva CEO Bruno Hix said . . .*

"Begovic?" Emerson pulled out the stolen phone, opened it to Carpenter's picture, and held it up.

Graeber said, "Or Carpenter. It's the same guy. No doubt about it."

The camera followed the guy in the suit as a couple of other men guided him into a waiting BMW. The car eased forward, slowly, because of the crowd.

Emerson said, "Look at the plate—MC1. Contact

Fassbender. He owes us a favor. Tell him to find out who owns that car. Like, yesterday."

An accounting thing, Angela had told Sam. Reacher had expected something complicated. Something that would require training and qualifications to unravel. But it turned out to be the simplest discrepancy in the book. *One too many.* One prisoner. One breakfast. One lunch. One dinner . . .

Jed jumped into the back of the VW and said, "How can you be so sure that wasn't my dad? You've never met him."

"I saw his photo from the day he was arrested."

"People change," Hannah said. She pulled an exaggerated, fake shiver. "If you saw a picture of me from sixteen years ago . . ."

Reacher said, "Part of the real Anton Begovic's ear is missing. Ears don't grow back. That's why the photo in the envelope in Angela's purse was so critical. Without it we would never have known the wrong guy just got released."

Hannah sped up a little. "Who did get released?"

"Someone who needed a new ID. We'll find out, if we can catch up to Hix."

"What if Hix doesn't go home?"

"I think he will. He wasn't expecting us to be at the ceremony, so he wasn't expecting to run. He'll either hole up or grab some supplies for the road."

"And if you're wrong?"

"I'll call Detective Harewood. Have him bring in the FBI."

Jed said, "Stop talking about this Hix guy. I don't care about him. I only care about my dad."

"We need to find Hix so we can find out what happened to your dad."

"What happened? Nothing happened. He's in prison. Still locked up."

Reacher didn't reply. Neither did Hannah.

Jed said, "Where else could he be? The wrong guy came out. My dad must still be inside."

Reacher said, "The wrong guy came out. That's all we know for sure."

"The guy took my dad's name." Jed started to cry. "You can't have two people with the same name. My dad's dead. Isn't he? That's what you're not saying. He's dead and I never even got to meet him."

Hannah cruised slowly past the big white house. The BMW was back in the same spot as it had been that morning.

"Thank goodness. He's there." Hannah pulled over to the grass verge at the side of the road. "But what can we do now? You can't buzz the intercom and ask Hix to let you in. I bet the gates are too strong to smash through. They probably have sensors that go off if you climb them. There's broken glass cemented on the top of the walls. And I bet there are sensors in the ground on the other side."

"Back up, close to the wall." Reacher took a gun from the pillowcase. The desert tan SIG P320 he'd captured from the second pair of guys at the truck stop on I-20. "Jed, look in the bottom drawer. I need five blankets. And the cushion from the couch."

Reacher tied two of the blankets corner to diagonal corner to maximize their combined length. He rolled them to form a makeshift rope, coiled it, and slung it around his neck. Then he tied the other three blankets together the same way. He secured one end to the VW's rear fender and climbed onto its roof. Hannah passed him the cushion. He set it down on the glass that was fixed into the top of the wall. He laid the blanket over the cushion and lowered it slowly to make sure it didn't touch the ground on the far side. He stepped onto the wall and stood with his feet on the narrow strip of brick without any shards. Checked that the blankets hung down far enough to grab if he needed to climb back out. Then he looked around. There was a clear band of grass, four feet wide, at the base of the wall. That's where the sensors would be buried. Beyond the grass, running the length of the property, there was a swathe of trees twenty feet deep. Reacher aimed for a gap between two of the thinner ones. He jumped, threw himself forward, rolled, and pushed himself up into a crouch. He listened. There were no alarms. No bells. No dogs.

Reacher straightened up and moved behind the tree line until he got to a point where he could approach the house on a diagonal, toward one corner. That way there would be no windows directly facing him. He crawled forward until he was at the limit of his cover. Then he lay for five minutes, completely still, observing.

There was a sound, behind him and to the left. A twig snapping. Reacher hustled back then got up and ran toward the source of the noise. He rounded a tree. And found a man. He was sitting at the base of the trunk, hugging his knees to his chest. He peered up at Reacher and whispered, "Please don't hurt me. Please don't hurt me. Please don't hurt me."

Reacher kept his voice low. "I'm not going to hurt you. Who are you?"

The guy straightened a little and when Reacher could see more of him he thought he looked like a young Che Guevara. The guy said, "My name's Maurice. You?"

"Reacher. What are you doing here?"

"I'd rather not say."

"You work for Hix? Or anyone at Minerva?"

"Hell, no."

"You going to call the police, or do anything stupid?"

"The police are the last people I'd call. And could I do anything more stupid than get stuck in this damn yard?"

"OK, then. Nice meeting you." Reacher turned and started back toward the house.

"Wait. Hix is home. So's his number two. And some other guy."

Reacher ignored him and kept moving.

Maurice scurried after Reacher. "Wait. Please. I have to ask you. Are you working on a story? Because if you are—"

Reacher said, "Are you a journalist?"

Maurice nodded.

"I'm not. I'm not going to steal your thunder. So stay here. Lie low. Keep quiet. Don't attract any attention. Somebody's life is at stake."

"Somebody's? Lots of people's."

"What do you mean by that?"

"You're here because of the drugs, right? That's why you're going after Hix. What happened? Did you lose a family member? A friend? In a Minerva prison?"

Reacher grabbed Maurice's arm and dragged him back, deeper into the trees. "Tell me what you know. All of it. Now. The nutshell version."

"It's like this. Minerva's an octopus, right? An evil one. On the surface all progressive and enlightened. But the truth? Tentacles everywhere. They cherry-pick inmates. Put them to work. All kinds of ways. Including refining drugs. They do it in their disused segregation units. Supply their own populations. Which is why their death rate is so high. They deny it, but it's true. And they've expanded. They supply other markets now, too."

Drugs made sense, Reacher thought. All prisons have a problem with them. Maybe Minerva saw it as an opportunity. It could be big business. And guys involved in that trade are the kind who find themselves needing new identities from time to time. He said, "Where's your proof?"

"Death rates. I've got that documented. Nothing else. Yet."

"I'm going to visit with Hix, right now. The subject may come up. Anything concrete I find, it's all yours."

Chapter 42

Reacher left the cover of the trees and approached the house from the southeast. Toward the rear corner. He climbed up onto the porch railing and wrapped his left arm around the column that supported the balcony. He used his right hand to slip the coiled-up blankets from around his neck. He held one end and swung the rest of the length around in an arc. Once. Twice. Then as it neared the top of its third rotation he snapped it in toward the house and straight back out, like a lion tamer with an oversized whip. The tip curled around the column and dropped straight down the other side. Reacher caught it with his left hand. He brought his hands close and gripped both strands together. He shifted the soles of his feet onto the face of the column. Moved his left hand up and pulled. Took a step vertically with his right foot. Moved his right hand. Stepped with his left foot. He kept going until he could grab the upper rail then he hauled himself up and over and rolled onto the balcony.

Reacher got to his feet. He stood still and listened. He heard nothing.

Along the side of the house a row of glass doors led out to the balcony. There were four. Maybe from bedrooms. They were all closed and, inside, white drapes were drawn across them. For privacy. Or to combat the heat.

Reacher moved around to the back of the house. The balcony boards were solid. His feet made no noise. He looked down into the yard. It was an even space, fifty feet square, carved out from the trees and covered with grass. Hix must have been getting ready for a party. There was a bar to the left with a line of silver buckets for ice, tables with trays of plastic cups, and two giant trash cans done up to look like Greek urns. In the center of the lawn a space had been covered to make a temporary dance floor. And there was a stage to the right with a drum kit, microphone stands, and a lighting gantry extending across its whole width.

Reacher continued around the balcony until he found what he was looking for. A sash window with frosted glass. A bathroom. He took out his ATM card and pushed it up into the jamb between the upper and lower panes. He worked it from side to side until the latch eased around and disengaged. He lifted the lower section an inch and looked inside. He saw a tub. A sink. A toilet. But no people. He opened the window the rest of the way and climbed through. He crossed to the door. Opened it a crack. Saw no one. He carried on to the landing. It was a broad U shape with an ornate rail around the open side, like an internal version of the balcony. The hallway was below. The stairs were at the far end. Voices were echoing up from the first floor. Three men. They sounded familiar. And they sounded angry.

Reacher crept down the stairs. He kept to one side, where the treads were least likely to creak. Made it to the hallway and crossed to the first door to the right. The men were yelling on the other side. Reacher recognized the voices from the ceremony at the prison.

Brockman said, "It's your fault. If you hadn't lost your nerve and hidden away like a scared little kid we—"

"You're blowing everything out of proportion." It was the guy who had emerged from the tent, pretending to be Begovic. "I was scared, sure. I'm not an idiot. But I was still working. Our contacts are reestablished. Deliveries resume this afternoon. I got better rates from two of our customers. There's no shortage of demand out there. And we have all the supply we could ever need. The only question is, how much money do we want to make?"

"But Reacher saw you."

"So?"

"And he saw the photograph. He knows you're not Begovic."

"Hasn't the photo been destroyed?"

"Yes."

"The fingerprint record replaced?"

"Yes."

"And there's no DNA on file for Begovic. So there's no way to prove I'm not him. You should have talked to me at the start. I would have told you. There's no danger. Especially since the real Begovic will be boxed up within the hour. By tomorrow he'll be in small pieces. There's nothing Reacher or anyone else can do to stop that."

Reacher opened the door and walked through. He found himself in a kitchen. It looked like it had recently been renovated. The surfaces were all marble and pale wood and stainless steel. Three guys were sitting on tall stools at a breakfast bar. They all spun around.

Brockman stood up. "Reacher? The hell are you doing here?"

Reacher closed the gap between them in two strides and punched Brockman in the face. He fell back, slammed into the counter, and slid onto the floor between his two buddies.

Reacher turned to the guy who was posing as Begovic. He said, "You. Real name?"

The guy climbed down off the stool. He said, "Bite me."

"Unusual. I bet you had a tough time at school." Reacher punched him in the gut. The guy doubled over. Reacher slammed his elbow down into the back of his head and the guy's legs folded and he hit the floor, face-first.

Reacher turned to Hix.

Hix stayed on his stool. His phone was in his hand. He said, "Don't look at me. I'm not telling you a thing."

Hix jabbed the phone three times. Reacher took it from him. There were three digits on the display: 911. But there was no call in progress. Reacher dropped the phone and crushed it with his heel. Then he walked around the counter to the business side of the kitchen. He opened the drawers in turn until he found one with utensils in it. He took out a knife. A small one. Its blade was only three inches long. But it was sharp. Designed for delicate work. Peeling. Mincing. Dicing. Reacher held it up for Hix to see. He said, "I watched you on the stage this morning. You looked like you were having fun. Like you loved the attention. The cameras. So tell me this: Would the cameras still love you if I slice your nose off and make you eat it?"

Reacher was inside the big white house for fewer than ten minutes. When he came out he was carrying a prison ID on a lanyard and a car key. He crossed to Hix's BMW and opened the driver's door. He leaned in and hit a button up on the ceiling near the rearview mirror. The gates started to swing back over the driveway. He called to Maurice and told him to come out from his hiding place in the trees. Then he walked to the end of the driveway and called to Hannah. He told her to retrieve the cushion from the wall and the blanket that was tied to the fender and bring the VW around to the front of the house.

Hannah parked at the bottom of the stairs leading to the front door. Jed had moved to the passenger seat. Maurice was standing nervously near the VW's rear hood.

"OK," Reacher said. "Here's the deal. Jed—your father is alive. I will try to keep him that way but I'm not going to lie. He's short on time, and he's in a lot of trouble. So no promises. Hannah—I need you to take Jed to the Riverside Lodge. Get a room. Use the name J. P. Slough. Pay cash. Call Detective Harewood. We do need him to get the feds involved. Tell him to start here, at the house. If I'm not at the hotel in two hours, leave town. Don't come back. Maurice— you were half right. Something is killing Minerva inmates. Maybe outsiders, too. But it's not drugs."

Reacher took the pillowcase and went back to the BMW. By the time he had figured out which switches and toggles to press and push to get the seat adjusted so he could fit behind the wheel, Hannah had slid into the passenger seat.

She said, "You're trying to dump me again. That's a nasty habit."

Reacher said, "I'm not dumping you. You just can't come with me this time. It's a one-person job. And I need you to keep an eye on Jed. If things go south, if his dad doesn't make it, he's going to need a lot of help."

"His dad's really still alive?"

"I believe so."

"Where?"

"In the prison."

"Who's the imposter?"

"A guy who goes by Carpenter. Might not be his real name. He's a middle man between Minerva and the clients they supply. He sold a guy out in Paraguay ten years ago. Expected him to die in jail. He didn't. He's back in the States and he's looking to get even. Minerva couldn't wash their hands of Carpenter because they need his contacts. So Carpenter needed a new ID. They took advantage of Begovic's pardon to make the switch. Carpenter was scared so he hid in the prison until the ceremony. Danny Peel noticed the discrepancy in the numbers. He dug. Joined the dots. Told Angela, who told Sam. The rest you know."

"Where are the Minerva guys now? Hix and Brockman and Carpenter?"

"In the house. The kitchen."

"We can't leave them unguarded."

"They're not going anywhere."

"Under their own steam, perhaps. But what if some of their other guys come looking for them?"

"That's why we need Harewood to bring the FBI."

"What if they get rescued before the feds show up?"

"That's a risk we'll have to run. I can't stay and watch them. I have to get to Begovic."

"I'll watch them. I'm not going to run and hide and leave them with the front door open. They killed Sam. I'm not going anywhere until they're in custody.

It's my decision. My risk to run. And I have my SIG. I'm not afraid to use it. You saw that last night."

Reacher said nothing.

Hannah said, "This other guy who's lurking around. Is he a revolutionary or something? Or does he just have bad dress sense?"

"His name's Maurice. He's a journalist. He seems harmless."

"He can babysit Jed, then."

"I guess."

"Jed was right. They are going to kill his dad. And I don't see how you can stop them."

"I have an idea."

"The guy's in a prison cell. You can't break him out. You do know that? Sam studied the ways people try to escape. You need months to plan. To observe. To find sloppiness in the guards' routines. Faulty equipment. Building failures. Staff who are vulnerable because they're getting divorced or they drink or use drugs or gamble or are in debt. You need luck. And even then, ninety-nine percent of attempts fail."

"My odds are a little better than that."

"Really? What makes you think so?"

"Harold wasn't wearing a wedding ring. And I saw four neat triangles of grass."

Reacher parked the BMW on Harold's driveway. His house was small and shabby. It was a single story with peeling paint, windows caked in dirt, a minimal porch, and a scruffy weed-filled yard. Reacher started with the mailbox. It was about set to overflow. He didn't pay much attention to the kinds of letters that were in there. He just took an elastic band from the first bundle he found and moved on to the back door. It wasn't hard to figure out which key to use from the collection in the pillowcase. It was the most scratched one. Reacher let himself in, crossed the kitchen quickly, and followed the corridor until he found Harold's bedroom. He opened the closet. There was only one suit hanging there. It was black. A white formal shirt was on a hanger next to it. And rolled up in a drawer, a tie. Also black. Funeral attire, Reacher thought. But that didn't bother him. It would be fine for what he needed. He changed into Harold's clothes and put his own things in the pillowcase. Then he moved on to the garage.

There was theoretically room in it for three cars but two of the bays were taken up by weight-lifting equipment. There were pictures on the wall of Harold in weird spandex outfits grappling with all kinds of heavy objects. Tractors. Tires. Farm animals. A wheel of cheese. Reacher had questions. The third vehicle bay was empty. There were oil stains on the floor. The remains of a paint spill. Dried-up residue from other fluid leaks. But no logbook. No meticulous records had been kept. Probably no meaningful maintenance had ever taken place in there. Reacher crossed to the tiny worktable. He took a knife. A screwdriver. A hammer. And a roll of duct tape.

When he was back in the car Reacher took all the remaining cash out of the wallets in the pillowcase. He rolled it up, secured it with the elastic band he had taken, and put it in his pocket. He emptied everything out of the pillowcase except for the tools and the SIG. Slung the lanyard with the ID on it around his neck. And drove to the prison.

The little crowd had disappeared. So had the security guards and the camera operators. The only people left outside the prison were the contractors, who were strolling around, shifting the chairs, and stacking the dismantled pieces of fence. The tent was still obscuring the entrance, though it was less rigid than it had been. Its roof was sagging and its sides were billowing in the breeze. The surface of the stage had been removed. It was piled up in the back of a truck that was sitting next to the exposed framework. Reacher parked next to the truck. He climbed out of the BMW and started to march around and stare at the contractors like a boss. The contractors looked away and pretended they hadn't seen him.

Reacher made his way to the entrance, leaned down like he was inspecting something, and gently set the roll of money on its side, next to the fence. Then he strolled back toward the BMW. When he was close he turned to the nearest trio of contractors.

"Hey," Reacher yelled. "You three. Stop loafing around. Get that tent taken down. We've got visitors coming soon. How are they supposed to get to the entrance?"

The contractors grumbled and muttered and drifted away to do as they'd been told. Reacher took the pillowcase from the car and carried it to the truck by the stage. He opened the door and put it on the passenger seat. Then he stood back and watched the contractors. He waited. After a couple of minutes one of them noticed the wad of cash. He stepped closer to it. He leaned down to pick it up. But his greed and surprise had overridden his memory. He'd gotten too close to the fence. The sensors under the ground detected his footsteps. They fired off instant signals to the security computers in the control room. A klaxon sounded. Red lights flashed. All the floodlights in the complex came on at once. And all the nearby cameras rotated on their posts to give the operators the clearest possible view of the cause of the problem.

Reacher jumped in behind the wheel of the truck, fired it up, and backed across to a spot near the fence at the foot of the closest watchtower. He grabbed the pillowcase. Gripped it in his teeth. Scrambled onto the truck's roof. Stretched up and took hold of the railing at the top of the tower's half wall. He pushed with his legs. Pulled with his arms. Poured himself headfirst over the railing. And was met by no one. There was no guard in the tower. No one with a gun or a uniform was in sight.

Reacher peered over the tower wall on the prison side of the fence. The grass triangle was below him, ahead around sixty degrees. It looked as green and lush as it had from the outside. From the higher elevation he could see the bricks surrounding it were painted red. A sign for people to keep away from it. Because of its purpose. It was a pit for guards to fire warning shots into. Its ground was soft. It was absorbent. It posed no danger of ricochets. There had been at least one riot recently. Hannah had told him about it. But there was no bullet damage in the neatly manicured grass. Therefore the towers were no longer used, except as window dressing when Hix was staging a publicity stunt. The heavy lifting in the world of surveillance was done by electronics now. Cameras and sensors. Reacher smiled to himself. It was like they used to say in the army. Sometimes there's no substitute for the Eyeball, Human, Mark One.

Chapter 43

The watchtowers were no longer regularly used, but they were still connected to the meshed-in walkways that crisscrossed the prison site. Reacher climbed down the ladder and started toward the building that housed the control center. He knew where it was because he had made Hix draw a diagram.

Reacher passed through five doors along the way. They were all secured. Hix's ID card opened all of them. The final one was the control center itself. Beyond that point the doors were designated operational, not administrative. That meant they could only be operated remotely. Which was the whole point of Reacher's visit.

There were two people on duty when Reacher entered the control room. Both men. Both in their late fifties. Both with enough miles on the clock to make sound decisions in times of stress. That was the theory. A hypothesis based more on the likelihood of escape attempts and riots than a one-man incursion. Even an incursion by one man who could do as much damage on his own as a medium-sized riot. But either way the theory held water. Reacher gave the guys instructions. They followed to the letter without argument. They didn't even balk when Reacher locked them in the storage cupboard and broke the key in the outside of the lock.

Reacher checked the display on the access control panel. It was rudimentary, but easy to interpret. The symbols representing all the doors between the control center and the segregation unit S1 were green. The other doors were all red. That was what he wanted to see so Reacher took the hammer from the pillowcase and smashed the controls. Then he smashed all the CCTV monitors. There was no way he would be able to disable all the cameras on his route. Not easily. And not quickly. But there was no sense in leaving any potential relief crew with the ability to use any of them.

There were five more doors to pass through before Reacher would get to Begovic's cell. The first two were in sections of the mesh walkway. Reacher was completely exposed while he was in there. He was in the heart of enemy territory. Massively outnumbered. Completely outgunned. If either of the doors didn't open he would have a serious problem. Or if there was some anti-infiltration system he was unaware of, ready to kick in and trap him. Or a backup control panel. Or an automatic reset procedure. He knew there were all kinds of ways he might not leave the place alive.

Reacher approached the first door slowly. Calmly. He stretched out a hand. Pushed. The door swung open. So did the second. The third led from the mesh walkway to a covered corridor. A smaller space. Completely enclosed. He would be like a rat caught in a drainpipe if the doors froze. The third opened. So did the fourth, which led into the segregation unit itself. Reacher was at the center of the cross, on the first floor. Above him were the three rooms that formed the unit's command hub. In the middle of each wall a door led to one of the cell wings. Reacher needed the west wing. He identified the door. The fifth. He pushed. It opened.

Reacher paused and looked at each cell door in turn. There were sixteen. Fifteen of these were always unlocked because the wing was not officially in commission. It was only being used for under-the-table projects. Hix had sworn that Begovic would be the only person locked up in there. But if he had tucked a couple of tame psychopaths away in the place, Hix might have thought it was a lie he could get away with.

Reacher listened. He picked up the sound of someone moving. Two people. In the first cell on his right. W1. Hix had described it as a transport preparation area. The door was standing open an inch. Reacher pushed it the rest of the way. Inside, there was an operating table. A metal trolley covered with surgical tools. A cabinet full of drugs. Two drip stands. A heart monitor. A person-sized metal box with a 12V car-style battery at one end to power the system that controlled its internal temperature, like a futuristic travel coffin. A defibrillator mounted on the wall. And two men wearing scrubs.

One of the men grabbed a scalpel from the trolley and lunged at Reacher. Straight forward. Going for Reacher's gut. But with no power. No venom. The guy was no knife fighter. That was for sure. Reacher knocked his arm aside, continued to spin, building momentum, and punched the guy just below his ear. The force hurled him across the operating table and into the narrow gap next to the wall.

Reacher turned to the other guy. He was standing with his hands up. He said, "Don't hurt me. I won't cause you any trouble. I'll do anything you want."

"You're getting ready to *prepare* Begovic?"

"I guess. They don't tell us names."

"You're going to chop him up?"

"God, no. The buyer does that. We send the bodies out whole."

"Who's the buyer?"

"I don't know."

Reacher stepped closer.

The guy said, "I swear. It's way above my pay grade. But there's a rumor. This one's going to our biggest customer. They work out of a ship. Off the Jersey coast. In international waters. Where there are no regulations."

"So the guys on the ship cut him up. And do what? Store his body parts until they're needed?"

"Eventually. He'll stay alive while only nonessential organs are harvested. You know. Corneas. One kidney. Skin. Some kinds of bone. The big joints. And blood. Blood replenishes itself, so it makes sense to keep him alive as long as possible."

"How much are all those things worth?"

"They use everything, once he's dead. It comes to $800,000, maybe."

"You send people to this place. People who are alive when they leave here."

"It's my job. I just do what I'm told."

Reacher felt the bile rising from his stomach so he stepped forward, butted the guy in the face, and went back out into the corridor.

Cells W2, W4, and W6 were empty. So was W3. W5 showed signs of recent use. There was a regular twin bed with a pale blue comforter and a TV perched on a footlocker by the far wall. The room smelled vaguely of pizza and Chinese food. It was where Carpenter had been hiding out before taking Begovic's place at the release ceremony. W7 was empty. And Begovic himself was in W8. He was on the bed when Reacher opened the door, lying absolutely still. For a moment Reacher thought he was dead. That the whole enterprise had been a trap. Then Begovic blinked.

"Anton?" Reacher kept his voice quiet. "My name's Reacher. I'm here to help you. To get you out. We have to get moving now. Can you stand up?"

Begovic didn't move. He didn't speak.

So not dead, Reacher thought. Just catatonic. Which was understandable. The guy had been wrongly locked up for years. Promised his freedom.

Then bundled back into solitary. Reacher felt some sympathy. But he could also feel the seconds ticking away. "Begovic!" he said. "On your feet. Face front. Forward, march."

Begovic stood and moved to the door. Reacher scanned the room for sentimental possessions but he couldn't see any likely candidates so he eased Begovic out into the corridor. Then toward the door at the center of the unit. They were halfway there when the lights went out. There was total darkness for six long seconds. Reacher heard two metallic bangs. One behind him. One in front. Begovic's breathing grew louder. Quicker. Shallower. Then there was a deep *clunk* and the light returned, only at about half the brightness.

"What happened?" Begovic's voice was soft and low.

"Main power went out," Reacher said. "It switched to the backup generators."

"OK." Begovic started moving again.

Not OK, Reacher thought. *Not in the same hemisphere as OK.* But he didn't say anything until he got to the door. There was no point raising the alarm if he was mistaken. Which he wasn't. It was just as he feared.

The door was now locked.

Chapter 44

Emerson and Graeber found the place they were looking for outside Winson with no difficulty. Graeber was driving the black van that was expected at the rendezvous. Emerson was driving the white one. They continued for a quarter of a mile after they spotted the premises then pulled over to the side of the road to figure out their next move.

They were in good time. The area was secluded. The layout looked straightforward. The only issue either of them could see was gaining entry. The site wasn't the most secure they had ever encountered but they were used to working in deserted buildings. Here they would be dealing with at least one person. Maybe more. And they needed to take supplies in with them. The barrel, in particular. Which meant getting the gate open. And doing it quietly.

The best scenario either of them could come up with was that the guy they were looking to surprise was already there. If he was, they could let the chloroform do its work then make as much noise as necessary with the gate. They could dynamite the damn thing if they wanted to.

They spent two more minutes kicking around their options then settled on a plan. A simple one, which was the kind Emerson liked best. They would leave the vehicles where they were for the moment. Take the lightweight stepladder, a tarp, and a rope from the white van. Climb the wall. Recce all the buildings in the compound. Bring the chloroform. And hope they would get lucky.

"What happened?" Begovic said again.

Reacher knew, but he didn't want to get into the details. He remembered hearing all about it from a tech-minded corporal he had met at Leavenworth years ago, when he was there for a prisoner transfer. The guy had explained that prison doors aren't naturally open with the ability to be locked if required. It's the other way around. Their natural state is to be locked, and they can be made to open if required. They work by having two competing magnets. One permanent. One electro. The permanent magnet is fixed into the wall. It naturally pulls a steel bar along a shielded channel in the door and into a socket in the frame, locking it. If the electro magnet receives current, it activates, and because it's set up to be stronger than the permanent magnet, it pulls the steel bar the opposite way, out of the socket in the frame, unlocking it.

The system has two advantages. Doors can easily be locked or unlocked remotely. It's just a question of applying or denying current to the electro magnet. And if the power is cut for any reason, even for an instant, the system fails safe and the doors automatically revert to locked.

Someone had figured out that Reacher had set all the doors on his route to be open. They couldn't lock them with the usual controls because Reacher had trashed them with a hammer. So they cut the power. The backup circuits were kept deliberately isolated from the locks. Reacher couldn't help admiring the simplicity of the solution. He also couldn't hide from the depth of the trouble he was in. Trapped in a place designed by experts to be escape-proof. The only possible way out was to restore current to the electro magnet in the door. Which was categorically impossible from where he was.

Unless . . .

The experts who designed the prison had not counted on one of the cells being filled with medical equipment. Reacher did a mental inventory of what he had seen in W1. He figured there might just be a chance, if his high school physics had stood the test of time. He spun Begovic around and told him to follow.

Reacher grabbed the roll of tissue off the weird one-piece, unbreakable stainless-steel toilet/basin/mirror assembly in the corner of the cell. He handed it to Begovic and said, "I need you to take all the paper off this. I want just the cardboard tube from the inside. OK?"

Begovic said, "Sure." He grabbed the roll, poked one index finger up into the center, and started to pull.

Reacher said, "Stay here a minute. I'll be back." He hurried into cell W3, took the hammer out of the pillowcase, stretched up, and used the claw to rip the metal conduit carrying the lighting circuit off the ceiling. He tore the wiring free and repeated the process in W5 and W7. He returned to W1 and found Begovic had the cardboard tube ready. Reacher took the knife from the pillowcase and cut a slit into the insulation at the end of the first length of wire he'd harvested. He gripped the plastic between one thumb and finger, and the copper between the other thumb and finger. He pulled them in opposite directions and the shiny copper emerged like a snake shedding its skin. He repeated the process with the other lengths of wire and ended up with three six-foot strands, which he joined together into one long piece by twisting the joints between his teeth.

"OK," Reacher said. "Hold out the tube. Grip it tight. Don't let it spin."

Reacher wound the copper around the cardboard again and again, up and down, back and forth, until he had a tight, thick coil with a six-inch tail at each end. He took the defibrillator off the wall. He bound one copper tail to each paddle with duct tape. Led the way out into the corridor and up to the door. Flipped the switch on the defibrillator that read *charge*. Waited for the light to turn from red to green. Turned the dial to the maximum discharge setting. Gripped the insulated handles that were attached to the paddles. Held the coil up to the doorframe on the side opposite the hinges, roughly halfway up. Then he turned to Begovic and said, "OK. When you're ready, hit the shock button."

Begovic said, "Ready." He stretched out a bony finger and jabbed the red disc.

There was a flash like a bolt of lightning. A buzz like a fuse box overloading. A sudden whiff of burning cardboard and scorched paint. And a soft *thud* when the coil hit the floor after the copper tails melted away.

Reacher said, "OK. Let's hope we just fried ourselves a magnet." He went to W1 and returned a moment later carrying the 12V battery from the body-sized box. "One way to find out." There was a metal conduit on the wall leading away from the frame on the hinge side of the door. Reacher used the claw of the hammer to tear it free. He pulled out about three feet of cable, doubled it over the knife blade, and sliced through. He trimmed back the insulation. Separated the two strands until the ends of the wire were far enough apart to reach the battery's poles. He made contact with the positive. Then the negative. Then he listened. He imagined he could hear the steel rod obeying the electromotive force and sliding slowly along its tube inside the door. Pulling clear of the frame. He held the wires in place for twenty seconds. Thirty. Then he dropped them and stood up.

He grabbed the pillowcase and turned to Begovic. "That's it. It worked. Or it didn't."

It had worked. Reacher pushed the door. It swung back. And he came face-to-face with three men. Two guards with AR-15 rifles. And a pasty-faced guy in a suit.

Chapter 45

Reacher grabbed the stock of the nearer guard's gun and pushed it up toward the ceiling. He kicked the second guard in the balls. Butted the nearer guard in the face. And kicked the second guard in the head before he could crawl away.

Begovic ran to the door that led to the exit corridor. It was locked.

The guy in the suit didn't move. He said, "You must be Reacher. Hell of an entrance."

Reacher collected the rifles and slung them over his shoulder. "Who are you?"

The guy didn't reply.

Begovic said, "His name's Riverdale. The warden. He's a complete asshole."

Reacher said, "Riverdale? OK. Time to redeem yourself. These doors need to open."

Riverdale stayed silent for a moment. Then he said, "No problem. I can do that. You just need to do one thing for me first."

Reacher said nothing.

Riverdale pointed at Begovic. "Kill him. Blow his head off. Then you can walk out of here."

Reacher shook his head. "I can see why you don't want him walking around, free. But that doesn't work for me."

Riverdale said, "This is one of those the-good-of-the-many-versus-the-good-of-the-few things. Shoot him, that's one dead person. If you don't shoot him, I can't let you take him with you. That's a given. So the doors will stay locked until more of my guys arrive."

"Have you got any more guys?"

"Plenty more. They'll kill both of you. You'll probably manage to kill me before you bleed out. So that's three dead people. Three dead is worse than one. It's three times as bad. That's ethics 101. So I'm asking you. Do the moral thing. Hell, even Begovic probably sees the logic."

Begovic said, "Screw the logic."

Reacher said, "Logic. No logic. It still doesn't work for me."

Riverdale said, "OK. I'll sweeten the pot. Kill him. We both walk. I give you a million dollars, cash. I hear you're broke. This is your chance to live like a prince."

"I have everything I need. Everything I want. Which makes me better off than any prince. So no dice."

"Look around, Reacher. Look at this place. Do you really want to die here? Today?"

"Everyone has to die someday. Someplace."

"But here? Now?"

"I don't see that happening. Not unless a random meteorite lands on us."

"No? So what's your proposal?"

"Open the doors. Watch us walk out."

"Be serious."

"Open the doors. Shoot yourself in the head. Don't watch us walk out."

Riverdale was silent for a moment, then he said, "Are you married, Reacher?"

Reacher said, "No."

"You ever been married?"

"No."

"Girlfriend? Significant other?"

"No."

"OK. Given you're homeless and destitute, I'm guessing you don't get much action. So I have an idea. Might tip the scales." Riverdale took out his phone and speed-dialed a number. When the call was answered he said, "Reacher's neutralized. I need to get back to my office. Turn the power back on and unlock the doors between S1 and there."

Nothing happened for twenty seconds. Then there were simultaneous clicks from all sides of the room and the lights stepped up a level.

Riverdale started toward the exit door. He said, "Come with me."

Reacher and Begovic followed through the covered corridor. The rat trap, as Reacher already thought of it. He was expecting guards to burst through the door behind them at any second. Or for Riverdale to hit the floor at some predetermined signal and bullets to tear into them from the front. They covered half the distance. Three-quarters. Took a left at the end. And finally made it into the next building. Riverdale led the way up a flight of concrete steps. He said, "This is the original admin block. Everyone else has moved to Hix's new, fancy building. But not me."

The steps opened onto a dingy corridor. It smelled vaguely of stewed cabbage and stagnant drains. There were windows on one side looking down over two of the exercise yards. And six office doors on the other side. At the far end a metal bar was fixed to the wall. Reacher figured it would be for cuffing people to, although it was in a very illogical place.

Riverdale ushered Reacher and Begovic down the length of the corridor and into the last office. The floor was bare concrete. There were fluorescent tubes in cages on the ceiling. Framed pictures of motorcycles on the walls. A couch against the far wall, covered in gold-colored velour. And a metal desk in the center of the room. Riverdale walked across to it and unlocked the top drawer. He took out a tablet computer, activated it with his thumbprint, opened a file of photographs, and handed it to Reacher. He said, "Take a look."

Reacher scrolled through the pictures. They were all of women. The youngest would still be in her teens. The oldest, maybe in her sixties. They were all naked. And the pictures had all been taken in that room.

Riverdale said, "Take your time. Pick your favorite. I can have her here within an hour. You can do what you want to her. For as long as you want."

Reacher said, "What's in it for you?"

"I get Begovic."

"And then?"

"You can go. Free as a bird."

"How?"

"Same way you got in, I guess. Whatever that was."

"You know how I got in. You figured it out from the doors I opened. You think I'm crazy? I'm not going back the same way."

"OK. If I can guarantee you a safe way out, do we have a deal?"

"What kind of safe way?"

Riverdale loosened his tie, unfastened his top button, and fished a key on a chain out from under his shirt. "This opens a gate. A private one. Nobody knows about it but me."

"Where?"

"Far wall of the warehouse. Brings you out on the safe side of the fence. Takes you to a path cut in the riverbank. All the way down to one of the old caves. It's been used since this whole area was French. Pirates. Smugglers. Bootleggers. Now me. I've got stores in there. Food. A boat. An inflatable."

"Bullshit."

"It's true. I was here when the prison was built. Added a few extras of my own. Had a feeling a day like this would come. When someone had to leave in a hurry. Thought it would be me, but hey."

Reacher nodded. "One more question, then we can shake hands. What time is Begovic due to be collected?"

"Why?"

"I have a thirst for knowledge."

Riverdale shrugged. "Twenty-five minutes from now, give or take."

Reacher held out his right hand. Riverdale stepped closer to take it. Then Reacher drove the side of the tablet into Riverdale's throat with his left. Riverdale's larynx collapsed. He fell backward and landed in a sprawl on the couch. He couldn't breathe. He couldn't scream. He clawed at his own neck. Tears streamed from his eyes. Reacher hurled the tablet onto the ground and stomped it into fragments. He crossed to the desk and rummaged through the open drawer. Took out a twelve-inch ruler. Moved back and grabbed Riverdale by the shoulders. Flipped him over. Pinned him to the couch with his knee. Slid the ruler between the back of Riverdale's neck and the steel chain that held the key. And started to turn.

The chain cut into Riverdale's skin. Blood dribbled onto the couch. Reacher turned the ruler again. The chain bit deeper. Blood poured over the fabric faster than it could soak in. Reacher turned the ruler again. And again. And again. The chain cut Riverdale's flesh. It tore his crushed windpipe. And finally sliced through his carotid. Blood sprayed right up the back of the couch and onto the wall. Reacher tilted River-dale's head a few degrees, pushed his neck down into the cushion, and held him there until his heart had nothing left to pump.

Reacher stood and looked at Begovic. He said, "What? I took a rational dislike to the guy. He got what he deserved."

Begovic didn't reply.

Reacher said, "You OK with what just happened?"

"Nothing happened." Begovic's face was blank. "I didn't see a thing."

Reacher nodded and started for the door. "Come on. Time to go."

Begovic didn't move. "What about the key? The secret exit?"

Reacher said, "We're not using it."

"Why not?"

"Either it doesn't exist, or it's booby-trapped."

"How do you know?"

"It's a universal principle. If something seems too good to be true, it is too good to be true."

"I guess." Begovic took one step, then stopped again. "I wish I'd understood that sixteen years ago."

"What happened sixteen years ago?"

"I got arrested. The first time."

Reacher stayed quiet.

Begovic said, "I met a girl. Wanted to buy her a ring. But I didn't have any money. So a guy loaned me some. More than I needed. A friend of my dead uncle."

"The money was dirty."

"Right. But that wasn't the problem. I didn't get

caught. He kept one of the bills with my prints on it. Said he'd tell the police I was passing forgeries unless I did something for him. And it was easy, so I thought, why not?"

"What did he want you to do?"

"Go certain places. Certain times. Where people would see me. That was all."

"You were his patsy in waiting. When he felt the heat, he framed you."

"Right. Then I got in more trouble. Most of that was on me. But it started with him."

"I'm sorry."

"Don't be. Not your fault. Just tell me, how are we going to get out if we can't use the key?"

"I have an idea. But we could use a diversion first."

Reacher smashed the square of glass with his elbow and jabbed the button that lay behind it. A klaxon spooled up and began to wail. Red lights started to flash. Reacher joined Begovic at the window and they looked down at the exercise yards. Inmates started to appear from two of the units. A and B. Slowly at first. The men looked tentative. Uncertain. Then the streams of bodies grew faster. More boisterous. The yards started to fill up. Inmates jostled and pushed. Guards appeared in the watchtowers. One had a bullhorn as well as a rifle. He started to call out instructions. They were muffled. Indistinct. Whatever he was saying, the prisoners took no notice.

Reacher turned to Begovic. "Why is no one coming out of C Block?"

Begovic shrugged. "Don't know."

"Is the block in use?"

"Think so. It was before I went back in solitary. Used to see guys from there in the chow hall. Doubt they closed it down since then. Why would they? Where would everyone go?"

Reacher thought about his conversation with Maurice, the journalist, outside Hix's house. About drugs. Maurice's theory that Minerva was making them. Then supplying them to the captive population. Reacher had dismissed the idea when he found out about the organ trading. Now he was reconsidering. Maybe this wasn't an either/or situation. Maybe Minerva was greedy enough to do both. He said, "These guys from C Block. Do you remember anything about them?"

"I guess. They were kind of cliquey. Sat together, mostly. Didn't talk to the other prisoners. Seemed friendlier with the guards."

Reacher led the way back down the concrete stairs and then along a bunch of corridors and walkways. It was a trial-and-error process. Three times they came to doors that wouldn't open. The fire alarm created a wider accessible zone than usual between the custodial units and the exercise yards, but that didn't extend to the perimeter of the prison. Its border wasn't predictable. Reacher and Begovic had to thread their way back and forth, sometimes doubling back from blockages, sometimes looping around obstacles. Reacher expected to run into a guard at every doorway. Around every bend. But in that respect the diversion was working. Everyone's attention was focused on the exercise yards. And Reacher didn't have to worry about the cameras. There hadn't been time for the monitors to be fixed. So after five long minutes, and a route only a drunk, crazy crow would fly, Reacher and Begovic wound up at the entrance to Unit C.

The door to the hub was standing open. It was wedged by a cinder block. Reacher led the way inside. The basic layout was the same as in the segregation unit. There was a square, central space with wings running perpendicular to each wall. The door to each one was open. The sound of voices and movement and activity was spilling out like they were in the foyer of an office or a workshop. The air was heavy with solvents and the hint of smoke.

Reacher started with the west wing. It was like the offspring of an art studio and a dormitory. There were six beds evenly spaced between areas full of easels covered with canvases. More were hanging on the walls. There were metal shelves overflowing with paint pots and jars of thinner and packs of brushes. Extra lights had been fixed on the ceiling. They were fitted with some kind of blue bulbs so that the whole space felt like it was bathed in daylight even though there were no windows. There were six guys in there. They had faded, stained aprons over their prison uniforms. They were all busy. One was working on a copy of a Monet. Two on Van Goghs. One on a Mondrian. One on a Picasso. One was flinging rough daubs of paint all over a long rectangular canvas that was stretched out on the floor. None of them paid any attention to Reacher or Begovic.

The north wing was the domain of four guys who were working on documents. Two with computers. Two by hand. Reacher looked over one of the manual guy's shoulders. There were two pieces of paper in front of him. They were the same size. One was filled with writing. It was someone's will. It painstakingly set out the names of people who were going to get a bunch of cash and jewelry and cars and a collection of antique shotguns. The second page was half-full. The script looked identical. It listed the same items. The same quantities. The same values. But the names of the people who were set to inherit were different. A woman who wasn't mentioned at all in the first document was set to clean up with the second.

Reacher said, "Could you write a letter in someone else's handwriting?"

The guy with the pen said, "Sure. Whose?"

"What if it was a suicide note?"

"'Course. Those are easy. No technical terms. Not too long. Not often, anyway."

The east wing was full of sculptors and jewelers. Three guys were chipping away at blocks of marble. One had clay up to his elbows. One was welding giant girders together. One was hollowing out a tree trunk. Five were melting yellow and white metals in dented crucibles and adding stones of all kinds of colors to make rings and bracelets and pendants. There were posters on the wall showing enlarged versions of signature pieces by Tiffany and Cartier and Bvlgari.

Some of the trinkets on the guys' workbenches were pretty much indistinguishable to Reacher's eye.

The south wing was home to six guys with computers. They were sitting on threadbare office chairs, staring at screens perched on beat-up, rickety desks and rattling away at cordless keyboards. Three of them were virtually inert, like robots, with just their fingers and eyes showing signs of life. The others were almost dancing in their seats like concert pianists or seventies rock musicians.

Reacher tapped one of the animated guys on the shoulder. He said, "Would you have a problem hacking into someone's email?"

The guy stopped fidgeting and said, "Yeah. Huge problem. I only do it like fifty times a day."

"You could read someone's messages?"

"Read them. Alter them. Delete them. Copy them. Whatever you want."

Chapter 46

The clock in Reacher's head told him it was time to leave. He grabbed Begovic and led the way out of Unit C. He was still convinced they would cross paths with a guard. Or a squad of guards called back on duty to deal with the ruckus that had resulted from the fire alarm. But again the unrest served their purpose. They made it to Unit S1 undetected.

The two guys who had been backing Riverdale's play were still on the floor. They were still unconscious. Reacher dragged them through the door he had disabled and shoved them into the preparation cell. He gave each another kick in the head to make sure they wouldn't make an unwelcome appearance any time soon. He did the same to the pair of medics he'd left there earlier. He removed the magazine and dumped one of the rifles on the operating table.

Checked the tan SIG. Then he went back out into the hub.

Reacher unslung the other rifle from his shoulder and said to Begovic, "Put your hands behind your back like they're tied. Look at the floor. Play along with whatever I say."

A minute later the door to the unit's south wing swung open. Two guys came through. They had a heavy-duty gurney. One was pushing. One was pulling. The guy in the lead said, "What's the story here? Why—"

The guy stopped talking. He was looking at Reacher. He couldn't understand why someone he didn't recognize was there. Apparently in authority. Who wasn't part of the program. He glanced across to Begovic. He couldn't understand why the prisoner was standing upright. Why he was still conscious. Why he wasn't boxed up, ready for transport. The guy's brain struggled for a second. It was trying to fit all the pieces together. Then it quit the puzzle. It didn't matter what the exact picture was. Because whatever shape it took, something was wrong. That was obvious. So he let go of the gurney and his hand darted toward his pocket.

Reacher didn't know if the guy was going for a gun or a phone. He didn't wait to find out. He stepped forward and spun the rifle around as he moved. Then he drove the flat end of its stock into the bridge of the guy's nose. The guy collapsed onto the gurney then rolled off its side. He crashed down onto the floor and lay still, facedown, with blood pooling steadily around his head.

"Don't move." Reacher reversed the rifle and pointed it at the guy who'd been pushing the gurney. "You can show us the way out. Or I can take you to one of the exercise yards. There are about a hundred guys there who would make you very welcome. That's for sure. OK. You have five seconds to decide."

Self-preservation won the day. Reacher and Begovic followed the guy through the unit's south wing. The cell doors were all open. There was no sound from inside any of them. Just the squeaking of three pairs of shoes on the concrete floor. A door was set into the wall at the far end. It was made of steel. Painted gray. It looked new. Shiny. The guy who was in the lead held his ID card up to a white plastic square set into the frame. The lock clicked and the guy pushed the door open. It led to a covered walkway. It was narrower than the other ones Reacher had been through. There were no lines painted on the ground. It had solid corrugated metal in place of open mesh. The air was hot and stale. It ran straight for thirty yards. There was a dogleg to the left. Then it ran straight for another forty yards. There was another gray steel door at the end, which opened into a kind of large shed. There were floor-to-ceiling shelves on two sides. They were full of janitorial supplies and prison uniforms and cans of dried food. A van was parked in the center. It was dark blue and shiny, like the one Reacher had seen outside the Riverside Lodge. It had been backed into the space. In front of it, in the middle of the opposite wall, there was a roll-up vehicle door. No other people were in sight. Reacher looked through the driver's window. The keys were in the ignition.

Reacher said, "What opens the exit door?"

The guy said, "There's a remote clipped to the visor. Hit the button, the door rolls up. Approach the gate in the inner fence. It'll open. Pull forward toward the gate in the outer fence. The inner one will close on its own. Then flash your headlights three times. The guy in the booth will let you out."

"Flash the headlights. Really?"

"That's the signal."

Reacher saw that the guy wouldn't meet his eye. So he opened the van's rear door and said, "Get in. You're riding with Begovic. When we're clear of here I'll come and let you out. But first I'll knock on the bulkhead. If the door opens and Begovic hasn't heard a knock, he's going to shoot out one of your knee-caps."

The guy shook his head and took a step back. "Wait. You don't flash your lights. You don't do anything. Just approach the outer gate. The officer in the booth has orders to let this van in or out, any time, no record, no search. Don't worry. You won't be penned in for long."

Penned in. Two words Reacher did not like the sound of. Not when they applied to him.

Reacher didn't make the guard get in the back of the van. Because Reacher didn't know Begovic well enough. He couldn't predict how Begovic would stand up to the pressure. If he got flustered or showed signs of panic there was too much danger the guard would go for the gun. He could make a noise. Alert whoever was on duty in the booth. Begovic could wind up taking a stray bullet. Or a deliberate one. So Reacher took a different approach. He knocked the guy out, rolled his body onto the bottom shelf at the side of the room, and piled a bunch of balled-up orange jumpsuits in front of it.

The van's engine started at the first turn of the key. The exit door opened at the first press of the remote. The gate in the inner fence rolled aside the moment the van approached. It slid back into place the second the van was through. Then nothing more happened. The outer gate stayed where it was. It was completely still. Inert. Like it was welded shut. Or it was just another fixed panel in the fence. The electrified fence. That was on their left. On their right. And now effectively in front and behind. There was no way forward. No way back. Nowhere to go even if they abandoned the vehicle.

The outer gate didn't move.

Reacher looked at the booth. He couldn't see inside. The glass was mirrored. Maybe no one was there. Maybe the fire alarm protocol required the guard to assist with the evacuation on the other side of the prison. Or maybe the guard was still at his post, waiting for some kind of signal. Something Reacher didn't know about. Something he had to do or the guard would raise the alarm. Reinforcements would come from behind, Reacher thought. Through the warehouse. Heavily armed. He checked the mirror. The roll-up door was still closed. For the moment.

The outer gate didn't move.

Reacher's foot was on the brake. He was thinking about shifting it to the gas pedal. There was no point trying to smash through the gate. It would be too strong. Designed to stop a much heavier vehicle. With a run up. Not from a standing start. Reacher had no doubt about that. But he figured he could cause a dent. Get some of the truck's metal in contact with the mesh or the frame. Then he could open the van's back door. The cargo space was fitted with shelves. He had seen them when he was getting Begovic situated. He could tear a couple out. Use them to connect the rear of the van to the inner fence. Maybe cause a short circuit. Maybe kill the power for long enough to climb over. If he could find something to cover the razor wire.

The outer gate didn't move.

Reacher looked down. There were mats on the floor. In both foot wells. They were made of rubber. Heavy duty. Made to protect the vehicle's floor from boots soaked with Mississippi rain. And thick enough to save a person from getting cut to ribbons. Maybe. There was only one way to find out. Reacher started to lift his foot. Then he stopped. And pressed down again for a moment.

The outer gate twitched. It shuddered. Then it lurched to the side.

———

Begovic switched from the cargo area to the passenger seat when they were a safe distance from the prison but he didn't say a word on the rest of the drive to Bruno Hix's home. He pressed himself back against his seat and stayed completely still apart from his eyes, which were constantly flicking from one side to the other. Reacher didn't speak, either. He didn't want to tell Begovic there was a kid waiting for him at the house until they were close. He didn't want to give him the chance to think about it too much. To freak out. But at the same time Reacher didn't feel right making meaningless small talk when he was holding back such a significant piece of information. The farther he drove, the less sure he felt about the choice he'd made. Then all of a sudden he was very glad he'd made no mention of Begovic's kid.

There were two vans parked outside Hix's house. One was white with Illinois plates. It looked to be a few years old. It showed plenty of signs of having lived a hard life and it was sitting at the side of the road. The other van was black. It had Mississippi plates. It looked new. Shiny. It was in great shape. All the way from its rear fender to its windshield. But its wings and hood and nose were ruined. Someone had used it to ram Hix's gates. Hard. It had shoved them open maybe four feet.

Reacher pulled over behind the white van. He told Begovic to stay put even if he heard noises from the house. He climbed out. He had the tan SIG in his hand. He checked both other vehicles' cabs and cargo areas. There were no people. Then he made his way through the gap in the gates, across the drive, past the VW, and up the steps.

The front door was open. Reacher peered into the hallway. He could see no one. He could hear nothing. He crept inside. Headed left, toward the kitchen. Where he had left Hix and Brockman and Carpenter, tied up and immobile.

The room was empty.

Reacher didn't care too much about the Minerva guys. But he was worried about Hannah and Jed.

He could see two possibilities. Whoever had arrived in the vans had a third vehicle, which they used to abduct everyone from the house. Or everyone, including the hostiles, was still in the house or on the grounds.

Reacher favored the second option. The first would involve a very large vehicle. It would need to hold a minimum of eight people. And it made no sense to abandon the white van. It looked serviceable and the back was crammed with all kinds of specialized tools and equipment.

There was a sound in the next room. A creak. It was quiet. It happened just once. But Reacher had definitely heard something. He crept to the door. Listened. Heard nothing else. Took hold of the handle. Jerked the door open. And jumped back to avoid getting hit by a guy who tumbled onto the floor, at Reacher's feet.

It was Maurice. The journalist.

Reacher said, "The hell are you doing in there?"

Maurice said, "Hiding. Waiting for you. What took you so long?"

"Where are the others? Hannah? The kid?"

"Out back. I think."

"You think?"

"I think they all are."

"All?"

"Hannah. The kid. Hix and Brockman. Carpenter. And two new guys."

"From Minerva?"

"No. They weren't here to rescue anyone. Definitely not. It was like they were looking for Carpenter. Like he was their target."

"Why did they leave you?"

"They didn't know about me. I was in the laundry room. I went in there hoping it was a pantry. I was starving."

"They didn't search?"

"I was hiding. I'm good at it. I've had plenty of practice."

"So did you see what happened? Or only hear?"

"I saw some. They didn't search immediately. They came crashing in. Hannah went for her gun. But they were too fast."

"Are they armed?"

"One guy, the younger one, he had a gun. The older one had a kind of flask and a cloth. He kicked Hannah's gun away then shoved the cloth in her face. She fell down. Jed tried to rush the guy. He kind of bounced off and the guy grabbed him and shoved the cloth in his face and he fell down, too. Then they searched. I only listened after that."

"What did they want with Carpenter?"

"One of them, the older one, I think, because he had this tone like he was in charge, he started questioning him. It was kind of weird. He said Carpenter had sold some liver that was bad and it had killed his son. He wanted to know where it came from. If Hix and Brockman were involved."

"What did Carpenter say?"

"Nothing. He wouldn't answer. The older guy said that was no problem. He had something better to loosen his tongue. Then I guess he used whatever was on the cloth to knock them out. I heard some thuds, then a bunch of slipping and scuffling. Five times. I guess they dragged everyone out back."

"Why out back?"

"Because I didn't hear any vehicles and they weren't at the front. I looked. To be honest I was going to run. Then I remembered you were coming back. Figured I should stay and warn you."

"You did the right thing." Reacher started toward the door.

"There's one thing I don't get." Maurice stayed where he was. "These guys want revenge for this fatal poisoning. What's that got to do with Minerva? There are no animals at their prisons. The company doesn't own any farms. Where are they getting the livers from?"

"It wasn't food poisoning that killed this guy's kid." Reacher grabbed the door handle. "And the liver didn't come from an animal. Not one with four legs."

Reacher crossed the hallway, ran up the stairs, and went into the center room at the rear of the house. It was a bedroom. It had a polished wood floor. Sleek, pale furniture. And three tall windows covered by white curtains, all closed, which hung down to the floor. Reacher crossed to the center window and peered around the edge of the curtain. He was looking through a glass door, across the balcony, and down onto the big square of grass he had seen when he first broke into the house. The difference now was the people who were there. Hix, Brockman, and Carpenter. Naked. Hanging by their wrists from the lighting gantry over the stage. Immobile. Hannah and Jed, on the grass to the right of the stage. Facedown. Dressed. Also immobile. And two guys Reacher hadn't seen before. They were ladling some kind of gel out of a large barrel and slopping it into ice troughs they'd taken from the bar.

Reacher ran back down the stairs, through the front door, and around to the rear of the building. He stepped up onto the porch. The new guys set the third trough down on the edge of the stage. They were standing on either side of the barrel. They heard the footsteps. Spun around. Pulled out guns. And aimed at Reacher.

The older guy said, "Drop the weapon. Then get on the ground. Facedown."

The breeze was blowing directly toward Reacher. Past the two guys. Past their barrel.

Reacher said, "Not going to happen. I have no

quarrel with you. I'm here for the woman and the kid. They come with me. The idiots you strung up? Do what you want with them."

The guy shook his head. "The woman and the kid are going nowhere. They saw us."

Reacher was picking up a faint smell. Something familiar. He said, "They caught a glimpse at best. They're no threat."

"Doesn't matter. They can put us at the scene. So can you."

Gasoline, mainly, Reacher thought. And benzene. And something else. Then he made the connection. The combination of ingredients. He looked at the barrel. It was almost empty. Almost. But not quite. He said, "Not my problem. I'm taking my friends and I'm leaving."

"You're in no position to be telling us what's going to happen."

Reacher said, "I'm in the perfect position." Then he fired. At the barrel. The bullet pierced the plastic and the remaining napalm ignited instantly. The sides buckled. The shock wave knocked both the guys over. And a tongue of orange flame engulfed the younger one. He screamed and writhed and squeezed off one unaimed round before he lost his grip on his gun.

Reacher jumped down from the porch, stepped forward, and shot the younger guy in the head. The older guy was on his back. He wasn't moving. He had escaped the flames completely. But there was a red stain on his shirt. Low down on the left side of his abdomen. It was wet. And it was growing. His buddy's bullet had passed right through him.

The guy rolled over and forced himself onto his hands and knees. He tried to crawl toward the stage. Reacher stepped across and blocked his path.

"Move." The guy's voice was somewhere between a croak and a whisper.

Reacher stayed still.

The guy nodded toward Carpenter. "Him. Got to make him talk."

Reacher said, "You're going to bleed to death."

"He killed my son. He has a supplier. I need a name."

"Your son got a transplant?"

The guy nodded, then slumped down onto his side. "His liver was toast. He went to rehab after rehab. Nothing stuck. The regular doctors wouldn't help. So I found a clinic. On a ship. They put in a new liver. But it was bad. Kyle died."

Reacher said, "The other guys you strung up. They're his suppliers. They run a prison. Find inmates no one will miss and sell them for their organs to be harvested."

The guy raised his head. "That true?"

Reacher nodded.

The guy said, "Help me then. Shoot them."

"No."

"Why not? You shot Graeber. My friend."

"That guy? He was on fire. It was a kindness. I'll make sure the prison operation gets closed down. Permanently. But I'm not going to kill anyone in cold blood."

"Please. For my son. His name was Kyle Emerson. He was twenty-two."

"No."

The guy struggled back onto his hands and knees and crawled another yard.

Reacher picked up a shirt from a pile of clothes at the side of the stage. He held it out and said, "Keep going and you'll bleed out. Stop, press this against the wound, call 911, maybe you'll have a chance."

The guy kept on crawling. He made it to the front of the stage. Stretched up. One hand scrabbled for grip on the wooden surface. The other grabbed the rim of an ice trough. The guy tried to haul himself up but only managed to pull the trough off the stage. It was full of cream-colored gel. The gel flooded across his chest. It flowed down to the front of his pants and mingled with the blood that had soaked into the material. He fell back. Rolled over. Clawed his way onto his knees. Straightened his back. Pulled a box of matches out of his pocket and turned to look at Reacher.

"Now I'm glad you didn't shoot these assholes." The guy took out a match. "Now they'll get what they deserve."

The guy struck the match. A flame flared at its tip. He seemed mesmerized by it for a moment. Then his knees buckled. He toppled backward again. He dropped the match. It landed on his stomach. It was still alight.

Reacher jumped away. It was an instinctive response. A reaction to fire that was baked deep into the back of his brain. Impossible to resist. He felt the heat on his face and arms. Heard a *crump* sound. Thought he heard the guy laugh. Thought he could see him smile. Then he raised the SIG and shot him between the eyes.

The guy's body lay still. The flames danced on.

Reacher heard two sets of footsteps approaching. Both were cautious. And they were separate. Maurice appeared on the porch first. Then Begovic. Maurice stood still. Begovic jumped down and headed toward the stage. Toward his former captors. Then he changed course. He crossed to where Jed was lying and stood and looked down at the kid.

Maurice said quietly, "Are they dead?"

Reacher pointed to the burned-up guys. "Those two are. The others are drugged. They'll be fine."

"Should we cut the Minerva guys down?"

Reacher shook his head. "Not yet. There's one more person hiding in the woodwork. Maybe more than one. We need these guys as bait."

Chapter 47

Reacher carried Hannah through the gap in the gates and laid her down in the back of the van he'd taken from the prison. Begovic followed and placed Jed next to her. Maurice trailed along at the rear. He didn't want to be left alone in the yard with the dead bodies.

Reacher closed the van's doors and turned to Begovic. "Can you drive?"

Begovic said, "I guess. I used to be able to. But that was fifteen years ago."

"The principle hasn't changed." Reacher held out the keys. "Go half a mile up the road. Then pull over and stay there until I join you."

———

Reacher waited until the van was moving then asked Maurice for his phone. He dialed 911. The emergency operator answered after two rings.

Reacher said, "I need the police. And if you can do it, a priest. A guy's had an accident in his yard. His name's Bruno Hix. He keeps talking about something bad he got involved in. Says he wants to make a confession."

The operator said, "Sir, what's the address where the accident happened?"

Reacher read the details from a plaque on the wall at the side of Hix's gates.

"Your name, sir?"

"Chivington. John."

"OK, sir. I can't help you with the priest. But I will send the police. And the paramedics. Hang in there. Help will be with you shortly."

Reacher ended the call and handed the phone back to Maurice.

Maurice said, "What now? Should I stay? Or go?"

"That's up to you. Are you only interested in Minerva? Or do you have time for an exposé on dirty cops?"

One police car arrived, seven minutes later. A Dodge Charger. Brand-new. Unmarked. It had a dome light flashing on the dash and it was moving fast. It slid to a stop at the side of the black van that had its nose embedded in Hix's gate. The driver's door opened. An officer jumped out. He was pushing sixty. His uniform was crisp. It was neatly pressed, but it was tight around his gut. He drew his gun and hurried toward the house.

The cop skirted the building and stepped onto the back porch. He glanced at the two burned corpses. Emerson's was still smoldering. Then he jumped down, hurried across the grass, and hauled himself up onto the stage. Hix was starting to regain consciousness. The cop slapped Hix's face. Over and over. A flurry of short, sharp blows. He said, "Bruno, what the hell happened? Who called 911?"

Hix didn't answer. He couldn't.

"Who are these dead guys? How come you're all strung up like this? Where the hell are your clothes?"

Hix managed to blink.

"Are there any more of them? Any who are alive?"

Hix grunted.

The cop lowered his voice. "Bruno, what did you tell them?"

Hix tried to shrug. He failed.

"Focus. Come on. Concentrate. This is important. What do they know?"

Hix shook his head.

"Do they know anything?"

Hix's voice came out harsh, but quiet. "They know everything."

The cop stepped back. He sighed. "Thanks for being honest, my friend. We had quite the run. I'm sorry it couldn't go on longer. But all good things come to an end." He slipped his gun into its holster. Took a pair of latex gloves from his pocket. Pulled them on. Leaned down and lifted the cuff of his pants. Unsnapped the strap on his ankle holster. Slid out a small silver revolver, straightened up, and held it to Hix's temple. "I'll make this quick."

"Stop." Reacher stood and stepped out from behind the bar. He was holding the SIG. It was leveled on the cop's center mass.

The cop raised his hands and stepped back.

"Throw the gun off the stage."

The cop did as he was told.

"Now the other one."

The cop tossed his official piece.

Maurice emerged from the other side of the bar. He was holding out his phone. He crept forward until he was close enough to read the cop's name badge. "Chief Moseley, congratulations. What a performance. When you're in jail and I've won the Pulitzer, I'm going to post it online. It's a master class in self-incrimination. I might have to pixelate parts of Mr. Hix, though. I don't want to turn it into a comedy number."

The smartly dressed kid at the Riverside Lodge was so happy to get his hands on the key to his VW, he told Reacher he could have as many rooms in the north wing of the hotel as he liked, for as long as he liked. Reacher said he'd take four, for one night. And that this time he only needed one key for his room.

Maurice had stayed at Hix's to wait for the FBI, then he was planning a trip to D.C. Hannah and Begovic stayed at the hotel. Reacher took Jed on a quick trip into town in Sam Roth's truck. They made two stops. The first was at a drugstore. Reacher went in alone. The second was at the burger place in the old gas station. Jed asked for a double with nothing green, just like Reacher, and he had finished before they got back to the Lodge's parking lot.

The following morning Reacher took Jed for another drive. They collected the bike Jed had been using from its hiding place and brought it to the Lodge. The messenger from Jackson was waiting in the parking lot when they got back. Jed climbed out. The messenger lifted the bike down from the truck's load bed and started to inspect every inch.

The guy said, "This is a disaster. You've scratched the paint. Crushed the saddle. Deformed the forks. Buckled the rims. It's worthless now. It's ruined. You little asshole."

Jed said, "I did my best to look after it. I'm sorry if there's any damage."

"What use is sorry?" The messenger shoved Jed in the chest. "You miserable piece of—"

Reacher got out of the truck.

The messenger grabbed the handlebars and scurried across to a station wagon that was parked by the porte cochere. "Hey, buddy, just a misunderstanding. Thanks for returning it. Guess I'll be leaving now." He fed the bike in through the tailgate and hurried around to the driver's seat. He started the engine and lurched backward, then changed direction and sped away toward the exit.

———

Reacher and Jed stood together until the car disappeared from sight. Then Reacher handed Jed a small paper bag from the drugstore. Jed opened it. He pulled out a folding toothbrush.

Reacher said, "For next time you take the Greyhound. Fits better in your pocket than the regular kind."

Jed said, "Thank you."

"Good luck with your dad. I hope you guys work it out."

"We're going to Colorado. Hannah said we can stay in Sam's house until Dad gets a job."

"Sam's house is nice. I bet you guys will be happy."

"Are you coming to Gerrardsville, too?"

"Me? No."

"Why not? You said it's nice."

"It is nice. But I've been there before. It's time for somewhere new."

If you enjoyed
Lee and Andrew Child's *No Plan B,*
read on for a thrilling preview of

The Secret

A Jack Reacher Novel

Coming in hardcover and ebook from

Delacorte Press

October 2023

Or he could take a nap.

Bridgeman was sixty-two years old. He was in rough shape. That was clear. He could debate the cause—the kind of work he had devoted his life to, the stress he had suffered, the cigarettes and alcohol he had consumed—but he couldn't deny the effect. A heart attack so massive that no one had expected him to survive.

Defying odds that great is tiring work. He chose the nap.

These days he always chose the nap.

Bridgeman woke up after only an hour. He was no longer alone. Two other people were in the room with him. Both were women. Maybe in their late twenties. They were the same height. The same slim build. One was on the left side of his bed, nearer to the door. The other was level with her on the right, nearer to the window. They were standing completely still. In silence. Staring at him. Their hair was pulled back, smooth and dark and tight. Their faces were expressionless like mannequins' and their skin shone in the harsh artificial light as if it was molded from plastic.

The women were wearing white coats over hospital scrubs. The coats were the correct length. They had all the necessary pockets and badges and tags. The scrubs were the right shade of blue. But the women weren't medics. Bridgeman was sure about that. His sixth sense told him so. It told him they shouldn't be there. That they were trouble. He scanned each of them in turn. Their hands were empty. Their clothes were not bulging. There was no sign of guns or knives. No sign of any hospital equipment they could use as weapons. But Bridgeman still wasn't happy. He was in danger. He knew it. He could feel it as keenly as a gazelle that had been ambushed by a pair of lions.

Bridgeman glanced at his left leg. The call button was where the nurse had left it. Lying on the sheet between his thigh and the safety rail. His hand darted toward it. It was a fluid movement. Smooth. Fast. But the woman was faster. She snatched the button then dropped it, leaving it dangling on its wire, almost to the floor, well out of Bridgeman's reach.

Bridgeman felt his heart quiver and tremble in his chest. He heard an electronic *beep.* It came from a piece of equipment on a stand near the head of the bed. It had a screen with a number in the center of the top half and two jagged lines that zigzagged across the full width of the lower half. The first line showed his pulse. It was spiking wildly. Its peaks were surging closer together like they were chasing one another. The number showed his heart rate. It was climbing. Fast. The beeps grew louder. More frequent. Then the sound became continuous. Insistent. Impossible to ignore. The number stopped rising. It began to flash. It changed direction. And it kept going down until it reached 00. The lines flattened out. First at the left of the screen and then all the way across until both were perfectly horizontal. The display was inert. Lifeless. Except for the desperate electronic howl.

It told of total cardiac failure.

But only for a moment.

432 | LEE CHILD and ANDREW CHILD

The second woman had grabbed Bridgeman's right wrist when the alarm began to shriek. She had yanked a square blue clip off the tip of his index finger and attached it to her own. The screen flashed twice. Then the sound cut out. The heart rate started to climb. The two lines began to tick their way from left to right. None of the values were quite the same as Bridgeman's. The woman was younger. Fitter. Healthier. Calmer. But the readings were close enough. Not too high. Not too low. Nothing to trigger another alarm.

Bridgeman clutched his chest with both hands. Sweat was prickling out across his forehead and his scalp. His skin felt clammy. He had to make an effort to breathe.

The woman with the clip on her finger lowered herself into the visitor's chair next to the window. The woman on the left of the bed waited a moment then looked at Bridgeman and said, "We apologize. We didn't mean to startle you. We're not here to hurt you. We just need to talk."

Bridgeman said nothing.

The woman said, "We have two questions. That's all. Answer them honestly and you'll never see us again. I promise."

Bridgeman didn't respond.

The woman saw him glancing past her, toward the door. She shook her head. "If you're hoping the cavalry's going to come, you're out of luck. Those clips slip off people's fingers all the time. And what do they do? Stick them right back on. Anyone at the nurses' station who heard the alarm will figure that's what you did. So. First question, OK?"

Bridgeman's mouth was dry. He did his best to moisten his lips then took a deep breath. But not to answer questions. To call for help the old-fashioned way.

The woman read his play. She put a finger to her lips and took something out of her coat pocket. A photograph. She held it out for Bridgeman to take. It showed a gloved hand holding a copy of *The Tribune* next to a window. Bridgeman could read the date on the newspaper. It was that day's edition. Then he saw two figures through the glass. A woman and a child. A little girl. Even though they were facing away from the camera Bridgeman had no doubt who they were. Or where they were. It was his daughter and granddaughter. In the home he had bought them in Evanston, after his wife died.

The woman took hold of Bridgeman's arm and felt for his pulse. It was fast and weak. She said, "Come on now. Calm down. Think of your family. We don't want to hurt them. Or you. We just need you to understand how serious this situation is. We only have two questions, but they're important. The sooner you answer, the sooner we're out of here. Ready?"

Bridgeman nodded and slumped back against his pillow.

"First question. You're meeting with a journalist the day after tomorrow. Where is the information you're planning to give her?"

"How do you know about—"

"Don't waste time. Answer the question."

"OK. Look. There is no information. We're just going to chat."

"No credible journalist is going to believe a whistle-blower without ironclad proof. Where is it?"

"Whistleblower? That's not what this is. The reporter's from a little weekly rag in Akron, Ohio. Where I was born. The story's about my heart attack. My recovery. It's a miracle, according to the doctors. Apparently people back home want to read about it. They say I'm an inspiration."

"Heart attack? That's what you're going with? When you're sitting on a much bigger story?"

"What bigger story?"

The woman leaned in closer. "Keith, we know what you did. Twenty-three years ago. December 1969."

"December '69? How do you know . . . ? Who are you?"

"We'll come to who we are. Right now you need to tell me what information you're planning to give this reporter from Akron."

"No information. I'm going to tell her about my recovery. That's all. I will never talk about December '69. Not to anyone. I swore I wouldn't and I keep my word. My wife never even knew."

"So you don't have any documents or notes hidden in this room?"

"Of course not."

"Then you won't mind if I take a look around."

The woman didn't wait for an answer. She started with the locker next to the bed. She opened the door and rummaged through Bridgeman's spare pajamas and books and magazines. She moved on to a leather duffel on the floor near the door. It held a set of clothes. Nothing else. Next she checked the bathroom. Nothing significant there, either. So she moved to the center of the room and put her hands on her hips. "Only one place left to check. The bed."

Bridgeman didn't move.

"Do it for your daughter. And your granddaughter. Come on. I'll be quick."

Bridgeman felt his pulse start to speed up again. He closed his eyes for a moment. Took a breath. Willed himself to relax. Then pushed back the sheet, swung his legs over the side of the mattress, and slid down onto his feet. He looked at the woman in the chair. "Can't I at least sit? I'm older than you. And I have one foot in the grave."

The woman held up her finger with the clip attached. "Sorry. The cable's too short. Maybe sit on the windowsill?"

Bridgeman turned and leaned against the windowsill. He watched as the other woman finished her search of the bed. Again she came up empty.

"Believe me now?" Bridgeman said.

The woman took a piece of paper out of her pocket and handed it to Bridgeman. There was a list of names. Eight of them, handwritten in shaky, spidery script. Bridgeman's was one of them. He recognized all the other seven.

The woman said, "Question two. A name is missing. Who is it?"

Bridgeman's heart was no longer racing. Now it felt like it was full of sludge. Like it didn't have the strength to force his blood into his arteries. He couldn't answer. It would mean breaking his oath. And it would be MAD to. Mutually Assured Destruction. That was what had kept them all safe for twenty-three years.

The woman handed Bridgeman another photograph. It was of his daughter and granddaughter again, this time on foot, halfway across a crosswalk. The picture had been taken through a car windshield. The woman said, "Bonus question. What happens next time? Is the driver drunk? Do his brakes fail?"

Bridgeman's heart felt like it was on fire. It felt like it was seizing up. It was only beating once every couple of seconds. He was getting light-headed. And then he had an idea. A desperate Hail Mary, but it was all he had. The woman had said *A name*. Not two names. And there should have been ten on that list.

Bridgeman said, "Buck. The missing name. It's Owen Buck."

The woman shook her head and said, "Nice try. You must think I don't know that Buck's dead. He died of cancer two months ago so you figured you could throw him under the bus without giving anything away. But unluckily for you it was Buck who wrote that list. So his isn't the name I need. It's the other one. He didn't know it. But you do. Don't pretend you don't."

Bridgeman didn't answer. He was trying to breathe extra deeply. And praying that the movement of his rib cage would help his heart to expand and contract.

The woman said, "Maybe the driver will be distracted? Maybe he'll be asleep at the wheel?"

Bridgeman stayed silent.

The woman said, "Maybe there'll be enough of your granddaughter left to bury. Maybe there won't."

Bridgeman was struggling for air. "Don't. Please. I can't."

"You can. You don't have to say it. You can do what Owen Buck did. Write it down. He gave me eight names. You only need to give me one."

She pulled a pen from her coat pocket and held it out. Bridgeman took it. But he didn't use it.

The woman said, "Have you ever seen a child's coffin, Keith? Because if you haven't I don't think anything can really prepare you for how tiny it will seem. Especially when it's next to the full size one your daughter will be in."

Bridgeman's hand started to shake.

The woman's voice softened. "Come on. One name. Two lives saved. What are you waiting for?"

Bridgeman took the list. He wrote *Owen Buck* at the top. He added another name at the bottom. Then he handed the scrap of paper back to the woman. She looked at it, then said, "Are you sure?"

He nodded.

She showed it to the other woman, then said, "You know who that is?"

Bridgeman nodded again.

"You know what they do?"

"Yes. And more importantly, I know what they did."

The woman shrugged then slid the list back into her pocket. "OK, then. I guess we're done here. You answered our questions, which means you're never going to see us again, as promised. There's just one last thing before we go. You asked who we are." She stretched out and touched Bridgeman's forehead. "Wait a minute. You feel awful. Let me open the window. Fresh air will perk you up."

Bridgeman said, "You can't. Hospital windows don't open."

"This one does." The woman leaned past Bridgeman, pushed down on the handle, and the window swung out on a broad arc.

"I don't get it. My daughter tried it the first time she came to visit. It was locked."

The woman scrabbled under the collar of her scrubs for a moment then pulled a fine chain up and over her head. The key to the window was hanging from it. "Here." She dropped the chain into the breast pocket of Bridgeman's pajama top. "A present. You never know. It might be a significant thing one day."

"But where did you—"

"The question's not *where did I*. It's *who am I*." The woman stood a little straighter. "Well? My name is Anita Sanson."

The woman with the finger clip climbed out of her chair. "And I'm her sister. Jennifer Sanson. Our father was Morgan Sanson. It's important you know that."

"I don't follow. Who is—" Bridgeman pushed off from the wall beneath the window. He tried to build some speed and dodge around Anita Sanson but he never stood a chance. He was too frail. The space was too cramped. And the sisters were too highly motivated. Anita shifted sideways. She blocked his path. Then she grabbed his shoulders with both hands and drove him back until he was pressed against the windowsill again. She checked that he was lined up with the open window. Jennifer bent down and took hold of his legs, just above the ankles. She straightened and Anita pushed. They pushed one more time. Two more times. Then they let gravity do the rest.

The following week Jack Reacher was in Seattle, Washington. On leave. The army hadn't given him much to get his teeth into recently and he had heard about some interesting bands coming out of the city. A whole new sound, people said. He figured it would be worth a little time and a few bucks to find out what the fuss was about.

Three days into the trip and Reacher had seen enough. The first band he caught was pretty good. The second was fine. The third was competent from a technical standpoint but it was nothing Reacher would call exciting. Nothing that was going to knock Howlin' Wolf or Magic Slim off his list of favorites. Reacher stuck it out for almost the whole of their set then realized he was more interested in the venue than the music. It was an old factory. The walls were brick. They were pitted and stained and riddled with holes and sockets and brackets where all kinds of equipment must once have been secured. Like industrial petroglyphs, Reacher thought, telling the story of the people who had spent their lives working there. He spent a few minutes trying to decipher them then gave it up and headed for the exit. That took him past the bar. It was a square area, separated from the rest of the space by a line of vertical iron pipes. There were a dozen of them, three feet apart, four inches in diameter, rusted almost black. Ten were lit from above. They all should have been. But the lamps over two of them had failed and left them lost in the gloom.

Reacher was almost at the door when he saw one of the waitstaff trying to deliver a tray of drinks. He was aiming for a table at the back of the bar. It was made out of an old beer keg with things that looked like upturned buckets as seats. Two twenty-something guys were perched there along with two women who looked a little younger. One of the guys gestured for the waiter to hurry up. Maybe he was thirsty. Maybe he was trying to show off. But whatever the reason, he wasn't helping. The waiter was doing his best. The space was crowded. The furniture was jammed in at all kinds of crooked angles. There was no set path for him to get through. There was no point trying to make him go faster. A couple of times he nearly dropped the tray. Once he skidded on a wet patch on the floor. And finally, when he was almost at the right table, he knocked into another customer. A guy who was hard to miss. He was six foot six with a huge beard, a baseball cap worn backward, baggy jeans, and a plaid shirt with buttons that were struggling to contain his gut. The guy glanced around. He was checking to see if anyone was looking. He saw that plenty of people were. So he shoved the waiter in the chest. Hard. The waiter stumbled back a couple of steps then lost his balance. The tray slipped out of his hands. Four drinks hit the floor. Three beers and some kind of fancy cocktail with an umbrella in it. The waiter tumbled over backward and hit his head on the base of another table.

There were a couple of dozen people closer to the action than Reacher. None of them lifted a finger. Not even to help the waiter back onto his feet. He finally rolled over then crawled forward to retrieve his tray. The fat guy pushed it farther away with his foot. Still no one did anything. Reacher took a step forward. Then he stopped. It was because of a similar situation that he'd been busted back to captain. Why he was stuck with the dregs of the cases that his new CO took pleasure in dumping on him. Which meant the problem would have to be handled in a different way.

Reacher backed into the shadows near the opposite wall. He waited for the waiter to return with a mop and a broom and a bucket. He watched him clean up the mess. He saw the fat guy take every opportunity to nudge and jostle him. Then when the waiter was done, Reacher strolled across to the bar.

The bartender looked up then took a step back. He hadn't noticed Reacher approach. He wasn't expecting to see anyone right in front of him. Certainly not anyone who looked like Reacher. Six foot five. Chest like a refrigerator. Arms like other people's legs. Cropped hair and two days' stubble. Head tipped quizzically to one side.

On the far side of the bar there was a metal tub about ten inches high and a yard across. At the start of the evening it had been crammed with ice and bottles of beer. Now it was mainly full of water with a few residual cubes floating around. Reacher pointed to it and said, "That thing? Give it to me."

The bartender blinked twice and said, "Why?"

Reacher said, "I want to borrow it."

"No," the guy said. "But you can rent it. Twenty bucks for a half hour. Driver's license for security. No questions asked. Do what you want with it."

Reacher shook his head. "I borrow it. For two minutes. You watch what happens. And when I return it, if you still think I should pay, I'll give you forty."

The bartender thought for a moment then called his buddy to help him heave the tub across to a spot close to Reacher. Reacher picked it up and headed toward the fat guy. The fat guy made a point of turning his back. Reacher closed in, paused to make sure the waiter could see what was happening, then lifted the tub and dumped the icy water over the fat guy's head.

The fat guy screamed. He howled. He flailed his arms and danced up and down on the spot. He huffed and gasped and finally spun around to face Reacher. His cap had been washed off. His beard was drenched. His shirt was clinging to his torso.

"The hell was that?" the guy spluttered.

Reacher said, "Training."

"What?"

"Like with a dog."

"You're saying I'm a dog?"

"I read somewhere, you have a dog and it misbehaves, you do something it doesn't like. Then it'll learn to mend its ways. Now, you're clearly not as smart as an average dog. Probably not as smart as a stupid dog. Probably a dog that started out really dumb and then had half of its brain removed is still smarter than you. So maybe I should stick around. Put this tub to work whenever you act like a jackass."

The guy frowned and shook his head. Droplets of water flew in a wide circle like he was a poodle that had been caught in the rain. He was quiet for a moment. Then his frown turned into a scowl. "Enough," he barked. "I'm going to kill you. I'm going to crush every bone in your body."

"You think?" Reacher was holding the tub low in front, base toward him, angled at about forty-five degrees.

"I know."

Reacher glanced down at the tub then ghosted across about a foot to his left. "You sure you're not going to break your own hand?"

"No. I'm going to break your face."

"Are you?" Reacher took a half step back and said, "Are there any bookmakers in the house? My money's on the lobotomized dog. That's for sure."

The guy flung himself forward and launched a punch straight at Reacher's face. No technique. No finesse. Just a whole lot of weight and momentum and fury. In some circumstances, that could have served him well. But not that night. Because Reacher stepped aside. Away from the unlit iron pipe he had been standing in front of. The guy's fist slammed right into it. His knuckles shattered. His fingers broke. All kinds of little bones in his hand and wrist and forearm were smashed. Tendons tore. Ligaments ripped.

And this time he didn't make a sound. The pain took care of that. It caused him to faint, right there on the spot. His knees buckled. His legs folded. He flopped backward and landed on the ground with his head six inches from the little umbrella that had fallen from the drink he had made the waiter spill a few minutes earlier.

Reacher carried the tub back to the bar and set it down.

The bartender said, "No charge."

Reacher didn't let go of the tub right away. He said, "Anyone asks, who hurt that guy?"

"No one. He hurt himself."

"Specifically, did I lay a finger on him?"

"You dumped water on him."

"Did I touch him?"

"No."

"Correct answer. Remember it. Make sure your buddies do, too."

Reacher stepped out onto the sidewalk and right away saw two men standing in the shadows near the wall. They were trim. Lean. Dressed all in black. Like French avant-garde philosophers who had become obsessed with exercise, Reacher thought. Although he knew what they really were. He could recognize soldiers in and around bars in his sleep. Years of experience had honed his instinct. And MPs were even easier to spot. No one else ever hung out with them. They were too unpopular. One thing Reacher couldn't figure was how they had got there so fast. Another was who had called them. How they had known to. And why they had bothered if all they had seen was a little spilled water and a busted hand.

The MPs stepped forward. The taller one said, "Captain Reacher?"

Reacher nodded.

"Could you verify that please, sir."

Reacher took out his wallet and showed his Military ID card.

"Thank you, sir." The MP pulled an envelope from his jacket pocket and handed it over.

Reacher tore the envelope open. Inside was single sheet of paper with the Military Police crest at the top. It informed him that the balance of his leave was rescinded and that he was ordered to report to an FBI facility in downtown Chicago at 11:00 A.M. the following day.

Reacher looked at the MP. "What do you know about this?"

"Nothing, sir."

"What have you heard?"

"We've been told nothing, sir."

Reacher smiled. It was clear that these guys were NCOs. The backbone of the service. And Reacher knew from experience that the NCO scuttlebutt was the most efficient communication medium in the world. "I didn't ask what you've *been told.* I asked what you've *heard.* And if you tell me you've not heard anything I'll have you locked up for impersonating a member of the United States Army. So let's start with this. I'm being sent to Chicago. How come?"

The MP glanced at his buddy then said, "Word is someone died there."

"Who?"

"Don't know."

"One of ours?"

The MP shook his head. "Business guy. Fell out of a hospital window."

"Fell out?"

The MP shrugged.

"If the stiff was a business guy, what's our angle?"

"Word is it's part of a bigger thing. Other agencies. Orders from the Pentagon."

"Then why are they sending me?"

"They wanted an O-3 or higher. No one else would touch it. I'm sorry sir, but this whole thing has *poisoned chalice* written all over it."

HAVE YOU READ THEM ALL?
The Jack Reacher thrillers in the order in which they were written: